Judy Astley was frequently told off for day-dreaming at her drearily traditional school but has found it to be the ideal training for becoming a writer. There were several false starts to her career: secretary at an all-male Oxford college (sacked for undisclosable reasons), at an airline (decided, after a crash and a hijacking, that she was safer elsewhere) and as a dress designer (quit before anyone noticed she was adapting *Vogue* patterns). She spent some years as a parent and as a painter before sensing that the day was approaching when she'd have to go out and get a Proper Job. With a nagging certainty that she was temperamentally unemployable, and desperate to avoid office coffee, having to wear tights every day and missing out on sunny days on Cornish beaches with her daughters, she wrote her first novel, *Just for the Summer*. She has now had eight novels published by Black Swan.

Pleasant Vices

Judy Astley

BLACK SWAN

PLEASANT VICES
A BLACK SWAN BOOK : 0 552 99565 7

First publication in Great Britain

PRINTING HISTORY
Black Swan edition published 1995

7 9 10 8 6

Set in 11pt Linotype Melior by
Phoenix Typesetting, Ilkley, West Yorkshire.

Black Swan Books are published by Transworld Publishers,
61–63 Uxbridge Road, London W5 5SA,
a division of The Random House Group Ltd,
in Australia by Random House Australia (Pty) Ltd,
20 Alfred Street, Milsons Point, Sydney, NSW 2061, Australia,
in New Zealand by Random House New Zealand Ltd,
18 Poland Road, Glenfield, Auckland 10, New Zealand
and in South Africa by Random House (Pty) Ltd,
Endulini, 5a Jubilee Road, Parktown 2193, South Africa.

Printed and bound in Great Britain by
Cox & Wyman Ltd, Reading, Berkshire.

For Barbara Forlani
and
Virginia Astley

The gods are just, and of our pleasant vices
Make instruments to plague us.

King Lear – William Shakespeare

Chapter One

'Mum, Mum what's oral sex?' Polly, with big-eyed, ten-year-old innocence that didn't at all suit her question, was gazing steadily at Jenny over the breakfast table. Slowly and sensuously, as if she already knew perfectly well the answer to her question, the child licked porridge from her spoon.

It wasn't the best way to start a Monday morning. The things the children asked Jenny on Mondays usually concerned the whereabouts of gym kit, swimsuits, lunch money and shoes. It was too early in the morning for it to be a joke, Jenny thought. The easiest thing, she knew, would be for her to say, 'OK Polly, I give up, what *is* oral sex?' and for Polly to give some witty, ludicrous reply, with no more complication than if she had asked how you could tell if there were elephants in the fridge. But Polly was waiting and watching.

Jenny folded her hands round her coffee mug, took a deep breath and prepared to give her daughter a direct, honest and textbook-correct answer, just as she had always tried to do with all her children's enquiries, though the questions about how long it takes for dead hamster bones to moulder, and what exactly were quadratic equations *for*, were easy peasy compared to this one. She and Alan had always agreed that scrupulous honesty in the family was to be the rule, none of those slippery evasions of their parents' generation. None of that 'You don't need to know that, not yet,' intended to put you off asking ever again. But Alan wasn't

9

there. He had gone early to the office and an important audit; he needed to avoid the traffic, he said, and questions like Polly's probably, Jenny thought crossly.

Just as Jenny was about to waffle her way into an answer, Ben got in first, his spoon clattering noisily into his Alpen. 'God, Poll, do we have to have this at breakfast?' Ben, whose face these days changed colour as often as a traffic light, was going rapidly into a red-for-danger/anger/embarrassment shade. He slammed his mug on the table, slopping coffee, scuffed back his chair and lunged for his school bag. Jenny could feel a draught – all Ben's movements seemed larger than life. The slightest of his actions caused the lists and bills pinned to the notice board to flutter nervously. Biggles, the ginger tom, slid to safety through the cat-flap.

Well, it's one way of getting Ben out of the house in the mornings, thought Jenny, getting up and moving automatically to the dresser to get his week's lunch money from her purse.

'Well what is it? Me and Harriet need to know!' Polly persisted, thumping the table with her spoon, her attention now on her escaping brother, and conscious of having lit an interestingly sparkly fuse.

Ben, crashing clumsily past her chair as he made for the door, leered down at her, his floppy hair swishing across the top of Polly's head. 'It's when you talk about it, OK?' he hissed. 'Like when you get French oral classes at school, and you discuss things, you know?' He grinned at Polly maliciously, anticipating gleefully the day she found out he'd lied. ' 'Bye, see you later, extra art after school . . .' And Ben was gone, slamming noisily out of the front door as he ran.

The kitchen settled into peace again. It looked much bigger without Ben's lanky presence and his dangerously windmilling arms. Surely, Jenny thought, at almost seventeen he should have lost that overgrown baby bird look, and that gawky lack of co-ordination?

Shouldn't he have grown into his body by now and become man-shaped?

Polly was calmly scraping the last of her porridge from the bowl and Jenny started dealing with the dishes, the question still hanging in the air, awkward as a bad smell in church. Jenny sneaked a wary look at the girl and wondered if and how she should burden her with the truth. Telling her wouldn't be the end of it. Polly's current fascination with all things sexual would lead her to ask more, like the dreaded 'Is that what you and Daddy do?' which Jenny suspected was slightly beyond even her honesty threshold.

But Polly, brain as skittish as a firefly, had blithely moved on and was out of the kitchen and half-way up the stairs to the bathroom before Jenny had decided exactly what to say. It wasn't her day for the school run and, as Jenny stacked the dishwasher, she had an irresistibly cheering vision of Polly climbing into Ceci Caine's Range Rover and loudly stating that she knew all about what oral sex was. Jenny could only hope that Ceci, kohl-lined eyes as round as records and prim mouth pursed up tight like a cat's bum, wouldn't drive straight up the back of a bus.

Good thing Daisy's already left, Jenny decided. She wouldn't have chickened out of sex-educating her little sister, no chance. She'd have sat Polly down for a long, informative and alarmingly accurate lecture, complete with fellatio demonstration using, Jenny knew as she cleared it from the table, the half-empty bottle of Marks and Spencer's freshly squeezed mandarin juice. Jenny quickly shut the bottle safely away in the fridge, preferring not to speculate on how Daisy, at only fifteen, came to know so much, so young, and trusting it was all theory so far and no practice.

*   *   *

It was true that Daisy had left the house unusually early, but she had not gone to school, not yet. Sometimes there were more important things than school. She and her friend Emma sat in the train heading in the wrong direction. They huddled into their vast Oxfam overcoats, big enough to fit comfortably over their school uniforms. Daisy's floppy green velvet hat, brim pinned up with a feathered brooch, was a bit creased from having been squashed among her school books, but as it was on her head and she couldn't actually see it, she didn't care. What she could see, gleaming on the grubby floor of the train, were her treasured Doc Marten boots, three weeks old and almost comfortable. At school, they'd have to be carried round all day in her bag, they were too precious to trust to the cloakroom, but that was a problem for later. With only registration and a free study period before 10.00 a.m., there was plenty of time for Daisy and Emma to go into town and have their ears pierced.

'My mum will kill me,' Emma said happily as the train sped between surburban back gardens.

'Mine won't. Never does,' Daisy grumbled. 'I know what she'll say, I know exactly. She'll smile in that dozy way she does and say, "Oh darling, how lovely!" Sometimes, it's like kicking a beanbag, getting her to disapprove. She probably wouldn't even mind if I got nose studs!'

'She'd mind if you got a tongue stud or nipple rings or something though wouldn't she?' Emma asked.

'Oh yeah, well that's different. She'd say that was politically unsound, not feminist enough. She's good at pulling that one. But I wouldn't do that anyway. It would hurt. Imagine them getting caught on something – or someone.'

'Well don't worry,' Emma consoled her, 'you can come home with me after school and share my mum telling me off. She thinks that ear piercing is only one small step up from wearing an ankle chain, so you can imagine what she's going to say.'

Daisy felt quite envious. Jenny's a useless mother, she thought. What was the point of a parent who absolutely refused ever to get really cross about anything you did? Even if I get caught skipping school this morning, she thought, *Jenny* will probably agree that I had a perfectly good reason, be willing to send a note. Hopeless. Jenny could get a first class degree in Understanding Her Children (whether they wanted her to or not). I won't treat mine like that, Daisy decided. I'll make sure they've got something to rebel against, then they'll know what's what.

By the end of the line, Daisy's mind was on whether to choose hoop sleepers or studs, and was therefore not as alert as usual at the ticket barrier.

'Ticket please, love.' A firm hand restrained her, the rest of the queue pressing impatiently against her back. Emma, who had a railcard, was already through the barrier and waiting, closely inspecting a half-clothed beautiful youth on a poster advertising jeans.

'Er, lost it on the train, sorry,' Daisy whispered, hoping the man would feel sorry for her. They always had before. But Daisy in her Doc Martens no longer looked as sweetly childlike as she had in the days when she'd first started playing this game.

The ticket collector stared suspiciously into her purple-shadowed eyes. There were too many trying it on these days. Daisy blinked hard, trying to make tears come, but the man had seen it all before. She was handed like a parcel to another official.

'Come on, let's get you out of the way,' he said with hostility, leading her firmly towards his office. A rumble of smug disapproval rolled from the rest of the held-up queue. Frantic, Emma hopped up and down uselessly, not knowing what she should do.

Daisy twisted her arm free from the man as they

13

went into the office, wondering if she should try to make a run for it. But she needed to use that station so often, and then there were the heavy boots and the huge coat – she wouldn't get very far. 'I think I must have dropped it down onto the line as I got off the train . . .' she ventured in her most reasonable voice, the one that came over as a convincing mixture of apology and authority when her mother used it to get refunds for faulty goods and not be fobbed off with credit notes. But the official was immune to her middle-class accent and to the uniform revealed beneath the scruffy coat that showed her to be a pupil of one of the area's many smart private schools. Such provocative signs of privilege made him reach for the phone with sweet satisfaction.

Oh God, thought Daisy, horribly aware that she had made his day, this is it.

Jenny liked Mondays, once the children had been persuaded to go off to school. Monday held the promise of a fresh new week, the opportunity every seven days to get it right this time. This was the only possible day for starting a new diet, giving up drink, paying bills and getting to the bottom of the laundry basket. Somehow, the rest of the week always managed to wear down Jenny's good intentions and slide away downhill out of control towards the inevitable chaos of the weekend.

She padded serenely round the kitchen (stylish cherry and maple fittings with no overdone, over-carved twiddly bits), doing comfortable housewifely things, alone with *Start the Week* on the radio giving her a vague feeling that she was listening to dinner party conversation without having to worry about choking on fish bones, or make any scintillating comments herself. The washing machine and dishwasher were humming busily. The floor was drying, and the swing bin, rinsed out with Flash (though Jenny thought she could still smell a hint of decaying prawn shell lingering from Saturday's supper party), was upside down on the Delabole slate worktop. Gleaming down at her from the rack above the Aga, Alan's precious Italian saucepans shone like much-loved family silver. Other men, she thought, polished their golf trophies. Alan's passion was reserved for his cookware. Watching him painstakingly cleaning it was like watching a proud new mother lovingly bathing her baby. Jenny guiltily eyed her shamefully tarnished flute in the corner of the conservatory. She had no pupils on Mondays, and as she peeled off her rubber gloves she promised herself a session with both the silver polish and the Poulenc Sonata later that afternoon.

As Jenny smoothed hand cream into her fingers, she consulted her wall calendar. Polly had written in her ballet, tap and jazz dance classes in thick red felt tip pen, which left little room for the rest of the family's activities. But tonight at 7.30, Jenny read, there was to be the first Neighbourhood Watch meeting. Typical idea of Paul Mathieson, she thought. Another attempt to rope the residents of the Close in for an evening of local bonding. It was always Paul and Carol, rounding up the inhabitants for the annual bonfire party ('Do come, such a lovely opportunity for us all to get together . . .'), the Christmas Eve bash, or a series of acrid barbecues on damp and dewy summer evenings that were never quite warm enough.

Sue at the corner house said she suspected him of having Northern roots. 'It's not in the blood of us Southern suburbanites,' she'd said to Jenny over a subversive coffee. 'We don't socialize collectively, not herded together in street parties. People like us would rather get a taxi to the All-Nite Supermarket than pop next door and borrow a cup of sugar. There's always that risk you'll have to look at someone's daughter's wedding photos.'

It wasn't so much the gathering together of the neighbours that bothered Jenny, it was more the idea of setting up something by which they were actively encouraged to keep an uncomfortably close eye on each other. It was like having an official excuse to peer out of the windows with a ghoulish sense of duty. Alan, over the weekend, had dismissed it all as pointless, on the grounds that any street organized enough to set up this kind of thing was obviously doing more than enough peering through its metaphorical net curtains already. In Alan's opinion, any baseball-capped teenager who dared to give an envious second glance to number 28's XR3i was already likely to be surrounded instantly by a posse of amateur law-enforcers. Old Mrs Fingell across the road at number 21, the only one in the street who actually had, shame of it, real net curtains to hide behind, must be tee-heeing with delight at the thought that her snooping would now be officially endorsed by police and a quorum of Close residents.

With her thoughts on that evening's meeting, Jenny had to remind herself that she wasn't actually spying when she went through Alan's pockets before sending his grey suit to the dry cleaners. It was really an act of virtue, especially when compared with the possible alternative of sending a wad of twenty-pound notes to be hand-finished, or a credit card to have its magnetic strip rendered lifeless. Jenny sat on the frilled bed, denting the crisp, white cut-work duvet with her still-slender hips, and selflessly sorted through a heap of crinkled Visa slips, fresh from Alan's wool-and-mohair mix pocket. It was always the same when he'd been away to a conference, as he had the week before. As she sorted the receipts into chargeable expenses and personal sections, she wondered fondly how an accountant could be so carelessly inefficient with his own finances. Cobblers' children syndrome, she supposed, like Sue who had always grumbled that her landscape gardener husband (before the divorce) could never be bothered to mow the lawn.

The receipt for the flowers was a surprise. What flowers? I haven't had any flowers, not lately, thought Jenny, holding the piece of paper and wondering why Alan hadn't mentioned them during the weekend. Surely if he'd sent her an Interflora bouquet from Bournemouth, he'd have expected to see one of her heavy-handed arrangements on the hall table. Quickly she shuffled through the receipts, looking for the one that corresponded with the Visa slip. Alan always kept a VAT receipt, just in case there was something he could claim. And there it was, a pale pink order form from a Bournemouth florist, the carbon-smudged message just readable. *Wonderful tonight, till next time, all love.* No signature, but Alan's pocket. Wonderful tonight, to Jenny, sounded vaguely familiar. She trawled her memory and scooped out of it a song of that title by Alan's beloved Eric Clapton. The words 'wonderful tonight' were preceded by 'My darling you were . . .' An everlasting loyalty to the music heroes of his youth had always before seemed rather endearing, touchingly boyish, as if a taste for the rock music of 1968–75 (Beach Boys, Pink Floyd, Rolling Stones et al), was something most men were expected to grow out of, like reading the *Beano*, and train spotting. This was one of the songs Alan would croon around the house late at night, drunk, while clearing up after a dinner party. It was a signal that he was on the way to feeling like sex. But this message: *all* love? Who was all this love allocated to?

Jenny sat on the bed, facing the big gilt mirror over the chest of drawers, the chest she had so lovingly tortoiseshelled with a foul mixture of stainers and vinegar after attending classes in decorative painting techniques the year before. The face staring back at her looked more puzzled than stricken. She reached out and got hold of the brass rail at the bedhead, feeling the need to steady herself, and that the safe level ground of marital harmony was tipping slightly.

Slowly and reluctantly, her brain allowed in the possibility that her husband might be having an affair. It wouldn't be casual sex because, dangerous as it was these days, that certainly wouldn't rate £45 worth of flowers – not from an accountant anyway, money conscious as they habitually were. Such a huge amount of money, too, when Alan had been worrying lately that the cash flow in the accountancy practice was a long way from healthy. Somehow he'd collected too many clients with diminishing incomes and a reluctance to pay their bills. And Alan wasn't the type of man to have an affair, Jenny told herself sensibly. But a little voice (sounding like Sue's) was also telling her that there was no such thing as the type of man who didn't. Here, maybe, was a torrid romance with someone he thought of as, if he followed the words of the song, 'Darling', whereas Jenny he tended to address, in moments of tenderness as 'Pudding'. Someone to whom he sent £45 worth of flowers, delivery and VAT extra, yet to Jenny he occasionally brought a limp bunch of tulips, grabbed in a hurry from the van outside the station, and never quite enough of them to make one of those generous over-blown arrangements that she admired in *The World of Interiors*, but couldn't do.

She inspected herself closely in the mirror. She was looking for what Alan saw when he looked at her, not for what she took for granted about her own face. She saw a woman who looked less than her age, could still pass for under forty; a woman who wore slightly too much red lipstick, as a hangover from her student days when she'd once been hungry enough to supplement her meagre grant and parental stinginess with what was politely described as 'escort' work. A woman who still thought it wasn't ageing to wear her fairish hair thickly hanging to shoulder length and who was probably wrong about that, as tying it back took another five years off and messily piling it up looked so drop-dead sexy that no-one noticed her age.

Jenny tried to imagine what Alan would think of her now if he was meeting her for the first time, say at a party. Had she now become depressingly housewifey? No longer fanciable? Peering at herself in the mirror, she searched for any trace of the girl Alan had first met, the thrilling, lemon-haired flautist, shimmering in black silk in the orchestra. Instead she saw a harassed middle-aged mother of three, a part-time flute teacher with tarnished hair and lines on her face that she liked to think were from laughing rather than ageing. What, these days, was Alan seeing? Had he met someone fresh, young and perfect, someone who, newly discovered, still found it more exciting to go to bed with him than with a gardening magazine?

Jenny wondered if she would ever move from the edge of the bed. Her fingers were frozen round the flimsy bits of paper, and her eyes, in the mirror, were dulling with the cloud of unanswered questions. Who was this 'Darling' who had been 'wonderful'? And which night? Age? Height? Brainpower? Surely to God, not another accountant? And not, oh please not, that desperate old cliché – his secretary?

She forced her reluctant limbs to unfold and walked stiffly down the stairs like someone recovering from flu, and into the sitting-room, wondering what was the right thing to do next. She thought about TV plays she had seen about this kind of thing, where wives set fire to their husbands' dearest possessions in a frenzy of furious resentment. The immaculate saucepans were reputedly indestructible and anyway essential – it was pointless to smash anything she might need to use again. The image of a blazing train set came to mind, even though Alan, as far as she knew, hadn't touched one since Daisy was little. He didn't play golf, so she couldn't test her angry strength bending a set of priceless clubs, and she used his camera and hi-fi just as much as he did. Anyway, maybe it was all a mistake, she thought hopelessly, feeling that she should at least go through the motions of giving him the benefit of the doubt before she made a bonfire with his clothes and his cookery books.

Then the phone rang, and immediately the news of Daisy's arrest pushed all thoughts of Alan from Jenny's mind. Clutching the phone, listening to the police sergeant, she could foresee, in the months ahead, Daisy in court, fined, expelled from school and abandoning her GCSEs half-way through the course. She asked to speak to Daisy, and through the window watched Carol Mathieson tripping along the Close with her determined high heels and shiny, stiff *Come Dancing* hair. She reminds me of one of the three Billy Goats Gruff, Jenny thought, watching her clicking along, trip-trap, trip-trap over the ricketty-racketty wooden bridge. Perhaps she'll be eaten by a troll lurking behind number 16's lime tree.

Carol, seeing Jenny watching her, trotted across the road quickly and mouthed an eager hello at her over the garden fence. Jenny, with the ruins of Daisy's life grasped in the phone in one hand, the wreck of her marriage among the bundle of receipts in the other, smiled rigidly while Carol made faces about the meeting. 'You are coming, aren't you?' she cooed persuasively over the fence. 'I'm just going to make a start on the finger foods!'

Jenny waved limply at her, wishing, not for the first time, that the local preference for knocked-through rooms and all-exposing windows didn't leave her feeling that her entire domestic life was simply a big-screen video, switched on for all to see, like watching opera with the excluded masses in the rainy piazza at Covent Garden.

When she heard the faint and sorry voice of Daisy saying, 'I'm sorry Mum, I didn't mean to . . .' down the phone, somehow she couldn't stop thinking about Carol's buffet. Troll-au-vents. Daisy heard her mother giggling down the phone and thought that it was sure to be entirely her fault that at last the poor old thing had flipped.

Chapter Two

'Whatever were you thinking of? You get enough money for fares, don't you? And why weren't you in school?' Jenny leaned back on the Aga rail, arms folded, facing her daughter with enough parental fury to satisfy even Daisy's high standards. Polly and Ben had fled quietly up the stairs to avoid getting caught in any crossfire in the kitchen, and Polly was taking advantage of the atmosphere of tension to seek comfort in Ben's room with his Sega Megadrive instead of doing her homework.

It had taken Jenny all afternoon to get round to confronting Daisy. In the car on the way home from the station her shocked brain was still reeling with thoughts of Alan's Bournemouth romance. Revving angrily at the traffic lights, she'd suspected she might burst into tears if she started talking. Daisy would just have to interpret her lack of communication as hurt silence. Daisy had waited patiently to be told off and had sat quietly in her room all afternoon, finishing some long-overdue maths. She had been surprised not to be taken straight to school, but hadn't dared ask Jenny why she was being brought home instead, as if her crime was a sort of illness that could be infectious to the other girls.

Jenny gave the tomato sauce a vigorous stir and turned to face Daisy again. 'You know what will happen now, don't you?' she said. 'You'll have to go to court, and you'll probably be let off with a warning, seeing as it's your first time. This *is* the first time isn't it? You don't make a habit of cheating British Rail do you?'

''Course not,' Daisy mumbled, staring at the pale wooden floor. It wasn't entirely a lie, it was the first time she'd been caught. She counted the knots in one of the wooden planks, not daring to meet Jenny's glittering gaze.

'And the worst thing is, you'll have a record. They'll make social reports on you. Social workers might start coming round. God, I suppose there's even a chance you'll be put on probation! It'll be either that or a caution or nothing at all, the sergeant said. And it won't be nothing at all, you can bet,' she said, waving the wooden spoon threateningly.

Jenny watched Daisy scuffing the floor with her foot and wondered if the thought of probation was actually as shocking to the girl as it was to her. Perhaps Daisy was secretly thinking it might add to her status with her friends at school. Boys might find it dangerously attractive. Suppose she was expelled? Daisy had changed into unfamiliar clothes, a neat white shirt and a red skirt that was not, for once, from a charity shop. She looked as if she was already anticipating her court appearance, trying to get round Jenny just as she would the magistrates by being as ordinarily presentable as possible. She'd even tied her hair back with a plain black cotton scarf. Usually her hair, with its irritating half-grown-out fringe, hung across her face like a lop-sided wedding veil, and was constantly being scooped back in that Sloaney gesture common to all girls whose parents paid for their education.

Jenny reached into the fridge and pulled out a pack of tagliatelle. 'Go and call the others, supper's nearly ready. You can do the table. And make sure Polly doesn't forget to wash her hands.'

Social workers. Jenny's body went through the motions of preparing the supper, briskly washing lettuce and flinging open cupboards and drawers as if she really was concentrating on nothing else, while her mind wondered what it would take to get everything in the family back to normal. Biggles, unfed and ravenous, seemed to know better than to complain, and waited silently on his fur-matted cushion for someone to remember he existed. Social workers didn't, Jenny knew, deal with families like hers. They existed, helpfully and rightly, for the abandoned, the feckless, the inept and the inadequate. Nice middle-class girls, surely, were never Taken Into Care, that bogeyman threat hung over the inhabitants of the council estate just the other side of the main road. Did social workers have those special labels stuck to their windscreens, like doctors, she wondered as she drained the pasta, *Social Worker on Call*? She could just imagine a neat little Vauxhall Nova parked outside the house by an efficient woman with a clipboard and a heap of scruffy buff folders, all the neighbours filing past to read the shaming sign perched on the dashboard.

'Why's supper so early?' Ben asked as he and Polly clattered into the kitchen.

'Mum's going out,' Daisy said in a whisper, terrified of attracting any more attention to herself. Then she added, 'I'll babysit Polly, shall I Mum?'

Jenny plonked the dish of pasta on the table and looked at Daisy's extraordinarily humble expression. 'Well you'll be home anyway, so you can hardly call it babysitting. Don't imagine you'll be allowed out for the foreseeable future, Daisy. I think you can take it that you're now what you'd call "grounded". Anyway, Alan should be back before nine.' Jenny stopped in the middle of the kitchen, salad bowl in hand, gazing unseeing out of the window. What a lot there was to confront Alan with; perhaps she should make a list. She sighed, 'God knows what he's going to say.'

Daisy slumped miserably in her chair and helped herself to a minuscule portion of tagliatelle. Jenny felt infuriated by her air of penitence – Daisy was normally so feisty. She hadn't said a word in her own defence about the fare-dodging, although she could usually be relied on to make a spirited effort at justifying any misdemeanours. It was almost as if the girl was acting, practising for a school play audition for the role of some mousy Victorian governess.

It was an enormous relief to everyone when Jenny and her cloudy mood left the house to go to the meeting. Ben opened his bedroom window and lit a cigarette to go with his chemistry homework. He sat in his room up in the attic, wondering if it was time to remove Michelle Pfeiffer from the wall and install someone else. He didn't feel the same about her since Luke at school had come back from Los Angeles after the summer and bragged that he'd actually met her, really truly spoken to her. 'She was only this high!' he'd said, pointing at the middle of his chest. He'd made it sound like they'd spent hours together, though it turned out Luke had merely collided with her for the briefest second in a restaurant doorway. It was hard to carry on fancying someone who might actually have spoken to greasy Luke, even to tell him it didn't matter that he'd stood on her foot; such an off-putting thought that she might have wasted one of her sensational smiles on such a creep. All the same, if Michelle was actually lying on his bed right this minute, instead of being blu-tacked to his sloping wall . . .

Jenny strolled slowly up the road towards the Mathieson's house at the end of the Close, where it sat importantly in central position, watching over the rest of the inhabitants like the responsible head of a family, which was rather, she thought, the role the

Mathiesons had taken on for themselves over the past few years.

The Close was a cul-de-sac, jutting like a fat thumb into the Common, giving the inhabitants a feeling almost of rural isolation. But across the main road at the end of the Close the council estate loomed high and huge. It was the mysterious hinterland from which all crime and chaos was generally assumed to originate. No-one from the Close had ever been mugged, threatened or harassed by anyone from the estate, but on dark evenings, mindful of terrifying newspaper reports of no-go areas and escalating violence, they automatically carried only credit cards or small amounts of change to the off-licence, and at night carefully took their in-car entertainment systems into their homes with them. When, through its owner's forgetfulness, a car stereo went missing, there was a man at the pub round the corner who could reliably supply and fit a replacement Blaupunkt within twenty-four hours.

The houses in the Close were big, sedate Edwardian villas, with attics Veluxed and occupied by teenagers or au pairs (Croatian was the current preference, they ate so little out of solidarity with their tragic compatriots back home, and Fillipinos always came expensively in pairs). Limed oak or pastel-sponged kitchens extended into pretty conservatories, and garages had been converted into freezing, unused, home offices and games rooms. The occupants, like a lot of the population of South West London, were an artistic collection. Apart from Alan the accountant, the stately Fiona Pemberton who happened to be Polly and Daisy's headmistress, and Paul Mathieson, who was something in software, the Close residents were mostly in TV, journalism and advertising. Several cars, all of which languished unwashed at weekends while their owners shuffled through the worthiest Sunday papers, displayed the prized badges of media success: BBC executive car park stickers on their windscreens.

Front gardens were well tended, with not an ugly spotted laurel or dull privet to be seen, but planted with choisya, philodendron, or a rare viburnum. Exotic varieties of clematis trailed around the porches, tangled with passiflora or cascades of excessively thorny but wonderfully scented Bourbon roses, all neatly under-mulched with weed-proof bark chippings. Standard bay trees stood like sentinels in ornate, frost-proof earthenware tubs by front doors and were decorated with oranges and cinnamon sticks at Christmas time. Fiona Pemberton had been horrified when hers had been stolen.

Most of the people who lived in the Close had done so for several years. They tended to buy the houses after living in smaller versions of the same thing, having developed a fondness for art nouveau stained-glass porch doors, generous room sizes and plaster acanthus cornicing that was hard to paint, imagining that they were on their way up to something even more impressive. The ultra-successful moved on to security-gated splendour on Barnes, Clapham or Wimbledon Commons or, if they could put up with the problem of parking, to something elegantly Georgian on Richmond Green.

Only old Mrs Fingell's house stood out from the rest, unmodernized, shabby, unkempt and rewarded for it by being placed in a cheaper band for Council Tax payments. Mrs Fingell, in her house that was unchanged since she had moved in in 1947, had greying net curtains haphazardly draped across her window, her grandson's rusting Volkswagen minibus perched for long-overdue repair on crumbling bricks, half in and half out of the garage, and a collection of dented dustbins that suggested a family of at least eight. Cats peed on her straggling lavender, and litter and cardboard boxes blew in through the gaps in her collapsing fence. At 79, she lived alone with her apricot poodle, unaware that pooper-scoopers had been invented, and her neighbours, who fumed quietly at the decrepit state of her house and garden, liked to think that by waving as they passed her window, they were doing their bit to keep an eye on her.

'You know what the Mathiesons and such are all worried about, don't you?' Jenny was startled from her gloom by Sue catching up with her just outside Mrs Fingell's house. 'It's the council estate. They think only two types of people come out of there – cleaning ladies and criminals!' Sue's springy red hair bobbed up and down as she walked, her face, lively with the anticipation of making fun out of a tedious evening, had a pleased-with-life radiance that Jenny had forgotten existed. Sue chuckled, 'That's why they want to set up the Neighbourhood Watch thing, to frighten away the common criminals and the common people, not to mention how good it is for insurance premiums, being hand-in-glove with the local police.'

The houses they were passing didn't seem to be lacking in burglar proofing. At number 5, in spite of protests to the council (a round robin organized by Paul and Carol Mathieson), Harvey Benstone had even cut down his prize camellias so as to deprive no-good joint-casers of a potential lurking place. Large metal alarm bells hung warningly over the ornate front doors, and powerful lights flicked on and off all night as foxes and cats strolled across inaccurately beamed flower beds.

'Will there be food, do you think? I'm starving. Last time I came to Carol and Paul's I had a McDonald's with the boys first, and then found I could have saved my money. I'm relying on Carol for dinner, there's sod-all in my fridge, 'cept the Martini of course. I hope I've guessed right this time,' Sue said as she and Jenny arrived at the Mathiesons' wrought iron gate.

'You have. I happen to know Carol's had an afternoon of finger-food preparation!' Jenny started to giggle. Sue always cheered her up. She had an impulse to confide in her about Alan, and about Daisy, but there wasn't time. Paul Mathieson opened his front door as the two women crunched over his gravel.

'We've got a Crime Prevention Officer!' he said excitedly, as if announcing that tonight's dinner would be a roast ox. 'He said a gravelled path was just the right thing, nice and noisy. Puts them off, intruders.' Paul, pleased with himself and eager as a boy scout, was wearing a multi-coloured sleeveless pullover, handknitted, with little houses on it. Jenny recognized it from the Kaffe Fassett knitting book that she had once bought. She had felt too intimidated by the degree of difficulty of the patterns to buy any wool. Carol, she saw, had not felt the same. Carol could also arrange flowers, she noticed, admiring the display of dahlias, lilies, carnations and unidentifiable greenery on the mirror-polished table in the hall, reminding her of the Bournemouth bouquet. Carol did everything neatly, even to the extent of producing, eleven years before, twin boys in one well-organized pregnancy. That, she had said at the time, got all that inconvenient childbirth business over and done with in one go. They had now been tidied away to boarding school, courtesy of a trust fund from a dead grandmother.

'Look in there, lovely grub!' Sue whispered loudly, prodding Jenny in the back as they went towards the murmur of voices in the lemon-and-white-stippled sitting-room. Plates of teeny smoked salmon sandwich wheels, cheesy scones and other savoury bits and pieces sat, elaborately garnished and forbiddingly clingfilmed, on Carol's best lace tablecloth, hovered over longingly by a collection of Close residents, clutching schooners of sherry. Then Jenny caught sight of the policeman, her second that day, sitting importantly on one of Carol's mahogany carvers, and whispered back to Sue, 'I think you'll have to wait till the floor show's over; you'll have to make do with a drink for now.'

'No problem!' said Sue, picking up the two fullest glasses of sherry from the silver tray.

Polly wasn't sure if it was a knock on the door that she'd heard, so she assumed someone else would answer it and carried on watching the television. Eventually, lured by the sound of male voices in the kitchen, she crept up to listen at the door. It wasn't her father, she realized, and it wasn't just Ben talking to the cat. She slid in through the door and sat at the table, unnoticed by the gaggle of teenage boys gathered together round the kitchen scales. The boys were very big, two were wearing expensive puffa jackets and another, who looked slightly familiar in a pulled-down baseball cap, had a biker's leather jacket with patches sewn on it. Ben was looking pale and nervous, not like when he was with his usual mates.

'What are you doing? Is it homework? What are you weighing?' Polly asked all her questions at once, before they could throw her out.

'What's she doing here? You said there wouldn't be anyone . . .' a gingery boy was staring coldly down at Polly.

She stared back, and gave him her best smile. 'I'm Polly. I live here,' she said. 'What are you doing? It looks like you're weighing out Oxo cubes. Is it homework? Have you got Home Economics?'

'Polly, get out, would you? Please?' Ben looked at her with an unusual amount of appeal in his voice.

'Well, I was just thinking about making some hot chocolate . . .' she said slowly, enjoying being infuriating. The audience of boys, menacing though their expressions were, didn't bother her. She was on home ground, bugging her brother and liking it. There might be something in it for her.

Ben broke away from the group, got hold of her wrist and marched her to the door. 'Just this once Polly, please will you do as I ask?' he said.

'And what if I do? What do I get?' she smiled confidently up at him.

Ben sighed, but knew the solution. 'If you look under my pillow, there's last month's *Playboy*. You can go up and borrow it if you like. And then I won't tell the parents if you don't tell the parents, OK? Deal?'

'OK, deal!' Polly squeaked, making for the stairs. With any luck he'd forget about the magazine and she could take it to school and show Harriet. Together they could try to make sense of the letters page, and try to find out more about oral sex. Harriet had said she was sure there was more to it than just talking. Polly, magazine in hand, darted into her room, grabbed her hand mirror and took off her knickers. While Ben, in the kitchen, bulk-bought enough cannabis to supply the lower sixth for a month, Polly lay happily among the soft toys on her bed comparing her fanny with that of the Playmate of the month, wondering if her own pudenda would ever be so glamorously photographed.

Jenny sat on Carol's squeaky beige leather sofa, listening to the police constable and trying to stay awake. The room was hot, crammed with Close residents, and Jenny wished there had been something more thirst-quenching than sherry to drink. In the yellow-and-white room, on the pastry-coloured sofa, Jenny was beginning to get the queasy feeling that she was inside a lemon meringue pie, baking stickily. The high turnout of residents was a surprise. Even Fiona Pemberton, whose evenings were usually filled with parents' meetings, school fund-raising sessions and

31

curriculum seminars, had turned up. Jenny didn't much like meeting Fiona socially. At the school they were always Mrs Collins and Mrs Pemberton to each other. It probably didn't do, Jenny assumed, for the headmistress to be seen to be on first-name terms with mere parents, not at a school as fiercely competitive as Polly's and Daisy's anyway. So on home territory, Jenny tended to wait, schoolgirl-like, till she had been addressed, still half formally, as 'Jennifer' and take her cue from there. She had always thought that, by the time she got to forty, she would no longer have that feeling that there was homework she'd forgotten to do, nor would she be intimidated by headmistresses, but she now realized it would probably never happen, at least not while she had children of her own being educated.

The policeman spoke slowly and carefully, repeating points about window locks and car alarms as if he wasn't sure they were capable of taking in all the information. Jenny, who didn't particularly want to meet the eye of the law again that day, stared at the figured cream carpet and was amazed to hear Sue's voice breaking in with a question.

'All this advice about security locks and burglar alarms,' she said. 'Are the police generally of the opinion that if we choose not to have these things, then we have only ourselves to blame for a break-in? Would it be what you'd call "contributory negligence"?'

Jenny stared across at Sue, who had her head tilted at an interested angle, and a smile of great charm aimed like a crossbow at the policeman. Jenny took a closer look at him. He was undoubtedly attractive, and Sue was twice-divorced, currently alone with her two teenage boys, and constantly prowling. Jenny paid close attention to his reply, interested for Sue's sake.

'No of course not,' the constable said, meeting Sue's smile with an equally charming one of his own. 'But our opinion is that there are precautions the house-holder can take, if he or she so chooses, and it's my job to point these out. Some of them are even free – for example, anyone can make sure they close their curtains when rooms are lit. There could be a potential felon hanging around outside: you think you see a bloke walking his dog a bit slowly, and what you're really looking at is some thief pricing up the paintings on the walls.'

There was a distinct shuffling in the room. Most of the residents had such elaborate and showy arrangements of window drapery, flounced, fringed and swagged-and-tailed curtains, arranged to fall in artistic pools of excess fabric on the floor, with bowed and rosetted tie-backs, that they found it tedious to close their curtains, and tended to leave their windows prettily exposed day or night. It hadn't seemed to matter, with the Close having no casual passers-by.

'Shall we have a little break now, and then more questions later perhaps?' Carol suggested firmly, already reaching across and tearing the first strip of clingfilm from the spinach and ricotta filo rolls. 'And I'm sure we could all manage another drink . . .'

'I'm surprised she wasn't trampled in the rush,' Jenny said to Sue as they collected plates full of Carol's dainty delicacies.

'Hmm . . .' Sue replied vaguely, gazing past Jenny across to where the young constable was being cross-examined by Fiona Pemberton.

The rest of the meeting passed briskly. Leaflets and window-stickers were issued, and Paul Mathieson was voted the Close co-ordinator. He volunteered to take charge of the 'Neighbourhood Watch' boards that had to be fixed to a few lampposts and get in a couple of handymen to put them up.

Jenny, relieved to be out in the fresh air but dreading going home alone to face Alan and his adultery, turned to Sue. 'Coming back with me for a drink? A proper one this time?'

But Sue had a look of girlish anticipation about her, and a big, pleased grin. 'Not just now, thanks, I'm being taken in for questioning!' she said, indicating the constable unlocking his Metro. 'Come to the tennis club tomorrow morning for coffee and I'll tell you what it's like being grabbed by the fuzz!' Sue winked lasciviously, and left Jenny to accompany the infuriatingly slow and mildly tipsy old Mrs Fingell to her front gate.

Alan's grey BMW was parked out in the road instead of in the driveway. Another quick getaway in the morning, Jenny assumed, wondering what and who he was really getting away to and from. Slowly she unlocked the front door, reluctant to confront a relationship that, once the accusing and excusing was done, would now be shifted, changed for ever. But there, in the warm hallway, Alan was coming towards her, arms out and innocently welcoming. He looked very big, almost filling the space between the stairs and the wall. All that scrumptious food he's always cooking, she thought, he's getting too bulky to be a good accountant. Clients with money problems want to see someone lean and mean.

'You look tired, Pudding. Come and have a drink,' he said, pulling her towards his cosy, familiar body. Impossible to imagine him calling someone 'Darling'. Jenny relaxed against him, automatically. Alan smelt of home, of family. Whatever would she say to him? And when? 'I'm afraid there's a spot of bad news,' he said. Jenny stiffened, wondering if he was going to get in first. Tell her he had just packed a suitcase and that the quick getaway would be for ever, not just the duration of the next audit. She looked up at him coldly, waiting. He laughed, maddeningly. 'Hey it's not that bad! Mrs McKinley phoned. She says she's terribly sorry, but the twins are giving up the flute lessons. They've decided to have a go at the violin. Pity, losing two pupils in one go like that.'

Jenny sighed, and headed for the wine bottle on top of the fridge. 'I've now lost four in a month,' she said glumly. 'I'll have to advertise.'

'What about Fiona? Why don't you ask if she needs another music teacher? Schools are usually pretty desperate.'

Jenny fidgeted around by the sink, still unwilling to look at him properly. 'Who's been weighing stuff?' she asked, noticing that the scales were drying on the draining board. 'Have you or the children been cooking?'

'Well, I had some pasta with the rest of your tomato sauce. It wasn't bad, in fact it was pretty delicious. Did you get those new season fresh plum tomatoes I told you they'd just got in at the Italian deli?'

Jenny smiled at him, indulgent of his hobby. 'No, of course I didn't! We don't all have time to stand around peeling and deseeding tomatoes! I opened a tin of them like most people do!' Good thing, she thought, as she reassembled the weighing machine, that he hadn't found the empty Sainsbury's pasta sauce jar guiltily hidden away at the bottom of the rubbish bin. It had added a certain piquancy to her own recipe. She started nervously wiping the draining board.

'Why don't you stop fussing and come and sit down?' Alan leaned back in his chair and patted the seat next to him. 'I think we've got something else to talk about.'

Jenny felt her stomach tighten again, churning Carol Mathieson's filo rolls and lukewarm sherry. He looked so comfortable, so guilt-free sitting there, a bit like an over-large elf in his baggy old sweater and with his hair curling at the ends. Biggles purred contentedly on his lap. If he doesn't tell me this time, Jenny promised herself, I'm not going to mention it, not ever. She was surprised by her decision that was on the side of cowardice. It was also, though, on the side of maintaining domestic survival, the security of her family. The question of whether or not the family collapsed into miserable fragments could be all down to her, or could depend on what Alan said next. She sat down next to him, picked at the white azalea plant on the table in front of her and took a long sip of wine while she waited to see if her marriage was about to come to an end.

'Daisy told me what happened,' Alan said.

The moment passed, and Jenny joined in the discussion about Daisy's arrest with something like relief. Perhaps, if she said nothing, it would all just go away, like she always thought with the first throat-rasping symptoms of a cold. In either case, it would be as well to buy a large box of tissues.

Chapter Three

'Well, if he's up to anything there must be some sort of clue,' Sue remarked the next morning. 'Are you two still doing it? Or is he avoiding sex? Does he suggest things like why don't you ever wear purple tasselled knickers or gold stiletto heels? He wouldn't be just the same as usual; you'd just know. I always did.' Recalling the past deceits of men, Sue allowed a flash of gloom to cross her face, and then took a packet of cigarettes from her bag. 'Let's go and sit on the balcony,' she said, tugging at Jenny's shirt. 'I'm dying for a cig.'

The two women took their coffee out onto the tennis club balcony, and sat looking down at the courts, where women enjoying off-peak membership and crèche facilities were firming their bodies and their backhands for the approaching spring.

'Sorry, I know it's a bit cold, but I hate it in there,' Sue said, lighting her cigarette. 'They're all blonde. When I first joined I thought it was a condition of membership. No offence,' she added, with a quick look at Jenny's hair.

'That's OK,' said Jenny, grinning. 'I'm only hanging on to the blondeness by what's left of my fingernails these days. I've just progressed to that stuff that "Covers All Grey". And no, honestly, there's nothing I've noticed about Alan that's different. He's just the same, just the usual, comfortable, very much husband-type person. I feel disloyal,' she added guiltily. 'I shouldn't be talking to you about him like this. I'd hate it if he did the same about me.'

'Probably does,' Sue said, inhaling happily. 'We've all got to talk to somebody, otherwise we'd all end up in therapy, like in America. I'm going to tell you about what I did with Constable Barry last night, parked up the lane by the end of the Common, and I'm not going to feel guilty in the least. After all, he's probably in the canteen right this minute telling everyone round the formica table that the suspect proceeded in a southerly direction till her mouth made contact with the victim's extended truncheon . . .'

'Sue you didn't! In a police car?' Jenny felt a vicarious thrill. Sue seemed to have the sex-life of a free-ranging teenager. Jenny realized it was years since she had had sex anywhere but in a comfortable bed, and it felt like another lifetime since she'd had it with someone other than Alan. Perhaps that was what he had realized too . . .

'Well why not? There's nobody at home who wants it. Besides, he bought me three large ones down at the White Swan, and a prawn sandwich. It was the least I could do.'

'You make it sound very business-like, bordering on prostitution!' Jenny said.

Sue laughed. 'Of course it is! Most sex is prostitution, isn't it? One or the other partner repaying a favour. Perhaps especially the cosy husband and wife sort. Even the producer of *Woman's Hour* thinks that's what marriage is. On past experience I think she's probably right.'

Jenny changed tack slightly. 'Are you sure you should? I mean, is it safe these days?' she asked quietly as the waitress hovered about, dealing with their coffee cups.

'What, AIDS, do you mean? You can use a condom for a blow-job too, you know, though I think it only matters if your gums bleed a lot. Anyway I never did like the taste.' Sue raised her voice slightly for the benefit of the waitress who had flicked her hair behind her ears in order to listen better as she wiped the next table.

Jenny giggled and could feel herself blushing. 'Long time since I did that in the back of a car,' she said with a slight sigh.

'Are you sure it's not a long time since you did "that" at all?' Sue asked her, with an intensely questioning look. 'That might be part of the problem . . .'

'I suppose sex is a bit samey, as it were. But then if you always do it with the same person, and you do more or less the same sort of thing, in the same bed, it's bound to be, isn't it?'

'Well that's probably where the purple tasselled knickers come in,' said Sue. 'Never mind him being at it with someone else, perhaps that's what you need – a little of who you fancy.'

'But I don't fancy, that's the thing.' Jenny gathered her bag and her jacket together. 'I used to feel quite smug about that, you know. I used to think, oh well I did all that stuff, putting it about a bit too much before I got married, well, we all did then, it was that time, few health worries, all that. I used to reason that it was better that way round, than wondering later what I'd been missing. Imagine being a virgin when you married. You'd always want to know . . . No I think my days of doing it in cars are well and truly over. Just something to read about in old diaries!'

'You don't know what you're missing!'

'But that's just it, Sue, I do!'

Ben, Luke and Oliver were taking a cigarette-break during a free study period. They sloped along the path behind the tennis club and sprawled on their favourite bench under the trees, overlooking the courts. Ben realized it was becoming quite a ritual, just checking to see if Carol Mathieson, with her unexpectedly schoolgirlish legs, was out there playing. Oliver didn't usually come with them. A bit adolescent for him, sneaking out of school to leer at half-dressed housewives. He didn't look as if he needed to, Ben thought. Oliver had looked 35 since early puberty, his solid, hairy, rugger-playing body overnight resembling that of a prosperous lawyer somewhere in the prime of life. He never had trouble being served in pubs, and on Mondays he bragged about girls from the High School who couldn't get enough. In the showers after games he so intimidated the others by his swarthy manliness that Ben, for one, felt no girl at a party would ever be pleading with him for anything more than a light for her cigarette.

'Look at them, just look at them. Ripe for the picking, like a tree full of plums,' Luke was saying, leaning forward and inhaling deeply on his Marlboro. Ben stared at the women on the nearest court and, fancying them not at all, still sensed the familiar rising feeling inside his trousers. He crossed his gangly legs and wished he didn't blush so easily. It was such a giveaway.

'What about that red-haired one?' Oliver said, taking a sudden keen interest.

Ben could sense Oliver's sexual antennae tuned in to the woman walking across the club balcony. 'God, not her, she's one of our neighbours,' he told Oliver.

'Married is she? Not that it matters.'

'Divorced,' Ben conceded. 'I know her sons . . .'

'All the better. Every woman's dream, that's what we are, when they get to that age. Look at this lot; if they've got time for tennis they've got time for sex. Only common sense they'd rather educate an innocent teenage boy than clean the windows. They think of it as social work!'

40

Ben couldn't fault Oliver's logic, but most of the women didn't attract him. It was Carol and her firm, gym-mistress bum he wanted to see. Even when playing tennis, her hair stayed strictly in place. He almost groaned aloud to think of the times he'd watched her running neatly around the court, with her crisply pleated skirt flashing sensible plain white knickers. He would be willing to bet she wore a dazzling white sports bra too. He could almost hear her saying 'spotless', a word that always triggered his mother into falling about with snobbish laughter. He had no time for all that lacy underwear stuff, all cutesy frills and come-on-look-don't-touch daintiness. All the teasing High School girls wore it, and flimsy though it looked, so far it had always proved impenetrable.

Jenny left Sue to have her daily run on the gym's high-tech machines, and strolled in weak sunshine across to her car. The car park was full of Mercedes Estates, convertible BMWs and Renault Espaces, reflecting the fact that the club members could afford a lot more than the astronomical joining fee. As she unlocked her Golf, she glanced back at the club. She could see into the gym, where a line of elegant, agile women in cutaway leotards ran, with expressions of determination, on rubber treadmills. They're just like hamsters on a wheel, Jenny thought. All around her was park land, the Common, miles of riverside towpath, and here were grown-up, sensible people, paying an annual fortune to do their running in a room.

She got into her car and switched on *Woman's Hour*, reflecting that she was getting very cynical. After all, she knew that no woman in her right mind would go and run alone on the Common, however much was to be gained from fresh air and inspiring surroundings. There was too much to risk in terms of flashers, rapists, murderers and muggers. Funny how it was more or less all right for dog-walking, though, she thought, pulling out on to the main road and heading for the shops. As if being accompanied by a bustling little Jack Russell, or a loping labrador, was any kind of protection.

Jenny parked outside her local newsagents and went inside for a packet of postcards. It wasn't a bad place to advertise for pupils – everyone seemed to do their local buying and selling there. The window was full of cards, some smartly computer-printed, selling everything from car parts and washing-machines to gerbils and baby buggies. She looked over the collection, working out what to say, and found herself counting the number of ways 'accommodation' had been spelt. Then a sudden thought occurred to her, a thought in the shape of Carol Mathieson, all-seeing Neighbourhood Watch Kommandant personified. Did she really want her advertisement to be that local, so local that no-one in the Close, unwrapping a wickedly fattening Dime bar outside the newsagents, could possibly miss this undignified bid for additional income?

Jenny shoved the postcards into her bag and got back into her car. She drove up through to the other side of Putney and found another branch of the same shop, with the same kind of ads in the window. No-one here, she was sure, would recognize her phone number, though it wasn't too far for pupils to travel to her house. And it was yet another area with enough spare money for music lessons. They were an essential part of the local kit, along with riding, ballet and the more obscurely philosophical of the martial arts.

Jenny drove home absent-mindedly, roughly working out how much extra income she would need to earn to compensate financially for being husbandless. It would have to be an awful lot, because an awful lot was what Alan earned, in spite of recent panic over the business, and what they as a family spent.

She wondered what the alimony rate would be if the worst happened and they divorced, Alan going off with Ms Right (mark 2) to raise an entirely new brood of expensive children. (Ms Right would be sure to want them; after enticing men like Alan into their temptingly uncluttered, child-free lives, they nearly always started drifting in and out of Mothercare round about their mid-thirties.) Lost in calculations, Jenny almost didn't see the blue-and-white ribbon stretched across the Close, and very nearly drove through it, like a sprinter winning the Olympics.

She stopped the car and stared into the Close. Police cars and vans were parked at angles so random as to suggest maximum speed and importance. The ribbon was the sort they used when they'd found a dead body. Whose, Jenny wondered, and where? She had a sudden vision of Mrs Fingell sprawled among her dustbins, one of Alan's stainless steel Sabatiers plunged hilt-deep into her back. Perhaps he couldn't face any more of her tedious teases as she caught him unloading Sainsbury bags from the car, all that 'Poor Mr Collins, is she making you do the cooking again? (cackle cackle),' which always drove Alan demented.

Returning to reality, Jenny realized it was most likely Laura Benstone at number 5, renting out her house for another episode of *The Bill*. She was always doing it, pleading poverty and school fees to pay, and hardly a fortnight went past without some film crew or other blocking someone's drive with their catering trucks. She might have let us know, Jenny thought, wondering if they really had to take over the whole street.

Ahead of her she could see a gaggle of policemen walking about in the road, shepherding a collection of reluctant residents towards the main road.

A police sergeant approached her, walking heavily and importantly to her car window. 'Sorry Madam, you can't come in here. I suggest you park over on

43

the estate. We have an Incident.' He said it proudly; this had clearly made his day. In her car, Jenny fled before the Close residents, collectively, could catch up with her. But having parked, she couldn't resist joining them on the patch of grass that separated the estate flats from the main road, just to find out exactly what was going on.

'I called them in,' Paul Mathieson was saying proudly. 'After Mrs Fingell came round and told me. You can't be too careful. Not with bombs.' Jenny peered past the group, which consisted of two young mothers and an au pair with a brood of toddlers, John Jordan the 'resting' actor from number 10, Laura Benstone's husband Harvey, who was furious at having been interrupted half-way through writing a vital scene in a TV sitcom (serve him right, thought Jenny, both for the catering trucks and for cutting down those camellias), Paul Mathieson, Mrs Fingell, and the rarely seen George Pemberton, semi-retired lawyer husband of Fiona. From balconies above, Jenny could hear the chatter of estate residents revelling in a rare visit from the police that was to the Close and not to themselves. More accustomed to police cars chasing suspected joy-riders round their labyrinthine lanes, they cat-called and gloated delightedly.

The police cars and vans had chosen a crazy place to park if something really was about to explode, dangerously close to what Jenny took to be the bomb. She also noted that the object in question was sitting on her own garden wall. Alan had built that wall. It had been the only use he'd ever found for his mother's final Christmas present, a Reader's Digest guide to DIY. It had been open on the path, like one of his cookery books, as he carefully measured out sand and cement. Jenny often thought he'd erected the wall as a monument to his mother, and at the time had half-expected him to top it off with a sculpted angel, and to carve her name and the dates of her birth and death on it, seeing as she, tidily cremated and secretly scattered at Blenheim Palace, had no gravestone.

Now it looked as if the police were going to detonate whatever device it was they'd found perched on it. Jenny shivered. What would have been a playful little breeze in the lush and sheltered gardens of the Close was, here under the looming blocks of flats, a freezing blast of tunnelled wind.

'Whatever made you think it was a bomb?' Jenny asked Paul. 'It's hardly IRA territory is it? Did you have a close look?' She peered past him, squinting against the weak sunlight. The object on the wall was hidden in what looked like a Waitrose bag. Someone, out of curiosity, must have been peering in to see what it was.

'You wouldn't think Hampstead was IRA territory either,' Paul was saying, 'but they had a bomb there, didn't they, just before Christmas.' He was smiling smugly, practically wagging a finger at her. 'It's a sort of square black thing with wires trailing. You can't take chances, not these days.'

Down in the sealed-off Close, blue lights on police cars were still going round and round. Just showing off, Jenny thought, wishing she could get home and go to the loo.

It was a very small explosion, what the police always referred to as 'controlled', but enough to wreck the wall. It fell almost willingly to the ground, crumbling with a shameful lack of resistance. Perhaps Alan had misread the recipe for the mortar after all. He is going to be furious, Jenny thought, wondering at the same time if the damage was covered by house insurance. Did it count as an act of war, malicious damage, accident or what?

'Bloody waste of time,' George Pemberton rumbled crossly. Overwhelmed usually by the presence of his wife, he was hardly ever heard to speak, and Jenny turned to look at him. 'I could see it wasn't a sodding bomb,' he said. 'The fool wouldn't bloody listen.'

'Did you see what it actually was?' she asked him. He looked such a mild sort of man, very beige in a wool shirt and old man's cardigan with leather buttons, the sort of man who would smoke a pipe and be good at crosswords, not the sort to have such fury bubbling away inside.

'Just a teenage thing,' he said, his glare, as he looked Jenny up and down, mutating into something unnervingly close to an ogle. 'One of those things they're always listening to when they walk into you on the pavement. Gives them a glazed look. Yours have them,' he finished, glowering at Jenny accusingly.

The police sergeant came back, walking even more slowly. 'You can all go home now. Panic over,' he said, with a hint of a smile.

'What about Mrs Collins's wall?' Paul stepped forward and asked.

'Are you Mr Collins?' the sergeant asked, puffing out his chest like a sparrow squaring up for a territorial battle.

'No, I'm not. As a matter of fact I'm the Neighbourhood Watch co-ordinator,' Paul replied, puffing out his hand-knitted chest to match the sergeant.

A small, knowing smile crossed the face of the policeman. 'So you'll be the one who called us in,' he said, looking Paul up and down as if he was exhibit A.

Paul beamed and nodded, proud as a schoolboy at a prizegiving. Confidently, he waited to be congratulated.

But the sergeant's grin was not a friendly one. 'So you'll be the person,' he hissed, coming very close to Paul and adding with the kind of sneer only achievable by a man in uniform, be he commissionaire or Colonel, 'Sorry, I'll rephrase that. What I mean is you'll be the

46

complete and utter dickhead who can't tell Semtex from a Sony Walkman. Tell me, Sir, am I right or am I right?'

There wasn't much scope for fantasy, being an accountant, even one with so many clients in the music business. Alan sat behind his impressive, environmentally hostile teak desk and tried to feel interested in the table of disheartening figures in front of him. On his walls in the cream-and-chrome office hung dusty gold and platinum discs donated by rock stars in their past prime, with gratitude to their money-minder. Often, Alan had been given tickets to see bands that he had long known he should be feeling too old to watch. He'd tried offering them to Daisy or Ben, who had scorned these heroes of his youth, pretending, he thought, that they'd never heard of them. Jenny never wanted to go either, unless, which was rare, he could promise her a flute player in the band, or a comfortable seat at the Albert Hall. All these things had served as excuses down in Bournemouth, driving Serena half-way across the county to see one of his favourite bands. 'I adore these old dinosaur bands,' she had said, referring to the fact that they'd been famous since her babyhood. Alan couldn't see the relevance to an extinct creature; dinosaurs died out, some old rock 'n' rollers, thank God even against overwhelming odds, never did.

The client in the chair opposite was unhappy, complaining that the Inland Revenue were claiming his blood and bones as well as what was left of his now meagre income. Alan found meetings like this more depressing than any other, for although his own long-ago fantasies of stardom remained just that – distant unreality – here at least was one who had, at the time, done all the fantasy-fulfilling for him, for him and his generation. At nineteen, after three blissful,

47

girl-pulling, schoolwork-wrecking years in an atrocious part-time band called Snakepit, Alan had given in both to the nagging of his frantic parents and the growing knowledge that he was an essentially inept guitarist, and sold his precious Telecaster. Sadly he had not, as he had daydreamed, been telephoned by Mick Jagger begging him to join the Rolling Stones in place of the dead Brian Jones. He was nowhere close to the Jimi Hendrix league when it came to sex appeal. So, worn down by a finger-wagging lecture from his headmaster that he had been undeservedly lucky not to fail his A-levels, Alan had been persuaded that one day he might want to live somewhere more secure than on a mattress in the back of a Transit van with a woman who would hang around for more than a torrid twenty minutes in the Watford Gap car park, and he had gone off to study accountancy for no worthier reason than that he was better at maths than anything else. It had felt like conceding defeat, abandoning his fantasies and joining the grown-ups, but at least there were still other, braver people who would do the rich and famous and badly behaved bit on behalf of him and the rest of the more cowardly conventional. Now he sat, comfortable in his well-worn leather chair, watching one of those whom he had relied on to fulfil his there-but-for-qualifications-go-I dreams, scratching round in a column of pencilled figures for the wherewithal to fund his next telephone bill.

Alan felt depressingly adult. He studied the lined face of the man opposite, a drug-ravaged face that looked as if it had lived three debauched lifetimes, and he felt sorry for him. Alan didn't like this feeling, he didn't want to feel pity for a former hero, that wasn't what heroes were for. The whole point about them was their indestructibility. They were supposed to be made of different, star-dusted stuff.

He sighed, promised to sort out the official receiver

and, charitably, did not point out that the lifetime earnings of the average middle management employee must have been sniffed up the client's nose during the past ten fame-diminishing years. There was no point, and it would make no difference now. Unfortunately for this client, cocaine was not tax deductible.

When Jenny eventually got into the house, there were already two messages on her answerphone, both of them from men enquiring about the flute lessons. Jenny was pleased that men were taking an interest in their children's music lessons. She was too used to pushy mothers, asking things like why hadn't little Petronella been entered for Grade 3 yet, surely she was more than ready. Fathers tended to keep out of the way, occasionally turning up to collect their children from the lessons, but as often as not hanging around outside in the car boredly flicking through their *AA Book of the Road* rather than coming in and risking a chat about progress and practice.

Jenny was just opening the front door to go and collect Polly from school when the phone rang again.

'It says flute lessons on your card.' Yet another male voice, this time sounding like he had a bad cold and was talking through a handkerchief, mumbled at Jenny.

'That's right,' she said brightly. 'Is it for a child?' Jenny tried to be welcoming, business-like. 'I normally charge £16 per hour, £9 for a half hour . . .'

'A child what do you mean, a child?' the man interrupted, spluttering down the phone at her.

'Well, I teach all grades of course, complete beginners too . . .' The phone went dead. 'Oh terrific,' she said into it. 'Thanks for wasting my time and making me late.' She flung the phone down and dashed out to the car, glaring at the ruined wall as she passed. It might be a good day for seeing Fiona Pemberton about teaching flute at the school. Biggles was sitting in a patch of sunshine on top of the rubble, washing his back leg. I wonder how long it will take Alan to sort that lot out, she thought. It could end up like Mrs Fingell's garden. She bent down to stroke Biggles, and picked up a blown-in Snickers wrapper.

'Pity about your wall!' Carol trilled at her from the window of her all-white Peugeot. Pity about your bloody husband, Jenny felt like shouting back.

Polly was looking unusually subdued, sitting big-eyed and wary out on the school steps, watched over protectively by her loyal friend, Harriet Caine. Jenny sensed trouble as she struggled to squeeze the Golf between a Nissan Patrol and a Vauxhall Frontera.

Harriet did the talking. 'Mrs Spencer says she would like to see you,' she reported quietly to Jenny, standing guard in front of the guilty-looking Polly.

Jenny gently moved Harriet aside. 'What have you done now, Polly? You know this is an important time, with your exams coming. I hope it isn't anything naughty.'

'Depends how you look at it. Not very naughty. I don't think so anyway, but I think maybe Mrs Spencer does.'

Jenny strode up the steps into the grandiose Victorian building, wishing she wasn't wearing her oldest jeans and sweatshirt but was one of those mothers who always dressed as if they were about to go to a charity lunch. The building was scruffy, a large converted house forming the tacked-on junior department of the High School. Few of the parents here had ever visited an ordinary modern primary school, but had they done so they would have realized that no state school would have tolerated the dingy corridors and lack of space that parents here were taking out second mortgages to pay for. What they wanted and got for their money was to have their little daughters grandly presided over by the formidable Fiona Pemberton, to learn French from the age of eight, and to scramble at eleven for the forty or so places reserved for them in the famously successful senior department of the school.

Ahead of Jenny a gaggle of the velvet headband brigade (pie-crust collars and cashmere to match) were discussing the forthcoming exams, which would weed out the no-hopers from those who would make it through to the senior school and safely on their way to Oxbridge, exams which would make lifelong enemies out of politely ruthless mothers. The crowded corridor, cheerfully lined with splodgy paintings, smelt of brown rice and chicken, overlaid with the soupy aroma of pre-pubescent little girls. The lino floor was scratched and filthy, and Jenny wondered, if it wasn't in the interests of keeping the place clean, why the uniform list required the girls to have three pairs of shoes each.

Jenny took a deep breath and knocked on the open door of Polly's classroom. She felt guilty herself, summoned like this to the teacher's presence. She should have waited and got some idea about what Polly had actually done before she rushed in, then she could have prepared an informed defence. Mrs Spencer, a brisk young woman with neatly bobbed, conker-brown hair, was sitting at her desk marking the day's maths.

'Ah. Mrs Collins,' she said, but didn't continue, and Jenny thought, Oh God, it's so serious, the poor woman doesn't know what to say. 'Ah. Mrs Spencer,' was the most tempting reply, which Jenny, wisely, didn't make.

'Polly tells me you want to see me,' she said instead, as evenly as she could manage.

'Yes. Mrs Collins, I'm afraid I found Polly and her friend looking at this during the lunch break.' Glancing nervously towards the open door, Mrs Spencer pulled the *Playboy* magazine from under the pile of exercise books. Jenny could feel her mouth twitching treacherously into a smile and fought to resist it. Mrs Spencer had put the magazine down and moved her hands down to her lap, as if not quite liking to touch. She's only young really, Jenny thought, early thirties perhaps. Where do teachers leave their sense of humour? In a staffroom locker every morning? Is it confiscated by the head teacher and kept in a cupboard till the end of term?

'She's just a typical little girl with a highly developed sense of curiosity,' Jenny said, getting in quickly with her defence of Polly.

Mrs Spencer regarded her coolly. 'There are plenty of things for little girls to feel curious about at ten, Mrs Collins. Pornography isn't usually one of them.'

You've been dying to say that, Jenny thought, you've been rehearsing that all afternoon.

'She says she found it in your house.' The teacher leaned forward slightly and stared at Jenny intently and with scarcely-hidden curiosity. 'Should you have left it lying around do you think?'

Oh no, thought Jenny, she thinks we're regular readers. She's sitting there wondering if Alan is trying to perk up a flagging sex life. Jenny had already realized the magazine must be Ben's (mustn't it?). Who but a teenage boy would want to gaze at these glossily sanitized gynaecological studies? Who but a teenage boy and blasted Polly.

Jenny felt as defenceless as when she herself had been caught smoking at her own school. 'I'll have a word with her,' she promised, giving in feebly and mindful of the exams. 'It won't happen again.'

Behind Jenny there was a brisk rustle and a slight breeze, and Fiona Pemberton, looking queenly in something floral and silky swept into the classroom. Jenny wished that she and the magazine could hide under the desk. 'Glad to see Daisy is feeling better. We missed her yesterday. You do know you're supposed to send a note of course, but as it's you . . . Trouble with Polly?' Fiona suddenly said, her face switching from all-purpose professional smile to furrowed concern as she caught sight of the magazine. She picked it up, thumbing through it with no hint of the genteel repulsion of Mrs Spencer. Her frown deepened, as her well-practised brain sorted out what was happening. 'Can't have this you know, Mrs Collins. Corrupting the other girls. I'd be sorry to see Polly turning into a Bad Influence.'

'Just a bit of childish fun, I expect, Mrs Pemberton,' Jenny said firmly, standing up both to leave and to feel on more equal terms with the headmistress. She'd never liked being loomed over. 'I must get back. I've got a pupil at 4.30.' Fiona was still flicking through the magazine and Jenny smiled at her as she walked towards the door. 'Do keep it if you like,' she couldn't resist saying, and then could have kicked herself. She could hardly add, after that, 'I suppose a job's out of the question?'

Chapter Four

Daisy was wrong if she imagined, on her return from school, that the destruction of her Walkman would result in any leniency in her punishment for fare-dodging. A girl at school was having a party a few Saturdays ahead, and Daisy was quietly desperate to go to it. Everyone else was going. She put on a desolate, wronged expression and wandered sighing round the kitchen, toasting a crumpet on the Aga and waiting for Jenny to feel sorry for her. The Walkman suddenly became her most prized possession, now lost for ever together with her new Senseless Things tape, her absolute unchallengeable favourite. She put on an expression that she hoped looked like deep mourning.

But, with an end-of-the-day headache from a hopeless Grade 1 pupil shrilling and stumbling over his scales, and no fruitful response to her advert, Jenny was adamant. 'No of course you can't go out to parties. You haven't even missed out on one single weekend yet. You skived school and you stole; you can't expect us to overlook it completely.' Jenny then smiled with some sympathy. 'Look, it won't be for ever. But it will be long enough for you to think about what you've done.' She reached for her jacket, hanging on the back door. 'Keep an eye on Polly for a bit will you, love,' Jenny went on. 'I'm just going round to tell Paul he needn't worry about replacing your Walkman.'

Daisy flipped from feigned misery to real anger, waving her crumpet in the air and dripping butter

54

onto the floor. 'Oh Mum, that's not fair! Why should I have to lose out on that too?'

'Don't jump to conclusions! I'll get it on the house insurance! Or from those trigger-happy police.' And she made her escape, before Daisy could wear down her resistance.

'Good thing I was home, really. Anything could have happened,' Paul Mathieson was bragging to Carol as he watched her chopping leeks. In the ice-white, germ-free kitchen she chopped fast and firmly; bits did not fall off the scrubbed board onto the floor, or stick to the knife in an undisciplined way. The knife was stainless steel, it wouldn't dare be otherwise, and the shining blade flashed up and down. Paul, flinching, put his hands in his pockets on their way to a gesture of protection.

'Anything could *not* have happened, Paul,' Carol said, stopping briefly to point the knife at him. 'There was nothing in that bag but Daisy Collins's Walkman. I think that Mr Hasty is going to have to volunteer to pay for that, isn't he?'

'Yes Carol,' Paul conceded meekly, wondering if it would be all right to help himself to the sherry, even though it wasn't quite time yet. He glanced into the sitting-room at the glass cabinet containing the decanter. If it wasn't locked, she wouldn't hear him opening the door. But if it was locked he was in trouble, for although the lock was tiny, it had a distressingly loud mechanism to it that no amount of oiling could silence. 'Can I tempt you to a teeny drink, my pet?' Paul said, thinking to entice her to early alcohol. He took a hopeful step towards the cabinet. A couple of sherries inside Carol, and she might be in the mood for a bit of conjugal access later on.

'Not until you've fed the cats,' she replied sternly, not even looking up from the chopping.

Paul turned back and dutifully opened the catfood cupboard. Ming and Mong, the matched pair of squint-eyed pale Siamese cats yowled at him from the kitchen floor, plaiting their skinny bodies round his legs. Greedy little buggers, he thought, why should their dinners get priority over me and my drink?

He held his breath as he scooped the foul-smelling Whiskas. The two food bowls had the word 'Pussy' in ornate script painted on them, bought in humourless innocence by Carol, but which never failed to bring a silly schoolboyish smirk to Paul's face. He bent to put the dishes on the floor, keeping the evidence of his dirty mind turned away from Carol, in case she caught him and gave him one of her looks. The cats, tigerish, hissed at each other over the food and jostled stupidly for the same bowl, ignoring the other one. Paul squatted on the floor to push them apart, getting scratched for his effort, then sat back on his heels and watched Carol's bum jiggling slightly in its tight mauve trousers as she vigorously cut carrots. It was a trim bum, apple-round and temptingly biteable, it seemed to Paul. He could see the imprint of her knickers showing through the fabric, and knew they were the blue lacy ones, cut high and trimmed with jaunty satin frills round the legs. Paul, influenced by the cats, bared his teeth in semblance of a lecherous snarl, just as Carol turned to look at him.

'What *are* you doing?' she demanded, incredulously.

'Er . . .' The doorbell rang, saving Paul from inventing an explanation. Rearranging his features into a twisted grin, he scrambled up from the floor and leapt into the hallway, almost falling through the frosted glass into the porch in his eagerness to be away from Carol's interrogation. 'Come in, come in!' he yelled into Jenny's surprised face. 'Come and have a drink.' He steered Jenny into the sitting-room and placed her firmly in front of the drinks cabinet, opening it (damn, unlocked all the time) with a flamboyant flourish and hauling out the sherry bottle.

'Er, actually have you got something else . . . ?' Jenny was saying, but found herself holding an engraved schooner, with copper-coloured liquid being slopped shakily into it.

Carol bustled through from the kitchen, wiping her hands on a flower-appliquéd towel. 'Jenny, Paul is *so* sorry about Daisy's tape player,' she purred, and then added waspishly, 'aren't you Paul?' as Paul was looking resolutely blank.

'Oh yes. Of course. Though it was an understandable error. You never know these days, crime is all around us, bombs, terrorists, drug dealers. It's a war out there,' he waffled, swilling down his sherry and reaching for a refill. 'Top-up Jenny?'

Jenny, who thought it wasn't really very understandable at all and had barely sipped her sherry, put her hand firmly over the top of the glass. 'No thanks, really, this is fine.'

Carol took over, guiding her to the squeaky sofa. 'Of course you know, Jenny, he's right in one way,' she said. 'The increase in crime, especially burglaries in areas like this, well it's appalling. I blame all those unemployed boys with nothing better to do.' She leaned forward eagerly, and then back again, frowning as she caught Paul's gaze homing in on her cleavage. 'Have you been in that estate up across the main road? All day long, absolutely heaving with people, all milling about with nothing to occupy them. We're heading for a revolution, that's what I think. They'll come pouring across that road and ransack nice, law-abiding places like this, just like Russia.'

God, she's mad, thought Jenny. Stark staring. Carol would never go across the main road into the estate, in case she was robbed both of her values and her valuables. How could she possibly have a clue what went on over there? But Carol, her spun-sugar hair jerking briskly like a rooster's crest, was just warming up.

'And the children, not a father present between them! No role models. I thank God we were able to send our boys safely off to a decent prep school where they can learn what's what. And there's a lot to be said you know, for joining the cadet force. Channels their energies.'

Into learning how to kill each other, crossed Jenny's mind, but she said instead, 'They could learn what's what here at home, surely, with both parents present?' suddenly keen to defend her own version of family life, 'if all you think they need is a father-figure?' Carol gave her a sly look, something conspiratorial, as if what Paul could teach her sons wasn't likely to be worth knowing.

'You know,' Jenny told her, 'the vast majority of crime by young people is done by boys. The same lone parents are also bringing up girls too. So surely it's the messages that are getting across to boys in society that are damaging, not necessarily their family structure.'

Carol, for a moment looked stumped, but soon rallied. 'Oh well, the girls, we all know what they're doing don't we? Getting themselves pregnant and straight up the housing list, that's what.'

In the face of such prejudice, Jenny could only give up. It was time to go before Carol progressed to the benefits of bringing back National Service. 'I must get back, I've got a chicken in the oven,' she said, leaving her sherry glass on the floor beside the sofa and hoping that one of the snaky cats would knock the dregs out of it onto the cream carpet. No wonder they had to send the boys away to boarding school, she thought, the pastel furnishings would never stand up to healthy wear and tear. In any normal family, that pallid sofa would have a generous quota of felt pen marks.

'We haven't paid you for the Walkman,' Paul said, pulling his cheque book out of his pocket. 'How much, about thirty quid?'

'Thirty-five should just about cover it,' Jenny answered, wondering why on earth she'd ever thought of going through all the bother of claiming on house insurance.

'Though, really I suppose,' Paul wavered, 'if it wasn't for Mrs Fingell poking about . . .'

'If you've got it, I think Daisy would actually prefer cash,' Jenny persisted ruthlessly.

'Oh, right.' Paul slowly counted out the notes. 'Here you are then, and do tell her it was only out of a spirit of neighbourliness, won't you?'

Alan felt self-conscious in the pub. It hadn't felt like this in Dorset, perhaps this time it was because he was still wearing an office suit. Serena was buying the drinks. He watched her queuing at the bar, her long legs in black lycra, her long body in an oversized cream silk shirt and embroidered waistcoat. She didn't look conspicuous – every girl in the place was dressed in some sort of version of what she had on. It was Serena's idea of what to wear to the office. A bit whacky for accountancy, Alan's partner Bernard had thought, but she was the most highly qualified of the new young applicants, as well as Bernard's niece, and as Alan pointed out, they weren't exactly offering the kind of salary that would run to power-dressing.

Alan felt he still smelt of the office, but worried more that when he got home he would smell of smoke and pub, and that Jenny would be needing an explanation. He worried, too, about Serena and the flowers; she hadn't said anything, perhaps his daft romantic gesture had embarrassed her. He imagined her giggling about them, heartless and youthfully brittle with her flat-mate. It wasn't likely that she had, in her shared basement flat, anything suitable to put them in; things like huge, expensive vases were accumulated by people like himself and Jenny over many years of organized domesticity. She'd probably dumped them in a plastic bucket. Maybe it was too much, they'd only gone to a casual gig together after all, not for a night of passion at the Ritz. It had been a rare spontaneous gesture, the result of relief at finding, right there in his own office, someone to share his interest. It was easy with his cooking, everyone could eat and appreciate the results and say all the right things. But music was a different matter. At home, it was only when he was drunkenly playing air-guitar to Free's *Alright Now* at the tail end of one of his own parties that he could feel uninhibited about his tastes. That they weren't shared by his family and friends usually became obvious as Ben and Daisy left the room in over-exaggerated embarrassment ('Oh *Dad*') and life-long friends started looking for their coats and car keys. He'd never, in all truth, shared Jenny's love for classical music, although years ago the sight of Jenny, dizzily blonde and slinky, playing her flute in tight black velvet had attracted him quite madly. There was still something sensuous about watching her play; the way she licked her lips and carefully prepared her soft mouth for the flute. But Mozart did not move him, Mick Jagger did. In polite company, where middle-aged, middle-class musical taste had settled at the point of unobtrusive Dire Straits CDs as dinner party background, he hoarded this secret as guiltily as if he still had a yearning to stand anoraked and train-spotting on Crewe station.

The pub was pretty sordid, with a brownish swirl-patterned carpet disguising goodness only knew what kind of stains. There was a smell of stale beer and air freshener and the walls and ceilings were murky with congealed fumes from micro-waved chips. Alan rarely went into pubs with Jenny; perhaps on holiday in Cornwall looking for a beer and a sandwich, always to somewhere clean, rural and picturesque with lavishly planted hanging baskets, where hearty, home-made bread and organic Stilton would be served. Outside this one, the traffic roared past on the North Circular and an ancient greasy roadie in the corner was sound-testing a microphone, murmuring the usual 'one, two,' into it. Alan liked that sound, it was like a comforting, long-familiar mantra. His suit felt ever more out of place as the bar filled, everyone else in jeans or leather or cords. He should have taken a change of clothes into work with him, he thought, like he had in school days, hiding his fur-trimmed parka in his bag for travelling home on the bus and trying to pull girls from the grammar school. You got detention if you were caught doing that, he recalled. He wondered what the punishment, if Jenny could catch him now, would be.

Serena brought over the drinks, and the band came on to the tiny stage and started flicking at their guitars. Alan looked around the room; he wasn't the only ageing rocker in the place, which wasn't surprising, seeing as the band had been in business 25 years. He caught the eye of a balding man, about his own age and they exchanged half smiles, acknowledging each other's long service as rock aficionados. Was he another refugee from an over-cultured home, Alan wondered? Just then the band, the tweaking and tuning satisfactorily completed, slammed heavily into their first number, and he felt the music, hard as a gut-punch, with just the same thrill as at his first Yardbirds gig back in 1963. Back then, he had suspected that not even sex would come close to this, and, if pressed thirty years on, would have to acknowledge that he had suspected right.

Jenny had never had an obscene phone call before.
You certainly didn't expect it in the middle of supper.
The awfulness of it, she thought, could only potentially be rivalled by a call from any woman hoping
to get Alan and then pretending she'd got a wrong
number. The man had been very specific about what
he wanted, though how she was supposed to provide
that kind of service down the phone she had no idea
– perhaps he, like Polly, also thought oral sex was some
kind of conversation. Back at the table, Jenny pushed
the remains of her chicken round her plate, bereft of
appetite.

'But what did he actually *say*?' Polly demanded
eagerly, wondering if oral sex, after all, actually
involved talking on the telephone. This would be
something to tell Harriet, as far away as possible of
course from Mrs Spencer and any other schoolteacher
busybodies.

'Yeah Mum, what did he say?' Daisy asked, wishing
she had taken the call. It was so rarely that she let anyone else answer the phone too, reasoning accurately
that most calls were usually for her.

'He wanted, er, well, wanted me to do things. Offered
money too,' Jenny said, brightening slightly and giving
a weak grin. Perhaps it would be best to make light of
it, especially in front of Polly. Lucky that Polly hadn't
picked up the phone, she'd have kept the man there for
hours, talking pornography and acquiring new depths
of knowledge.

Ben, trying to stay calm and wishing some woman
would call him and offer to pay him for rendering
obscene services, reached across and spooned up too
many potatoes from the dish, messily dropping some
of them onto the pine table. 'Isn't that the sort of thing
you're supposed to tell your vigilante group about?'

he asked. 'Won't you have to report the crime to your leader?'

Jenny shuddered at the thought of repeating the details of the call to Paul. He'd write them all down, verbatim, and file them away in one of the folders Carol said he kept neatly shelved in his attic den. She could just see him, licking the tip of his biro and saying, 'Now can we just go over that again, make sure I've got it right. What was it exactly he wanted you to do?'

'No, because it's no threat to anyone else in the road. I won't be telling anyone else. Definitely not.' Except Sue, she thought privately, who could be relied on to lighten the sordidness of it. Then she grinned at him. 'Oh and Ben, don't call them vigilantes, it's only Neighbourhood Watch. Can you see Paul and Harvey and old Mrs Fingell wandering round with cricket bats, defending the Close and beating up suspected villains?'

'I can,' said Daisy, 'especially Mrs Fingell, and Carol even more. I think she'd like a uniformed man with a barrier across the end of the Close, letting in no-one but people like her in sequined Italian tracksuits, oh and perhaps the postman and the John Lewis van. None of my friends would get near the place, not ever.'

'You still haven't told me what he said,' Polly grumbled into her cauliflower. 'If I don't know what a dirty phone call sounds like, how am I going to know if I ever get one?'

'You'll know, Polly, believe me. And let's hope it never happens.'

Polly hoped for no such thing, and was determined to spend the rest of the evening hanging around as close to the telephone as she possibly could, even if it meant missing *EastEnders*.

Even though it was after midnight when Alan came home, Jenny was still awake. Eager to get on to the next day and hope it turned out better than this, she had gone off to bed early, tried to sleep but couldn't. Daisy's music, essential accompaniment to homework, was still thump-thumping from her room. Jenny wondered if it might be better to ask her to turn it up till it was identifiable, rather than having to lie there trying to guess what she was playing from the heavy bass rhythm. Then there were her thoughts: two odd phone calls in one day, the first one about the flute lessons, where she and the caller seemed to be talking at bizarre cross-purposes, and then the blatantly obscene one. She wondered about the postcard in the newsagent's window; perhaps there were pervs out there who simply wrote down a few numbers at random and gave them a call, on the off-chance. Did that happen to the people trying to sell old sofas, or their wedding dress? Perhaps her handwriting had looked too distinctly feminine; next time she'd type her advert. She had at least, thank God, not put her name and address on it.

She heard Alan at about 12.30, pulling up into the driveway, the handbrake giving its characteristic whine. Something else that would need expensive fixing, she thought. Snug under the duvet with a novel, she knew she should really go downstairs and talk to Alan, explain about the demolished wall, tell him about the phone call, and about Polly and the *Playboy* magazine. If it hadn't been for that damned florist's receipt, she would have looked forward to sharing the day's disasters with him, lightening the drama by laughing and having a late glass of wine together while he picked at the cold chicken at the kitchen table. Jenny lay wide awake, propped up like a glamorous invalid on the big blue-and-white-striped square pillows, wondering where on earth he'd been till this time, with whom and doing what. I never used to give it a thought, she realized, having assumed that when he said he had a client to audit who could only by seen during the evening, and thirty miles away, that he would have no reason to be telling anything but the truth. Now she could feel herself turning into the kind of wife she had always loathed, the sort who sniffs the air, cat-like, for unfamiliar perfumes, inspects jackets for stray other-woman hairs. She could hear small noises of Alan creeping about downstairs, obviously hoping not to disturb anyone. Every floorboard in the kitchen seemed to have been reawakened, and Jenny could track his progress by the creaking as he walked from door to fridge, to the sink, to the table, and back to the warmth of the Aga.

As sleep wasn't possible and curiosity grew, Jenny pulled her dressing-gown from the back of the door, wrapped herself cosily into it and went downstairs. Alan was drinking tea, chewing a chicken leg and looking lonely, she thought, sitting on the wooden rocking chair by the Aga, Biggles curled up on his lap. He smelt of pubs, and she tried not to think who he might have been to one with. Was it marginally better, she wondered, than smelling of expensive restaurants? Or was She the type (rather like Sue, much as Jenny loved her) who was anyone's for a half of lager and a bag of pork scratchings?

'You're late; too much work?' she asked as lightly as she could manage, switching on the kettle and reaching into the cupboard for a mug.

'Yeah sorry about that, though I did find time to grab a sandwich and a pint later on. This chicken's good,' he said, making Jenny immediately suspicious. Usually he would comment that just a little more tarragon would have been a good idea, or irritate her by asking if she'd crushed the garlic before she'd chopped it.

'You saw the wall?' she asked. Alan nodded, looking sorrowful. Jenny grinned at him. 'I'm afraid it was our Neighbourhood Watch being over zealous. Mrs Fingell and Paul thought Daisy's Walkman was a bomb and the police blew it up. It was quite dramatic. I got £35 off Paul for it. I'm not sure what to do about the wall.'

Alan's chicken leg stopped half-way to his mouth and he gave a blast of incredulous laughter. Biggles stretched his ginger face up towards the chicken, in hope. 'You're not serious! Stupid buggers! Actually I thought you'd backed your car into it or something, hardly dared mention it in case you got all upset.'

Jenny leaned on the Aga, cupping her hands round the mug and warming her back. Alan was looking tired but affectionate. Was that guilt, or was he becoming horribly adept at running two lives? Earlier in bed, brooding on the possible depths of his deception, she had started him off having a one-nighter with some stranger at the Bournemouth conference, and had progressed in the space of thirty seconds to having him set up in somewhere, say, St Albans, with an entire extra family.

He was still giving her a fond and familiar look. 'You know we could take this tea up to bed, in fact I think we should, don't you Pudding?' He got up slowly, nudging the cat gently to the floor.

'Why Pudding?' Jenny asked suddenly, switching off the kitchen lights behind her as they made for the stairs. 'And what sort of Pudding? A Roux Brothers special, say a difficult *millefeuille aux framboises avec crème fraîche?* A solid sticky toffee pudding? Delia Smith's wholesome apple pie? Or something fiery and exotic by Marco Pierre White?'

Alan, his hand fondling her bottom as they climbed the stairs, laughed. 'You've got nothing on under this. Delicious. I'd say that makes you right this minute, a highly appetizing crème brûlée. Sweet, with a deceptively crisp surface and deliciously creamy inside.' Jenny giggled quietly. At the top of the stairs he gently bit the back of her neck. 'But of course,' he went on, 'I'll have to taste you and see.'

He can't have been doing it this evening, then, Jenny concluded with relief as she cleaned her teeth, brushed her hair and splashed on some Diorella, because if he had he'd never have the energy to do it again, not these days. She climbed back into bed and Alan wandered around the bedroom, off to the bathroom and back and shed the trappings of the day, till all that was left was a pale, slightly flabby, vulnerable body confidently expecting to sample the pleasure of his wife's. Alan got into bed beside Jenny, smiling happily, snuggling up to her like a guilt-free child and laying a heavy arm across her breasts. God I hope he hasn't caught anything dangerous, Jenny thought, feeling suddenly chilled. With her highly efficient contraceptive coil she could hardly ask him to start using condoms without giving a very good reason. She wished she'd been quick-witted enough to pretend that along with the other disasters of the day, the thing had unexpectedly dropped out, but it was too late now, his hand was rediscovering its familiar map-references on her body, so, praying silently, Jenny crossed her fingers and prepared to risk her life.

Chapter Five

'I can't miss Sophie's party, I just can't bear to. What am I going to do?' Daisy, freezing cold on the games field, kicked the goalpost and thrashed at the grass with her hockey stick, complaining to Emma from the depths of despair.

Emma tried sympathetically to think of past tactics that, with her highly exacting parents, had usually worked. 'Have you tried reasoning with them? Say you've learned your lesson and swear you'll never do it again? Have you tried cleaning your room and promising to keep it all horribly tidy for ever and ever? That kind of thing even works with my mother, and you know what a stroppy cow she is.'

'No. No point. This time they're outraged, they feel "disappointed" as Mum put it. She has this "how could you let us down like this" expression whenever she looks at me, as if she regrets being so understanding all these years. She looks really miserable and it can't be *all* my fault. I can't help it if all her pupils suddenly don't like playing flutes any more.' Daisy gave a deep sigh. 'I'll have to come up with some mega plan by the end of the week. Perhaps she'll relent and let me stay the night with you, if I swear we're going to stay in and revise physics.'

'Got to be worth a try,' said Emma. 'You can't miss a good party, it isn't healthy. All those boys from your brother's school are going, so we should be there. Getting off with them is good for us, with all our adolescent hormones rushing about. I'm sure they'll give up and disappear for ever if we don't give them something to do. Hormones I mean, not the boys. Think of it, back in the olden days, girls were having babies and amazing orgasms by our age. It can't be right to suppress all that.'

Emma had a slightly off-the-wall grasp of biology, Daisy felt, but she probably had vaguely the right idea: if nature made you feel like mucking about in a sexual way, then who were they to argue with that? They could leave out the having babies bit of course. She could try putting that one to Jenny, that being grounded was getting in the way of her essential sexual development – though on second thoughts perhaps she couldn't. Jenny, when Daisy was younger, would occasionally let slip that she herself had had a wild time in her own youth, and that it was no bad thing either. Just lately, though, she had been careful not to talk about it, as if she rather regretted mentioning it. Daisy blamed AIDS.

From up at the far end of the pitch, Emma and Daisy could hear the rest of the hockey match shrieking its way to a finish. Daisy always managed to get picked to play left back for the better team on games day, along with Emma in goal, both of them perfectly content that all the squalid, muddy battling for the ball would take place at the opposite end of the field and they would be left in peace to shiver and gossip.

'Where are all the blokes then?' Emma said, folding over the top of her games skirt so its hem was up to the bottom of her navy blue school games knickers. 'There's usually at least six over by the gap in the fence.'

Daisy swivelled round to look. 'Not one,' she said. 'We must be losing our appeal. Probably too old. I expect they turn up in droves to watch year eight, all

those twelve and thirteen-year-olds, just on the turn.
We're cooked, finished, and obviously of no interest
to the pervs.'

'No you're wrong,' Emma said, suddenly perking
up and running her fingers through her wind-ravaged
yellow hair. 'Look, there's that one from Ben's lot, the
one who looks more like someone's dad.'

Daisy recognized the description before she actually
saw Oliver, and immediately started arranging her long
legs in a decorative pose, leaning, seductively she
hoped, against the goalpost with her skirt 'accidentally'
hiked up and showing her gym knickers. They were
baggy and truly horrible, and always referred to as
'bloody bloomers', but nevertheless, Daisy reasoned,
they *were* knickers, and from what she heard Ben
saying, that was what boys all wanted to have access to, visually or manually.

Daisy had a soft spot for Oliver; there was an Italian
look about him, very dark and knowing. Holidaying
at Lake Como when she was thirteen, Daisy had been
thrilled by the attention she had attracted from waiters,
cab drivers and strangers in the street – a constant
stream of exotic, appreciative noises, hissings through
dangerous white teeth, low, sly whistles, deliciously
rude-sounding foreign words, then the covert squeezes
and prods. 'Don't take any notice,' Jenny had instructed
her, appalled that her baby daughter was already being treated as a sex object. 'Don't meet their eyes
and they'll leave you alone.'

But Daisy had gazed brazenly into every passing
velvet-dark eye, so different from those of cold, gawky
English boys, who blushed to the roots of their acne if
she so much as blinked at them. Two years later, on a
chill English hockey pitch, Daisy could feel the glint
in Oliver's eyes from a hundred yards and suddenly
sensed ice-cream and sunshine.

'Don't hog it, Ben,' Oliver ordered, reaching out his hand. Ben inhaled deeply and passed the loosely rolled spliff over to Oliver, who took a well-practised toke. 'Not bad, this stuff. Usual supplier?' he asked Ben.

'Yeah. But they're putting the price up for next time. Unless we order more, that is.'

'Don't really need it do we?' Oliver leaned contentedly on the fence. 'Not when we can get off on watching totty like your little sister. I like a girl who hitches her skirt up instead of down when she knows a bloke is looking. It's a very promising sign.'

Ben was watching Emma who was jogging up and down on the spot to keep warm, her games skirt flashing her navy blue underwear at him. It was amazing, he thought, how those awful regulation knickers, so unappealing when left drying stiffly on the laundry room radiator at home, could actually become quite sexy when they were on a non-family bottom.

A laugh rumbled from Oliver. 'Another time, we should bring binoculars, pretend we're doing a survey on the incidence of black-headed gulls in London's open spaces or something. A good way of combining A-level biology with, well, A-level biology.'

'I'm spending my life spying on sporty women,' Ben muttered. 'I'm getting a taste for it. God what will I be like when I'm sixty?' Emma's legs were even firmer than Carol Mathieson's, but under those awful knickers he knew there would be a barbed wire fence of deceptively flimsy frills from Knickerbox.

'By sixty you'll probably have been arrested for it,' Oliver concluded, stubbing out the remains of the joint and making a private bet with himself that he would personally dispose of Daisy Collins's virginity before the end of the school year.

*   *   *

'Do say if you'd rather not, won't you?' Laura Benstone's pretty, ski-tanned face was peering anxiously at Jenny round the lilac tree by the front gate.

Jenny, stiff from thinning out the dead bits of lavender in the hope that it would last through the coming summer, stood up and tried to straighten her back. 'Rather not what?' she asked Laura warily. Why did Laura always do this, she wondered, start talking to her as if they'd already had half the conversation?

'Your house of course!' Laura said, with a smile as if she was about to give Jenny a huge present. Jenny flicked earth from her gardening gloves and waited, smiling encouragingly. 'The people filming, they can't use mine because I've booked it out for a fashion catalogue, all stills. So they said could they possibly use yours, as it's almost identical?' Laura looked worried, as if it had suddenly occurred to her that Jenny might not want two tons of film equipment and thirty total strangers taking over her home. But then she cleverly pulled the plum from the pie: 'You do get an awful lot of money for it,' and then she whispered, as if Neighbourhood Watch might be all-hearing, as well as all-seeing, 'cash, if you prefer.'

Jenny laughed.'That's not the sort of thing you're supposed to say to the wife of an accountant!' she told Laura.

Laura looked momentarily confused and then grinned. 'Could be worse, darling,' she replied pertly. 'You could be married to a tax inspector. Anyway, will you do it? Pretty please? I hate to let them down, they might use someone else next time and then I'd have to go out and get a proper job. And we are trying so hard for another baby . . .'

Jenny really wished people wouldn't say things like that. Into her head rushed an unstoppable vision of Laura and Harvey having frenzied sex in their kitchen against their vast Bosch Gourmet Food Centre, magnetic plastic fridge letters clattering to the floor around their feet like multi-coloured rain. Jenny fiddled guiltily with her trowel and tried to concentrate.

Laura, huge eyes staring appealingly out from under her dark fringe, was looking alarmingly as if she might cry, making Jenny feel personally responsible for the eventual size of Laura and Harvey's family.

'OK, OK, I'll do it,' Jenny told her. 'Or at least, they can come round and talk about it so I can find out what's involved. It'll have to be a stupendous amount of cash if it means weeks of disruption, though,' she warned Laura.

'It won't, I promise. They only usually take one day. Oh super, you're wonderful!' Laura gushed delightedly. 'I won't forget this, you and Alan must come to dinner.'

Well if she couldn't get flute pupils, this would have to do instead, Jenny thought as she scrubbed earth from under her nails in the kitchen. The spectre of a future on half the income with the same expenses briefly chilled her again. But just then the phone rang. Perhaps it will be one of the answerphone parents ringing back at last, Jenny thought, as she hastily dried her hands.

She liked the man's voice, there was a sense of humour in it. She didn't get much of that in the usual music-pupil parents. Usually they were too concerned with instrument prices, making sure they got their full half-hour, and the whereabouts of the nearest Royal Academy examination centre to waste time with friendly badinage. It would be nice to teach a grown-up for once too, someone who was learning to play because they had chosen to.

'Is my being disabled a problem? Or, sorry, I should say, "physically challenged" shouldn't I?'

'As long as you can hold a flute, it doesn't make any difference,' Jenny told him, which for some reason made him laugh. 'How mobile are you?' she then asked, wondering if he intended to travel to her house and would need a ramp for a wheelchair to get over the front doorstep. There was probably something in the shed that Alan could rig up.

'Oh, pretty mobile. It's just the new feet, well you'll see.'

Jenny rather hoped she wouldn't, not seeing their relevance to music. 'Have you got your own instrument?' she then asked, and the cheery man laughed again.

'Certainly have, love. Never go anywhere without it!'

'You got him from an advert? Flute lessons in a shop window? Are you mad? You might as well have put "Friendly fellatio, thirty quid a blast"!' This wasn't the response Jenny had expected, when she went to see Sue to show off about her new pupil. Sue was in her kitchen, stirring their lunch – Waitrose lentil soup from a carton – and looking over her shoulder at Jenny with an expression of complete astonishment. 'Are you the only person on the planet who doesn't know what 'flute lessons' means when it's on a sleazy postcard?'

'It wasn't a sleazy postcard! And no, I may be ridiculously naïve but I didn't know. There's obviously a gap in my education,' Jenny retorted from Sue's kitchen table, where she was slicing the Waitrose garlic bread (also from a carton). 'I put an ad, as I told you, in a perfectly ordinary newsagent's window. I didn't notice any French lessons, Swedish massage or lists of Miss Whiplashes, anything like that!' Then she stopped slicing abruptly, and, knife poised, stared horrified at Sue. 'Oh God what have I done?'

'Why, what *have* you done? Given him your credit card number as well?'

'Apart from booking him in for a lesson next

Thursday at two, I asked if he'd got his own instrument. No wonder he laughed.'

'Not surprised.' Sue took the soup to the table and giggled happily. 'I expect he said he was incredibly attached to it!' She gave a delighted snort, relishing the joke.

Jenny thought she could feel her face going pale. 'Don't laugh, he actually did say something like that. Whatever is he going to expect?'

'A blow job of course, and a good one. What will you charge him?'

Jenny still looked pale, and also determinedly prim. 'For a flute lesson I charge £16 per hour, £9 for half an hour. I wouldn't do *that* to a stranger for any amount,' she told Sue archly. Sue's eyes twinkled, disbelieving. Not these days, anyway, Jenny added to herself. It had been different back in the days when she'd once found it the only way to keep herself in food and music papers. For a couple of weeks, well into an end-of-term overdraft, it had been that or give up college altogether. In terms of payment she'd have been happy, if the clients only knew it, with just the sumptuous meals they'd provided. But that had all stopped when she met Alan and he'd taken pity on her empty fridge. She'd never told him. Whatever would have been the point?

Jenny made a decisive start on her soup, but Sue was waving her spoon about and had a hard-thinking expression. 'You could charge a lot more than that, and it would only take a few minutes . . .' she calculated.

Jenny's spoon splashed into her soup. 'No I couldn't not for any price!'

'Bet you would! Bet you'd do it for £50.' Jenny stared back coolly at her, but Sue didn't give up. 'OK, but you'd do it for a thousand.'

Jenny laughed. 'Oh well, for a thousand, I suppose most people would, unless they were filthy rich already.

Yes, OK, I'd do it for that. But I'm not being offered a thousand, I shouldn't think anyone would be. And I'm not doing it, I'm not a tart.'

Sue had a triumphant grin on her face as she ripped apart a slice of garlic bread. 'Ah, but it's like that old joke isn't it? If you say you'll do it for a thousand quid, then we've already established that a tart is what you are, now we're just haggling about the price!'

Half an hour and the best part of a bottle of wine later, Sue and Jenny were in the sitting-room, each reclining on a kelim-covered sofa and clutching mugs of coffee. Jenny liked the room, it reminded her of the hippy dens that she and fellow students fashioned for themselves at university long ago. The walls were a cosy womb-red, though hung with vivid, driftwood-framed abstract art rather than the concert posters she had had, and the floor was swathed in a collection of ancient rugs. Divorced from her pair of husbands, and with her sons away at a famous public school, Sue lived, also student-like, in a state of perpetual clutter; no-one had ever seen the surface of her desk, so strewn as it was with letters and documents. It only needs the smell of joss-sticks, Jenny thought, and we could be way back then . . .

Sue broke into her thoughts. 'I mean, it's not as if you've never done it before, what could it hurt?'

'My dignity, integrity?' Jenny countered. 'Plus the fact that I'm supposed to be a happily married housewife?'

'Doubly titillating for your customer. You could dress the part in floral crimplene, fluffy slippers and a pinny,' Sue argued. 'And where did the "happy" come from all of a sudden? What about Alan and whatever he's been up to lately? Can't you think of it as sweet and lucrative revenge?'

The wine and the warmth from Sue's log fire were making Jenny sleepy. She looked out of the window across the main road to the ever-lively estate. No wonder Sue had a broader outlook on life, because, compared with staring over the never-changing Close to number 15's neat festoon blinds, a wider view was literally what Sue had.

'I did a lot of it in my teens – for free I mean,' Jenny admitted, thinking aloud. 'It was to do with being Catholic. We all knew we couldn't have sex, that was a sin. The nuns never mentioned the oral stuff, well they wouldn't would they?' Jenny smiled to herself at the very thought. 'As long as we didn't actually go all the way – remember when it was called that? – anything else was fine. By the time we'd made it into the sixth form, there were girls who'd seen as many dick-ends as weekends and could still call themselves virgins.'

'Well there you are then,' Sue said, as if it was game, set and match to her. 'And if you use these,' she fumbled under the sofa and pulled out a packet of condoms, 'they're labelled "assorted citrus flavour", you'll be able to close your eyes and pretend you're sucking a fruit gum.'

I'll just have to explain it's just a dreadful mistake, Jenny thought several days later. She hadn't been at all organized, not even taking the man's telephone number. Even with a real music pupil she should have done that, in case she had to cancel for some reason. She should have taken far more details. She'd actually booked time to be alone in her house with an unknown man; he could murder or rape her, and she was every kind of fool for being so casually negligent. He'd *said* he was called David Robbins, though if he was looking for something other than a music lesson, it wasn't very likely to be his real name. Jenny had a cursory look in the phone book, but couldn't bring herself to phone any of the twenty-seven possible numbers. What could she say? 'Hello, this is Jenny Collins, sorry but the service I provide isn't actually fellatio after all'? Suppose she had to say it to twenty-seven different answering machines? Would it be worse than saying it to his face, as she would obviously have to?

Wherever she went, driving Harriet Caine and Polly to school, trailing round Waitrose, restocking at the garden centre, Jenny searched for cheerful-looking youngish men in wheelchairs. The few she saw looked miserable and ancient, wrapped up in hand-crocheted blankets and pushed by weary women. They looked more in need of a square meal than anything furtively sexual. She eyed drivers with 'disabled' stickers on their cars, but couldn't see which bits of their bodies weren't in full working order. She even crept up behind a man on crutches outside the local greengrocer's and started talking wildly about the inflated price of cauliflowers, just so she could hear his voice. Jenny thought she'd recognize the sound of David Robbins's voice anywhere, a slight Welsh lilt on the edge of breaking into a chuckle. But the man on crutches, possibly because his leg hurt, was devoid of humour and sourly remarked, in an accent that was pompously London SW, that caulis were always that price in February, hadn't she noticed?

On the day of David's appointed visit, Jenny could barely think straight for nerves. Always quick to take advantage of a lapse in concentration, Polly complained over breakfast of feeling a bit ill.

'It's like a cold starting,' she said, putting on a pained look and trying to make her voice sound croaky. 'You wouldn't want me to infect the whole class, would you Mum, not with the entrance exams coming up?'

'What have the exams got to do with it?' Jenny asked, determinedly packing Polly's break-time snack for her and shoving it firmly into her school bag.

Polly had a ready answer. 'All the other mothers

would know it was your fault, for sending me to school ill. They'd say you'd done it on purpose, because I'd be better by exam time and their children would all be horribly ill. And they'd All Fail!'

'They'd only know it was my fault if you told them,' Jenny pointed out, refusing to be threatened. Polly was trying not to grin, relishing her attempt at blackmail.

'She's only putting it on. She's always doing it. Spends half the day up in the nurse's room pretending she's got a headache,' said Daisy, wishing she'd been that resourceful at Polly's age. In five years' time, she could foresee, Polly would never get caught doing something as mundane as fare-dodging. She'd be more likely to get away with hijacking the entire train.

Polly pulled a face at Daisy. 'It's true,' she bragged loudly, 'I *do* get headaches. Sister Hamilton says I'll have to have a brain scan if I go on like this.' She passed a dramatic hand across her brow and fluttered her eyelids. Jenny and Daisy laughed.

'That was Sister Hamilton's idea of a threat,' Daisy said. 'Poor woman doesn't know Polly very well, or she'd realize all that special attention would be just what she would love.'

Eventually Polly gave up, trailed reluctantly out to Ceci Caine's car and Jenny had the house to herself. All she could do now was pray that Polly wasn't really ill enough to be sent home from school. Hard-heartedly, but excusing herself on the grounds of protecting her child from something worse, she switched on the telephone answering machine so that if the school nurse called to demand that Polly be collected and brought home, she could pretend to be out.

Pretending to be out, or actually *going* out were options that crossed her mind more than once that morning as she did fervent house-cleaning in an attempt to take her mind off David Robbins. She phoned

Sue. 'I can't face him, not even to tell him there's a mistake. Why don't you come round and tell him for me?' she pleaded.

'Not a chance. I think you should go ahead and do it. Think of the money, think of the naughtiness of it, God knows you've behaved yourself well enough over the years, you deserve a bit of fun.'

'If you think it's such fun, why don't you come and do it instead? After all, he won't know.'

'Sorry, got a bikini wax booked up at the Club. Anyway, there's just an outside chance he really wants to learn to play the flute, and then what would I do? I got chucked out of recorder class at nine!' Sue argued, laughing down the phone. 'Either do it, or tell him you can't. I bet you haven't even taken that card out of the newsagent's window yet have you? That should tell you whether you want to or not . . .'

At lunch time, Jenny was on her way out of the house to do exactly that when the phone rang. With the front door open, she hovered in the hallway, bag and car keys in hand, letting the machine do the answering, but listening in case Polly had developed genuine pneumonia during the morning and had been rushed to hospital.

'Alan, it's Serena,' she heard. 'Look, sorry to ring you at home but I can't make Thursday night. Do you think we could do it next week instead? I hope you haven't already got the tickets . . .'

The voice was young, breathy and eager. Jenny froze. So 'darling' had a name, she was reality, flesh and blood and voice. She was being taken somewhere by some-one else's husband, somewhere that required tickets: theatre? a concert? So Alan was besotted enough to arrange something. It was usually Jenny who did all this – Alan seemed to think that turning up at the right place in more or less suitable clothes was an adequate contribution to their social life. Now he was showing himself capable of organizing one of his own, 'playing away' Jenny had heard hearty rugby types calling it.

'Hope I'm not too early.' Jenny, through heart-pounding misery, heard a voice by the door. 'I didn't expect this place to be so easy to find.'

With a choice of doing her explaining right there on the doorstep, with, just yards from her front gate, Carol Mathieson bossily supervising the erection of Neighbourhood Watch placards to one of the Close's three street lamps, or foolishly inviting the stranger into her home, Jenny instantly opted for danger. David Robbins, firmly supported by a pair of sturdy crutches, lumbered into her kitchen and heaved himself into the rocking chair. He didn't, Jenny noticed heart-sinkingly, have a flute with him.

'Tea or coffee?' Jenny asked, resorting to the safety of social graces while she decided what to do. 'Tea would be nice,' he said, giving her an odd, attractive smile. He looked, she thought, as if he was beginning to think he might be the one who had to come up with an explanation for a mistake. And no wonder, she realized, filling the kettle and bustling around in a domestic sort of way. How often do people visit tarts in cosy, affluent suburban homes, children's paintings on the walls, cat on the window ledge and homework abandoned on the kitchen table? Then she remembered Cynthia Payne and the luncheon voucher parties in Streatham.

'I parked round the corner, and staggered up the road. Never know which to do really,' he said, grinning at Jenny. 'Can't work out which one draws less attention, not with these.' He prodded at his legs.

'If you don't mind me asking, what happened?' she asked. 'And do you want sugar in this?' I can't believe this is happening, she thought. It's like one of those near-death things, I feel like I'm watching myself from the ceiling. He was a good-looking man. Sue would be kicking herself if she saw him, not one she'd imagine having any trouble attracting women. What was he *doing* here?

'Accident with a train. I did think of telling people it was a Falklands landmine, or frostbite from guiding Ranulph Fiennes across Antarctica, but the truth tends to come out.' David Robbins stirred his tea thoughtfully and looked at Jenny. 'Wife went off after that. We're in the last stage of divorcing now. At first she made jokes about me being permanently legless, but it was all a front. I think there was someone else anyway.'

'You live round here, do you?' Jenny asked tentatively, nervous that she might come across him some time in the Waitrose car park.

'Cardiff. But no-one fits limbs like they do at Roehampton. They made my new feet. I feel like Douglas Bader. Now and then I come up for a spot of adjustment, and for this sort of thing. Suits me right now not to look for anyone long-term.' He gave her a shyish grin and Jenny could feel a blush. She wanted to ask him why he thought he had to pay for sex, but was afraid to cross over from the safety of small talk. There was a silence, broken only by the busy sounds outside of Carol and her workmen, scrabbling busily about with ladders and hammers.

'You haven't done this before have you?' David Robbins said softly. He was looking slightly past Jenny to where her flute was in its usual place in the conservatory. 'But you know what it's all about. It's not music.'

'No, it's not music,' Jenny agreed, knowing this was the moment to explain the mistake.

In the end it was quite easy. It wasn't music, and Sue had been right, it was much more profitable. Jenny had forgotten how exhilarating feeling truly, secretly wicked could be. In plenty of time to collect Polly from school and rush her on to a ballet class, she spent twenty minutes in the shower washing away any lingering feelings of guilt, counted her money and stashed it, together with the rest of the citrus-flavoured condoms, in a rhinestoned evening bag at the back of her underwear drawer. Must remember for next time, she thought, towelling her wet hair, the lime flavour isn't up to much.

Chapter Six

Jenny spent several days hugging her shameful secret to herself, hardly daring to leave the house in case she blurted it out to someone in the street. She felt that if she allowed herself out, let loose in public, she would be sure to be accosted by someone doing a survey, and would confess, when asked, her new occupation. 'I fellate strange men for money,' she could hear herself announcing loudly to a bored student with a clipboard trying to sell insurance in a crowded shopping precinct. To keep herself under some sort of control she stayed home and fed the family on long-stored, unlabelled casseroles from the freezer, and when the cat food ran out she extravagantly opened a can of best dolphin-friendly tuna for the delighted Biggles.

From the safety of her window she watched Paul Mathieson looking proudly up at the Neighbourhood Watch sign on the street lamp outside his house, and gleefully she thought, here's one crime you haven't spotted yet, right under your nose. How ecstatically horrified Carol would be, too. A few months ago she had walked down the Close with them as Jenny was taking Polly to one of her disco classes ('Make-up already at your age dear?' Carol had commented, eyeing Polly's dazzlingly lurid lycra outfit set off by Barbie-pink lipstick) when a teenager from the estate had crossed the road in front of them wheeling frothily-frilled twins in an absolute Rolls-Royce of a pram. 'Three guesses how she paid for that,' she had sniffed, shocking Jenny.

'Can't guess, you'll have to tell me!' Polly had piped up, earning one of Carol's Looks.

'Her mother, hire purchase, or borrowed?' Jenny had suggested, refusing to play.

Jenny expected a suitable feeling of guilt to creep up on her in time, as she imagined it should, but every time it threatened, she thought of Alan and how effortlessly he was running his new romance along-side his wife and family. His was the greater betrayal, Jenny concluded, for she wasn't involved with anyone, merely propping up the faltering family finances. Every now and then the name 'Serena' popped menacingly into her head, with its connotations of home-counties nice-girl, someone clean, placid, undemanding and unchallenging. The thought of her rival left Jenny with a compulsion to work at being defiantly the opposite. She hadn't mentioned the message on the answerphone to Alan. If challenged (and how likely was that?) she would simply shrug and tell him it must have got lost or forgotten or something. Daisy tended to monopolize the phone and its accoutrements, considering them by rights her personal property, so Alan would not be too surprised.

'Can't you just imagine what she's like?' Jenny asked Sue days later, reluctantly emerging from the house to meet her for Polly's tennis lesson and after-school tea at the club. 'I bet she's thirtyish, thinnish, dimmish, and wears co-ordinating shades of beige. And I bet she's got a blue-rinsed widowed dragon-mother in Surrey who plays bridge in the afternoons.'

Serena – the name had an unquestionable, middle-class self-certainty to it, like Fiona and Arabella, Melissa and Camilla. They were names of posh girls recalled from Jenny's childhood, girls in fiction, or from the intriguing boarding school hidden away behind trees on the hill near her home. Her own friends at the grammar school had had names like

Christine, Wendy and Sandra, with at least three other Jennifers. It was galling to think that the name Serena still could make her feel socially inferior, when it was Serena, not her, who seemed to be prepared to have an affair with a married man. On the other hand, Jenny then grudgingly reasoned, it was a Jennifer, not a Serena, who was sitting here on the tennis club balcony, having spent a suburban afternoon working as a prostitute.

Sue, who was far less interested in Alan's love life than in Jenny's professional one, did her best to be consoling. 'Well if she's really that dreadful, he won't be interested for long, you can guarantee. It's just one of those symptoms of the male menopause, something young and pretty and impressionable. Men just like to check they've still got the old pulling power. Once he's feeling reassured that he has, it'll be all over.'

'Yes, I know. I just have to wait it out and he'll be back to lolling sleepily in front of the fire all evening like an ageing labrador. What I'm afraid of is that I won't like him at all by then, for having felt he had to do it, and it will all be too late,' Jenny said with a sigh. 'Why can't he be like other men and just go in for buying purple shoes, or fast cars? The male menoPorsche, it should be called, seeing as that's what they start wanting in their forties.'

'Well don't worry, it doesn't last. Now tell me all about the customer!' Sue said with indecent impatience. 'I got a good look at him, he parked outside my house. Utterly gorgeous, I thought. I'd have done it for nothing. Is he coming back for more? Will he get to be a regular? And if he does, will you introduce me?'

Jenny squirmed, and wished she was safely alone in Waitrose, or doing a shift in the school library, anywhere but here with Sue and her vicarious fascination. She really was worse than Polly for wanting to know intimate and lurid details. Polly at least was safely out of earshot, having her first outdoor tennis lesson of the year down on the court below with five other ten-year-olds. She should just tell Sue nothing had happened, that she really was too much of a prissy little housewife to consider prostitution as a viable career option. But whenever she thought of David Robbins and what she had done, a distressingly uncontrollable smile spread across her face, along with the certainty that she was blushing. In an attempt to keep her face straight, she looked down at the women and the children's class on the tennis courts, all dressed in similar regulation little white outfits, with the latest Air-Wear tennis shoes, none of them the sort to challenge the club rules by breaking the dress code. A bunch of Serenas, all of them, she thought, opting to tell the truth, and be damned.

'It was good fun. Just like being young and free again,' she said decisively, giving Sue a smile of pleased radiance. 'Extremely free,' she added, feeling the happy blush coming on – white was too dazzling a colour for tennis, she thought, reaching down into her bag for a disguise of sunglasses. Something else was dazzling her, too, little flashes of sunlight as if someone was using a mirror to catch the light and was shining it in her direction. Perhaps a magpie in a tree with a stolen piece of jewellery, she wondered, maybe the dinky kind of slim gold bangle she imagined a Serena would wear.

Carol was dusting Paul's attic study, spraying jets of polish and rubbing firmly at the veneered surfaces. Mrs MacNee did the rest of the house, but Carol always told her firmly that Paul wouldn't have anyone touch his study, no-one but her. She didn't trust anyone not to peek into the box containing his sacred Masonic kit, or go investigating the files relating to his honorary treasury of the sailing club, or poke about among the drying prints hanging in his darkroom. Radio Two trilled beside her as she worked, and every now and then she glanced out of the high window to check who was coming and going in the Close below. Paul's telescope, with which he studied the movements of the planets, kept getting in her way as she polished and tidied, banging her on the shoulder and prodding her neck as she moved briskly round the room, sorting Paul's crisp new Neighbourhood Watch files (one for each household) into street-number order on the new Ikea shelving unit. She took a quick look into the one marked 'Number 14, Collins', found no entries yet, and wondered if she should make a note of the rather attractive hobbling man who had called on Jenny several days before. Perhaps he was just reading a meter or something, she decided, Paul's Parker pen poised in her hand. Or perhaps he was from the insurance company, calling about the ruined wall. She rather hoped he'd call on her next time too, she thought, as she wrote *blond handsome visitor (male – early 40s?), purpose unknown, 1.45 p.m. on 21st'* in the folder. She filed it away with the rest and looked down into the road. Mrs Fingell was putting a newspaper-wrapped parcel into one of her many dustbins. Whatever was in that, Carol wondered, knowing in reality that it was probably nothing more sinister than potato peelings.

That was the trouble with taking on responsibility for the neighbourhood, it made you exceptionally suspicious about other people's behaviour. But then, she reasoned, someone had to be, crime figures were rising all the time, and some people weren't even bothering to report domestic burglaries any more, as the police were so unlikely to catch the culprits. Every night, police sirens wailed past the end of the Close, heading for some thieving villain gone to earth in the depths of the estate. Every week she scanned the local paper, counting up the number of charges brought against the crooks who lived so near, propping up her firm belief that a whole criminal culture was born and not made. Reading, she gave a little sigh of grateful relief every time she saw the words 'remanded in custody'. That was what they deserved. She didn't for a moment believe what Jenny had once told her, that many people, innocent or not, spent home-destroying months in remand centres simply because, unlike perhaps multi-million pound fraudsters, they had no owner-occupier families who could promise bail-money. She and Paul, wondering if they were right to trust their burglar locks, lay awake and watchful in the noisy nights, picturing the sordid, syringe-littered stairways, the graffitied walls, certain that chaos and riot were only a half-brick's throw away.

Carol finished her dusting and filing, and adjusted Paul's telescope. By standing on an upturned box, she managed to focus it, not as it usually was on the heavens, but on houses and gardens around and below her. Heady with authority, she inspected all the gardens within range, noting the appalling weeds in Sue Kennedy's, practically a jungle, she thought, clicking her tongue with disgust, making a mental note to have a little word at the next opportunity. Then, with some adjustment she could, she found, focus right into the Collins's conservatory and after only the smallest hesitation, with self-righteous delicacy she focused right out again, over beyond the edge of the council estate towards the river and, to her surprise, on to the tennis club balcony. So that's what they do in the afternoons, she thought primly, watching Jenny and Sue giggling together over cups of coffee. Sue was smoking too, which, Carol thought, rather defeated the point of expensive membership of a health club. I do wish I could hear what they're saying, she thought, with fervent curiosity.

*   *   *

'Why are we going to Laura and Harvey's? We've never been there before, and they haven't been here, so they don't owe us.' Dressing for dinner on a Thursday night, Alan was reluctant to go. He very much preferred being the one who did the cooking. Other people's cooking, unless it was a sanctified, Michelin-starred chef, was unlikely to be up to his own standard. He tried hard, but he couldn't enjoy an under-spiced stew masquerading as *Daube de Boeuf*, or soy-drenched Anglo-Thai messes adapted according to availability of ingredients, from a selection of currently fashionable cookbooks.

You'd bloody well want to go if sodding Serena asked you to, Jenny hissed at him from the safety of the bathroom, and then said, 'It's because of the film people; I agreed we'd talk to them, remember? It's just Laura being grateful.'

'I just hope she's grateful enough to know I can't face any chi-chi attempts at squid in its own ink. No-one gets it right, they always cook it till it's the texture of car tyres,' Alan grumbled.

'You're very hard to cook for, you realize that don't you? Soon no-one will invite us to eat with them at all,' Jenny said, emerging from the bathroom to rummage in the wardrobe for her black silk skirt. She wondered whether to combine it with her comfy chenille sweater or her translucent cream shirt, and if it was worth making an effort to look good at all, with Alan in such a mood. She tied her hair back with a yellow scarf and immediately, with her angular jawline exposed, felt about ten years younger. 'You put people off – they're afraid of your ludicrously high standards. It's like asking bloody Escoffier round for supper. I think Laura's very brave.'

'You said she was very grateful. So she should be,

these film people mean we'll be mucking up our tax returns. Once you start admitting to that kind of free-lance operation going on in the house, they'll never be off our backs. Every year they'll bung in an estimated assessment, you'll see.'

Jenny zipped up her skirt, and pulled the chenille sweater out of the drawer, opting for comfort over glamour, seeing as Alan was giving no sign that he was the slightest bit interested in what she looked like. Time was, she recalled, he'd have fondled her gently as he fastened her zip for her, or commented on the transparency of the shirt. Instead he was looking grumpy, searching through a drawer for cufflinks.

'Is there somewhere else you'd rather be?' Jenny suddenly asked bravely, challenging him in the mirror, hairbrush in her hand. 'I mean, if you'd rather not come out with me, please do say. We're not chained together, I can go on my own.' Here's your chance, she thought, take it or forever leave it. Alan left it.

'No, no I'll come. It's been a tough week, that's all, and the next one looks like being no better. Accountants' bills seem to come last on everyone's priority list.' He smiled, and ruffled Jenny's newly brushed hair. 'Sorry, Pudding. I'll stop complaining and I'll do my best to be sociable, and anyway I want to know about these film people, and how much they're going to be messing up my kitchen.'

'I'm sure they won't mind if you load your entire batterie de cuisine into crates and get Harrods to take it into storage.' Jenny smiled sympathetically at him. 'Just try to think of the money; even after tax it could be a whole term's school fees.'

'What I am thinking,' Alan confessed with a sly grin, 'is that if we do have to go out for dinner, at least Laura and Harvey are within staggering distance of home and we can drink as much as we like.'

Laura and Harvey lived in one of the prettiest houses

in the Close. It was the same, structurally, as Jenny and Alan's but maintained, like a model always ready for the photographer, in the most pristine condition. Looking at the fresh clean paintwork, Jenny wondered if it was really true that film companies who found something lacking in the décor of their chosen locations, actually did repaint at their own expense. Thinking about her flaking front door, she hoped they did. It would also be a good persuasion point for Alan. The Benstone's front garden, with the camellias gone, was rather exposed, but the front windows and porch were charmingly trailed with clematis in spring followed by tiny, delicately scented pink roses in the summer. Tubs of topiaried box-hedge stood squarely each side of the front doorstep, underplanted with white anemones, which would be followed later by Cambridge blue trailing lobelia. Miraculously slug-free delphiniums and foxgloves grew in front of the sitting-room windows, giving the impression in the early summer of a cottage garden of Gertrude Jekyll-style opulence. The feeling of effortless extravagance continued inside the house, with generous swathes of crisp Designers' Guild chintz at the windows, polished blond wood floors, and a pair of elfin daughters appealingly dressed in multi-coloured layers of exorbitantly priced Oilily clothes.

Jenny, trailing the reluctant Alan, rang the Benstone's doorbell, and was welcomed in by Harvey wearing a limp and faded rugby club sweatshirt, which didn't at all go with the elegance of his surroundings.

'Do come in!' he bellowed at them, waving a half-full glass of wine. 'Lovely to see you!' and then towards the kitchen he yelled, 'Emily, keep hold of Pushka!' Laura, spring-fresh in Monsoon voile, drifted gracefully out of the kitchen, closing the door on a small daughter clutching a struggling tabby cat, and the usual pantomime of air-kisses followed.

Laura took Jenny and Alan into the sitting-room and started pouring glasses of wine. 'Do sit down. Sorry one of the sofas is missing, we had a Mothercare shoot in here yesterday and it had to look like a playroom. You should have seen it, rocking horses and blu-tacked bunny pictures everywhere! Fiona and George Pemberton should be here any minute. Did I mention that they were coming too?'

'No, actually you didn't,' Jenny said, her social smile congealing, dreading facing Fiona for an evening of light entertainment. Which of them would get drunk enough to mention the incident of Polly and the *Playboy* magazine she wondered, hoping it would be Fiona and not Alan, who, when she had told him about it, had found the tale boyishly amusing.

'I did think of asking Sue from the end house, make it a real neighbours' evening. But we couldn't think of a suitable man.'

'Sue can usually dredge one up all by herself, given ten minutes notice or so,' Alan said.

'Not that they're essential of course, even numbers,' Laura said doubtfully, glancing towards her dining-room and her carefully balanced table arrangements.

A few moments later, Fiona made her usual majestic entrance, followed by a rather droopy-looking George. 'Sorry we're late,' Fiona boomed, sidestepping Harvey's attempt to kiss her by thrusting her jacket at him, 'George fell asleep watching the golf. He's no good at late nights, likes to have a little nap first.' George smiled placidly enough, but Jenny noticed him take a vicious kick at a stray piece of Lego.

'Well actually,' Laura went and stood next to Harvey, linking her arm through his and smiling winsomely, 'we can't have *too* late a night, if none of you mind.' She gave a little giggle and peeked out from under her fringe. 'I'm ovulating, you see.'

Harvey, pink to the edge of his greying moustache,

disentangled his arm and busied himself with the drinks tray. 'Her and the bloody cat,' he said, clinking ice. 'Have to keep her shut in, or she'll get herself up the duff with the nearest tom. Spends all day yowling and rolling around,' he said, with an embarrassed attempt at a laugh. The entire group froze, collectively imagining the elegant Laura, not the cat, rolling on the Afghan kelim and howling out of the window in a frenzy of sexual longing.

'Probably something to do with the moon,' Jenny contributed at last, glancing across at Fiona and thinking surely a headmistress could be relied on to find a subject to change to. 'Women in one house do tend to synchronize. Perhaps it even extends to cats.' Alan, she noticed, was downing his drink rather fast, staring fixedly beyond the group and through the open door towards the dining-room. She followed his gaze and together they watched as, on the immaculately laid table, all shining silver, polished glass and artlessly casual flower arrangements, the said cat was slyly picking its delicate way towards the butter dish, and finding it, was then licking rapturously.

'Trying for a boy,' Laura, clutching a glass of mineral water, confessed coyly. 'I do think men like to have a son, really, deep down, don't they?'

'Can't think why. Not much sense in men, really,' Fiona argued. 'I spend all my time teaching girls that they can achieve anything that they want without relying on men.'

Laura gave a small laugh. 'But not making babies they can't!' she said. Fiona gave her a cool grin. 'It's only a matter of time . . .' she said with foreboding, looking sideways at George, who was studying Laura's maple-wood bookshelves full of fat blockbusters.

'Shall we eat? Just a simple peasanty meal tonight, I bet you haven't tried tapenade, sort of squashed olive thing, I made it to go with the lamb . . .' Harvey was confiding to Alan as he led him towards the dining table. Jenny crossed her fingers and willed Alan not to mention that this was the third dose of highly fashionable tapenade he'd been treated to in six weeks, none of which so far had measured up to his own version. She also prayed he wouldn't start wittering on about the lamb – rare breeds were his current passion, and he was quite likely to baffle poor, well-meaning Harvey with questions about whether the sheep was a Soay or a Shetland, when it was most probably shamefully anonymous. Jenny had a close look at the butter dish as she sat down – the butter along one side looked suspiciously serrated, presumably the pattern of the cat's tongue, and it was now too late and totally impossible to mention it. She tried not to think about what else might have gone on, cat-wise, while they were cooking in the kitchen.

'. . . And the poor little sod's fanny, all swollen up and bloody. Randy little animal keeps licking it, and rolling around on her back. Moggy masturbation I suppose.' Harvey, well into the pudding and heading for a state of drunkenness that wouldn't help his chances of procreation that night, was clutching the struggling tabby cat on his lap as he ate the strawberry tart. Any moment now, Alan thought with nausea, Harvey would raise the cat's tail and show them its genitals, right there across the table. The cat escaped to the floor and Alan flinched as Harvey finger-fed dollops of sumptuous home-made ice-cream to it as it padded round his chair and Jenny tried not to link thoughts of blood with the raspberry coulis on her plate. George was keeping up a constant chortling rumble, as if he couldn't believe his luck, coming out for a neighbourly supper and stumbling on such a madhouse.

'And how is your music coming along?' Fiona asked

Jenny, rather as if she was talking to one of her fourth formers. Jenny, nevertheless, appreciated Fiona's effort to switch the topic from the Benstone family's collective fecundity.

'Well I've lost a few pupils just lately. I'm in the process of finding some more.' This was the moment to ask about teaching at the school, while she had Fiona captive in a state of dinner-party good manners. She hesitated, knowing that if she was going to get a job at the High School, Fiona would have to be given a moment to come up with the idea herself, but the pause was scuppered by Alan.

'Need another flute teacher at your school, Fiona? Recorder and piccolo chucked in free, so to speak?' he chipped in clumsily. Jenny lashed out at him furiously with her foot and connected instead with something soft and yielding. There was a bitter yowl from under the table.

'There she goes again! I can get my whole next episode of *Keep It In The Family* out of that cat!' Harvey yelled delightedly, poking about under the table to retrieve his anguished pet.

Fiona glared around the table, her gaze coming to rest on Alan, seeing as Harvey's head was under the tablecloth. With her full command of grandeur she answered him. 'I'm afraid we have our full quotient of peripatetic staff, just at the present,' she said. Jenny smirked and bit her lip so as not to giggle. She could just imagine Alan later that night, mincing about the bedroom stark naked, putting on Fiona's air of majestic pomposity and quoting her words.

'Very Brontë-esque, your daughters' names: Emily and Charlotte,' George suddenly said to Laura. 'If you do get a son, will you be calling him Branwell to match?'

'Absolutely not,' Harvey answered for his wife. 'Wasn't he a drunk?'

'Certainly was. Probably felt in awe of the over-achieving women folk in his family,' George said, winking at Jenny and helping himself to a large portion of Brie.

'Names are so important,' Fiona chimed in. 'At school I come across some sadly unsuitable choices. Parents should be far more careful and think ahead. Take Grace, well that's asking for trouble. The ones we get are invariably vast and clumsy creatures and honestly, I mean, can you see a Talullah for example, taking up quantum physics, and being taken seriously at it?'

No, Jenny thought suddenly with pain, you need a name like bloody Serena for that kind of thing.

'I always think your girls have such pretty names,' Fiona went on, turning to Jenny. 'Polly and Daisy – they always remind me of Victorian parlourmaids.' She gave a tinkling little laugh, and Alan said to Jenny with a grin, 'Well there go our daughters' chances of a Nobel Prize for biochemistry. Doomed from the font.'

The party broke up when Laura, having served coffee very quickly after the cheese, became clearly fidgety. Any moment now, Jenny thought, she will be checking her temperature and going to splash on some more Giorgio. Fascinated, they all watched as Laura gazed lovingly into Harvey's unfocused eyes and crooned, 'I don't think you should drink any more, darling.'

Bit late, Jenny thought, obeying the signals, and gathering her thoughts and her handbag together. George, amused and bloody-minded, sat back in his chair and started chatting amiably about half-hardy annuals, until Fiona stood up and stated briskly to him, 'Time to go, it's getting late. Charming meal, you two, you must come to us soon.'

Alan repeated a similar version of the same words and suddenly the four of them were on the doorstep. Jenny, just about to turn off towards her own house, suddenly felt George's hand on her arm. Looking up quickly she caught George grinning slyly at her.

'You could try advertising your flute lessons,' he said quietly. 'Though you know what you might get instead of pupils don't you?' He had a very cunning look in his eyes.

'Yes I know exactly what I might get,' Jenny told him quietly, and then added recklessly, 'and it pays a hell of a lot better than bloody music.'

Chapter Seven

'They won't be back till at least eleven,' Ben promised Daisy. 'You've got plenty of time to try getting out and back in again. You don't actually have to go anywhere.'

'I might as well, once I'm out. I'll go and see Emma for an hour. I don't intend to risk my life and then waste the effort.' Daisy pulled on a pair of ancient and terminally uncool trainers, hoping no-one out in the dark would recognize her in them. The Doc Martens wouldn't do at all, not for climbing out of her window down via the conservatory roof to the back garden. They were much too heavy and inflexible. On the night of Sophie's party, she'd have to change into them at Emma's. Even getting over the back fence would be difficult, with the mouldering compost heap, the honeysuckle threaded through with lethal blackberry thorns and the gate double-locked against intruders from the Common.

'You look just like a burglar. Where are you going?' Polly, her face peering with intense curiosity round Daisy's bedroom door, couldn't bear to miss out if something was going on. 'You're not going *out*, are you Daisy?' she said with thrilled relish. 'You're still *grounded*! You're not *allowed*!'

'I'm not going out Polly, not exactly,' said Daisy, wondering what kind of a bribe it would take to get round Polly.

'No, she's not going out,' Ben joined in quickly. 'She's just, er, just practising for, um, the Duke of

Edinburgh award. She has to learn how to do some climbing, that's all. It's called an initiative test.' Polly looked disbelieving, so Ben tried appealing to her sense of conspiracy. 'Only don't tell Mum, because Daisy's trying to make up for being bad by doing this as a surprise. Think how pleased they'll be when Daisy gets a medal.'

Polly's expression was of deep calculation. 'No-one gets a medal for being able to climb out of a window,' she said, with a knowing look. Then she conceded, 'I'll think about it. A Snickers bar would help,' she said eventually.

'I'll pick one up at the shop on the estate,' Daisy promised, opening her window. 'Now don't forget, Polly, it's a surprise. OK?'

It looked an awfully long way down, really. Much further than it looked from down below. It had seemed such a good idea when she and Emma had discussed it at school. Now it seemed ludicrously Famous Fiveish, scrambling down the drainpipe dressed in camouflage black, to escape the villainous captors. Except that in this case the captors were her terminally insensitive parents. It would be more of a giggle if Ben would do it with her, but he had refused, saying that two of them would make too much noise, and besides, when he went to Sophie's party he intended to go the easy way, out through the front door. With immense care, Daisy put a foot over the window-sill and felt around in the dark for a foothold on the ridge pole of the conservatory.

'You OK?' Ben called from the safety of her bed.

Daisy glared at him. 'Seeing as I've still got most of me inside the room, yes Ben, I'm OK so far, thanks for asking,' she retorted with sarcasm. 'You should try this, it isn't that easy.' It was all right for him, she thought, lying there all limp and gangly like an abandoned string puppet. He was so long, he could probably step straight out of the window down to the ground, though he'd probably manage to knock out every pane of glass from the conservatory on the way.

'You should try paying your train fares, then you wouldn't have to try this either!' he snapped back. 'I'm on your side, remember.' And mine, he admitted to himself, knowing for certain that if Daisy made it to Sophie's party the next weekend, her desirable friend Emma would be sure to be there too.

Holding on to the loo window ledge and levering herself carefully across the conservatory roof, Daisy jumped down to the ground by way of the upturned pile of flower pots on the garden table. For a few moments she stood leaning against the wall, shaking with nerves and fear. It would be all right next time, she knew. It was only that first attempt that would unnerve her. Next time, she'd be down from her window as lithely as Biggles.

Daisy now wanted, really, to go back into the house lie around on the sofa for the evening and watch TV, but bravado, and the need to appease Polly, made her stride off up the road towards the shop on the corner of the estate. She felt more than slightly silly, dressed all in black and with her face streaked with charcoal from the barbecue kit. She was sure that anyone who saw her would think she was some kid playing Let's Join The SAS. But Ben had insisted, saying that she must minimize her chances of being seen, especially with the Neighbourhood Watch on constant alert.

She phoned Emma from the payphone on the corner and was quite relieved to discover she was out. It was nearly ten already, and if the parents got sudden food-poisoning at the Benstone's, or had a row with Harvey about the overall dismal quality of the British sitcom, they could be home any time now. Daisy hung around in the shadows outside the estate newsagent's until she was sure there were no hostile crowds of ragga boys inside who could mistake her, in her black disguise, for a Goth and beat her up, bought the Snickers bar and strode back down the Close, keeping tight in against the hedges and overhanging trees. As she climbed up to the roof of the conservatory again, using the terrace bench as a step-ladder, she started to relax. This is quite easy, she thought, just so long as the parents assume I'm in my room doing homework, I could get away with this.

She'll never believe me, Paul thought to himself as he peered down from the attic, eyes screwed up against the dark. She'll accuse me of crying Wolf, especially after last time, with the bomb that wasn't a bomb. Only his terror of Carol's scorn kept Paul from rushing straight to the telephone and dialling 999. And perhaps she was right, it might be as well to double-check.

He squinted down into the Close again, wishing his telescope and his multi-lensed Nikon camera had the wonderful kind of night vision that made such brilliant TV programmes about badger-watching. Then, when the police asked him to inspect a line-up of potential felons, he would be able to astound them with his unswervingly precise identification, or even an amazingly sharp photo. He would put together a Photo-fit picture that would have the villain skulking in his home, terrified to go out. He could just imagine it, the local police chief emerging from the courtroom and congratulating him personally: 'We dream of witnesses as observant as you, Sir.' There would be something in the local paper; he might be described as a community leader. Excited now, Paul made a note of the time in the file for number 14 (Collins). He then had another look down into the Close. The dark figure was still there, struggling a bit, halfway up the Collins's conservatory and heading for one of their bedroom windows. And

Jenny and Alan, he knew, were at the Benstones, he'd watched them go earlier. Their poor defenceless children, alone in that house, at the mercy of a ruthless cat burglar. It was no good, even if he had to drag Carol up to the loft so show her, and so waste precious time, he would have to get the police. Wasn't that what Neighbourhood Watch was all about?

The police car, blue light whirling and making eerie shadows on the trees, passed Alan and Jenny as they walked up the Close towards home.

'Hope it's not old Mrs Fingell,' Alan commented. 'Poor old thing, all alone with that smelly orange dog, anything could happen.' Jenny hoped it wasn't her, too. Like everyone else in the Close, she put a generous amount in the annual Help the Aged envelope, and had once shovelled snow off Mrs Fingell's path (leaving it treacherously icy), but when it came to real helping, on a day-to-day shopping-and-mopping basis, they all quailed before the rank seediness of Mrs Fingell's existence. The Close residents who actually ventured inside number 21 tended to be those who, out of curiosity, or a desire to reconstruct original decorative features, wanted to see what their own houses had looked like in the days before modernization. Awestruck, they had all reported a magnificent claw-footed bath, original but crumbling cornices and an odour of pre-war squalor that quite took the breath away. Everyone who had been in Mrs Fingell's kitchen agreed that the council should provide her with at least a Home Help.

Jenny and Alan arrived at their gate at the same time as the police car which screeched to a halt beside them. Suddenly a far more appalling scenario than an injured Mrs Fingell sprang to Jenny's mind. Suppose David Robbins had really been an undercover vice squad member? Was she about to be arrested for keeping a disorderly house as the quaint old-fashioned charge called it? Or, as was more likely (the wearing of two false feet being quite an extreme disguise for even a plain-clothes cop) had he discovered that he could get services such as Jenny had provided for a quarter of the price and twice the expertise in King's Cross, and grassed on her in a fit of outraged consumer pique? Jenny felt prickles of perspiration and her heartbeat rocketed up to danger level.

'Report of attempted burglary,' a bearded policeman said, pushing past them and up their path. 'Got a key?' he asked, as Jenny and Alan stood on the path unmoving and puzzled.

'Yes, of course, but there are three people in there. Or at least there should be,' Jenny told him, shaky with relief but suddenly fearful that only vulnerable little Polly might be in the house, alone facing a ruthless team of professional robbers, Ben and Daisy having callously abandoned her for the sake of some unmissable teenage jollies.

'We got someone round the back, they won't get away,' the policeman said with commendable confidence as Alan opened the front door.

'What's the matter, what's Daisy done now?' Polly in her Mickey Mouse pyjamas hovered at the bottom of the stairs, riveted by the sight of the policeman.

'Why?' the policeman asked her, speedily picking up on a possible line of enquiry. 'What has Daisy done before?'

'Nothing!' Polly lied, spinning out the word into at least six emphatic syllables. She clutched her biggest Snoopy, looking suspiciously like, Jenny thought, an innocent little girl who was over-acting the part of, well, an innocent little girl and determinedly justifying £70 per term spent on Extra Drama. She was also standing firmly on the bottom step, blocking any possible progress up the stairs.

The policeman asked her questions about what she might have heard, and Alan asked her where Ben and

Daisy were. 'Oh they're upstairs doing some home-work,' Polly said. 'Have been most of the evening,' and then she added, 'except when they watched telly,' as if she had realized she was going too far.

'What's wrong? What's happening?' Daisy and Ben appeared together at the top of the stairs.

'Come down a minute,' Alan called. 'The police think we've got burglars.'

'Do I have to?' Daisy hissed, 'I'm doing a face-pack!'

'No-one out there, Mick.' Another, younger, police-man emerged from the garden. 'A pot with a plant in it knocked over, though. Bloke probably saw a cat clambering about. Sorry you've all been disturbed. We'll go and have a word with the informant.'

'Can you tell me who it is?' Alan asked.

'Not really Sir, we're not supposed to . . .'

'We don't need to ask,' Jenny put in crossly. 'Bloody Paul Mathieson, I'd bet anything. Our over-enthusiastic Neighbourhood Watch co-ordinator,' she explained to the police.

'Can't be too careful though, can you?' the bearded policeman said.

'That's the kind of thing *he* says,' Alan told him, glumly.

'You've gone and done it again haven't you?' Carol, pummelling Estée Lauder Night Repair into her face, sat at her flounced dressing table and glared at Paul via the mirror. She wore a lilac chiffon scarf to protect her hair from the cream, and her eyelids were puffy from over-zealous application of make-up remover. Around her shoulders frothed an ocean of pink organdie frills.

She looks like an alien, Paul thought. If she suddenly took it into her head to go walking on the Common in the night, she'd be reported to the Parapsychology people and they'd be flocking from all over to get a look

105

at her, trying to log a sighting in a book, like twitchers after a lesser spotted albatross. 'No, I haven't done it again,' he said wearily, sitting on the boudoir-blue, ribbon-threaded duvet and risking another telling off. 'I really did see someone climbing into the Collins's house. Whoever it was must have hidden in the airing cupboard or something and sneaked away. At least they won't have had a chance to take anything; it will be all they could do to make an escape.'

He was still quite proud of himself really, and hurt that Carol didn't share the feeling. If only the police had caught the intruder, then things would be different. 'My hero,' she would call him, and there'd be none of this messing about with face creams at bedtime either.

'I hope you're going to keep this Neighbourhood Watch business under control next weekend when the twins are home,' Carol warned him. 'I don't want them making a nuisance of themselves in the Close, and you know what you're like with a New Interest.'

Paul made a private decision to show the boys his files and make up a rota for them to keep watch with the telescope. Perhaps they could all go out together and photograph everyone's garden furniture – too much of it was being stolen all over London, he'd read in the papers. He ought to check out the iffy merchandise at car boot sales too, which might be fun with the boys. She didn't have to take over everything, after all, did she? It was always Carol who, in the holidays, took them for their swimming lessons, to riding and to karate. She said it was because it clashed with his working hours. This would be something the boys and he could all get involved in together, something just for them, a Boys' Own adventure.

Alan, with a mild but bearable hangover, said a brief goodbye and left early for work the next morning, which left Jenny to deal with a letter from the police about Daisy.

'You can go down to the police station for an official Caution, it says here, but that means you have to be prepared to admit you did it. Otherwise I suppose we'll all have to endure some sort of court hearing.'

'Not much doubt which you'd prefer,' Daisy mumbled rudely through a mouthful of Crunchy Nut Cornflakes. Ben nudged her, warningly, and Daisy slopped milk on the table.

'Stop it you two, you're like a pair of babies!' Jenny said to them. 'Obviously it would be more convenient to get it all over and done with, and you *are* guilty, aren't you Daisy? They don't actually believe you really just lost your ticket, and it's impossible to prove.'

'Didn't think it was up to me to prove I'm innocent. We're always being told that the great British justice system works the other way round. And they can't prove I didn't pay,' Daisy said, pertly.

'They found you without a ticket. Case over!' Jenny snapped. 'Either way, you'll have a criminal record, we'll just go down to the police station and then afterwards we can forget all about it.'

'God, do you have to come? Can't Emma come instead?' Daisy asked, horrified that she might have to be marched along, flanked by parents, like a small child. They would probably make her wear sensible shoes.

'Don't push it, Dais,' Ben muttered, looking sideways at Jenny's increasingly furious face. She never used to be like that, he thought suddenly, she used to be all sort of benevolent and understanding. Perhaps it was her age.

'While we're all here, and talking of crime,' Jenny said, leaning forward and stirring her tea thoughtfully, 'Does anyone want to tell me anything about last night? About why the police thought we might have burglars?'

'Wasn't the police thinking it,' Ben cut in. 'It must have been Paul Mathieson again.'

'Yes but why? Even Paul must have had some sort of reason. I'd like to hear what it was that he saw.' Jenny sipped her tea and waited patiently.

Daisy gulped down the last of her cereal and pushed back her chair. 'Going to be late . . .' she said, getting up and glancing warningly across at Polly sitting at the table, still with her aren't-I-a-good-girl expression. She looked so puffed up with smugness, Daisy thought, she might burst any moment, scattering little nuggets of truth all over the table like spilled Rice Krispies.

'It was probably just Biggles, trying to get in Daisy's window. Wasn't it Daisy?' Ben said, taking his bowl to the dishwasher so as not to have to show his reddening face and quakey hands to Jenny. She could always spot lying a mile away.

'I heard him, all the way from my room, he was miaowing and miaowing,' Polly contributed dramatically, eager to join in with the conspiracy.

Daisy glared at her over-acting sister, but had to continue, 'Yeah, that's right. I leaned out of my window to call him in off the conservatory roof. Paul must have seen me.'

While Jenny was pondering how Paul could have mistaken a small old ginger cat for a full-sized human, Polly chipped in with an interesting thought. 'Why was he looking, do you think?' she suddenly asked.

Why indeed? thought Jenny.

Serena was wearing an old leather biker jacket. Not a soft and subtle designer version, but a genuine, heavy-duty zipped and studded one, with the leather worn to greying scuffed patches and bits of the sleeve-fringe curling up with age. She wore it, Alan noticed, with a

thin cream silk skirt, an endearing contrast of tough-
ness and vulnerability. He wondered if that kind of
jacket would suit Jenny and decided it wouldn't. It
shouldn't really suit Serena either, he realized; at work,
she should be putting across the serious-accountant
image. But at the photocopier she passed close by
him, and he caught a hint of the leather-smells of
the past, of dangerous Rockers and their greasy hair
and engine oil, of the warlike threat on the Brighton
beaches, of his group of scootered Mods, preening
and flaunting in their slick mohair suits. From outside in the hectic London streets, he thought he could
hear seagulls, and The Who.

'Sorry about the other day.' Serena's soft voice
melted into Alan's thoughts. 'I had to stay on at
home and take care of Mummy's flu. She's been
getting rather frail and cancelling her golf just lately.
OK for next week, though. Joe Walsh is at the Mean
Fiddler. What do you think?'

What did he think? He thought that right now he
wanted to push her roughly against the photocopier
and ravish her. Somehow, enticingly, there was about
being with Serena the secret of regaining lost youth.
Alan was starting to need to be closer and closer to
her, as if to inhale the magic scent. As middle-aged
women put their trust in ever more expensive cosmetics, so Alan put his into absorbing Serena, and
while she was prepared to spend some spare social
time with him, he wallowed in the glorious feeling
that, just a touch and a breath away, was the elixir of
eternal youth. He no longer would have agreed with
the wish to die before he got old, now he wanted not
to get old before he died, and it was nothing to do
with how many years he lived.

Of course it would be all right for next week. Alan
put out a tentative hand to stroke Serena's leather-
clad shoulder, but she slid away, unnoticing, into her

office. Should he touch her at work, though, Alan wondered. Should he touch her at all? Did this count as having an affair when all they did was spend the odd evening drinking beer and watching ancient rock 'n' rollers in seedy pubs and clubs? So far, Alan had convinced himself that all was innocent, simply because he assumed an affair was not a matter for guilt until he climbed into a woman's bed and body. But what, he thought, with a twinge of something that surely wasn't guilt, would Jenny call it?

'Of course I'll never do it again. That was a kind of accidental one off. Events just took over,' Jenny said to Sue in the changing room after a fast game of tennis. 'It was rather like being twenty again, back in the days when sex was so easy, simpler and more fun to end the evening in bed with someone who'd just bought you dinner than to find a reason why you shouldn't.' She looked up quickly from loading her tennis shoes into her bag; anyone could be in the loo cubicles, ears flapping.

'Did you do it because you were angry with Alan, do you think?' Sue asked her.

'Probably. And you know, I've realized I'm not really, apart from flute-teaching, not really employable. I have no *skills*. Half the orchestras that existed when I was playing have been made redundant, so I can't go back to that. Most of the musicians I worked with are now unemployed.'

'You could do a course in something?'

'I could. And if Alan and I really do separate, I'll obviously have to. He's an accountant, with years of practice at making sure estranged wives don't get more than their due. I just suddenly feel so vulnerable, not being able to earn some money. Not *for* anything, not yet anyway, just running-away money, like Jessica

110

Mitford. Though the way Alan's work is going, it's going to be needed to keep the kids in school. The idea that he might have someone else makes me realize how dependent I am on him financially. It's hateful. We've just slipped into it. Women like me don't work as prostitutes, not really,' she said, thankful that she was pulling her sweater over her head at that moment.

Sue made a disappointed face at her. 'Well you know what I think about that: one way or another we all do if we're married. And I seem to manage to be quite a lot like one even now I'm not! Hey ho, no such thing as a free lunch . . . !'

The two women walked out to the car park together. As Jenny unlocked her car she said to Sue, 'You know, I can't imagine Alan going off and renting sex, but really, you wonder don't you? No-one knows what any of them get up to when we're not there. I mean, I'm still getting some very odd calls, so who *are* all these men who phone? Do you think they've got lovely wives and sweet broods of children at home?' She felt suddenly anxious for these unsuspecting families, as if she was personally responsible for tempting their husbands.

Sue said, rather sadly, 'With both my husbands I always used to imagine the absolute worst. I was rarely disappointed by being wrong. There's probably many a generous, kind woman just like you, or men too, of course, out there providing the kind of thing blokes got used to in their pre-wife days, maybe something quirky they got a taste for at boarding school or whatever. It's probably what keeps some marriages together in the end, having somewhere nice and anonymous to sneak to for a spot of harmless spanking and wanking or whatever Matron's speciality with the Upper Fourths in the dorm used to be.'

'Social services, with a difference . . .' Jenny giggled. 'Thank God I'm in the private sector,' she said laughing, 'at least I can say yes or no. And from now on it's decidedly no!'

At home, the phone rang twice. The first sounded unpleasantly sleazy and Jenny hung up, telling him firmly that he'd got the wrong number. It was definitely time to advertise somewhere safer than a shop window, she thought. The second caller was a bit worrying . . . a vaguely familiar man's voice simply said, 'Oh good, I was checking you were in. I'll be round,' and then hung up abruptly. Jenny looked at the clock: almost time for Polly to be dropped off at the gate. The doorbell rang and Jenny went to open the door, a welcoming smile on her face ready for her daughter. But on the doorstep stood George Pemberton, slightly smarter than usual in a tweedy jacket with the buttons wrongly fastened as if from hurry and nerves, and clutching a bunch of tight-budded pink roses, the sort that needed an aspirin in their water if they're ever going to open properly.

'Oh hello George,' Jenny said, the smile fading a little. 'I was expecting Polly.'

'Oh. Sorry,' he said, 'does that mean you haven't got time?'

'Time?' she said, trying to get her brain to interpret what he was saying. Vaguely, she recalled what they had said to each other as they left the Benstone's dinner party. Good grief, she thought, suppressing an urge to giggle, surely he wasn't thinking . . . oh surely not, not George.

George was through the porch and into the hall-way. 'Fiona isn't very keen on "music". Tone deaf in fact you could say,' he told Jenny, with an unfamiliar lopsided grin that was well on its way to being a leer. 'So I thought I'd get my flute lessons somewhere off the premises, so to speak.' George started fumbling in his trousers and Jenny, appalled, thought he was already undoing his flies, there in the hallway, where anyone could see in through the open door. Thankfully, she suddenly saw that what he was exposing was only a wad of notes.

'Fifty quid shall we say? Cash do you?' he asked expectantly.

Chapter Eight

'No, George, cash certainly *won't* "do me"!' Jenny said firmly, watching with a twinge of sympathy as George Pemberton's face took on a childlike expression of acute disappointment. At least he didn't ask if she took Visa. Her face felt twitchy, as she very much wanted to laugh, but she stopped herself. He looked quite forlorn, standing dejectedly in her hall, his bunch of roses and handful of banknotes now a pair of embarrassments.

'But I thought . . . you said the other night . . .' George began. 'And it isn't at all unusual you know,' he continued, regaining confidence as Jenny had neither slapped his face nor threatened him with the Vice Squad. 'You read about it all the time, women making a bit on the side by having a bit on the side,' he gave a watery grin.

'You're reading the wrong newspapers then,' Jenny told him briskly, appalled at the idea of mixing business with neighbours. 'Now, why don't you come into the kitchen for tea and flapjacks. Polly will be home in a minute.' Thank goodness, she thought, leading George, now mild as a spaniel, into the kitchen, she hadn't had crumpets in the bread bin – she could imagine his rising hopes (and not just hopes) if she'd offered him those.

'You won't mention this to Fiona?' he said, with an expression of panic.

Jenny laughed. 'I wouldn't dare! Polly was caught

reading *Playboy* at school, I'm in enough trouble already for being a terrible parent!' At that moment, Polly came crashing in through the back door, pulling Harriet Caine and her reluctant mother Ceci into the house after her. 'Mum, Mum, me and Harriet want to go to Laser Leisure on Saturday and Harriet's mum says it's only all right if you say it is.' She then added in an intense stage whisper and a covert glance at Ceci, 'She thinks it might be violent. It's not. Tell her,' Polly insisted, pulling persuasively at Jenny.

Ceci Caine's elegant Ferrari-red nails pushed back her mane of streaked blonde hair and she grimaced apologetically at Jenny. 'Sorry and all that,' she said in a rich, purring voice and smiling at George with polite interest. 'I'd never heard of, what is it Polly? Laser Leisure?' She had another quick look at George, parked in the rocking chair, his bunch of pink roses still on his lap, and her smudgy black-rimmed eyes widened questioningly. If he was Polly's grandfather, surely she should be introduced? Jenny picked up on both Ceci's curiosity and the sub-text of what she was saying; what she had clearly meant was, 'Is Laser Leisure common?'

'I'll take them on Saturday afternoon if you like, Ceci. Polly's been before, as part of a birthday treat. It's not as dreadful as it sounds.' Ceci looked only slightly reassured, wondering if she should trust the judgement of a woman who entertained unknown, rose-toting men in her kitchen. But at least she would be getting Harriet off her hands for half a day. She smiled, giving in graciously.

'Oh, well all right then, thanks awfully. Come on Harriet darling, time to go,' she said, and gave a mock despairing look over her shoulder to George. 'So much to do,' she gushed. 'Suzuki violin tonight, ballet tomorrow. Byeeee!'

'Pity it's not flute as well, Mum,' Polly said,

wondering why her mother and George both went an interesting shade of pink as she said it. 'You keep losing all your pupils, don't you?'

On Friday evening, travelling home from their prep school on a weekend *exeat*, the Mathiesons' twin sons received their usual list of domestic instructions. The boys didn't listen, as the list never varied. They called it the 'not' list, as it consisted entirely of things they were not to do. It covered such things as not playing football in the flower beds, not going to the Common or (God forbid) the estate, not shouting from one end of the house to the other, not forgetting to wash their hands (before and after just about any activity) and not teasing the cats. Carol was still in full flow as they arrived at the house and the boys climbed out of the pristine Peugeot and stood mutely, waiting for her to run out of orders, shuffling their feet and kicking at the gravel outside the front door.

'And no eating cereal in the lounge,' she said, waving the door key at them in a slightly threatening way. 'You can watch TV after breakfast, not during it.' She unlocked the door, but still wouldn't let them past her into the house. 'And feet, of course,' she added, looking down despairingly at the two pairs of grubby and fast-growing feet on the doormat. 'Your slippers are right here, ready for you behind the door, so you can change out of those shoes.'

Sebastian, older of the two by ten authority-giving minutes, groaned. 'Oh Mum, I can't wear those old bunny slippers! I'll get my trainers out. I mean, suppose somebody comes?'

There was a smirk and a smutty snort from Marcus. Sebastian nudged him into silence and Carol looked at them, puzzled.

'You can't wear those,' she said, with a dismissive

little laugh. 'Your tennis shoes must be kept for tennis, as usual! I've booked a lesson for you both tomorrow morning up at the Club. You'll like that.' It sounded like a command, so the boys didn't feel they needed to reply. They changed, reluctantly and silently, into their despised furry animal slippers and then, collecting their bags, padded softly upstairs to reclaim their much-loved, but over-clean bedrooms.

'By the way, boys,' Carol called, breaking her own rule and shouting up the stairs to them, 'Polly's mummy says she will take you out tomorrow afternoon, with Polly and her little friend Harriet. Something called Laser Leisure, she said. Now don't complain about it being educational on your weekend off. A bit of extra science will do you no harm at all!'

'Laser Leisure! Grrr-eat!' 'Brrrill!' the boys yelled as loud as they dared, in the safety of Sebastian's room, bouncing high and delightedly on the bed, firing imaginary laser beams at each other in a manner that would have had Carol hauling them downstairs for an hour's compulsory piano practice.

'Hope Polly's mum doesn't tell her what Laser Leisure really is,' Marcus said at last, looking worried.

' 'Course she won't. She knows we'd never be allowed out with her again. And she needs us for playing with Polly in the holidays,' Sebastian told him.

'And we need Polly, too,' Marcus said ruefully, only too aware that one of the worst things about being sent away to school was a lack of local friendships for casual weekend and holiday play. He sighed, and looked longingly out of his window towards the estate at the end of the road. How he envied those roaming gangs of kids, allowed out on the streets for football and fun, all strolling daily to the nearest school and with a vast choice of partners in crime (sometimes literally) only a block away. 'You're so lucky, you've got each other,' Carol was always saying to the twins. But they weren't convinced. They knew they were missing out. They'd give up all the dubious privileges of their smart and isolated school to be able to wander along in a shambling gang to the local comprehensive, their shirts hanging out of their trousers, breakfasting on chocolate bars, an illicit Coke and experimental cigarette in their hands. They dreamed of joshing and pushing at bus stops (annoying old ladies), lounging against shop windows (annoying shopkeepers), and play-fighting all over the dusty pavements (annoying pedestrians). At their disciplined, over-organized boarding school there was very little opportunity, apart from covert and cowardly attempts at bullying, to be anything other than depressingly Good.

Saturday mornings usually followed a comfortable pattern for Alan. He got up early, showered, had a quick but futile glance at the crossword, enticed by the once-a-week chance to win a decent bottle of whisky, and then took to the shops. Saturdays were for cooking, for stock-brewing, squid-disembowelling, meat-marinading, lobster-murdering – whatever took his fancy with which to delight Jenny and frequently a collection of dinner guests.

This Saturday, Alan was going out, but not to the thrillingly-scented food shops of his choice. Small neighbourly comments along the lines of how long it took to rebuild Coventry after the war made it quite clear that it was time to mend his bombed wall, and he was heading with enormous reluctance towards a vast branch of B&Q, hoping that, amongst its huge range of stock, he would recognize the right ingredients with which to salvage his only attempt at building.

He posted a Rolling Stones tape into the car player and turned the volume up loud. The sun was shining and he tried but failed to capture a mood of optimism to go with the exalting music. He would far rather be in his beloved fish shop, poking at the scallops or weighing up the possibilities for a *bouillabaisse*, or perhaps considering a simple, barbecued fennel-stuffed, Pernod-drenched sea bass. The fishmonger was among a row of small, friendly, specialist shops, prettily painted in a tree-lined road near the station. On Saturday mornings, Alan looked forward to meeting like-minded men, unashamedly carrying vast French shopping baskets full of clumps of fresh coriander and discussing exotic cheeses and the advantages of Xeres vinegar over balsamic. Instead, he miserably turned the BMW off the dismal dual carriageway somewhere beneath the M4 flyover, and joined the DIY brigade collecting the components for a constructive weekend.

In the car park, Alan sat for a while in the car, listening to the end of *Satisfaction* and drumming rhythmically on the steering wheel. He could see whole families visiting the warehouse, which was as huge as a Heathrow hangar, in search of mysterious (to Alan) slabs of pine-cladding, brass-effect door knobs, pastel-coloured lavatory seats, Georgian-style window frames and flat-pack wardrobes. Some customers, he thought, awestruck, were probably buying entire fitted bedrooms or kitchens, which they, unlike Alan, could probably actually fit all by themselves. Overcome by the enormity of the task ahead, he wondered if he should simply finish the job the police had so carelessly started and destroy the rest of the wall, getting a man in from the garden centre to replace it with a pretty little white picket fence like the one the Benstone's had, or some good, solid larch-lap that would stop the litter being blown in.

Eventually, no longer able to put off the moment, Alan collected a trolley that was easily big enough to accommodate the raw material for half a house, and launched himself into the store. He had to ask the way to the bricks and when he found them realized he should not have expected to find the same old, carefully reclaimed Edwardian-stock bricks he had originally used. Should have gone to the architectural salvage place, he thought, too late and frankly not interested enough, choosing something spanking new and having an approximate guess at the right colour. Perhaps no-one would notice the difference.

The back of the car now felt strangely heavy, reminding him of summer holidays, lumbering towards a French *gîte*, overloaded with luggage, sundry heaps of sports gear, Polly's surf-board and Jenny's usual box of holiday books. Could do with a break, he thought, absent-mindedly driving on to the M4 and then missing his turning back towards home. He joined the flow of cars heading towards Hammersmith, and when he got there, instead of going back across the bridge towards home, drove on towards Kensington, thinking at first vaguely, then more positively, about Serena. He now knew where she lived. After an evening of Joe Walsh's seductive, relaxed, country rock on Thursday night she had allowed Alan to drive her home instead of striding off in her usual independent fashion towards the nearest tube. He'd spent the evening sweatily preparing to persuade her, too, as she lived only a few miles from him and there they both were, miles out in north London. In the end, though, she'd been quite happy to jump into his car, the fringes on her leather jacket swinging as Alan nervously lurched round corners, desperately trying to keep his hand from stroking her slim, lycra thigh.

It was no longer possible to pretend his interest in her was less than carnal. He'd put *Sympathy for the Devil* on the cassette player and managed, for once, to keep himself from singing along with it. Outside Serena's flat, he had switched off the car engine, waiting without breathing, to be invited in for coffee and whatever else the night and Serena might offer. He'd felt weak with longing for her supple body as she turned to open the car door, and the leather of the jacket had squeaked faintly. Just at the moment when she turned to smile a sweet goodbye at him, Alan had noticed a basement door open and a dumpy, blonde, spike-haired figure ran up the steps and stood silhouetted against the light. She looked, he had thought at the time, like an irate wife, arms folded firmly into the 'where-have-you-been-till-this-time' position. Guiltily he had thought of Jenny, who had never been that sort of wife and had never failed to trust him, and reluctantly he'd surrendered Serena to her fuming flat-mate. Another opportunity lost, he thought, feeling old and that time and chances were both expiring fast.

The car swung heavily into Serena's street and Alan could hear a clunk as the bag of ready-mix cement fell over onto the bricks in the car boot. He stopped the car opposite Serena's flat, switched off the engine and then wished he hadn't chosen a spot so close. He also wondered if he ought to get out and check that the cement bag hadn't split. He knew that there were also a couple of old bottles of mineral water rolling around in the boot, and had a vision of the bricks and cement and water building themselves into a haphazard wall of their own. A woman, not Serena, emerged from the basement of the building opposite and terrified him into restarting the engine. Was that the small, cross woman from the other night, he wondered, risking a quick glance. Attracted by the sound of the car, she glared across at him and Alan, panic-stricken, pulled away sharply, finding that his hands on the wheel were trembling as he turned back towards the centre of Hammersmith and the bridge across the Thames, to home and safety.

*　　*　　*

At that moment, Serena was talking to Jenny on the telephone. 'Sorry, Alan is out at the moment,' Jenny was saying, icy cool and almost secretarial. From the conservatory she could hear eleven-year-old Georgina Smythe and her flute murdering Glück's *Dance of the Blessed Spirits*, and wondered why it wasn't pupils as hopeless as this one who chose to give up learning the instrument.

'Awful of me to bother you I know, only I think I left my scarf in Alan's car the other night. I'd hate to lose it, you see it's a super Chanel one I borrowed from Mummy.' Serena's silky, rather child-like voice continued. Jenny promised to look for the scarf, privately thinking what an appropriate weapon it would be for strangling her husband. Was this, she thought, returning to supervise Georgina's lesson, a heavy hint from Serena that an affair was definitely going on? Or was it a double bluff, as in – the affair was on but Serena was pretending everything was innocent by being so up-front about it? Either way it got Jenny hopping mad. She picked up her own flute to show Georgina how the piece should be played, but with shaking, furious fingers managed to play almost as badly as the child. 'We'll both practise it for next week,' she said, giving up the attempt and trying to make a joke of it. 'Perhaps one of us will get it right by then.'

'Have you ever been before?' Polly was asking Sebastian and Marcus in the car on the way to Laser Leisure.

'No, but just about everyone at school has. We've been dying to,' Sebastian told her eagerly.

Polly gave a lordly grin to the boys and Harriet, relishing her superior status as an experienced Laser-shooter. She looked forward to leading the ensuing battle, and to being the overall winner at the end of the afternoon. The twins looked a bit nervous, thought Jenny, smiling in the driving mirror at them. And well they might, she realized, knowing that it wasn't fear of the game that worried them, but the fear of what Carol would say if she knew where they were really going. Unbeknown to their mother, the only scientific enlightenment the boys were going to get was from the flash of the ultra-violet as teams of hyper-excited children zapped each other with laser beams, recording the hit-score on responders strapped to their bodies. Good exercise was the only possible redeeming feature she would be able to find to appease Carol, Jenny decided, even though Carol thought exercise could only be done under conditions of rule-bound sport outside, in good fresh air. At least Carol believed firmly in competition, she thought, turning into the Laser Leisure car park, and perhaps one of the twins would win.

Alan was well into rebuilding the wall by the time Jenny and the children got home. As she turned into the driveway, Jenny's car wheels whizzed up dust and grit which fell, irritatingly, into Alan's mortar, as carefully mixed and prepared as a delicate *Hollandaise*. In the blast of air from the car, the Reader's Digest DIY guide fell from its propped-up position on the heap of bricks and landed in Alan's bucket of water, rendering him furious and dripping. Marcus, who was interested in anything that looked messy, clambered out of the car and came to inspect Alan's progress and see if he could join in. 'The bricks are a different colour,' he pointed out.

'I'm hoping no-one will notice,' Alan replied, slapping another trowel full of mortar on the wall.

'Well Marcus noticed,' Polly said smartly, watching her father turn interestingly brick-coloured himself.

Alan gritted his teeth. 'Why don't you kids go into the house and get something to eat?' he said, his eye on Harriet, who was inspecting her shoes after walking into a cementy puddle.

'We had lunch. We had McDonald's,' Sebastian said with great pride. Poor kids, thought Alan suddenly, Carol and Paul probably make the twins avert their eyes from hamburger bars. Probably think they'll catch something nasty in there, like an undesirable accent.

Jenny called the children in and then, seeing the state of their shoes from treading in the wall debris, promptly sent them outside again, round to the back of the house to play in the garden. She stood in the doorway watching Alan stirring the cement and decided that, from her point of view, it was not the ideal moment to mention Serena's phone call. When she did tell him, she wanted him to have nowhere to look but straight at her, no possibility of shifty guilt being diverted into concentrating on lining up the next brick.

'Let's go out on to the Common!' Polly yelled, dashing off and making for the back gate. Sebastian and Marcus hesitated, looked at each other and at the sprinting bodies of Harriet and Polly far down the garden, and followed.

'She'd better not find out,' Sebastian warned, thinking of his tyrannical mother, as he and Marcus jogged nervously down the path after the two girls towards the open gate and the forbidden Common.

'She won't find out from me,' Marcus retorted. 'But she won't like my shoes.' As he ran he looked down at his feet, where a thin crust of cement was dulling the highly polished leather.

'It's her own fault, she should have let us wear our trainers. Anyway, she won't blame you, she'll blame Polly's dad for making such a mess. He's got that stuff

124

all over the pavement. It's worse than dog.'

Out of the garden on to the Common the boys stopped, and, like puppies, stood sniffing the unfamiliar air. There were smells of bracken and blossom, and damp, oozy grass. Padding after some unsuspecting prey, one of the Mathiesons' Siamese cats, enviably free from parental rules, stalked through clumps of early bluebells.

'We're over here!' called Polly's voice from behind a hawthorn bush.

'Come and find us!' added Harriet in a taunting sing-song.

Sebastian and Marcus took a swift look round to make sure there wasn't a marauding parent in sight, and leapt into the dense shrubbery.

Harriet pounced out from behind the hawthorn and grabbed Marcus, twisting his arm. 'You're Marcus. I can tell because you're wearing the red sweatshirt. What happens when you haven't got any clothes on? How do people tell the difference between you then?' Marcus, unused to fending off girls and somehow sure he'd heard that you shouldn't have to, stayed passive as Harriet wrestled him to the floor and sat on his chest.

'That's the whole point, stupid. We're identical,' Sebastian told her smugly. 'You can't tell.' He kept a wary distance from Polly and grinned at Harriet, sitting down and pulling at dandelion heads.

'Seb's hair is a bit longer,' Harriet judged, inspecting them both closely. 'And I think he might have more freckles.'

'I'm a roundhead. Seb's not,' Marcus, in a slightly strangled voice gasped from his position as Harriet's cushion. She had her legs apart and across him, crushing him solidly, the rivets on the back of her jeans digging into an exposed piece of flesh under his sweatshirt. His back would be all grass-stained, he thought, desperate to be allowed to his feet.

'What's a roundhead?' Polly asked. 'Do you mean

like Cavaliers and Oliver Cromwell and history?'

'Being a roundhead doesn't make you look different,' Harriet said scornfully. 'Not in this century anyway,' she added grandly with all the authority of a recent school project.

'Oh yes it does!' Marcus protested, suddenly catching sight, too late, of warning signals from his brother.

Sebastian groaned. 'Shut it Marc!' he yelled, as he felt Polly watching him blush. Her inevitable next remark was, as he knew it would be, 'OK show us then! Which bit of you is it that is a roundhead?'

The two boys were silent. It hadn't occurred to Marcus that there were people on the planet who didn't know his school's terms for circumcised and uncircumcised cocks. He and Sebastian looked at each other, and the two little girls waited. Their silence told Polly exactly which bit she needed to see. She was perfectly used to seeing Alan casually and uninterestingly naked around the house, though not Ben these days, who scuttled rapidly from bedroom to bathroom, with his bathrobe belt tightly knotted, just in case. Polly's curiosity was on full alert. She knew what a penis looked like, and was haughtily scornful of girls at school who dared admit they didn't but she had never come across the possibility that some penises were different from others. In the interests of research she knew it was crucial to find out how. Suddenly Polly leapt on Marcus and started tugging at his tracksuit bottoms.

'Gerrofff!' roared Marcus, wriggling desperately under the bulk of Harriet.

Sebastian hurled himself on top of the heap and the four of them fought intensely for a moment in a tangle.

'If you show us, we'll show you something interesting, really, truly interesting,' Polly coaxed, sitting up and pulling dandelion seeds from her hair. 'So interesting you'll be able to show off to all the boys at your school about it.'

Sebastian, from the safety of the far side of an oak sapling, thought about the bits of girls he hadn't yet seen, that probably no-one at school had seen, and wouldn't they all be jealous if that was what Polly was promising. Harriet was giving her a doubtful look, as if she wasn't sure she was prepared to go along with this. Sebastian didn't really mind showing his willy, his mum and Matron at school looked at it all the time, just to see if the end was getting tight like Marcus's had and would have to be trimmed.

'OK what will you show us?' he asked, prepared to bargain.

'Well,' Polly said slowly, 'have you ever seen . . .' she looked across at Harriet, making sure she could count on her joining in. The two boys leaned forward, eagerly, and Polly asked in a loud, excited whisper, 'Have you ever seen a dead body?'

Marcus gasped, Seb looked sceptical and Harriet stared intently at Polly, wondering which way to play it. She rather thought, on balance, she'd prefer to show the boys her fanny than have to go with them and look at a corpse.

'Yeah. I know where there's one, really near, near where you're sitting now!' Polly continued, her eyes blazing with dramatic importance. 'And it's only me that knows, so you have to do what I say if you want to see it.'

Marcus felt prickly with fear. He didn't at all want to see anyone dead, but even more he didn't want Polly to know this. There was a moment of silence, while decisions were made.

'OK,' Sebastian said simply, standing up and lowering his trousers. 'Come on Marcus, get it out.'

Reluctantly, but with a sigh of inevitability, Marcus stood up and fumbled with his trousers. He wondered if Polly would touch it, and if it would go up at all. He reminded himself how envious the boys in his form

127

would be when he told them. He hoped he could rely on Seb to exaggerate a good bit, make it all sound infinitely ruder than the cool, silent, clinical inspection that Polly and Harriet were now making.

After a few minutes, Sebastian shoved Harriet, who was peering horrendously closely, back into the grass and hurriedly re-dressed himself. 'That's enough. Now let's see this dead person,' he demanded.

'Oh, I didn't say it was a person, did I? I'm sure I didn't . . .' Polly said, sneaking away towards the garden fences and giving the boys a sly look.

Harriet, relieved, caught on, and giggled. 'No, she didn't say it was a *person*, she never said *that*!' she told the boys contemptuously, skipping towards Polly and safety.

'I will show you a body though. There's a bit of old rabbit that a fox left . . .' Polly called, laughing, over her shoulder. It's round this corner . . . and she disappeared at a run behind a clump of blackthorn. Sebastian and Marcus dashed after the girls, hellbent on revenge. From out of sight there came a blood-curdling duet of screams.

'They're putting it on,' Marcus said. 'You just wait till we get you!' he yelled.

'Yeah, we'll get their knickers, they deserve it,' Sebastian said, hurling himself painfully through the blackthorn. Then he stopped, and looked at what had made the girls scream. Harriet had her hand over her mouth, looking as if she might be sick. Polly's eyes were wild with terror. The four of them stood and gazed at the stretched-out, gape-mouthed, twisted body of old Mrs Fingell.

Chapter Nine

'Mugged,' was Paul Mathieson's immediate and authoritative verdict, although Mrs Fingell showed no obvious sign of injury. Paul, Carol, Jenny, Sue and the four children stood around the still and solid body like a silent gathering at a wake. Harvey and Laura Benstone were picking their careful way across the damp grass towards the group, respectfully shushing their oblivious little girls who whooped and shrieked in the unaccustomed freedom of the great open space. Sue's dog, an aged and bad-tempered Airedale, whined and tugged at its lead, furious at having its daily snuffle through the rabbit warrens interrupted, and irreverently eager to take curious sniffs at the body.

'Alan's phoning the police, and an ambulance,' Jenny whispered, shivering and rather frightened in the presence of the corpse.

'Not much use, getting an ambulance,' Paul commented bluntly. 'The police will bring their own mortuary van. Of course not yet, seeing as it's murder . . .' he said, proud of his extensive knowledge.

Bloody know-all, Jenny thought, moving closer to Sue and sliding her arm through hers for warmth and comfort.

'Are we sure she's dead?' Sue suddenly asked. 'I mean, should we do the kiss of life or something?' There was a distinct rustling of the grass as feet were guiltily shuffled. No-one was actually prepared to touch Mrs Fingell and check for signs of breathing and pulse. Even when alive, she had carried a certain aroma of decay.

'Oh God, I feel awfully faint,' Laura Benstone squeaked feebly, pressing a limp hand to her forehead.

'We'll go home, darling. Take the girls away from this. They really shouldn't see,' Harvey said eagerly, pulling at Laura's arm. Then he turned to the others, feeling he should apologize for shameful curiosity. 'We only came in case there was anything we could do . . .' he murmured. Jenny felt Sue's body twitch slightly, and realized she was, typically, trying not to giggle. 'We could take her dog perhaps?' Harvey continued, desperate to be useful, and bumbling off after Mrs Fingell's scuttling little orange poodle which was happily sniffing around the base of an oak tree.

'They'll have to cordon off this part of the Common,' Paul was saying, gazing around. 'One of those little tents they'll have, too, to cover the body. We shouldn't really be here, you know, trampling on Evidence.' Jenny was watching Paul's face, which was vibrant with excitement and importance. 'As your Neighbourhood Watch representative,' he started to say pompously, getting well into his stride, 'I feel I should recommend that you all return to your homes and wait to be summoned for evidence. I'll have to wait here, naturally. The police will no doubt wish to interview you all in due course . . .' He was interrupted by a loud sniff from Carol, who, to Jenny's amazement, was actually crying.

'Oh what is happening to the world?' Carol suddenly wailed dramatically, putting a protective arm round the shoulder of each of her highly embarrassed twins. 'A poor old lady can't even walk her pet on the Common without being mugged and murdered by a bunch of louts from the estate!' She looked up, as if appealing for a response from the heavens.

Sue covered her face with her hand and shook helplessly, and Paul smiled across with unctuous

130

sympathy, not realizing she was hiding an attack of the giggles. Jenny nudged her to stop, feeling a sinful and inappropriate smile creeping over her own face. Some people, she recalled, do have this nervous reaction to terrible things, an outrageous and uncontrollable desire to laugh.

The police arrived, swarming across the Common in a number large enough to satisfy Paul. He strode off to meet them, proudly confident that this time, at last, he had something that wasn't a waste of their time.

'Shouldn't we cover her up?' he heard the voice of Polly saying as he came level with the now-familiar police sergeant. An angry yowl of protest and series of shocked screams followed, and Paul and the police rushed to the little group. Sue was now laughing openly, clutching Jenny for support. Carol's tears had halted abruptly and she was now staring with silent fury at Mrs Fingell, who was thrashing around beneath Jenny's Barbour.

'Where's the corpse?' the police sergeant asked Paul.

'She was dead . . . ! Really, a minute ago . . .' he babbled.

'Dead drunk more like,' said a young constable, winking at Sue. He bent down to take a closer look at Mrs Fingell and she rolled on to her side, revealing an empty sherry bottle.

'Thought it was getting a bit uncomfortable,' she said, grasping the bottle and hurling it into the shrubbery. 'One less for the bin,' she said, cackling wickedly.

'Anyone here going to walk this lady home?' the sergeant said looking round. Carol's mouth was pursed up tight with disapproval, though at Paul, Polly or Mrs Fingell, Jenny couldn't be sure.

'We'll take her,' said Sue, bending to pick up one of Mrs Fingell's skinny arms and guide her to her feet. 'Come on, love,' she said. 'We'll make you a cup of tea.'

'Bugger tea,' Mrs Fingell retorted, scrambling to her feet and squinting through the trees to check the angle of the sun. 'Looks to me more like time for a gin.'

Jenny and Sue each took one of the old lady's arms and escorted her carefully back into the Close, followed at a safe distance by a trail of dogs, neighbours and children. Polly marched ahead, one hand on her hip, the other twirling a stick, pretending she was leading the Putney Shangri-la Majorettes. Alan was still sitting on the pavement, smoothing off the last of the mortar as the small procession drew level with him. 'Oh. Glad to see you're all right,' he said rather fatuously, grinning up at Mrs Fingell.

'Oh don't you worry about her, she's all right,' Carol said grimly, and then looked at the wall closely, taking comfort from what she saw. 'Did you realize those new bricks aren't *quite* the right colour?' she asked Alan sweetly.

'I'll put the kettle on,' Jenny volunteered as she and Sue tugged a happily swaying Mrs Fingell into her sitting-room, and parked her on the sofa. 'I think gin would probably really finish her off.'

'Good idea,' Sue agreed. 'Anyway, I fancy tea even if she doesn't.'

'No need to talk about me as if I'm not here,' Mrs Fingell grumbled, shifting her bloomered thighs up onto the tatty sofa and settling comfortably into the cushions. 'They all do that, my daughter-in-law, her kids, the people from the Welfare . . .'

'Sorry,' Sue said. 'Now, are you hungry? Can we get you something to eat?'

Jenny, searching in the kitchen for tea and milk, made a face at Sue through the open door. The cupboards, like Mother Hubbard's, were almost bare. 'I'll go down to the shop for you if you like,' Sue volunteered.

'No need. My son's coming later. Taking me over to his place for supper. One thing that wife of his can do is cook.' Then Mrs Fingell sniggered. 'About all she's good for, certainly no good for the other. Even walks with her knees glued together.'

Jenny, still bustling in the kitchen, heard her and laughed, wondering why it always seemed so outrageous when old people showed evidence of a filthy mind. After all, she couldn't imagine either herself or Sue suddenly becoming all prim and proper the minute they got to bus-pass age.

'Here's tea,' she said, bringing the tray and putting it on a dusty little table next to an equally dusty ancient grand piano. 'I found some biscuits, too.' The small, smelly dog, returned by Harvey, whined to be fed and Sue took him off to the kitchen where she found a stained tin opener and a can of Chum. Jenny poured tea and had a quick, fascinated stare around the room. The curtains had a very 1960s pattern of bold brown and orange flowers, the sort that were now only seen in run-down hospital out-patient departments. The carpet had obviously been a good one in its long-ago day, and was grass green, with darker patches that might indicate the incontinence of the orange dog (or Mrs Fingell, Jenny wondered squeamishly). On the beigey-yellow wall over the bleak fireplace hung a vast flag, an American Southern Cross. Looking round at the piano, Jenny also noticed a large, silver-framed collection of black-and-white photos, about twenty of them, which on close inspection were all of cheerful young men in US army uniform.

'Looking at my boys are you?' Mrs Fingell said fondly, turning a little on the sofa.

'Yes. Who are they? Friends of yours? Relations?'

Mrs Fingell chuckled. 'You could call them relations. Of the carnal sort. One of them is my Lance's dad.'

Sue joined Jenny, and together they peered at the photos. 'Oh, that's interesting, which one?' Sue asked. Mrs Fingell gave a delighted snort in her tea.

'Goodness love, how would I know? Could have been any one of them. Or one or two others, who didn't have a photo on them at the time. I did like to collect the photos.' She sighed, remembering.

Sue and Jenny looked at each other, wondering if they'd heard right. 'But surely . . .' Sue began, and then stopped. Deciding which of two or possibly even three men could be your child's father was just about an understandable quandary, but which of a possible twenty or more . . .

'Shocked you have I?' Mrs Fingell, pleased with herself, looked at Sue. 'You young things don't know the half of it. How do you think we all got by in the war? Did you think rationing and all that was really done on a fair shares basis?' She pulled herself up on the sofa and reached over for her tea, dunking a custard cream biscuit messily into it. 'My family was bombed out of the East End. By rights I should have gone into a prefab, and then if I was lucky by now I might be stuck on the top floor of one of those prison blocks on the estate. But you don't just think, you know for sure, that you might as well live as if there's no tomorrow, and you'll do anything. Just for you and yours. Everyone did. All that love thy neighbour stuff, I never saw much of that. It was dog eat dog. And people eat dog, I even saw that.' She leaned forward, a look of bitter recollection on her face. 'Do you know, my aunt actually cooked a piece of cocker spaniel she found in a bombed terrace. When you've seen your family down to that, it's no hardship to trade a quick shag for a pound of sausages, I can tell you.'

*   *   *

'The wages of sin, this house,' Sue said to Jenny later as they carefully closed Mrs Fingell's rickety front gate.

'I wonder when she retired?' Jenny mused, looking at the rotting window frames and the ramshackle garden. 'Puts my little venture into humble perspective doesn't it?' she went on. 'There was me dabbling in a spot of paid naughtiness, just so I could go on having life's little trimmings if Alan decides to take off, and down the road all the time is a woman who took to prostitution just to survive.'

'Well she could have got another kind of job after the war,' Sue reasoned. 'Though with tarting you can choose your own hours and take time off if your kid's ill. I wonder if she was ever actually married, or if she just calls herself "Mrs" like cooks always used to.'

'Imagine,' said Jenny, 'what the Mathiesons would say if they knew. Not just one, but two houses of ill-repute in one small suburban cul-de-sac!'

Alan was lying on the sofa. As she walked up the path, Jenny could see him through the sitting-room window, feet up, beer in hand and his eyes half-closed. He looked as if he intended to stay there all night, slumped and exhausted from his efforts with the wall. Jenny went into the house, and was immediately pounced on by Daisy rushing down the stairs pursued by Ben, who tripped and missed the last couple of steps, landing in an untidy heap at Jenny's feet.

'Hey, slow down!' she said, pulling Ben upright. 'What's the panic?'

'She's got my headphones,' Ben said, reaching across to grab them from Daisy's hand.

'Well you're going out, you won't be needing them.'

'I need them while I get ready!' he snapped at Daisy.

Jenny felt that at their age she shouldn't have to be refereeing, and marched straight on into the kitchen

where she banged about looking for things for supper, wishing she couldn't still hear every word of the din.

'No you don't,' Daisy snarled, 'you'll get toothpaste or something all over them. And what's that poovy pong?' she added, wrinkling her nose.

'Aftershave,' Ben told her, blushing and making for the stairs.

'After what? Do me a favour!' she snorted.

'She's only jealous because she can't go out.' Ben leaned over the banisters and loudly appealed to Jenny for support.

'I don't want to know. Just carry on arguing amongst yourselves!' she shouted.

No wonder Alan is looking elsewhere she thought, finding enough ingredients for a *Salade Niçoise*. He must be lying on that sofa right now wishing he was somewhere quiet and peaceful, with someone quiet and peaceful. As she boiled eggs and chopped tomatoes, she imagined Serena in a pale and tranquil apartment, surrounded by the trappings of a grown-ups-only life, tasteful and delicate sculptures, intricate, unchipped glass ornaments, creamy, unmarked silk cushions. She thought of a high, wide bed, perhaps of elegant blond wood, hung with drapes of sheer silk that ten-year-olds hadn't wound themselves in to giggle and hide from their scruffy friends. A bed piled with Floris-scented white antique lace cushions that a teenager hadn't flumped carelessly into as a handy nest from which to watch *Neighbours* or monopolize the phone. Jenny sighed and whipped up a fast salad dressing, knowing it wouldn't be as good as Alan's, but reluctant to play the useless wife and disturb him. Serena wouldn't have any problem with curdling walnut oil, Jenny concluded, whisking the dressing more in hope than expectation. Viciously she tore some leaves from the nearest of the four basil plants lined up on the window ledge. Blinded by love,

Alan would probably be thrilled to be served ready-made Paul Newman stuff-in-a-bottle by the object of his desires.

Ben suspected he'd overdone the aftershave. If you can smell it yourself, he thought, it's probably too much, even if the stuff is right under your own nose. There was supposed to be just a hint, just enough for Emma to scent appreciatively as she nuzzled close to his neck. There wasn't supposed to be enough to make her eyes water. He started to feel hot at the thought of Emma as he trudged down the Close on his way to Oliver's house. He didn't want to get sweaty, and his armpits were safely stiff with a triple spraying of Right Guard, but the picture that kept creeping into his mind of her adjusting her games skirt and showing off her thighs was quite irresistible. He could feel the stirrings of an erection even as he walked, and wished it would go away. He tried instead to concentrate on the other feeling he always got on the way to Oliver's, a certain amount of stark terror, as Oliver, with a full scholarship to their expensive school and a council grant for his uniform, lived right in the middle of the estate, as overlooked by tower blocks as was the Close. His house had four bedrooms, and his family was large – six children – run on chaotically anarchic lines by ex-hippy parents, a dedicated mother who educated three of her younger children herself at home and a session guitar player who was using his increasing bouts of unemployment to take over more and more of the surprisingly large back garden for organic vegetables. The fence, to stave off residents who were too idle to get as far as the greengrocer on the edge of the estate, was of coiled barbed wire like a military base.

As Ben walked, his right hand was clutched tightly

round the clingfilmed three ounce stash of dope in his pocket. He couldn't afford to be mugged for that, or there'd be no profits for him and Oliver to share. Crossing the main road in front of Sue Kennedy's house, he took a deep breath and entered the estate, treading carefully round the mountainous heaps of dog shit from the estate's enormous and free-ranging population of Dobermanns and German shepherds. Ben wished he could borrow Sue's grouchy Airedale, just to get him safely across the open space ahead, where teams of circling boys with heavy-duty mountain bikes, state-of-the-art trainers, bandanas and backward-facing baseball caps eyed him with interest and suspicion.

'You going to Mick's?' one of the boys called out.

Startled, Ben looked round to check it was really him the boy was talking to. 'Yeah you, you look like one of his brother's mates.' The boys were cycling closer to him now, starting to weave slowly and expertly round him, just close enough to intimidate. It was impossible, with the spotted, drug-runner style bandanas covering the lower halves of their faces, to see their expressions. His hand on the stash in his pocket grew hotter and he wondered if the stuff would melt.

'Yeah, I'm going to Mick's,' he answered, as casually as he could manage. The kids were no more than Polly's age, he reminded himself, wondering if the Right Guard was going to last out the evening.

'Well tell him we've been waiting for him and we're getting pissed off,' another of the boys said.

'OK, I'll tell him,' Ben replied, walking across the last bit of the square and wondering if they'd grab him as soon as he got to the deserted narrow passageway by Oliver's house.

'Cheers,' the boys yelled, and cycled off across the square again. I'm getting like Carol Mathieson, terrified of anyone who isn't exactly the same tribe as me, Ben

thought, angrily correcting his politics from the safety of hindsight.

'Going out' for Ben and his friends mostly involved finding somewhere to gather where the maximum number of girls could be found. All places of teenage entertainment had been closed down either by people fearful for their furnishings, or those chasing fatter profits. Even on the estate they were banned after 7 p.m. from the community centre, which was taken over for bingo sessions. The two local discotheques charged £2.50 for a bottle of mild Mexican lager (including slice of lime) and wouldn't allow in anyone under 25, or in jeans, trainers or leather. In the town, the police patrolled in pairs, separating groups of bored teenagers looking for fun from nervous proprietors of hamburger bars, where occasional knifings took place between groups whose sole difference was the chosen shape of their trousers.

Ben and Oliver, each now also equipped with a night's supply of booze, headed for the river towpath, beside the bridge, watching carefully to see if they were being followed by hostile raggas or goths. Both were aware that their hair was the unmistakable public school style – floppy, and over-long at the front, and their clothes, despite a fashionable hint of unkemptness about them, were too clean.

'Do you think she'll be there?' Ben asked Oliver for about the fourteenth time, as the group of kids on the green next to the bridge came into sight.

'She might, she might not,' Oliver said, unhelpfully. His attitude, it seemed to Ben, was rather casual: if one girl wasn't available, any other would probably do. The group by the bridge consisted of about fifteen teenagers with nowhere better to go. There was a homogeneity about them, the girls being a giggling, confident bunch mostly from Daisy's school, and the boys a brash, showing-off contingent from Ben's. By some form of

139

consensus this was where they all knew to congregate, in the absence of a party or any other firm venue. A couple of dawdling policemen hung over the bridge parapet, just checking that no-one was yet about to fall drunkenly in the river, and being snobbish enough to think that from this group, at any rate, no real drugs or knife trouble could be expected.

'No Daisy then?' Oliver checked with Ben, before he could feel free to aim his one-night affections at a small, curvy fair-haired girl called Lucy.

'No. Not for a while. Except that she's got a plan to sneak out on the night of Sophie's birthday party, even if she dies in the attempt, she says.'

'Well as you know, ideally I'd like to save my-self for her till then,' Oliver said, grinning past Ben towards the foxy little face of Lucy. 'But you know how it is, got to get the practice in . . .' He shrugged, and left Ben to go and offer a swig from his cider bottle to the giggling Lucy.

Emma arrived with Sophie about ten minutes later. Ben, who had been feeling pretty big-time, having sold all his stash except a bit for himself, suddenly wished he had Daisy there so he could be artlessly chatting to her, and Emma could join them. Now, with only himself to rely on, he felt overheated again as he watched her picking her way down the grassy slope. She was wearing a floaty, translucent flowered long shirt over black leggings. As she came closer, Ben could see through the frail fabric that she wore a cropped black top that left a tantalising strip of naked flesh round her middle. It's about a hand's width, he caught himself thinking, feeling that his own hands were becoming flopping, uncontrollable lettuces on the end of his ape-like arms. The evening was fairly cold, Emma had obviously chosen fashion over comfort and would be needing to be kept warm later. Ben could hardly wait.

*   *   *

Carol and Paul took the twins to an early showing of *Jungle Book* at the Odeon.

'It's important we give them something to take their mind of this afternoon's events,' Carol told Paul after the fiasco on the Common. Paul had been hoping to start some bowling practice with the boys in the garden, ready for the summer. He looked forward to sitting in the sun outside the school pavilion, proudly watching them star in the first eleven, and had vague fantasies of a queue of leading public schools offering sports scholarships to the twins, renowned throughout the English prep school world as, perhaps, 'those marvellous Mathieson boys', regardless of their efforts in Common Entrance a year or so ahead. Half-lost in a dream, he flexed his bowling arm and caught sight of himself in the hall mirror, looking strangely twisted and odd. Reflected behind him was one of the Siamese cats, sitting complacently on the table next to Carol's militarily precise arrangement of scentless carnations. Strange that the cat was allowed to shed its fur over any surface it chose, whereas he, a grown-up human, could only expect a hail of abuse if he so much as left a stray hair in the shower. He looked closer at his reflection and ran his fingers carefully through his hair, checking to see how much of it fell out on to his hand. Quite a lot of it did these days. He had another go at his bowling position and felt a twinge in his shoulder that hadn't been there the previous season and hoped he wasn't in for a painful and expensive spell with the demon chiropractor up at the Club.

'So we are going out then?' Carol did not wait for the inevitable gesture of agreement, and was already reaching into the cloakroom for her coat. 'Something undemanding and light. I think they ought to laugh.'

141

You can't laugh to order, thought Paul, rubbing his shoulder blade.

You had to be fit to be a policeman, Ben reflected as he ran, wondering if his rugby training would be up to enabling him to escape. It was all Luke's fault, trying to make a greedy profit, selling on the ounce of dope he'd scored off Ben and Oliver to a bloke they didn't know.

'Raggas know when they're being ripped off,' Oliver had warned him, and this had proved to be horribly true.

'What's this garbage cut with?' the boy wearing the world's hugest trainers had demanded, sniffing suspiciously at the wodge of dope.

'Nothing, stupid,' Luke had replied riskily and somehow, magically, about ten of the boy's mates had appeared from the towpath beyond the arch of the bridge, their oversized clothes giving them an alarming illusion of bulk.

'Run!' Oliver had yelled, unnecessarily, as he and Ben and the others in their group took off up to the top of the bridge and across into the Saturday night crowd in the town. Police, alerted on the way by the sudden frantic flurry of movement, joined in the chase.

Ben seized his chance, the moment and Emma, dragging her into an alleyway at the side of the Odeon. Looking back briefly over his shoulder, he could see one of the ragga boys hesitating on the corner back at the main road, his baseball cap clutched in his hand for better running power. Fearful that the boy was about to spot him, Ben pulled Emma into a doorway and started kissing her thoroughly. As she broke away to protest, he put a restraining finger to her soft lips and glanced over her shoulder.

'It's only till they've gone. They'll think we're just

another couple,' he explained, wondering if he'd get away with that one. Thankful that he could put his heavy breathing down to the exertion of running, Ben started kissing her again, thrilled that she was now enthusiastically joining in. Suddenly, just as Ben was edging his thumb under her cropped tee-shirt, a door opened next to them and a family of cinema-goers rushed out. A young boy was noisily sick on the pavement.

'You should have told us you'd already had junk food for lunch!' Ben heard the outraged voice of Carol bleating at Sebastian. Paul was standing around, shifting from one leg to the other, worrying in case Carol ordered him to clear up the pavement, the way she would have done if Sebastian had been a dog. Ben peeked over Emma's shoulder, watching Carol bend to wipe the face of her son, her pale pink leggings stretching taut over her bottom. For a moment, in the dark, she gave the impression of being naked below the waist and Ben felt a familiar lurch in his already over-stimulated groin. He sighed deeply into Emma's patchouli-scented hair. So many women, he thought, so little time.

It had been a tedious evening. Jenny had found nothing to interest her on TV, had finished the crossword and couldn't face straining her eyes doing needlepoint in the lamplight. Daisy made sure everyone knew she resented being still grounded, flouncing around the house, sighing and unsettled, ostentatiously writing her diary on the sofa and glaring at her parents as if thinking up new and vitriolic ways to describe their cruel treatment of her. Alan had drunk most of a bottle of priceless claret and fallen into a deep and unattractive stupor. Jenny wished she'd taken Polly to see *Jungle Book*, even though they'd both seen it before. Eventually she decided sleep was the only interesting

prospect, and on her way to the stairs opened the front door for the miaowing Biggles.

'You've got a perfectly good cat-flap in the kitchen,' she told him, bending to give his velvet-soft marmalade ears a rub. Looking out into the chill night, she noticed Alan's car parked too near the front door. It reminded her of the conversation with Serena about the scarf. In the confusion of the afternoon, the 'murder' of Mrs Fingell and the bickering of her children, Jenny had forgotten her plan to confront Alan about the phone call. She stepped out into the cool air and opened the driver's door and looked in both glove compartments, finding only a map book, a hotel guide and a torch that didn't work. She flicked through the guide, wondering if she was looking for little intimate country inns, marked perhaps with a damning asterisk, but there was nothing. The scarf was in the back of the car, just under the edge of the front passenger seat. Jenny picked it up and held it by a hand-hemmed corner with the tips of her fingers, as fastidiously as if she'd come across a used condom. In the warm sitting-room Alan, sprawled plumply on the sofa, was starting to snore. Impatiently Jenny shook him and held out the scarf.

'A friend of yours, Serena I think she said, called, wanting her scarf back. She left it in your car.' Jenny let go of the scarf and it floated delicately past Alan's face and draped itself across his chest. Grunting his way out of a doze he picked it up, then dropped it abruptly on the carpet as if terrified of leaving incriminating fingerprints on it.

'Whose did you say it was?' he blustered, rubbing his sleepy eyes. Jenny watched him calmly, trying to be objective about whether he was reacting guiltily or not. She was too tired to tell. There was a brief and thoughtful silence. 'Oh right! Serena!' Alan suddenly stated, as if he'd not quite worked out who she was.

'Hardly special enough to recall', was the message he seemed to be trying to convey – how many women was he used to chauffeuring around? He reminded Jenny of Polly when confronted with something mysteriously broken: 'Oh *that* plate! Oh *now* I remember!'

'Yes. I gave her a lift home from work the other night.' He got up quickly, too quickly and staggered slightly. What did that mean? Jenny wondered, low blood pressure or lack of concentration? He was picking up empty glasses from the coffee table, not looking at Jenny. The scarf lay like a pool of something colourful and spilt that no-one wanted to clear up.

'Ah. You work with her, do you?' Jenny asked, casually conversational as she fluffed up the cushions on the sofa, almost as unwilling as Alan to have honest eye contact. Alan yawned and stretched languidly.

'She's a trainee, Bernard's niece. Shameless nepotism, don't you think?' Alan grinned brightly at her, picked up the glasses and the empty wine bottle and took them to the kitchen. So Serena was simply a mere junior colleague.

'I'll put it back in the car, then you won't forget it,' Jenny called to him as she picked up the soft silk square. She went quickly out to the car and shoved it onto the front seat, then went back into the downstairs cloakroom to wash the scent of Serena off her hands, rubbing and rubbing at them like Lady Macbeth. Two things bothered her more than slightly, in fact they made her heart beat with alarming heaviness. The first was why had the scarf been in the *back* of the car? Would it be charitable or naïve to pretend it fell from the back of Serena's sleek pony-tail (if indeed she had one), silkily and unnoticed as Serena travelled innocently in the front seat? Or would it be more realistic to assume that Alan and Serena had been frolicking, teenager-style, in the back of the car, parked, like

Sue did, in one of the many lanes on the Common?

The other thing which crossed Jenny's mind was a simple matter of mathematics. If Alan was intending eventually to keep Serena in Chanel accessories, there would be precious little income left over to support his family.

Chapter Ten

Alan knew he was in trouble; he'd known all night, ever since just after he'd cleaned his teeth and started automatically packing his wash-bag and realized he'd completely forgotten to tell Jenny about the audit in Leicestershire, and that he'd be staying away from home for two nights. It had been a very edgy Sunday, too. Polly had refused to eat the beef he'd so painstakingly cooked, simply because he had reassured his family that he was protecting them from mad cow disease by announcing that this particular joint was from a herd of guaranteed BSE-free Red Polls.

'Now look what you've done,' Daisy had grumbled at him as Polly burst into immediate anguished tears out of solidarity with the cattle that shared her name.

'Oh the poor, poor things!' she had wailed, pushing the succulent slices of beef messily off the edge of her plate.

It wasn't his fault he forgot the audit either, Alan thought. With all that business over Mrs Fingell on Saturday, and the rebuilding of the wall (and had anyone been appreciative? congratulatory? grateful?) things that mattered had slid from his mind like roof tiles in a gale. The office hadn't yet said who they were sending with him. He hardly dared think about that. Jenny didn't usually fuss. She'd always joked that his absence gave her an opportunity to have a quick couple of days dieting and to do all those woman-things like root-retouching and pussy-waxing or whatever it was they were supposed to pretend they never actually did.

She'd never been the kind of wife who minded about having to be alone at home, and in fact had always scorned the ones who did. Carol Mathieson used to complain she was too nervous to sleep at all unless Paul was in the house, though she hadn't been heard to say this lately, since George Pemberton, drunk at a Christmas drinks party, had sidled up and quietly offered his services as night watchman. This time, though, Jenny had looked at Alan as if he was planning a permanent absence from home life, or sneaking off to Brazil for a dozen years, perhaps with the takings, meagre as they were at the moment, from the office bank account.

'Why didn't you tell me?' Jenny had said. 'A bit sudden isn't it?' as if he was sliding off on the spur of the moment to get up to no good. All he was doing, he reflected dolefully, sliding quietly out of bed on Monday morning, was yet another depressing analysis of an under-employed musician's finances, another attempt to persuade a client that his rapidly diminishing income would no longer cover a stay at the Ritz every time he popped into London to buy a shirt or two. Alan had to go, it was how the ever-increasing bills got paid. He didn't want to wake Jenny, but feeling sudden guilty fondness for her soft and sleeping body curled up warmly into the centre of their bed, leaned over and kissed her.

'What time is it?' she mumbled, half-opening her eyes.

'Only 6.30. You've got ages yet,' he whispered, reaching under the duvet and squeezing her warm thigh, and wishing he could stay longer.

'Oh God! And it's Monday!' she exclaimed loudly, sitting bolt upright and holding her head which was spinning from the abrupt movement. 'Laura's film people, they're doing the stuff in the kitchen today! I promised we'd all be out of the way by 7.30!'

Jenny was clambering out of bed, Alan's imminent departure suddenly of no importance at all. 'I could do without all that today, with Polly's exam as well and everything.' She grabbed her dressing-gown and hurtled towards the attic stairs to wake Ben, then whirled in and out of the girls' rooms, tugging at their duvets, opening curtains, and leaving them in no doubt that it really was time to get up. Back in the bedroom, grabbing leggings and underwear from drawers, she caught sight of Alan complacently naked in the bathroom, noisily peeing in his favourite pose, no hands, pelvis thrust forward and his hands occupied with pulling his hair down over his forehead towards the style he had favoured in his youth. He was watching himself in the mirror set into the tiles behind the loo and cheerily whistling *Honky Tonk Women*. I hate it when he does that, she thought, what does he think he looks like? Bet he doesn't do that when Serena's around. And if he does, she thought, with a grin and a dash of merry spite, I hope her loo is carpeted in pale pink – the very worst thing to have on the floor when there's a man of unreliable aim around the place.

'Sodding exams,' Polly grumbled in the kitchen, drooping over her Coco Pops.

'Polly! Don't say things like that.' Jenny hovered over Polly, who could eat agonizingly slowly on occasions.

'What, exams?' Polly asked impudently, opening her eyes wider and infuriating her mother.

'Poll, not today, please,' Jenny said, whizzing round the kitchen with a damp cloth, inefficiently trying to clear and wipe surfaces while the others were still eating. The film people were likely to take one look round and zoom off up the road to Carol Mathieson's permanently sterile kitchen.

'I might not do very well,' Polly warned, a sly look on her face. 'I might still be In Shock.'

'From finding someone having a sleep two days ago?' Daisy asked her with weighty sarcasm. 'What do you want Mum to do, send a note?' She giggled. 'I can just see Mrs Pemberton's face . . .'

Jenny laughed, picked up Daisy's school bag from under the table and thrust it at her. 'Here, time you were all out of here. This kitchen's going to earn its keep today. Ben, take another slice of toast with you,' she added, habitually worried that he would soon be the longest, skinniest human on the planet.

'And don't worry, Polly,' she said, scooping the child out of her chair and hugging her, 'the worst that can happen is that you really don't do all that brilliantly. Just as long as you try your hardest. There are plenty of other schools, and if this one doesn't want to keep you, it's their loss.' She gave her a kiss, and sent her off to climb into Ceci Caine's car. Polly trailed slowly trying hard to look pitifully close to tears; when she waved from the gate Jenny for once wished it was her turn to do the school run. 'I'll collect you this afternoon!' she shouted suddenly, knowing that Polly was tweaking deliberately at the heart-strings. 'Tell Ceci!'

'They're just coming round the corner!' Jenny heard Laura's voice calling out to her as she watched Ceci do a gear-crunching three-point turn in front of the Mathiesons' house. Laura trotted up the path, already, at that ungodly hour, wafting a gentle smell of cosmetics. No early morning flung-on leggings-and-sweatshirts for her, Laura was already pin-neat in frill-collared blouse, floral needlecord skirt, pale green tights and principal boy shoes with little gold buckles. As Laura had said, they really were just coming round the corner. What seemed like a self-important motorcade of four or five rather scruffy vans and buses, piled into the Close, taking up enough space to annoy every resident who wasn't being paid for their presence. A large silver truck with *Picture This!* emblazoned on the side pulled up across next door's driveway, and Jenny backed nervously into her hall as she caught sight of Carol Mathieson up at her window, opening her bedroom curtains. A gun-metal grey Porsche swung confidently through Jenny's gates just as she was about to hide behind the door.

'Hi, you must be Jennifer,' the driver called to her, switching off the engine. 'I'm Hugo Hamilton, director on this shoot.'

'Hello Hugo.' Laura emerged from behind Jenny as they both went out on to the drive and she smiled winningly at the attractive, slightly greying man.

He was seriously good-looking, Jenny decided, and well aware of it, unfolding himself slowly from the Porsche as if to emphasize that there wasn't a car built that could truly accommodate his impressive, hulky body. As if someone (a wife? boyfriend?) had decided to dress him up as an archetypal Advertising Man, Hugo was wearing stonewashed jeans (with signs of impressive over-strain round the crotch), a denim shirt that looked suspiciously newish and an expensively distressed leather jacket. On his feet were cowboy boots of such extravagance that if Carol Mathieson were there she would feel obliged to warn him he could easily be mugged for them if he ventured on to the estate. Jenny and Hugo shook hands, and then with a grin that showed perfectly capped teeth and a 'Hi darling, how are things?' Hugo indulged Laura in a spot of air-kissing.

'Sorry, but I'm afraid you really can't let them park there,' Jenny told Hugo, who looked blankly out of the garden at his company's truck. 'The neighbours might need to get in and out. Block this drive by all means, for now though,' she added, worried that he might, after all, take off and use another location. In her head, Jenny had already accounted for Polly's next term at school.

'My lot won't be arriving till 8.30,' Laura said, peering with frank curiosity into the house past Jenny to make sure she had tidied her kitchen according to instructions and not suddenly repainted it purple since she'd made the booking. 'My own venture. Catalogue for next Christmas. Already!' Laura explained to Hugo, glancing at her watch. 'I could really do without it all today,' she said, skipping sideways as vast aluminium cases were hauled into Jenny's porch. 'I think I just might be pregnant!' she hissed loudly. 'Either that or my period is due right now, right this minute.' A large bearded man carrying lights made a grimacing face which only Jenny could see, and bolted back out through the front door, away from the awfulness of women's talk. Laura was prodding her left breast, oblivious to the bustle behind her. 'Because they do hurt, don't they, at either time. I can't tell. I'll have to do a test. I just can't while the house is full of people.'

'Perfect darling, well done as always!' Hugo was calling to Laura from inside Jenny's kitchen. He started, without ceremony, to rearrange furniture, piling up chairs and shoving the table towards the conservatory. 'It will fit all right in there, I should think,' he said to the bearded man who was doing intricate things with a silver parasol.

'Would you all like some coffee?' Jenny thought she should offer, at least.

'No, no you mustn't *give* them anything!' Laura immediately reprimanded her. 'That's what the Katy Katerer truck is out there for. They provide everything, but everything. If you're here,' Laura added in a voice that suggested Jenny should definitely go out and spend the day in the Tate Gallery, 'they might give you lunch.'

'Should I not be here then?' Jenny thought she'd

better get it clear. 'What if there's an emergency, or they need to know about plugs, or the phone rings?' (Oh God, she thought, men who might want flute lessons . . .)

'Frankly, Jen, I find it's best not to watch what they do to the house,' then she added quickly, 'though of course once they've gone, you won't know they've been, so to speak. It's just at the time . . .'

'Table over here I think, Kev,' Hugo was saying to the bearded man, who was single-handedly struggling through the doorway with the top half of a large round pine table, followed by a scowling blonde girl lugging a pair of bentwood dining chairs.

'What's wrong with my table?' Jenny asked Laura.

'Just something to keep the stylists and the props people occupied. Don't worry about it, and for heaven's sake don't take it personally,' Laura instructed her.

Jenny watched her kitchen being dismantled around her, thinking murderous thoughts about Alan, who had once more escaped up a motorway on the grounds of work, and took herself off to have a peaceful shower and make herself feel human again.

Emerging from the bathroom wrapped in a towel, deep in thoughts about what Alan's business trip might really involve, she was startled to see Sue sitting cross-legged on her bed, calmly reading *Country Living*.

'God, you scared me,' Jenny told her. 'I thought you might be one of those film people, trying to take over my bedroom.' Alarming bangings and crashings and shoutings were drifting up the stairs.

'I've come to move you out of the house, actually,' Sue said. 'You can't possibly stay here with this lot, you'll go mad worrying about your paintwork. I thought I'd take you out to lunch and we can pretend to be Ladies who Shop.'

'OK, but I have to be back in time to collect Polly. It's the day of the Great Exam.' Jenny pulled a long

153

pink shirt out of the wardrobe and Sue inspected the cosmetic collection on top of the chest of drawers.

'Does this stuff actually work?' she asked, reading the instructions on the cellulite treatment bottle. She squeezed a bit out onto the back of her hand and massaged it in, sniffing at it.

'Does anything?' Jenny asked, giving her a backward grin in the mirror. '£25 for a spot of fantasy cream. They saw me coming.'

'You and a million others. Let's take it back for a refund,' Sue said, shoving the bottle in her bag.

'Don't be daft! How can we prove it didn't work?' Jenny asked her.

'Wait and see,' Sue said mischievously, 'I've got a plan, but I can't do it on my own.'

'Oh God,' Jenny groaned, 'are we going to make trouble? I've got enough already with Alan and Daisy and Ben and those people downstairs, and Polly's exam . . .'

'No this is fun, I promise. You expect justice to be seen to be done, don't you? Well you bought something that wasn't any use and I've thought of a way of getting your money back, that's all,' Sue said, in a deceptively simple way, her eyes twinkling at Jenny. 'And after that we can buy a little treat for old Mrs Fingell, and go and see how she is.'

'Anyway, how's business?' she asked. 'Loads of offers of tasty, sorry should I use that word? Tasty clients?' she giggled.

'No! Of course not!' Jenny said, rather wishing she'd never let Sue know the awful truth. 'I told you that was just a one-off – but goodness, we could do with the money. Accountancy isn't what it was; if no-one out there is earning anything, they haven't got any money that needs accounting, if you see what I mean. Alan is forever having to hand their stuff over to the Receiver people. That's why I'm renting the kitchen out today. Loadsa cash. I'd rather rent the house out than myself – I don't have to worry about it getting diseased, murdered or blackmailed.'

Inside the department store, Sue led Jenny firmly through the cosmetics area to a counter staffed by a nail-filing assistant who took little notice of browsing customers playing with the test samples. Sue produced the plastic cosmetic bottle from her handbag, handed it to Jenny and prodded her. 'Go on,' she said, 'tell her.'

'Excuse me,' Jenny said politely, but loudly enough to get the attention of three counters-worth of staff. 'This stuff, for cellulite, that it says you just put on and the fat fades away. It doesn't work. So can I have my money back please?'

The assistant, spun-sugar strawberry-blond hair as brittle as candyfloss, and her immaculate eye make-up glossy as a *Vogue* cover, smiled professionally at Jenny and took the bottle from her.

'Sorry madam,' she said, 'but you appear to have used almost all of it. I can't possibly give you a refund.'

'You have to use it all to find that out,' Sue pointed out. 'It doesn't do what it claims to. So can my friend now have her money back please?'

Jenny, fiddling with the eye-shadow testers and making a muddy mess on the back of her hand, could hear a slightly menacing tone in Sue's voice. The assistant, her smile now as fixed as her lip-gloss, was trying to be placatory, fully aware that several customers were now lingering around, sampling perfumes and sensing entertainment.

'I'm afraid these things aren't really quantifiable,' the girl said, savouring the long word as if she'd got it straight from her training manual. 'We have a policy of not refunding unless there's actually skin damage.'

'Consumer rights. An item has to be fit for its intended use,' Sue insisted. And then, to Jenny's horror, Sue turned to her and said loudly, 'Go on, Jen, show the girl your bum!'

'Hey, hang on a minute!' Jenny hissed, watching the gleeful crowd collecting around them.

'Yeah, go on, you show her,' encouraged a plump woman pushing a double buggy. 'I bought that stuff too and it's a rip-off. I'd like to see someone getting their money back for once!'

The support of the crowd and the feeling of being in the right were getting to Jenny. Sue often made her feel like she was part of some daft comedy act. Jenny quickly considered her underwear: quite respectably pretty, high-cut navy-and-white flowered M & S knickers, and her thighs weren't that unpresentable, just a bit lumpy . . .

'OK, why not?' she said. '£25 of water and fancy chemicals and I should have legs as smooth as a teenager, but instead . . .' Jenny announced to her audience, slowly raising her skirt, hiking it up at the side teasingly like the opening seconds of a bawdy nightclub act.

'Da da da, de da da dum,' someone starting singing *The Stripper* quite loudly and Jenny, enjoying the moment pulled up her skirt higher and turned round to give the girl behind the counter a good view of her bottom and the tops of her thighs. She glanced mockingly over her shoulder, daring the assistant, whose thickly mascaraed eyes were as big as bath-spiders, to refuse her request.

Jenny's skirt was up to her hips by now and Sue, like the straight man in a double act, was prodding at her flesh. 'Look at that!' she demanded, as everyone stared. 'Lumpy cellulite! That stuff's a con!'

'Give her the money!' yelled a voice from the crowd.

'Yeah, go on. They make a fortune on this!' came a cry of support.

The assistant hurriedly opened the till and shakily counted out the notes, handing them, with the fastidious tips of her lacquered nails, across to Sue.

Jenny, suddenly coming to her senses, lowered her skirt, patted it decently into place, and felt a blush coming on. 'Thank you,' she said, with as much dignity as she could muster, and the little group gave her a round of applause. Only when she dared look up and take the money from Sue did she notice that one of the figures now hurrying away, the only one not laughing delightedly, was Carol Mathieson.

'Oh good grief, did you see? That was Carol. She's everywhere, that woman. Now it will be all round the Close.'

'Who cares?' said Sue airily. 'And anyway, isn't the fight for justice one of the Mathiesons' favourite themes? And just think,' she whispered loudly, 'you got the price of half a blow-job just for showing your knickers!'

Carol was still trembling when she got home. She carefully eased the white Peugeot past the trucks parked in the Close and parked as near to her front door as she could. Quickly she hauled her Marks and Spencer carrier bags full of economy packs of chicken into the kitchen and flung them crossly into the depths of the freezer without the thorough labelling (re date of purchase and intention of use) that they usually got. Those two, she thought, Jenny and Sue, they just didn't care how they behaved. She felt offended that she, Carol, who had chosen her home with such care, should have ended up living a stone's throw from the sort of woman who was prepared to flash her bottom in a respectable department store just for the sake of a bit of a refund. If the twins had been with her, imagine what they'd have thought! Grown-up people were supposed to have standards, grown-up people of a certain background were supposed to *set* standards. Carol filled up the fridge haphazardly with packs of dolly-size vegetables, miniature carrots, baby beans and tiny, embryonic cauliflowers, and then went upstairs to the attic. The telescope was already focused on the Tennis Club and there they were, those two careless, wicked women, giggling on the balcony and tearing recklessly into great slabs of what looked like garlic bread. They were laughing, probably, at their own cleverness, Carol guessed in outrage. Well they'd better not behave like that in the Close, she thought, resolving to have a Little Word. She swivelled the telescope round and refocused on Jenny's conservatory. Whatever they were doing in her house, those *Picture This!* people, it seemed to involve putting most of Jenny's kitchen furniture into the garden. What a pity it wasn't about to rain.

Outside the school it was easy to see which mothers, that day, had daughters taking the school's own entrance exam. Smiles were fixed, there was much hearty laughter and fake dismissal of their own children's chances of success. Jenny, climbing out of her Golf, heard one mother boasting that her daughter, in the car that morning, had *completely* forgotten her entire six times table. Another was saying that she had spent the whole evening before working out how to do Venn diagrams and was still none the wiser, her child having had no clue either. It was immoral, really, putting these girls through such a distressing selection process, Jenny considered, taking her place anxiously at the foot of the school steps. Ceci Caine, too eager to hear what Harriet's day had been like to let Jenny drive her home, came and stood next to her.

'You know, it's not right is it?' Jenny said, glad to have someone to hear her thoughts. 'The school

158

willingly took on all these little girls at the age of four, not knowing which would turn out to be the infant prodigy and which, as they put it so tactfully in school reports, the late developer. It's as if they've reached judgement day, where only those who'll be absolutely no effort to teach will get to stay on.'

Ceci looked wary, as if Jenny had confessed to sympathy with the wrong political party. 'Yes, but surely you want Polly to go through school with girls who can match her ability, don't you? It's so much more *stretching*.'

Jenny saw Polly elongated, pulled like elastic between her family and the stringent academic requirements of Fiona Pemberton. All those dance classes Polly loved so much, would she have time for them in the senior department, where homework was supposed to take God-given priority? To Ceci she said, 'I'm not sure. I mean they've all been OK together this far, haven't they? And anyway, maybe Polly is one of those who won't be staying.'

'Oh surely not . . .' Ceci murmured automatically, bored with the ritual comforting that had been going on for weeks among all those mothers who had doubts.

'Mum, Mum! It was really hard!' Polly came shrieking out of the main doors and hurtled down the steps. Jenny hugged Polly, relieved that she did not look too concerned by the difficulty of the exam. How worried should anyone of ten have to be?

On the way home, Polly wheedled for chocolate eclairs and a banana milk shake, taking full advantage of Jenny's sympathetic mood.

'Well, I'll buy some eclairs, but I think I'd really like to go home and see what they're doing to the house. Apparently it's an ad for breakfast cereal.'

'Perhaps I can be in it,' Polly said eagerly, pulling down the vanity mirror in the car and making actressy faces into it. 'I'd really love to, more than anything!'

Jenny was touched by the child's shiny-eyed enthusiasm. 'OK, let's forget the cakes and go and see what's happening.'

Since that morning, the population of trucks and vans had increased as Laura Benstone's drive now also overflowed with vehicles. How many people does it take to photograph one Christmas gift catalogue, Jenny wondered, quickly telling her brain not even to think about it as she started adding up the stylists, props people, designers, directors and multitude of hangers-on that could well be leaning against Laura's limed-oak kitchen units at any one moment, fingers artistically curled round coffee mugs.

The scene in Jenny's own house bordered more on the chaotic than the creative. Somewhere offstage, probably in the conservatory, there was shouting. Hugo strode about in the hall crossly, his expensively cut hair was up on end from frantic runnings-through with the fingers, exposing thinning patches of scalp, his mobile phone poking rudely from the waistband of his jeans. A greeny-pale, ginger-haired girl of about Polly's age was sitting on the stairs looking tearful, and being inadequately comforted by her worried-looking mother, who listlessly patted her child on the shoulder and whispered unheeded encouragement to her.

'Everything all right?' Jenny called brightly to no-one in particular as she hung up her jacket, well aware that everything was obviously far from all right and hoping someone would tell her what was going on. Ominous bucket-clankings came from the kitchen and Polly dashed in to have a look.

'Ugh puke! Someone threw up!' she yelled, backing out again.

'Sorry about that. Don't worry, Belinda's mopping.' Hugo smiled wanly at Jenny, who wanted to get past him into her kitchen. With practised skill he blocked the doorway and treated her to one of his less convincing smiles. 'Spot of trouble with our little star,' he hissed viciously, glaring towards the unhappy child on the stairs. 'It seems milk products don't agree with her terribly well.'

The child's mother, sensing criticism, glared back. 'That much milk wouldn't agree with anyone. My Gemma may be sensitive, but she *is* a professional. You should have got all you needed in less than five takes.'

'If she could have *done* all I needed in less than five then obviously I would have done,' Hugo snarled back. 'Now I'm stuck with the set, the product, the crew and no actor. What am I supposed to do now?' He bellowed into the kitchen, 'Kev! Call Castakid would you? Get me another brat!'

Polly slid out of the kitchen doorway, and smiled winsomely up at Hugo. 'You've got me, if you want me. I'm not allergic to anything, and I could *live* on breakfast cereals,' she purred, willing him to see her as a perfect solution. Hugo looked Polly up and down with hostile speculation and her smile widened into her version of a cute-kid grin. Hugo made a speedy executive decision.

'Get the Carmens out, Belinda!' he yelled into the kitchen. 'I've found us another little star!'

'Wait a minute,' Polly said, turning suddenly business-like, possibly at the thought of having her hair curled. 'How much do I get paid?'

Chapter Eleven

'A hundred pounds! You're getting a hundred pounds just for gobbling down a bit of breakfast!' Daisy was appalled and trembling with envy. By the time she got home from school (late because of gym club, she claimed) the house looked boringly like home again. Daisy would have liked to give Hugo Hamilton the opportunity to see and discover her; perhaps he'd have been captivated by her excellent high cheekbones and long, slender legs. Instead, she was faced with Polly swanning around the kitchen being maddeningly big-time. Daisy stamped about crossly, chucking her school bag onto the rocking chair and kicking at the books that came tumbling out.

'Well I deserved it,' Polly retorted, tossing her head carelessly so that her unfamiliar mane of tubular curls bounced. 'After all, everyone I know will see me on television, looking like this!' she made a mock-mortified face and ran her fingers through the curls, secretly enjoying the springy texture and glancing sideways into the mirror to see if she really did resemble the tousled temptress she imagined herself to be. She pouted at her reflection and gathered the curls up onto the top of her head. If she started a career now as a child model and actress, she'd be well used to it by the time she was old enough for the real stuff. How impressed they'd be when she turned up for sessions and stripped off to pose with no fuss about anything but hiding a slightly bored yawn . . .

'You know you look like bloody Shirley Temple!'

Daisy said rudely. 'I wish I'd been here. They'd have had to use me then.'

'Oh no they wouldn't have, you're *much* too old. And spotty.' Polly made a sensible dash for the door and escaped just as Daisy was taking aim with a heavy maths textbook.

Jenny was vaguely listening to all this from the depths of the fridge as she searched for something to give them all for supper, and felt rather proud of Polly. The ginger child's mother, outraged that Polly had so easily taken over her daughter's job, had complained that her darling Gemma had been picked out of 200 at the initial audition and had trailed into town for three recalls before the final decision had been made. Perhaps Polly, who had got it right for the exasperated Hugo in just two takes, really was a natural. Gemma's mother had confided that Gemma paid all her own school fees out of her modelling and acting earnings, thus financing herself at a well-known stage school which would otherwise have been beyond the family's means.

As she slowly grated some cheese, Jenny wondered how much it would cost to have a basic portfolio of photos done so that Polly could be enrolled at Castakid and join the family workforce. At Daisy's age she had been starting a Saturday job, sweeping up in a hairdressing salon. She would never make the children pay for their own schooling, of course, but it would help if Polly's constant demands for dancing lessons and Megadrive games could be met from some of her own efforts. It might teach at least one of their greedy, all-consuming children the value of money.

Daisy was sulking up in her bedroom. She had had a dreadful day. Emma and Sophie had a secret and had been exchanging sly giggly grins. She'd tried to interest them in her forthcoming trip to the police station, and confided, in a bid for attention, her dread of being trailed along with a full set of parents to the depths of the Interview Room where she would have to come up with a promise to be law-abiding for ever and ever. The glamour-value of her crime, however, had now diminished, and whatever it was that Emma had done at the weekend, and that Sophie knew Emma had done, overshadowed poor Daisy. Daisy blamed her parents. She shouldn't still be grounded. She was getting left out of things and would need to be more extreme to get people to notice her. Her parents would only have themselves to blame if she turned to more serious crime.

She gazed miserably out of her window and up the Close towards the Mathiesons' house. Someone was in their attic, Paul probably, she thought. Carol had once mentioned that he had an office up there. She'd said it in a grand sort of way, as if Paul was so much in demand he had to have work-premises wherever he was. Daisy thought he didn't look much as if he was working, more as if he, too, was gazing out of the window. Knowing Carol, Daisy thought, poor old Paul was probably grounded as well.

Absentmindedly stir-frying vegetables, Jenny looked around the kitchen to see if there was any damage. The peach-and-cream-dragged paint on the skirting was very scratched, but she couldn't honestly remember whether or not it had been like that for years. That was one of the pluses of fançy paint finishes, they did very usefully blur imperfect textures and unevenness – rather as expensive foundation was supposed to do for skin. Ben shuffled into the kitchen, shoving the door open heavily so that it crashed against the wall next to it.

'Ben, please take care, there's a dent in the wall where you keep banging that door. The paint keeps flaking off around it.'

'Sorry,' he mumbled and grinned at Jenny, pushing his hair away from his forehead and revealing eyes that, unusually, for him, had a lively twinkle.

'What's got into you Ben? And who were you phoning?' Daisy, back in the kitchen and ever-suspicious, caught sight of his expression on her way to the cutlery drawer in the dresser.

'How did you know I was?' Ben taunted her, grin widening involuntarily.

'Heard the one in here go ping, that's how. And Polly is singing *The Good Ship Lollipop* in the loo, so it couldn't be her.'

Ben's smile was now accompanied by the kind of light blush that would have been becoming in a small child. Daisy slammed knives and forks on to the table, which made them spin wildly, so that they settled facing all the wrong way. The blush was the same kind Emma had had all day. So was the smirk.

Jenny smiled broadly at the vegetables as she stir-fried them, thinking hey-ho another cheery supper of stimulating conversation and repartee coming up. She had read in a magazine somewhere that the act of arranging your face into a smile stimulated happy-triggers in the brain, so that you really did feel better. She tried it out, waiting to feel good and for the sound of background hostilities to fade to insignificance.

'What are you grinning like that for?' Ben asked, catching sight of her manic face.

'Yeah, you look like someone's told you a joke you don't really get,' Daisy added, looking at Jenny as if she suspected her of major craziness. 'Oh and by the way, there was this note, it fell off the top of the fridge when Ben wafted into the kitchen.'

Jenny handed over the stir-frying to Daisy and looked at the tatty scrap of paper. *Man phoned, called Robbins, says is Friday at 2 OK for extra flute lesson, told him probably yes, 'cos he said he'd been before. Oh and he said could his friend come at 1.30. Love Belinda.* She read it twice more, as if the note would suddenly reveal David Robbins's phone number so she could ring him back and say no, he certainly couldn't come and neither could his friend. Whatever did they think she was? She knew exactly what they thought she was. A feeling of panic flickered in her stomach. She could say no when the men arrived, or she could relax and earn herself an unexpected hundred pounds for a few minutes' effort. On balance she'd much rather, she thought, as she drained the rice, and wondered about mint-flavoured condoms, earn it like Polly, for eating breakfast cereal.

Alan tried hard to pretend he had asked for Serena to be sent to join him as an essential part of her training, just as the trip to Bournemouth had been. He could feel how near she was, just the other side of the wall. He put his hand flat against the gently flowered wallpaper, next to the antiqued brass light switch. The hotel was the sort that described itself as 'country house' in style, which meant that the room dividing was of the thin, block--board sort, making little more than expensively frilled and flounced cubicles out of stately old bedchambers. Serena could be just inches away, perhaps lying on her bed, shoes off, skirt rumpled, flicking through one of those raunchy magazines for women, the sort they had to put on the top shelf. Or perhaps she was doing the *Financial Times* crossword. She was fearfully clever, really knew her stuff, much more so than Alan, he had to admit. Because of this he wondered, an hour later, when he was pouring her a very large vodka and tonic in his room, if she'd seen right through his look of concern as he casually called her in to go over a couple of worrying points in the client's list of tax claims.

'I'm afraid I've got it all laid out on the desk in here.' Alan smiled apologetically at her, ushering her, like a fly towards a web, into his room. 'So I hope you don't mind . . .' Serena was giving him an oddly amused look, as if thinking it was typical of men of his age to think a girl would only normally go into a man's hotel room in order to make immoral use of the bed. As if in defiance, she sat pertly on the edge of the bed, crossing her legs and allowing her skirt, which had buttons all the way down the front, only half of which were fastened, to fall away each side.

'Sorry there's no lemon,' he said, clumsily tumbling ice into Serena's drink.

'No problem,' she said, her voice now coming from right next to him, suddenly, not from the bed. She stood by the desk, her eyes roving confidently over the columns of figures in front of her. Alan took a large, loud sip of his drink and slid his trembling hand along her arm to her shoulder, wondering in which direction he should go next. 'He should have waited till March to buy the car, that was mistake number one.' Serena pointed a clean, square-cut nail half-way down the page, insultingly oblivious to Alan's touch. He had, literally, made no impact. She probably thought he was leaning on her while he looked at the figures. His hand ached to move to the soft warm place at the back of her neck, to untie the velvet bow that held her hair back. He dared himself to reach for the end of the ribbon, and then the phone rang.

Someone was with him. Jenny sensed it before he spoke, something in the hesitation and the way he breathed – shakily. 'Hi, Alan? Are you all right?' she asked, wishing she hadn't phoned. What you don't know can't hurt you, wasn't that how the old saying went? What about the things you suspect, but don't know for sure? Jenny thought they were the things, perhaps, self-inflicted though they might be, that hurt you most of all. Alan chatted suddenly, about the journey, about the hotel and its shortcomings, gabbling in a jocular way that was unlike him. 'And it's three quid for a shot of mini-bar vodka!' he heard himself exclaiming, and then wished he hadn't with Serena there next to him, probably thinking now that her stingy boss grudged her a drink.

Jenny heard a soft laugh, the chink of ice, lots of it, not just one drink's worth and knew for sure that Serena was with him. She had to ask. 'Who have you got there with you?' she said as casually as she could manage.

'Oh, just a colleague, going over some of tomorrow's work, you know how it is,' Alan said, 'all go.'

If it had been a male colleague, he'd have mentioned him by name.

It was dead, definitely dead, stiffening even – one of its front paws was sticking out, making it look as if the cat had keeled over in mid-prod at a mouse. Paul was tempted to go into the house and tell Carol that this time he had, really had, found a corpse, make her come out and look. He didn't think she'd find it very funny. Someone would have to go round and tell the Collins family, though. He thought it should be Carol, really, women having the gentle touch when it came to things like that. Polly might be there, and be terribly upset. It was probably her cat. Carol came out on to the patio at that moment, to water the hanging baskets she had been planting for the summer. Just now they were naked mounds of green polythene, cut-up bin liner, stabbed with holes and stuffed with seedlings of lobelia, begonias, primulas and a riskily early geranium or two.

'A riot of colour, they'll be by June,' Carol declared, stepping back slightly as she poured water, so it wouldn't spill on her beige suede shoes.

'The Collins's cat is dead,' Paul said, failing to admire Carol's efforts. 'It's down there, under the lilac. Old age by the look of it, there's no sign of a fight.' He pointed vaguely down the garden, as if showing Carol where she could find it. Not looking up, she continued ministering to her plants, trying not to recall Jenny in that shop, showing her fancy underwear. She frowned. 'Nasty great ginger thing. Do you know I caught him spraying, *spraying*, mind you, our dianthus. The Mrs Sinkins, I think it was. I didn't think cats did that, once they'd been neutered.'

'One of us will have to go and tell them,' Paul hinted.

'Yes. They can come and collect it. After all, it might have had a disease,' Carol said, wrinkling her nose. 'How dead is it, exactly?' She wondered how dead it would have to be before Ming and Mong started showing an unhealthy interest, perhaps even dragging the smelly thing up to the house and attempting to force it through the cat-flap, like they had with the run-over pigeon last summer. She shuddered. She'd also seen how far an untidy fox could scatter a dead rabbit. 'Better get them to remove it now, Paul, then it won't attract vermin in the night.'

It was an order, no doubt about it. Was there *ever* doubt, Paul wondered, obediently trotting through the house on his way to break the sad news to the Collins family. He didn't want to take the dead cat with him, they'd all be having supper, and the last thing they'd want to see would be a Sainsbury's bag containing their beloved pet being dumped on their back door step.

Jenny was playing her flute when Paul arrived. She looked very graceful, he thought, with her long eyelashes shadowing her cheek as she concentrated intently on the rippling music. He tapped lightly, reluctant to disturb her and she saw him hesitantly pushing his head sideways around the conservatory door. She felt cross with him for his apologetic inter-ruption, his awkward self-effacing posture as he slid his torso into the room, making a grotesque attempt at being inconspicuous. Having just achieved escape from her worries, deep into the music, she was abruptly dragged back into hearing the washing-up squabbles in the kitchen again as the children messily cleared up.

'I'm the bearer of bad news I'm afraid, Jenny,' Paul began formally, wondering if he should advise her to sit down in case of shock. Not that she'd shown much shock when Mrs Fingell had been 'dead'. But then Mrs Fingell hadn't shared her hearth and home for the past ten years or so. Jenny watched him shuffling his feet and looking past her out of the window.

'What's happened Paul? Are you going to tell me?' Jenny reminded him gesturing him to sit on the window seat. He looked quite shaky, she thought, starting to worry. Perhaps Carol was ill, or one of the twins.

'I'm so sorry, but your ginger cat has passed away in our garden. Natural causes by the look of him. I didn't like to bring him with me, because of your children, well, you know . . .' Paul had delivered his bad news, all in a rush, and without the vicarish tones of comfort he had rehearsed in the Close on his way.

Jenny put her flute back in its stand. Poor cat, she thought. Poor old orange thing, old Biggles.

'I could bring it round tomorrow, if you want to bury it in the garden,' he volunteered quickly, not wanting to give her the chance to start crying. He wouldn't know what to do if she did, Carol never needed much in the way of comforting, so he hadn't really had the practice.

'Thanks Paul, but do you mind if I collect him from you in the morning?' Jenny said softly, sinking on to the window seat next to him. 'I'll bury him under the strawberry patch. He used to love lying there on hot days. I'd rather Polly at least was at school while I do it. She was very fond of that cat.' Jenny felt a quiver in her voice, at which Paul got up quickly and bolted for the door.

'Must go, Carol's cooking something. Sorry and all that,' he called over his shoulder as he shot down the steps. Jenny followed him out through the door and picked weeds out of the terrace pots. Biggles had been Alan's cat. Would everything that linked him to the family gradually disappear, strands unravelling all over the place, till he was cut free like a drifting boat? True, he hadn't given up on his wall, had rebuilt it with as much care as he could be expected to spare for that kind of thing. But they both associated the wall with his mother, the last person, probably the only one, who had loved him totally, unconditionally. Jenny had never thought it such a good thing, really, that kind of obsessive mother-love, the sort that makes sons the world over think that, however appallingly, however downright evilly they behaved, there'd always be that one person who still loved them and would forgive them everything. No wonder wars, in spite of civilization, still went on. She hoped she didn't inflict that kind of devotion on Ben; she also hoped that, as a man, he'd be able to cope without it.

It was getting dark. Jenny was anxious that the little pile of foliage she'd collected really was all weeds, not Alan's precious rocket seedlings, which she should have brought indoors for the night. She picked up the pot and brought it in to the conservatory, placing it tenderly on its usual shelf. Fixing a fine rose-spray head to the watering can, she then went, not to the kitchen tap, but down the twilit garden to the water-butt by the shed and filled the can with the foul-smelling, but nourishing rainwater, the better to encourage the little plants. She couldn't do anything about the cat, and already she missed him trotting along beside her as she walked back up the garden; but there was still hope for Alan's plants.

By morning, Jenny still hadn't found the moment to tell the children about the death of Biggles. She was exhausted from a restless night spent half-waking and wondering what Alan was up to in his executive queen-size double bed. She, in the lethargic dawn, had imagined him somehow inspired with rejuvenating vigour, uninhibitedly cavorting with Serena through the night, overjoyed that he hadn't felt that good in years. Too far into sleep to drag herself awake and so choose something else to think about, Jenny had a bizarre vision of the occupants of the room next to Alan's tapping furiously on the interconnecting wall and demanding some peace and quiet.

Thankful when it was at last morning and her worst rambling thoughts could be put to the back of her mind to sleep, like Dracula in his coffin, Jenny got up early and automatically paced through the morning rituals. Still thrilled with her performance, and oblivious to domestic atmosphere, Polly went off to school eagerly, running to Ceci Caine's car joyously free of exam worries, and absolutely bursting with her new-found stardom. Jenny had kissed her goodbye and felt slight trepidation that, by the end of the day, Polly could be coming home wailing dramatically (as befit a newly qualified actress) that *everyone* – the *whole* school – hated her, and she had *no* friends, not *one*, all because she'd made them so envious. Eventually, only Ben was left, lolloping round slowly, collecting his school stuff together from every corner of the house.

'You'll be late, won't you Ben? Or have you got a free morning?' Jenny said, hoping he had, and wondering if he would collect and deal with the cat for her.

'S'OK, I can get the next bus. No leftover homework to finish in the common room.' He didn't look at all shifty for once, as he so often did when letting his work drift, so Jenny realized it must be true. It seemed unfair to reward such virtue with bad news

172

about Biggles, but there was little choice.

'You know when Paul came round last night?' she started saying, before feeling unexpected tears creep up again. Suddenly Ben was hugging her, and it felt so good to be comforted that she simply gave herself up to the misery and wept. 'It's the cat, he's dead!' she howled, crying for Biggles and her disintegrating marriage.

'I know,' Ben said, tenderly stroking her shoulder. 'I overheard Paul, but I didn't want to say anything that close to Polly's bedtime. You know what her imagination's like. I thought she'd wander round all night in the dark looking for cat-spirits out on the roof.'

Jenny laughed damply at his so-accurate summing up of Polly's inclinations and Ben, with a newly grown-up sense of the practical, and the hope of seeing Carol Mathieson, collected a bin liner from the dresser drawer.

'I'll go and collect him. Double biology can wait.'

Jenny blew her nose and wiped her eyes, and decided suddenly that she should be doing this herself, not automatically foisting on Ben the role of Alan-replacement for all the more repugnant domestic jobs. That was the other thing that mothers did, she realized, allocating gruesome tasks to the nearest male, everything from hauling out the garbage to unblocking the drains. Perhaps that was what you exchanged all that unconditional love for. She took the bin liner from Ben. If things like burying dead pets were what lone mothers had to get used to, she might as well start putting in the practice.

'No, really, it's OK, you go to school, I'll deal with Biggles,' she said firmly, giving him a small but fond push in the direction of his school bag.

He gave in, feeling, however, that he should have insisted, and wondering why his father wasn't there to tell him whether he should have or not. On his way down the Close he looked back at the Mathiesons' house. No-one seemed to be home. The white Peugeot wasn't in the drive, and on his way to the bus stop, Ben came to the conclusion (also a newly grown-up one) that collecting a dead cat from her garden would not have been the most erotic type of encounter he could hope to have with Carol.

When Jenny rang the Mathiesons' doorbell no-one answered, so she prowled around the front of the house, wondering which was the best way to get through to the back. She didn't want to go home catless, and therefore have to rely on Paul to bring it round and have him fuss about the right depth for the grave. She wouldn't put it past him to recite the ashes to ashes bit as if it was a real funeral, or tell her there were government statistics concerning the proportion of sadistic children who enjoyed torturing cats. The clean, smear-free windows of the Mathieson house stared blankly at Jenny as she tried the high wrought-iron gate through to the back garden. She should have known better than to imagine it could be left carelessly unlocked. Undeterred, Jenny dragged from its place on guard by the front door, one of the pair of stone pigs, whose necks and ears, in summer, would be cutely twined with climbing nasturtium. It weighed enough, therefore she decided it had to be strong enough to be stood on. Or perhaps it wasn't real stone, she then reasoned when, levering herself up to the precarious top of the gate, the snout dropped off. She'd have to sneak back later with super-glue. The cat was still under the lilac where Paul had found it, though decently covered, like a TV corpse, with an old cot-sheet. Jenny felt suddenly squeamish about picking up the little body, and tried to tell herself it was only Biggles under there and she'd picked him up a million times in his ten years.

'Pity you didn't really have nine lives,' she murmured to him as she used the edges of the sheet to scoop him into the bin liner, not looking at him too closely, preferring to remember him as a skittish young cat when the whole family had collected him from the RSPCA animal shelter, leaping four-square and wide-eyed into the air at every startling leaf-flicker, every thunderous clunk of a cupboard door.

Jenny hauled her sad bundle back up the garden towards the gate, surprised by how heavy Biggles, in death, was. She used the freshly painted, white iron-work garden table to stand on to climb back onto the gate, and sat on top of it for a few moments, wondering how she was going to jump down holding the bag. There was no question, somehow, of flinging Biggles to the ground ahead of her, as would be sensible. She had the ridiculous idea it might hurt him, or otherwise be disrespectful. Eventually gathering courage and simply jumping down the eight feet, she cursed as her foot caught the ear of the stone pig and it, too, snapped off.

'Shit,' she muttered, picking up the ear and the snout and laying them neatly by the front door, ready for sticking later. Jenny heaved the bag over her shoulder and lugged Biggles home to be buried, looking for all the world like a burglar with a bag of swag. No-one stopped to question her, no-one seemed to notice that she had climbed into the Mathiesons' garden, or that she had vandalized their pig. So much for bloody Neighbourhood Watch, she thought.

Chapter Twelve

'I'd have brought him round for you myself, if you'd only waited till lunchtime.' Paul was reproaching Jenny for having collected the cat herself. He stood watching her, arms folded, face sulky, as she filled in the little grave in her garden. He looked disappointed, Jenny thought, though whether it was because he'd been deprived of a job that suited his position as street watchman or because she'd proved capable of breaking into his carefully fortressed back garden, she couldn't really tell. Perhaps it was because of the stone pig.

'I'm sorry about the snout and the ear,' Jenny told him as she patted the earth flat over the cat and smoothed it gently, as if making a soft bed for him. 'I'll come round later and fix them back on for you; will that be OK? Or shall I get Alan to do it when he gets back?' That should get a reaction, Jenny thought, sneaking a teasing smile towards Paul, the threat of Alan let loose for more DIY.

But Paul wasn't listening. 'Are you sure it's deep enough?' he asked, as she knew he would, hands on hips and staring at Jenny's spadework. 'I mean, if you're going to carry on growing your strawberries here?' He looked doubtful, as if strawberries would be somehow cat-tainted. Perhaps he'd thought they'd be bright ginger and furry.

She laughed. 'Think of it as good old-fashioned humus! The stuff you pay a fortune for down at the garden centre.' Paul frowned thoughtfully, considering the lack of vegetative matter in Biggles, albeit that he was

100 per cent organic, and Jenny couldn't resist teasing him some more. 'A pity we don't recycle people like this too,' she said, raking a mouse-shaped pattern over Biggles's grave.

'Oh well, with people there are certain regulations,' Paul said pompously, safely on home ground, talking about rules. 'After all, you can't just plant them anywhere, can you? I mean, where would it end?'

Jenny leaned thoughtfully on her spade and considered the miles and miles of cemetery dismally sprawled across the outskirts of London. 'The only good thing about cemeteries is that they are open spaces. Pity to keep it all just for the dead, though. I'm sure I'd rather be buried over there under the cherry tree than lost in those anonymous miles over at Mortlake or Putney Vale. I can't see it would be any less healthy.' She picked up a large stone and hurled it at the hedge. 'Did you know you can get cardboard coffins, completely biodegradable?' she said to Paul. 'They come in a flat pack, like kitchen cupboards. We could do our own funerals. Quite legal.'

Paul looked worried, all furrowed around the brow, as if he had suddenly formed the suspicion that several generations of uncertified and uncoffined Collinses might already be quietly rotting under the suddenly suspiciously lush flower beds. What was going through his head, she wondered. Was it the thought of his beloved police force, blue shirt sleeves rolled up, digging rows of muddy trenches in her garden to see what was lurking down there? Biggles safely buried, she let Paul take the spade from her and watched him put it away in the shed, hiding her smile as she caught him glancing round at its contents as if checking for proper bags of garden-centre compost. Perhaps he half-expected, she thought, to find her own concoction, a sort of John Innes Number 5, Alan's-dead-mother mixture. It gave a whole new interpretation to 'bone-meal'.

While Jenny was clearing up Biggles's food and water dishes and putting them into the dishwasher, Mrs Fingell rapped on the kitchen window.

'You got the men in for something?' she asked, hauling herself across the doorstep and sniffing round the kitchen as if for the aroma of paint and carpentry.

'No, why? What men?' Jenny asked her. Still bending over the dishwasher, she filled up the appropriate plastic compartment with Rinse-Aid, checked the filter and poured in some salt. 'Why do gadgets that are supposed to save you time need so much attention?' she muttered, as she topped it all off with the washing liquid and switched it on.

Mrs Fingell had come into the kitchen, plonked herself down heavily in the rocking chair and was toasting her thick-stockinged toes on the Aga. She looks very comfortable, Jenny thought, flattered suddenly that this woman was making herself thoroughly at home. It wasn't that kind of place, really, the Close, where people were encouraged to make themselves feel snug in a room that wasn't theirs.

'Just that there's been a good few of them in and out of here lately, that's all,' Mrs Fingell went on, her sharp eyes inspecting the kitchen calendar. Jenny felt chilled. So Neighbourhood Watch was effective after all. Mrs Fingell could only have seen Mr Robbins and George Pemberton (plus roses) and the film crew, but Jenny felt as guilty as if she'd been caught in suspenders and a basque loitering in her doorway under a scarlet lamp.

'Just been getting a few quotes for this and that,' she lied, wondering why she bothered, taking refuge by the sink and filling the kettle. She fiddled with the taps, taking too long. 'Polly's getting a bit old for her wallpaper, all those pink ponies. Are you keeping notes for Paul Mathieson or something?' she asked, brazenly turning to face Mrs Fingell with a challenging grin. After all, what business was it of hers, *especially* hers, who she entertained, when and for how long?

'Not going in the supermarket direction this morning are you by any chance?' Mrs Fingell suddenly switched topics and shifted her awkward weight in the creaking rocking chair. 'Only if you are, I wouldn't mind coming with you.'

It wasn't a suggestion or a request, simply an order. There was nothing sinister, Jenny reasoned to herself, about an old lady wanting a bit of help getting her groceries. It only felt like a spot of blackmail because her conscience wasn't as clear as it should be. A mocking chant from childhood, 'We *saw* you, we *saw* you', hung between the two of them, unsung in the room. Jenny felt cornered but fairly safe. Mrs Fingell couldn't possibly know what had gone on that day when the conservatory blinds were down, and certainly, considering her own past, she couldn't possibly be passing judgement. Jenny told herself all this as she searched obediently under a pile of junk mail for her car keys.

'I do need one or two things,' she said to Mrs Fingell. 'We could get something to eat in their coffee shop too, if you like.'

The old lady grinned with satisfaction at the prospect of the outing and hauled herself out of the chair. She waddled with surprising speed back to the door. 'Come on then love, or the dog will be waiting for his walk,' she said. Jenny, grabbing under the sink for her collection of used carrier bags, gave her a sharp look. 'It's all right, I can manage to trot him round the common by myself,' Mrs Fingell called out, mockingly.

This is the sort of thing Carol Mathieson should catch sight of me doing, Jenny thought as she gently helped Mrs Fingell into the front seat of the Golf, not showing my backside to a shop-load of customers. Not that Carol's opinion mattered, she considered, wondering if Neighbourhood Watch was intended to make people feel more paranoid than secure.

179

Hesitating by the store entrance with her trolley, Mrs Fingell looked as if she was half-hoping that Jenny would be prepared to supervise her shopping and do the reaching up to high shelves and delving into freezer cabinets for her while she pointed regally to biscuits and bananas. Jenny wasn't playing this game – she'd seen how agile the old woman could be, and determinedly she reached for a trolley of her own and launched Mrs Fingell into the first aisle.

'I'll see you by the check-out and then if there's time we might go to the coffee shop,' she told her, and then relented. 'Make a note of anything you can't reach and I'll come back and get it down for you. Or you could ask someone else, staff or whatever,' she added.

'Been shopping here since the day it opened. I'll manage,' Mrs Fingell called over her shoulder as she marched off towards the cigarette counter.

'Shop till you drop' was the phrase going through Jenny's head as she piled food into her trolley. It must be fun to be one of those people who could apply that phrase to the whole-day excursion type of shopping, the clothes-and-shoes type. Instead, she wondered if you could *die* of supermarket shopping, the dismal blank that paralysed her head whenever she tried to recall what the family usually ate, which breakfast cereal to choose, just how greyish recycled lavatory paper could acceptably be. Even on the days when she went in, highly organized and efficient with a list, there would come a madness-point, something perhaps to do with the too-low, threatening ceiling, at which the slyly manipulative vendors would win, and she would start randomly hurling into her trolley bargain multibuys and special offers of syrupy orange squash, pungent floor cleaners and irresistible, ready-cooked chicken dishes that would end up welded to the iceberg at the back of the freezer. I must be the ideal customer profile, Jenny sometimes thought, detachedly lucid even at these out-of-control moments, so easily swayed, so easily – by the second aisle – losing track of sweet reason.

Jenny furiously fumbled the loading of carrier bags to keep pace with the speedy check-out girl, wondering how she could possibly have chosen ten cans of cat food when they no longer had a cat, when she heard the breathy excitement of Laura Benstone's voice behind her.

'It was positive! Isn't it thrilling? Due in time for Bonfire Night, just!' the voice gushed, and Jenny mustered enough social grace to look up and say congratulations. A brief and smiling glance at Laura took in that she looked pretty as a baby herself, in a bonny-blue mohair sweater cutely oversized and with her dark, feathery fringe caught up on the tops of her eyebrows. 'We haven't told the girls yet; we thought, you know, they'd want it *now*. You know what children are like, just can't wait!'

Jenny triumphantly stuffed the last bag of carrots into a bag just as the stolid check-out girl rang up the total. She wondered if this job was a sort of race for her too, each time trying to outrun the customer so that she could sit and pick at her nails while the fumble-fingered or the terminally slow laboriously stowed their unwieldy purchases. She vaguely recognized the girl, taken back suddenly by the big placid face to infant school days when she (with Ben in tow) and this girl's chirpy young mother had discussed reading schemes and sports kit.

'Ninety-six pounds fifty please,' the bored voice stated and Jenny fished around in her purse for her Switch card.

'Ninety-six quid! Bloody hell, whose army are you feeding?' Mrs Fingell, followed by a droopy youth carrying her pair of immaculately packed bags, appeared in front of Jenny, tempting her to reply, 'The entire USA, 1944?' Instead, an ugly squawk of rejection came from the till.

'Sorry madam, this card won't take,' the check-out girl said, yawning widely and gazing expectantly at Jenny for an alternative means of payment. It was too late, now, to call on past shared times, remind her that she and Ben had started school together. How unfair it would be too, to talk about Ben's A-level courses when Jenny knew for a suddenly recalled fact that the girl's brother (only months older than Daisy) was spending the rest of his teen years in a young offenders' institute for the apparently incurable theft of fast cars.

'Oh dear!' breathed Laura behind her, adding, 'How frightful!' as if she had heard of nothing more tragic in her life.

'I'll have to give you a cheque then,' Jenny said, rummaging through the debris in her bag and wishing she didn't keep every receipt she was ever given. Something to do with being an accountant's wife, she thought. The girl, however, knew the rules of the job.

'Only if you've got another cheque guarantee card,' she said, handing back Jenny's useless Switch card. 'S'no good for anything else once it's been stopped.' She pursed her lips and waited, staring out towards the delicatessen counter, not unhappy to be held up.

Jenny started to wonder if the girl was getting some kind of sweet revenge. The infants' school on the edge of the estate had been one of those that the middle classes describe as 'excellent, wonderful start, *fascinating* mix of people' until the children reached eight, at which point they abandoned it (and the fascinating people) in droves and took off for their long-awaited places at the choicest prep schools.

Faintly aware of a queue build-up and an atmosphere of niggling impatience, she stopped rifling through her bag. 'Well it's the only card I brought with me actually,' she tried the confident smile, and the reassuring tone. 'There's sure to have been a mistake anyway, and I've got plenty of identification if you'll just take my cheque.' She started laying out a selection of documents like a deck of cards: child benefit book, driving licence, tennis club membership card.

'Not allowed, sorry,' said the girl, unimpressed. Jenny wondered if she had recognized her, noticed the name of the cards, but there was no flicker of interest in the large blank face.

'Oh but surely . . .' started Laura in support.

'Look, I shop here all the time. Isn't there a manager or someone I could talk to, explain the situation? Obviously I can't just abandon ninety-six pounds' worth of shopping, simply because of bureaucracy and a silly mistake by the bank,' Jenny said, adding, threat-like, 'and some poor person would have to put it all back on the shelves.' She felt that if she had to walk out now without her trolley-load of stuff, she would never be able to face shopping again. Salvation, in the form of a smartly suited man with a clipboard, strolled up and the situation was explained.

'One of your most regular customers,' Jenny heard herself saying, not exactly grovelling, but feeling pulled between that and an assertion of some heartfelt right to leave the shop with the goods she wanted. She won; it was easy, what with her manner and her accent and her tennis club membership number and address scrawled on the back of her cheque.

'You was bloody lucky there,' Mrs Fingell told her as they walked back to the car.

'Why? My cheque won't bounce, and they can't expect me to have that much cash on me, I might get mugged. I suppose I could have gone home and picked up another of our cheque cards.'

'Oh no, you couldn't have,' Laura, still with them, said. 'Not if there's any dairy stuff. They can't let it out of the store if it's been off the shelf for more than about thirty minutes. In case you get food poisoning and sue.'

'It *could* bounce though, couldn't it. It's only because you're posh. They got no idea really,' Mrs Fingell, infuriating Jenny, persisted. 'Strictly speaking, you just walked out then without paying. Catch them taking that sort of chance with people like me. Or people from the estate,' the old lady snorted. Jenny heaved all the bags into the boot of the car and slammed it shut. Mrs Fingell waited to have the car door opened for her, still ranting on. 'When it isn't your sort of people, when it's people like me and the estate, it's called something quite different. It's called shoplifting.'

'Hang on, are we talking about the same Ben? My *brother* Ben? You snogged *Ben*?' Daisy's voice rose, and girls in the nearby lunch queue were staring with interest. Emma looked shifty, playing with her mashed potato, but couldn't hide her grin. Daisy put her fork down and considered her lunch finished (school ravioli, too disgusting to eat anyway). Sophie was sitting next to Emma, smiling her confirmation that the awful tale was really, actually true: Emma was now going out with Daisy's brother.

'But he's my *brother*! How gross!' she exclaimed. 'How could you?' and then, getting her priorities sorted, added, 'And why didn't you tell me before?'

'Because I knew you'd react like this,' Emma replied. 'I know it must be hard to think of brothers as humans, but if you took a distant, real-life look at him, say when he's with his mates, sort of mixed up in a group of them, he's actually not at all bad looking. And he can snog,' she said with undisguised lust. Daisy shuddered. She couldn't even begin to contemplate her brother doing all that stuff with anyone, let alone her best friend. Somehow it was, well, indecent. The smell of school

184

lunch and schoolgirls was making her feel queasy. 'Anyway, what he told me, the important bit,' Emma went on, hoping to get Daisy back into a better mood, 'was that his friend Oliver really fancies you. He's going to be at Sophie's party on Saturday, isn't he Sophe?' she said, appealing for help from Sophie who had made a start on her treacle pudding, the dramatic revelation safely over.

'Oh, yeah. Oliver's coming, definitely,' she confirmed. 'So you've got to find a way of getting there, Dais. He was asking about you last weekend too.' Just in time she stopped herself adding, 'before he got off with Lucy.'

Daisy wandered back to the counter and picked out the greenest apple. The hall was shrill with girlish voices that maddened her ears. She longed for the day when she could leave, desperate to escape after her GCSEs, and take her A-levels at the sixth form college. She knew all the statistics, her parents and their friends quoted them like some written-in-stone biblical text, all about how girls do so much better in a girls-only school. 'Without the distractions,' they always added euphemistically, meaning boys. How much they didn't know, Daisy thought. After all, what did they think the girls at school talked about and thought about every waking moment they were together? Boys distracted you whether they were actually there in person or not. Though she had to admit that it was probably easier in a physics class not to be in a school like the one Ben said Oliver's brothers went to, where they gobbed on the floor all the time and called girls slags every time they asked or answered a question. But then if she and Ben were at the same school, maybe she wouldn't see him as belonging to some kind of separate species with no right to be of any romantic interest to her closest friends. She comforted herself with remembering the wicked warmth that shone from Oliver's dark eyes as he'd watched her on the hockey field.

'Sorry Emma,' Daisy said, sliding back into her seat and trying out a smile 'It's just a bit of a shock. No wonder Ben's been going round with such a huge grin on his face the last couple of days.'

'Not just his grin that's been huge, I should think,' Sophie tittered, with a lascivious smirk.

'Oh please, spare me that,' Daisy groaned, pushed beyond her limit. She needed time to get used to the idea of Ben, awkward, flailing-limbed, blushing Ben, as an object of desire. Probably, she thought, a lifetime.

'It's a bit short notice I know,' Carol was saying to Jenny on the Collins's doorstep. 'And I'm sorry. But we thought it was time for a quick meeting, just to *recap*, as it were. *Do* try and come.' Jenny floundered for an excuse and couldn't find one. She thought of inventing an emergency pre-exam pupil, but couldn't trust the Mathiesons not to organize a keeping-watch rota for the entire evening to check her story, take photos and then challenge her later. 'Your friend Sue is coming,' Carol persuaded, tightening her lips automatically at the thought of Sue's capacity for sherry-consumption.

'Can't you just send a newsletter round?' Jenny suggested, wondering suddenly why there hadn't been a daily report, published to almost professional standard on Paul's attic computer.

'Oh no, that wouldn't do. We need the personal *input*, and suggestions from the *floor*,' Carol insisted. She licked the end of her pencil (which was tied with lavender ribbon to the top of her clipboard) and ticked off Jenny's name on her list. 'I'll put you down for a yes then,' she stated, and was half-way to the gate, clacking busily on her little heels, before Jenny could argue. As she shut the front door, surprised not to have been issued with a secret password for the evening's meeting, she heard next door's gate (resting actor) open, and felt sympathy for her unseen neighbour.

'I'll come with you tonight if you like,' Ben announced casually, sauntering down the stairs. 'Not much homework, and it's something to do.'

Jenny looked at him, suspiciously. 'It won't be any fun, only the neighbours. Won't you be bored?' She imagined Ben, fed up and growing more and more horizontal, slumped in one of Carol's armchairs. He'd pick at the fringing on a cushion, and probably unravel it. Carol would frown and hiss at him and he'd be miles away, dreaming and fidgeting . . .

'No, 's' OK, I'll just come and see what it's like,' he mumbled, ambling back up the stairs.

'Do you think it's something we've done? It's like being back at school, summoned to see the Head,' Sue whispered to Jenny as they gathered in the Mathiesons' sitting-room later. 'And where is everybody?'

It wasn't as good a turn-out as the first meeting had been, Jenny had to admit. Fiona Pemberton had apparently sent a note of apology, pleading a parents' evening. She hadn't mentioned George, who was now sitting on the arm of Carol's leather sofa smiling furtively across at Jenny and softly patting the cushion next to him in an inviting way that made her want to sit anywhere but there. Mrs Fingell was there too, smiling her witchy, knowing smile at no-one in particular from the cosiest armchair by the drinks cabinet. The resting actor and some BBC wives were gathered by the French windows, chatting about the best way to prune rambling roses, so far drinkless and wondering what to do with their hands. A power-dressed young couple looked repeatedly at their watches. Jenny waved to Mrs Fingell and smiled a greeting to the actor, then said to Sue, 'Novelty's worn off. There's not really anything new to hear. Everyone's got their window stickers and fitted their burglar locks. Probably can't think what else they're supposed to do. I certainly can't.'

'Oh look,' said Sue with interest, peering out of the window. 'Here comes Harvey and no Laura. Perhaps he'd like to come for a drink after.'

'Sue, you can't, not Harvey,' Jenny warned. 'Too close to home, and Laura's pregnant again.' She pulled her firmly away from the lace-frilled window and they both sat down, as close to the door as they could for a possible quick getaway. A smell of freshly cooked sausage rolls wafted temptingly from the kitchen.

'Listen, if you're talking close to home,' Sue retaliated, pointing past Jenny towards the hallway, 'Check out your Ben, then tell me, hand on heart that he always, but *always* volunteers to help in the kitchen . . .'

Jenny got up, crept to the open door and looked. Through Carol's kitchen door she could see the highly unusual sight of Ben loading glasses on to a tray. Carol was close to him, murmuring instructions, and Ben, when he turned to face them, looked quite flushed. The glasses tinkled dangerously as he carried them extra-carefully into the sitting-room and managed to put the tray on the coffee table without Carol's entire crystal collection sliding to the floor.

'Drink everyone?' Paul said, waving the sherry bottle. 'And then we'll start.'

Everyone sat, attentive as a schoolroom, waiting for Paul to put them in the picture. Ben lounged on the floor in a corner from which he had an uninterrupted view across to the tan sofa on which Carol was sitting. Hoping his mother (or worse, Sue) wouldn't notice, he stared blissfully at Carol, whose skirt was pulled tightly across her thighs so he could gaze up towards a glimpsed triangular pennant of white underwear. He hoped, quite desperately, that no-one would ask him to go and fetch something from the kitchen. He didn't think he'd be able to walk.

'Now the problem is,' Paul was saying, pacing about the room importantly and waving his orange Neighbourhood Watch brochure, 'that no-one is doing any reporting in.' There was a collective sighing and shuffling. Harvey reached across to the table and helped himself to a pair of sausage rolls, and Mrs Fingell could be heard noisily crunching nuts. No-one wanted to spend the evening being told off. 'The Close has been full of strangers for the past few weeks, what with film crews and all.' Everyone looked at Harvey, most with sympathy. 'And various cars have been parked here that we all know don't belong to any residents.'

'What exactly are we supposed to do about that, though, Paul?' Jenny chipped in, eager for him to get to the point. 'Surely it isn't anyone's business who we all choose to have visiting us?'

'Well, the point is to be *alert*.' Paul whirled round and pointed his brochure at her menacingly. 'Take down car numbers, check who goes into which house, and whether they come out again and maybe try another door. That kind of thing. They could be burglars, checking for regularly absent householders.'

'Or they could be Jehovah's Witnesses,' Harvey added as he reached across to the table and casually topped up his drink.

'Or bailiffs,' Sue said passing her glass across so he could refill that too.

Jenny felt twitchy, uncomfortable, as if every aspect of her personal life was under constant scrutiny. It was horribly like being a teenager again, with her mother checking and snooping on her every move, and marauding schoolmistresses stalking the town every lunchtime for out-of-bounds sixth formers illicitly meeting their boyfriends.

'Actually,' she said, decisively, 'I think I'm going to opt out, if you don't mind. I find the idea that every visitor to my house is going to have their description and car number logged, like some kind of police state, horribly intrusive, just not on. On balance I think I'd rather be burgled.'

'Me too,' Mrs Fingell added, emphatically banging her walking stick on the carpet. Hostility gathered, as the group clung to the remains of its privacy.

'But what does it matter if you've got nothing to hide?' Carol peered savagely into Jenny's face, as if any second she would try to gouge out a deadly secret. Jenny flattened herself against the back of the chair, alarmed.

'Oh, now come on, everyone. No-one wants to spy, just to look after each other. It's caring, not snooping.' Paul tried his best to pacify them, waving his arms around in his version of an all-embracing manner.

'It's horrendous,' Jenny persisted, slightly diverted by the fact that Ben was going dreadfully pink. Surely he agreed with her? This time it couldn't be that she embarrassed him. She got up and groped for her handbag down the side of the chair. Perhaps she should employ Paul and Carol as private detectives, get them to check up on Alan and what he was up to – that would keep their minds off non-existent crime in the Close.

'Er, sit down for one more minute, please Jenny.' Paul took hold of her arm and pushed her gently back down into the chair. 'It's not just car numbers and things. What I mean is that people aren't noticing when things *are* unusual. Like when you climbed over our gate to get the cat.'

Sue giggled and snorted. 'Like Burglar Bill. Swag and all,' she laughed.

'*Exactly* like Burglar Bill. That's *it*,' Carol stated, leaning forward and jabbing an accusing finger at

Jenny. '*And nobody noticed.* Not a single one. No-one in the entire street . . .' The finger was shaking with fury now as it roamed the room, accusing them one and all. The BBC wives stared guiltily at the carpet. 'No-one reported her climbing over the gate and back again, blatantly with a sack.' She leaned back on the chair again, her skirt rucked up even further from the excitement, much to Ben's delight.

'Carol,' Jenny said gently, as if to someone close to the edge of madness, 'Carol, that's because it *was* only me. If anyone did see me they probably wondered what I was up to, felt a bit curious, but they know me. I'm not worth a crime report. And I've apologized about the broken pig.'

'But you could have been anyone! Someone from the estate!' Carol wailed.

'But I wasn't! I was me! And the people on the estate do more nicking from each other than from anyone else! Why do you think half those doors up there are boarded up? Don't you ever read the papers? Oh this is ridiculous. I'm going home to watch telly.' Once again Jenny got up to leave; Sue greedily swigged the last of her sherry and got up to join her. Carol was looking daggers, and irresistibly Jenny jibed her some more, announcing to the room in general, 'I'm going just across the road, Carol. Don't feel you need to watch or take notes.'

Outside in the Close, Sue and Jenny took gulps of free, fresh air. 'Is it just me, or is Carol getting control-crazy?' Jenny asked. 'And what was all that about "if you've got nothing to hide". What was that supposed to mean?'

'No idea,' Sue said, yawning. 'What I'd like to know, though, and call me a nosy-cow neighbour if you like, but why is your Ben still in there?'

Chapter Thirteen

Alan drove home very fast from Leicestershire, relieved, somehow, that he hadn't been able to persuade Serena to accept a lift home and that she'd insisted on going back to London alone, by train. She told him she'd got a book she was dying to finish, apologizing for being anti-social and hoping that he didn't mind. No he didn't mind. He'd rather be alone with his thoughts and his music than have to make a hundred and fifty miles' worth of conversation. He'd be sure to end up relating cosy anecdotes about the family, turning himself inevitably into some humdrum avuncular figure who would come over as lovable but not libidinous. He hadn't tried too hard to entice her into his car, conscious as he was of having been far too cowardly to seduce her. He'd failed even to make a wholehearted attempt to, counting too much on her to realize what he was getting at and somehow join in as he clumsily skirted round her body and plied her with vodka. The very small consolation was that as nothing had happened in reality (everyone dreams don't they? he reasoned, fantasy life doesn't count) he didn't yet have to feel guilty, and could at least go home still just about able to look Jenny in the eye.

As he sped down the M1, Led Zeppelin's *Stairway to Heaven* was playing on the car radio, whisking Alan immediately back to his first meeting with Jenny. Enthralled by her playing in the college Mozart concert, to which he'd reluctantly accompanied a dull cousin, he had been amazed when Jenny had agreed to have dinner with him. He'd felt as foolish as a backstage hanger-on, callously ditching the cousin and sidling round to the stage door, not even knowing what name to ask for. Back at his flat, and hardly even able to believe his luck that Jenny had agreed to go there with him, he'd put his precious new Led Zeppelin album on the record player and then cravenly apologized for his musical taste; but from the shelf next to his chaotic desk Jenny had picked up his old school recorder and played the haunting opening bars of *Stairway to Heaven*. They'd been in bed by the guitar solo. He'd been incredulous at his success, by how easy it had all been. Now, an attempt at seduction, even the thought of an attempted seduction, left Alan with dry-throated, heart-pounding terror. He tried to put it down to lack of practice, adrenalin and the adventure of the chase. It felt dangerous, life-threatening, and the compulsion to see it through was like a death-wish. It was probably horrendously bad for his blood pressure, and he hated the feeling that he had actually reached the age where he had to consider his health. When media doctors wrote of mid-life stresses, they meant *him*. It was too depressing. Did getting older mean spending the rest of his life with a careful lack of over-excitement? And somewhere deep inside was a suspicion, though nothing to do with the pain and potential disaster from being found out, that the ludicrous biological urge to do all that sexual fiddling about with a new person's body might just not be worth it. He was setting himself up, surely, on the day he managed to make his lust known to Serena, for pitiless rejection and toe-curling humiliation. And if he succeeded what would be his reward? Only sex, nothing different, and as the saying went, he could get all that at home. But, he reasoned, muttering to himself as he turned at last on to the M25, what about rejuvenation? He was feeling old, greying, thinning and losing what small measure of charm and attraction he had clung to, and which had for years buoyed up his schoolboyish lack of confidence. If Serena could make him feel better about all that, then that really would be something he couldn't get at home.

It was just as well Alan was late getting back, Jenny thought at 1.30, wishing the man David Robbins had sent had got himself thoroughly lost. Why, she wondered as the doorbell rang, do people manage to be so punctual, so capable of finding the right address on time when it's for something illicit. She could hardly begin to count the number of people who turned up late for dinner at the house, all flustered and apologizing that they'd taken a wrong turning after Putney Bridge, or ventured accidentally into the estate, as if she and Alan lived in the back end of nowhere and the A-Z was written in Sanskrit.

To the immaculately pin-striped businessman now standing expectantly on her doorstep Jenny said firmly, 'I won't pretend you've got the wrong address, but I just don't do that sort of thing any more.' There was some apologetic murmuring from the disappointed client, and then from the road, the approaching click-clack of Carol Mathieson's unmistakable shoes.

She stopped and peered with frank curiosity at Jenny's visitor and, with no introduction forthcoming, said, 'I forgot to say last night, I was so sorry about your poor pussy! What a shame!'

'Oh good grief, what a thing to come out with,' Jenny muttered under her breath, smiling as steadily as she could manage at both Carol and the pinstriped client. Jenny realized she was still wearing her yellow rubber gloves from wiping down the kitchen cupboards, and suddenly thought the man might suspect, especially after Carol's bizarre comment, that she was lying, and that she'd got a customer for more bizarre practices already inside, perhaps tied naked to a chair prior to being beaten with the floor mop.

If she'd ever thought she might be tempted to continue earning cash from servicing men, the Neighbourhood Watch meeting the night before had killed all such ambitions stone dead. There had to be less risky ways of making a living, ones that didn't have the neighbours writing down doubtful car numbers and making you lie about having the decorators in. There must also be ways that didn't involve cheating on Alan, too. The possibility that he was up to something was so painful to her that she didn't want to risk having him feel that way as a result of *her* behaviour. He could hardly be expected to think that, just because she had done it for money, it didn't count as infidelity. If Alan left, there was mini-cab driving, or mail-order delivery, any old job till some full-time teaching could be found.

When David Robbins arrived half-an-hour later, Jenny started her speech while he was still half way up the path. 'I'm sorry,' she told him, 'I really can't go on doing this.' She laughed at his mock-crestfallen expression. 'I'm retiring to a life of virtue. You'll just have to make an effort and go and join a dating agency or something.'

'Oh, don't you worry, footloose and fancy free, that's me. Foot*less*, anyway. Actually I just called to say thanks but I've met someone,' he said with a happy grin, making Jenny feel she'd been over hasty and made herself look rather silly. She then wondered about offering him a cup of tea, but could foresee conversational complications. What on earth would they talk about? So, supported now by only a pair of sticks, David walked on his new plastic feet back towards the corner, round which he had been so careful to park. No chance of Paul Mathieson logging that particular number at least, Jenny thought, feeling, as she closed the door and prepared to be a scrupulously honest wife again, that she was saying goodbye to a friend. Full of good intentions, she spent the next hour running off copies of her CV on Daisy's computer and sending them out on spec to all the local schools. Somewhere out there, she reasoned, there must be the chance of a proper job.

When Jenny returned from collecting Polly (and Harriet, back with them for supper) from school, Alan was home and in charge of his beloved kitchen once again. The rich aroma of the Madeira sauce that he was gently reducing on top of the Aga wafted out welcomingly and filled the hallway. The smell of enjoyment-cooking, as opposed to the more tedious necessity-cooking so thrilled Jenny's taste-buds, she had to suppress a greedy groan as she and the girls tumbled into the house. 'Ooh yummee,' she said, following the smell into the kitchen, 'that smells just so scrumptious!'

Alan was settled comfortably in the rocking chair, pots and pans gleaming around him, full of vegetables and herbs, ready to go. He looked solid, happy, pleased to be back, the newspaper open at the football page and the cat purring on his lap. Jenny leant forward to kiss Alan and then jumped back in horror.

'Biggles! What's he doing here?' she exclaimed, clapping a startled hand to her mouth.

'Oh thanks, Jen, so good to know you're pleased to see me!' Alan said, grinning accusingly at her.

'But Biggles is dead!' Polly stated baldly. 'That's a ghost!'

Jenny wanted to smack her, suddenly; after all, he'd been Alan's cat, and the awful news could have been broken to him more carefully than that. She had thought it too cruel to tell him over the phone, even as a punishment for nesting cosily in a smart hotel with slinky Serena. Except that

Biggles, (unmistakably Biggles) ecstatically purring and rubbing his great big head against his favourite person, was clearly very much alive.

'He's dead. You buried him, Mum. Didn't you?' Polly went on, looking hard at Jenny for a sign that she might be going mad and have made the whole thing up.

'I buried something. I was waiting till you got back to tell you,' Jenny said doubtfully to Alan, eyeing Biggles suspiciously as she went to hang her coat up by the back door. She kept looking at him, as if any minute he was going to turn back into a damp and earthy corpse, and she peered at the floor for muddy footprints (and possibly the old cot sheet in which he'd been draped) leading from the cat-flap. Harriet hadn't budged from the kitchen doorway, but stood gawping with her amazed mouth dropped wide open.

Polly patted the very grubby cat on the head. 'You'll have to be renamed Jesus,' she announced importantly. ''Cos it's the third day, isn't it, and you've risen again.'

Jenny and Alan looked at each other and burst into incredulous laughter. 'Well I can't think where he's been, must have been locked in an oily garage somewhere. He's absolutely filthy. I didn't even think to check the other cat's collar. I couldn't bring myself to see if it even had one,' Jenny was saying. 'Some other poor person out there must be missing their pet.'

Polly, looking like she'd had a brilliant idea, suddenly grabbed Harriet, and, bored with the subject of dead and alive cats, the two girls scrambled out of the room and thundered up the stairs.

It felt strange to have Alan back at home. Jenny had spent so much of the previous night vividly picturing him *in flagrante* that she found his familiar, daytime self rather odd, as if it was something of a disguise. At any moment she expected him to shove the cat

197

to the floor, put down his drink and start the end-of-marriage announcement. She had a tight, tense feeling inside, and was finding it hard to breathe in the warm kitchen.

'Just going to get something from the car,' she told him, needing a moment to get used to how unchanged, how *ordinary* he was.

Out by the BMW, Jenny was tempted to open the door and sniff the air for girlish perfume. There was nothing on the seats, no giveaway glossy magazines, no abandoned lipstick. The back window had acquired a new sticker proclaiming *No to Terminal Five*. Half the cars in the Close had them (as well as ones about aircraft noise), even though most of the residents expected to be able to rush out and catch a plane at any old time to dash off for business meetings in far countries. That way the tax-free (legitimate business expense) travel could accumulate enough air miles to take their families on lovely foreign holidays. They were forever complaining about the crush at the airport, and Jenny thought they should be delighted to get a new Terminal building.

She looked in her car for something she could have gone to fetch and saw Polly's French dictionary on the back seat. Just as she unlocked the door, there was a splintering crash of breaking glass from across the road. She wandered into the Close and dutifully strolled across to look.

Harvey Benstone came sprinting out from number 5, mindful of his neighbourly responsibilities. 'It's the Pembertons' house I think,' he said, catching up with Jenny. 'Probably kids from the estate after the video and stuff so they can buy drugs. Bit bloody much in broad daylight.' He was so puffed up with the certainty of being right that Jenny could only admire the way this seemed to make him totally oblivious to the possible danger of being beaten senseless by several large, strong teenage thugs. But when they got to the Pembertons' garden, behind their pair of lilac trees was only the contorted figure of George trying to climb in through the hall window.

'Bloody woman didn't leave the key,' he huffed at them, bright pink with wasted effort. Jenny left him and Harvey to sort out a way of getting in and trailed back to her own house. At least it was something to tell Alan.

'Are you sure this is going to work?' Daisy asked Emma, up in the bathroom. 'And why aren't you having yours done?' Very carefully, nervous that it might dissolve the floor tiles, Daisy opened the bottle of hydrogen peroxide, sniffed it cautiously and winced. 'It smells dangerous.'

Emma took the bottle and sniffed too. 'No, it smells effective,' she pronounced. 'I'm not doing mine because I'm already blonde. And blondes have more fun, isn't that what they say? I've been thinking for a while that you're a bit, well a bit *mousy*, hairwise. This'll be good.'

'Well at least Mum won't mind, being the way she is. Though I don't know, can't be as sure of her as I used to be,' Daisy said, laying out the collection of equipment on the bathroom shelf. She opened the precious pot of Atlantic blue dye and sniffed at that too. 'As long as it's only the ends, at least I can cut them off if it looks dreadful. Yeah,' she said, perking up and finding enthusiasm, 'come on, let's do it!' Daisy perched on the side of the bath and Emma separated her hair into about thirty small sections and applied peroxide (using one of Alan's pastry brushes) to the end inch of about fifteen of them.

'It's like doing someone's roots, but in reverse. You'll look like you've got the ends of a load of 'blue-tipped paintbrushes dangling from your head,' she said, grinning at Daisy in the mirror.

'Gee thanks, can't wait,' Daisy told her doubtfully. 'I hope I can trust you with this.'

'Trust me with your brother, don't you?' Emma teased, looking over her shoulder towards the door in case Ben had crept up the stairs and was listening.

'Don't start. You promised. I need time for getting used to that,' Daisy warned her.

Emma secured all the peroxided bits of hair in strips of Bacofoil and put tiny elastic bands (stolen from her sister's orthodontic kit) round them. 'We'll finish the colouring bit after supper,' she told her. 'Your hair will take a while to bleach out.' She heard a set of footsteps thumping on the stairs to the attic, and the sound of a door closing firmly. 'I think your brother's home,' she said, abandoning Daisy's hair and fluffing out her own in front of the mirror. 'Got any lipstick?'

Over supper Jenny told the family about George Pemberton smashing his own window. They all laughed in the right places, but she still felt odd, as if everything she said had to be rehearsed first mentally to filter out anything that might trigger Alan into telling her something she didn't want to know. It was easier to talk to the children.

'What are you doing to your hair?' she asked Daisy with interest, watching the silver-papered strands dangling dangerously over the potato dish. 'I don't suppose, whatever it is, that Fiona Pemberton is going to approve,' she giggled, earning herself a dose of Daisy's scorn. In her opinion it wasn't part of the function of parents to join in the antagonizing of headmistresses.

'My mum would never let me do mine blue. You're so lucky, Daisy,' Emma said with a wistful sigh.

'*Blue?* Those bits under there are going to be blue? Good God!' Alan said, disbelievingly. Ben said nothing, ate little and sneaked blushing glances at Emma, to whom, in the past, before Saturday's electrifying physical contact, he had never had any trouble finding something to say. Jenny, with a mother's perception, noticed, felt maternally tremulous for him, and had to bite her tongue not to comment. For once the thought of youthful romance didn't make her eyes want to fill with envious tears. What was there to envy? All that tension, embarrassment, uncertainty and some hopeless fumbling if you were very, very lucky.

'I thought we might go out tomorrow night,' Alan said to Jenny, pouring her a third glass of wine. She was looking flushed and bright and rather jumpy. Time he took her out somewhere special. 'Just the two of us, a place I read about in *The Sunday Times* last weekend. You can babysit Polly, can't you Daisy, and we'll make that the last weekend of your being grounded.' He waited for her to look pleased, let-off and forgiven at last, but she and Emma were staring at him, still and shell-shocked, as if he'd just informed them that he was a serial killer and they were next.

'What's wrong?' Jenny asked Daisy. 'Won't you be happy to get your freedom back? I don't even mind paying you for tomorrow, either.'

Polly was staring backwards and forwards at the two girls, wondering what was going on, and piecing together some remembered bits of knowledge that seemed to start with the sight of Daisy climbing out of her bedroom window. She nudged Harriet and said, 'Mind if we skip pudding? We're just going out in the garden for a bit.'

'But it's dark now. Whatever do you want to go out there for?' Alan asked her.

'Oh nothing, just looking around. We'll take a torch,' she told him, busily not looking at him, but grabbing

Harriet's barely-finished plate and making unusually quickly for the dishwasher. She scuttled about the kitchen, pulling Harriet after her, grabbing wellingtons and coats and hissing 'Hurry up!' at her friend.

'Wanted to get out of clearing the table I expect,' Jenny said as she piled up plates, and for once she was prepared to be indulgent. 'Just leave them for tonight,' she told Daisy and Ben, 'I'll do them. I expect you've got things you want to be doing.'

On behalf of Ben and Emma, Daisy blushed furiously at Jenny's heavy-handed tact, and snarling ungraciously, dragged Emma towards the stairs so that her hair-dyeing could be finished.

'Now what have I said?' Jenny asked Alan.

'No idea, thought you were doing them a favour actually. Now about dinner tomorrow night . . .' he was saying, closing in for a hug. Jenny was just wondering if he'd notice how tense her body was when the phone rang. 'Bugger,' he said, kissing Jenny's ear and reaching across to take the call.

'Bugger,' he said again as he hung up a few minutes later.

'What's up? Work problems?' she asked. He looked nervous, she thought, shifty even, though she tried not to think it. It was all too exhausting, trying not to interpret every one of his gestures and expressions. No-one should have to do that much scrutiny, or be subjected to it.

'Tomorrow night. Dinner's on, if you want to come, but not just the two of us I'm afraid. Senior partner thinks we should get together before Monday and have a chat about the financial situation. Suggested dinner out at some place out near Watford. More convenient for him than us, but then he's paying.'

'Dinner on the company won't help its cash flow,' Jenny commented. 'Why can't you just have a meeting early on Monday at the office?'

'Walls have ears. Some of them electronic,' he said mysteriously, making Jenny think for a moment that the place must be bugged, like an old Eastern Bloc embassy. 'All those fancy phone systems and computer stuff. Not to mention the cleaning lady who knows what's going on before the rest of us do. And she's about as good at keeping secrets as a tabloid journalist.' He looked morose, his good-intention family feelings slipping away. Who else would be at the dinner, he wondered? Not Serena, he prayed – though she was Bernard's niece and it was a possibility.

As if Jenny was reading his mind she asked casually, 'And who else is going to be there? Bernard's wife, Monica, isn't it? Any others from the staff?' she wasn't looking at him, folding the tea towel with more care than she ever had before, draping it carefully over the Aga rail as if it was a precious cashmere sweater.

'Don't know. Sorry, I didn't think to ask,' Alan said, stacking glasses into the dishwasher, wondering if he was imagining any other questions unasked and un-answered between them. 'Anyway, you like Monica, don't you? I'm sure it won't be so bad. Sorry, though, I did intend it to be just the two of us, but you know what work has been like lately.'

Jenny did know, all those awful bank statements. She also knew that Bernard's wife Monica, a matronly and energetic chairwoman (no man, person, or simply 'chair' titles for her) of her local Townswomen's Guild, would exhaust her within half-an-hour with an intimidating list of her latest Good Works and charity events. She would have to spend the entire evening being impressed.

'Got any candles?' Polly and Harriet burst excitedly in through the back door, gasping plumes of cool, fresh air.

'Yes, cupboard under the stairs. Take the power-cut supply,' Jenny told them, watching them scatter mud flakes all over the wooden floor, and not particularly caring. She rinsed out the sink and went about inventing a couple of sponsored runs and a charity bike ride with which to do her equal share of impressing, and made up her mind to have quite a lot of anaesthetizing alcohol.

'Now what are they up to?' Paul was asking himself up in the attic. Carol wanted to watch a video of *Oklahoma!* the version recently produced by the local operatic society, so he felt banished from the sitting-room and was taking refuge with his telescope. He'd given the All-Clear to the rest of the garden that he could see, and it seemed to be all quiet, too, up at the Tennis Club and on as much as he could see of the estate. But the Collins's back garden was full of the kind of torchlight activity that only usually went with Bonfire Night. There was a flickering circle of what looked suspiciously like candlelight too. If only he could see what they were up to, and who was actually up to it. He opened the window and let in an unwelcome blast of chill air. He listened carefully, head sideways like a budgie, ear cocked for clues. There was traffic roaring from the main road and some loud car-music from the estate as usual (he sometimes thought that a fast car was considered a viable party venue for those people), but not much else. He was startled by a cat or a fox bashing at one of Mrs Fingell's many dustbins and hit his head on the window catch trying to crane further out. Suddenly the still air was filled with blood-curdling shrieks of terror. The torchlight in the Collins's garden was waving chaotically up and down and racing for their back door. Most of the candlelight went out, kicked over in the rush probably, he imagined. Whatever Satanic rites that unruly family had been practising, it served them right, felt Paul, they'd obviously called up evil spirits and frightened themselves half to death. He took the relevant file down from the shelf and filled in yet another entry for number 14. Theirs was the fattest and most frustrating file he'd got, stuffed with dates and dealings but nothing more positive than a sure as hell hunch that something was going on.

Alan thought the phrase 'bats out of hell' didn't seem inappropriate as the two girls came like whirlwinds crashing in through the back door.

'Polly! Tell me! What's happened, who's out there?' Jenny tried to peel the shrieking, clinging child from her neck. Harriet looked calmer but was alarmingly sick-looking and grizzling woefully.

'Come on girls,' Alan entreated them gently, 'tell us what happened out there.' He went and stood by the back door, peering out into the bleak darkness for some sort of clue. One or two of the candles still fluttered unreliably in the dark and he thought, but couldn't be sure, that some of the garden tools were littered across the lawn. 'I'll go and have a look,' he told Jenny, sounding more brave than he felt. Their screams had been truly blood-freezing.

'I think they've seen something. Or someone,' Jenny whispered, gathering the pair of trembling children into her arms.

'He's in there! He wasn't supposed to be!' Polly whimpered, and Jenny felt the back of her neck tingle. Someone in the garden? Daring to spy, or chasing her child? Maybe there was a point to Neighbourhood Watch after all, unless, and she felt slightly sick, there was a Neighbour out there, doing some off-the-records unofficial Watching.

'Daisy! Take care of Polly a moment will you?' she yelled up the stairs. 'And ask Ben to come down too please!' Sensing emergency in her voice, Daisy, Emma and Ben clattered immediately down the stairs, Daisy swearing slightly and dripping blue hair dye onto a pink towel. Leaving Daisy and Emma to comfort the sobbing Polly and quaking Harriet, Ben, Alan and Jenny set off into the garden with torches and collective courage.

'Can't see anything. What did they say it was?' Ben asked. Jenny got hold of Alan's hand, preparing herself against the moment when the mad axeman leapt out of the viburnum. The shed door banged open in a sharp breeze and Jenny gasped.

'Oh God, look what they've been doing!' she said suddenly, shining her torch on to the vegetable patch. Spades had been abandoned on the ground next to the strawberry bed and heaps of earth were dug out and piled loosely around. She giggled, slightly hysterically. 'The little ghouls have been digging up that poor cat!'

'Looks like they found him, and spooked themselves to bits,' Alan said, shining his torch into the hole and pulling a rather sickened face. 'Or what's left of him anyway. You go in and take care of them, and we'll fill this in again before the foxes get him.' In what was left of the candlelight, Alan looked cold and shivery and Jenny, once again, thought of the unfairness of women foisting the awful jobs on to men.

'No, Ben can go, I'll help you,' she said softly, picking up a spade. 'After all,' she told him grinning, 'I'm the one who's had practice at this lately!'

'Too late now, I suppose, to check if this cat had an identification disc?' he said, looking closely at Jenny and willing her to agree that it was.

Jenny hesitated; if she'd truly started to hate him, she could insist he dug up the cat and had a look. She hoped she'd never loathe him that much. 'Definitely too late,' she told him, shovelling resolutely and fast.

'You're so stupid Polly! Why did you do it?' Daisy

and Emma doing their reluctant bit to take care of the little girls, had made them rush back up to the bathroom with them so that Daisy's blue hair dye wouldn't be ruined. Harriet and Polly sat forlornly on the landing being shouted at. 'AND I've got to babysit you tomorrow. That's not fair. You'd better do everything, and I mean *everything*, that I tell you.'

She started hissing furiously at Emma, Polly craned her neck to hear what she said over the noise of the shower. 'What am I going to do now? It's wrecked, completely *wrecked* my brilliant plan! I'm trapped with little Miss Macabre here, with the best party of the whole year happening without me just a mile away!'

Oklahoma! was still blaring away downstairs; Paul could hear it two flights away. If the twins had the TV on that loud Carol would have had something to say. He could just picture her now, down there on the sofa, feet up and the paper in the box of All Gold crackling as she reached in blindly for one chocolate after another. Sporty people, he could see down the telescope, were leaving the Tennis Club. It was getting late, and even from this far away he could hear car doors being thoughtlessly slammed. A Range Rover glided smoothly into the Close and cruised along towards him. As the lights from the house mingled with the headlights on the car he could see the driver as she inconsiderately reversed into his drive to turn back down the Close. It was the big blonde woman with hair like tiger stripes, who was always doing that – usually in the morning when she picked up Polly. One day he'd be down there in the hall and catch her at it, crunching carelessly across the pavement right on to his gravel. Where was she going?

Focusing on the Collins's garden once more, he could see shadowy figures shuffling about, bending and moving and looking ridiculously (for the time of night) as if they were gardening. Two of them, Paul counted, and watched them digging and working together. If it was anywhere but in the Close, he'd have suspected they were burying a body. Perhaps Jenny hadn't been joking about do-it-yourself funerals after all, though he was sure even she, odd as she was, wouldn't hold a burial without the proper sort of ceremony (drinks, bits to eat, flowers) that went with it. It was far more likely she'd been up to the Garden Centre and bought some shrub that would flourish best if planted out on a waxing moon.

'What *are* they up to?' he asked the night air, his eyes sore from the strain of peering. Now they looked like they were doing something romantic, all wrapped round each other. Had to be the teenagers, he thought, turning to get the Collins file down again and put the Range Rover woman into it. Grown-ups never do things like that.

Chapter Fourteen

'If you want coffee or tea, I hope you don't mind helping yourself. I'm a bit stuck, as you can see,' Jenny said to Sue who came strolling in through the back door. Jenny, on that Saturday morning, was aware that she looked perfectly ridiculous, perched at the kitchen table listening to *Loose Ends* and reading the paper with each elbow squished into half a scooped-out lemon. She had a million and one other weekend things to do, starting with the clearing up of the ruined strawberry bed and the planting out of a batch of campanulas. Lazily she settled her arms deeper into the lemons. 'The things we do to be beautiful. Can't possibly be seen out with crumpled elbows,' she sighed, thanking her stars that Alan, in spite of knowing he was dining out that night, had been unable to resist going out for his usual social round of food shopping.

'Why don't you just wear something with long sleeves?' Sue suggested with simple logic, settling herself opposite Jenny and stealing half the newspaper.

'I thought of that, but I've got that lovely black velvet thing with the short, tight sleeves, not too short that they show the flabby armtops, but somehow thin-making. Why on earth do *elbows* go?' Jenny asked her. 'I can see that chins and bums will drop and expand with use and age, but how worn-out and ancient-looking can an elbow get? What does it *do* for heaven's sake?'

'I can think of some men whose elbows must be just about corrugated with overuse,' Sue muttered darkly.

'The ones I've tended to know, anyway. And talking of men . . .' she flung the paper down hard for dramatic emphasis, 'guess what?'

Jenny looked suspiciously at the vibrant, I-know-a-secret face, and groaned at her friend. 'Oh not again Sue,' she laughed. 'Don't tell me you've met another Mr Wrong!'

'No. Well yes!' Sue was beaming like a lovestruck teenager. 'Only he's Mr Right, this time I'm sure of it.'

'Sue, you're always sure of it, every single time!' Jenny laughed and shifted and dislodged the left lemon, sending it skidding to the floor. 'Bloody thing.' She peered round at the back of her arm. 'Look at this, it's as pink and rough as a ninety-year-old charlady's kneecap. Do you think lemons are really any use?'

'Can't tell you. All the magazines say so, though. Like cucumber for puffy eyelids. You could lie around all day looking like a glass of Pimms and see if it makes any difference.'

'I'm beginning to suspect it's just that lemons are the right shape to fit elbows, just as cucumbers are the right shape for eyes, and avocado is the right texture for mashing up and slapping on your face. We should probably have it all the other way round for it to work.'

'No, you're way off the mark.' Sue scrabbled in her bag for a cigarette. 'You're supposed to have a go at all these natural remedies, the ones they dig out every six months or so for the makeover pages, and then after you've made a horrible mess and your nails are full of pith and pips, and you smell like a leftover salad, you can't wait to rush out and spend a fortune on the kind of cosmetics that simply melt into your grateful skin.'

'Not me. Not after that cellulite stuff. I'm permanently cynical about it all now. I'd like to claim I'm no longer a cosmetics victim, but if that were true I wouldn't be sitting here doing this. It's getting harder and harder to know what I should wear, too. I wish there was some way of being absolutely sure what I look good in, so I wouldn't make expensive mistakes,' said Jenny.

'Well don't ask a man, whatever you do,' Sue advised. 'Last one I asked what I looked best in said "A darkened room". I divorced him. Well I had to, after that, didn't I?'

Jenny started giggling, glad that she wasn't also wearing a face pack that would now be cracked like an old plate. 'Anyway, tell me about Him, who is he, where did you meet him, and what makes him different from the rest of your collection?'

Sue took her time inhaling and thinking, and said, 'Well, he's certainly different, not local, just someone I met by chance.' She waited, avoiding Jenny's questioning eye and staring at the pots of herbs on the window-sill, as if deciding how much she should be revealing. Jenny was just considering this unusual reticence when Daisy walked in.

'God, Mum, what are you doing?' she said, slouching into the kitchen in Jenny's cream satin dressing-gown and making straight for the kettle.

'Good morning Sue, how nice to see you. Isn't that how it goes?' Sue reminded her.

'Sorry Sue. How are you?' Daisy conceded.

'I'm extremely fine thanks, and I quite like your blue bits of hair, but not an awful lot,' Sue replied. Jenny drew a sharp intake of breath, waiting for Daisy to stamp out of the room or say something fearsomely rude.

'T'isn't permanent, it's just for a, er, a laugh for a while,' she said instead.

What's she up to? was Jenny's immediate thought. The predicted reaction should have been for Daisy to scowl and snarl, 'well *sorree*' with as much heavy sarcasm as she could dredge up and then stamp around the kitchen, pointedly making a drink only for herself. From the activity around the cupboards and the fluttering of tea bags all over the floor it rather looked like Daisy was making a rare pot of tea for the whole household. I hope she's not going to ask me a favour, Jenny thought warily, trying to guess what it might be. Money? A friend to sleep over? Both of those could probably be accommodated, just so long as it wasn't the loan of tonight's black dress. But then, she reminded herself, Daisy wasn't going anywhere that night.

It wasn't any use thinking of appealing to Ben. He wouldn't be able to come up with a solution. He was going to Sophie's party whatever happened, he and Emma, playing at sick-making cosy couples. Daisy took her tea back up to her room and wondered how she could iron her dark blue dress with the gold stars on it without arousing suspicion. 'You never iron anything! What's going on?' would be the instant reaction of her mother, who, with her trouble-seeking radar, would suspect the worst and get Securicor in to guard her for the night. Or worse still, stay in and keep watch herself. One teeny crime, one tidgy mistake, and Jenny was turned instantly into the kind of mother that everyone else at school had. It just wasn't fair. Daisy collected together her new Senseless Things tape, a couple of joss sticks in a wine bottle and her Happy Hippy bath gel and went into the bathroom to make a start on the day-long process of getting ready to go out. She prayed it would not be for nothing.

Alan was in heaven, oblivious to life's cares, drooling over the Provolone and Dolcelatte on the cheese counter at the Italian deli in the same entranced way the other men were doing over the soft-porn video display round the corner at Rentavid. Like them, he was in no mood to be interrupted, and visibly leapt when Paul Mathieson tapped him on the shoulder.

'You been sent out shopping too?' Paul asked him in a sheepish bid for sympathy. He was clutching a two-tone leatherette shopping bag, holding it in front of him as if determined not to learn the easiest way of carrying it.

Alan felt immediate antagonism, and fought down the feeling that this was perfectly reasonable – after all, Paul was just being friendly. 'No, I enjoy it. Something of a hobby really,' he confessed. 'Very restful, cooking,' he added, gazing back at the display of buffalo Mozzarella, 'though I don't suppose Jen would agree, when she's dashing around trying to feed the kids between picking them up and dropping them off at all their various after-school activities.'

Paul could think of no reply. Cooking was something Carol did with vigour and adeptness but no real sign of delight. Offhand he couldn't think of anything she *did* do with delight, unless he counted petting those skinny cats. Relaxing was not a word he would have applied to the atmosphere in their kitchen when Carol chopped, mixed, sliced and stirred. He thought of the sheer brutality with which she broke and beat eggs, the awe-inspiring violence of her dough-kneading.

'Just look at that Parmesan,' Alan was murmuring. 'D'you know that here they sprinkle it between the layers of fresh lasagne before it's packed ready to sell?'

'Well, no, I didn't. Doesn't it go all over the floor when you unwrap it?' Paul asked, thinking of Carol's outraged face when confronted with an unexpected mess.

'Yes, of course, but who cares? It's well worth it!' Alan told him, turning to the pasta cabinet and picking up a couple of packs of the stuff. He shoved some into

Paul's hand. 'Try some!' he said expansively. 'Or what about the cuttlefish tagliatelle?'

Paul looked disbelievingly at the jet black pasta, which seemed even worse than the blue Smarties that Marcus was so fond of. He thought he'd wait till Alan left, sneak the lasagne back on to the shelf and collect a pack of their usual dried version from the supermarket. Meanwhile, there was something he was aching to know, the reason for which he'd entered this terrifying shop. 'What was going on in your back garden last night?' he said, then tittered nervously in case the reply was something too honestly sensual. 'Looked like a witchcraft meeting – the Close Coven perhaps!' An alarmed feeling was creeping up inside his head that he might have got it accidentally correct. They might put a curse on him. He'd never quite stopped half-believing that people could be changed into frogs, which was probably why he never could stand up to Carol. He stared around the shop, waiting for Alan to laugh it off, pretending he was studying the jars of sun-dried tomatoes and wondering why they hadn't removed the cloudy bottles of Podere vinegar from the shelves; surely it was looking slightly off?

'How on earth could you see into my back garden?' Alan asked him with quiet menace. 'And for what reason would you be looking?'

'Oh well, it was just the noise and the lights flick-ering, you know, could have been burglars, anything, kids got in from the estate, you know . . . Happened to be in the attic . . .' he bluffed lamely, guarding his chest with the shopping bag, aware that the shop had gone very silent and several customers in the shop were openly listening. Most of them were men, large men-acing ones. He felt suddenly like an unwelcome intruder, an epicureally-challenged gatecrasher in this haunt of gourmets. It would be ages till he was served, priority customers being Italian speakers or, like Alan, friends of the owner. He'd be much happier in Sainsbury's, in the single basket, cash-only queue. He smirked nervously. 'Just taking a neighbourly interest.' Alan, grinning coolly, hit him none too playfully on the head with a large olive-stuffed ciabatta loaf.

'Well don't,' he told Paul.

The doorbell rang just as Jenny was coming down the stairs. 'You can stay up till 10, just for once, but no later,' she called back up to Polly, as she glanced into the hall mirror. Her hair, which had taken thirty-five minutes to pile up, was collapsing already, but with the deep and gooey red lipstick and plenty of mascara (eye-care by Estée Lauder this time, not the greengrocer), she looked and felt quite gorgeously tarty.

'George!' she exclaimed, surprised to see him standing rather shamefacedly on the doormat. 'Fiona sent you over to borrow a cup of sugar?'

'No. I've come to see you,' he said, staring intently at the rather low front of her tight black velvet dress. Jenny put a protective hand towards her cleavage.

'Me? Oh look George, I've told you before. It's no. And it'll be no next time you ask too, just to save you the trouble,' she hissed firmly, pulling the door behind her a little so no-one could hear, then realizing she had enclosed the two of them into the dusty intimacy of the porch. She could smell over-wintering geraniums and George's pungent anticipatory aftershave.

'Oh look, I do make an effort,' he pleaded like a schoolboy excusing inadequate homework. 'I try them all, from King's Cross knee-tremblers to colonic irrigation. All I want . . .'

'You sound like a walking health hazard. I know exactly what you want,' Jenny told him, glad that she was wearing high heeled shoes and had the authority of being slightly taller than him, 'and I'm sorry, but you're

215

not getting it from me and that's that!' Her harsh treatment of him was having the wrong effect, she realized, he was now looking positively lascivious. Another minute and he would be drooling on the doormat.

'You look wonderful. Edible,' he told her breathily, looking her up and down and licking his lips. Jenny shuddered, though mostly at the thought that he must at one time have said things like that to the formidable Fiona. She wondered how Fiona had reacted. With commendably firm discipline, she imagined, for which George had probably married her.

'Look George,' she said, changing over to reasoning sweetness, 'we're just going out for the evening. Alan and I. You'll have to go away.' Jenny opened the front door a bit wider, trying to frighten him off, and the hall light exaggerated the hangdog pallor of George's mournful face. It looked as worn out and hopeless as his corduroy jacket. Then the sound of Alan on the stairs startled them both and George muttered a quick goodbye and shambled off to the gate. Poor old soul, Jenny thought, making a half-hearted effort to salvage her hair in front of the hall mirror. The world seemed full of men like him. She couldn't take them on – if she wanted to get more actively involved in charity work than running the local Help the Aged collection, she could think of much worthier causes.

'What did he want?' Alan asked, checking his tie in the mirror.

'Just my body,' Jenny told him with a cheeky wink as she went back upstairs to say goodnight to Polly.

'Long way to go for dinner with people we wouldn't really choose to go out with,' Alan said apologetically in the car.

'I don't mind, it's just good to be out, and the food

there is supposed to be miraculous,' said Jenny. 'I'm beginning to feel I'm living in a goldfish bowl in the Close, with Paul and Carol and their obsession with watching everyone. It's getting beyond a joke. I feel like writing up a list for them of exactly what I do in one particular day – everything including the times I go to the loo and what junk mail the postman brought. Perhaps they'd get the hint then.'

'No they wouldn't. Paul thinks we've taken up witch-craft. He told me in the deli, he was watching the candles in our garden last night and thinks we were calling up the devil.'

'Makes me want to hold naked rituals out there and mix up spells in a cauldron,' she laughed. 'We could invite him to join. I bet Carol would jump at the chance. There's sure to be something interestingly repressed and seething under her M & S bodyshaper.'

'She'd make a good Head Witch,' Alan agreed, nod-ding solemnly. 'Very good at keeping order. Dominatrix type.'

Must remember to suggest her to George Pemberton, thought Jenny, next time he comes round wanting to buy some sexual services. Perhaps they'd suit each other nicely.

At the traffic lights, Alan reached into the door pocket for a suitable tape. He came across the Beach Boys, but rejected it, remembering how irritated Jenny used to get with his out-of-tune attempts to join in with the irresistible harmonies. It was all right for her with her perfect pitch. All the same, ooh-oohing his way through *Good Vibrations* was something best kept for the privacy of lone motorway journeys. Rummaging about, he finally found a dusty old Fleet-wood Mac album, the first cassette tape he'd ever bought after finally conceding that the 8-track car stereo was, like Betamax, unlikely to have a future.

'You used to look a bit like the singer, Stevie Nicks

was it?' he said to Jenny as they cruised through Wealdstone High Street. 'Remember?'

'Do I ever!' she said, wrinkling her nose. 'Perilous platform boots and hanky-point floaty skirts. Not bad, those skirts. I should have kept one. Daisy would probably have worn it.'

'This week isn't it? Her appointment with the Chief Constable. Do you have to get her out of school early?'

'No thank goodness, so there's no need for Fiona Pemberton to know anything about it. Though she probably does; the staff must have heard the girls gossiping to each other about it.' Jenny felt uneasy, thinking about Daisy's brush with the law. Perhaps these things really were genetic. She wished she could ask Alan to take time out from the office to go instead. It was worse for her than going to the dentist. Many years ago, she had been arrested on the one time she had called at the escort agency to collect her commission and tell them she wouldn't be working for them again, and the police had chosen that moment for a raid. The thought of the long-ago detective leering and sneering into her face with a mixture of disgust and lecherous curiosity still gave her a nauseous shiver. 'We could have you up for being a common prostitute,' he'd threatened. 'Must turn some of them on, a bit of posh. Prostitute you may be, common you're not.' Jenny shuddered at the memory and turned up the car heating.

'I think you over-estimate staff-room loyalty,' Alan tried to be reassuring, 'if you think they'd report what they heard to the headmistress. I'm sure she'll be the last one to hear. And it won't be the worst thing that's ever happened at the school; I heard a thirteen-year-old got pregnant a couple of years back, and they're always dropping out of the sixth form because of drugs, and being passed on to those extortionate crammers in Kensington.'

The restaurant was a famous one, written about in countless weekend newspapers. Food writers liked going there; it was far enough from their office to necessitate taking an entire day out just to go and do their report. Glowing references to its meals were overlaid with more than a hint of incredulous journalistic wonder that such culinary skill could be found beyond the boundary of the M25. They wrote things like *Well worth driving out of London for,* as if the whole world resided in SW3. Alan tended to read out the more irritating quotes over breakfast on Sunday mornings. 'Listen to this Jen: *"Rather* a clever little *terrine de bouillabaisse"*. What exactly's that supposed to mean? Patronizing bastard,' he would grumble across the toast and Jenny would murmur a soothing 'Mmmm' in agreement from deep in the Books section.

The restaurant sounded full when Jenny and Alan walked in, but it was, in fact, more than half empty, only noisy with the strident sound of regular customers braying greetings to each other and loudly ensuring that everyone in the place knew that the head waiter had remembered which tables they preferred. 'So clever of you, Henry, to remember about Barbara's contact lenses and the air conditioning,' Jenny overheard. Turning her attention away from the unpretty sight of a portly weekend executive schoolboyishly rubbing his stomach and exclaiming 'Yum yum!' as he read the menu at the bar, she had a quick look at the décor. Someone had been reading the right magazines: no dated, over-chintzed floral frills here, just plain, straight-hung calico curtains tied to simple iron poles, pale cream walls lightly overwashed with burnt sienna, and on the floor, seagrass carpeting, which must be hazardous to high heels on less than sober customers. Even the stylish Laura Benstone had refused to have it in her house on the grounds that if the children were sick on it, it would be a bugger to clean up.

Bernard and his wife Monica, a chunky, comfortable couple in late middle-age, with matching hair cut short and striped in shades of grey, were already at a round table, which was laid for six. There was also one younger woman that Jenny did not know, though it took just the briefest heartstopping second to realize that this elegant girl with sleek, nut-brown hair tied back with a purple scarf and wearing a dusty pink silk jacket that could almost be Armani could only be Bernard's niece Serena.

'Frankie's just gone off to the loo, won't be a sec,' Serena said as the introductions were being made. Jenny sat down and fiddled with her napkin, glanced at Serena's overloaded handful of heavy rings, and wondered why it had never occurred to her that Serena might even be married. What kind of evening was it going to be, making dinner-party conversation with the woman she suspected of dallying with Alan? Did her own husband, if that's what he was, this Frankie, have the same painful suspicions? She resolved to take safe and childlike refuge in appreciating the food.

At too many dinners the deliciously extravagant flavours eluded her in the tension of meeting new people, keeping the chat going and simply getting through an evening. Sometimes, late at night, on journeys when Alan was raving over the supremacy of one sauce or another, she could hardly recall a thing she'd tasted. She looked across the table at him sitting between Monica and Serena. She noticed that he seemed positively exuberant, beaming broadly and already calling a waiter to order drinks. Perhaps, she thought venomously, he was excited by the juxtaposition of wife and mistress. Surely he couldn't have known about this?

'Always a bit nerve-wracking, going out to eat with an expert such as yourself,' Jenny heard Bernard confessing to Alan, 'so I thought, just to be on the safe side and make sure everything's up to scratch, I'd bring this along.' Jenny watched a flicker of incredulous dismay pass across Alan's face and looked at the tatty, torn-edged scrap of pale blue newsprint that Bernard had fished out of his pocket. 'It's an old Restaurant Watch notice from *The Sunday Times*,' he explained to those who didn't know. 'You put it on the table so the waiters know that you expect only the very best service. Knew you'd appreciate that.' Jenny knew that Alan, who thought such a thing the height of insulting rudeness, did not, and was feeling grudging sympathy for him as the last guest slid into the seat next to her. 'Hello, I'm Frankie,' Jenny heard, and turned to look at Serena's friend, who was fair-haired, stocky and thirty-something. Interestingly, the friend was also female.

It was Emma in Daisy's bathroom who came up with the solution to the big problem. 'We'll take Polly to the party with us. Simple. We'll be back before your parents, they've gone absolutely miles away and they'll never ever know,' she declared optimistically.

'We can't,' was Daisy's immediate reaction. 'Polly will tell. Besides, I don't want to go to a party towing my baby sister along. Whatever kind of twit will I look?' In spite of her doubts she was still getting ready. There had to be a way, some last-minute salvation. She'd wondered if she dared ask Mrs Fingell to babysit, but hadn't enough left of her allowance to pay her with. Besides, Daisy could hardly ask her not to mention it to Jenny. If she did, Mrs Fingell might not only refuse to come, but might tell Jenny anyway. It just wasn't worth the risk of asking her. Daisy would get out somehow though, with or without Polly. The dress with the stars on was neatly ironed, she'd found a pair of black tights that only had one ladder in them, and now she was carefully sticking on a pair of rainbow-coloured false eyelashes. 'Do these look stupid?' she asked, blinking hard at Emma's reflection in the bathroom mirror.

'No they look great. Hurry up, we've only got to fix Polly and then we can go; it's gone eight already.'

She's dying to get at Ben, thought Daisy, appalled that she was about to spend the evening at the same party as him, and no doubt have to watch him snogging her best friend. Taking Polly looked like being the only possible thing to do. 'How much fun am I going to have with Poll watching my every move?' she moaned, wondering how Oliver would ever get the chance to pounce on her.

'Well at least you'll be there – you won't be missing it, that's what matters. She'll probably fall asleep under a table or something. Stop worrying and let's go and persuade her to come. Will we need to bribe her?'

'Threaten maybe. She likes to watch *Casualty* on Saturdays, counts how many patients get rushed into Crash and never come out alive. Nearly all of them, she says.' Daisy fluffed out her hair so that the desired amount dangled over her left eye. The blue ends looked just the right shade against the dress. She couldn't waste all this effort.

Polly knew something was going on, and one way or another was planning on profiting from it. Daisy wasn't spending hours getting ready for a quiet evening in, that was for sure. She was just dialling Harriet's number to consult with her on suitable blackmail charges when Daisy and Emma marched importantly into the sitting-room and switched off the television.

'Hey, I'm watching that!' she shouted at them.

Daisy took the telephone from her and replaced the receiver, then took her hand and led her to the sofa. Polly felt nervous, Daisy was being quite gentle with her, which left her unsure how to react. Daisy being stroppy and demanding, she could deal with – she

222

was used to that. Daisy and Emma sat each side of her on the sofa, and Polly waited for the worst, possibly a thorough beating-up.

'Polly, how would you like to go out to a really good party? With us,' Emma asked, smiling sweetly at her as if she was offering her a treat.

'Yes. But it has to be a secret. You mustn't tell the parents,' Daisy added.

Polly pretended to consider for a long moment, trying not to smirk. They thought she wouldn't want to go, that she'd need persuading. How stupid of them. She slowly curled her legs up underneath her to look more settled for the night. 'But it's *Casualty*. I always watch that.' Defiantly, she folded her arms, wondering how far she could go with making Daisy furious.

Daisy bit her lip. 'We'll set the video. You've got to come Poll, I can't leave you here on your own.'

'No, you can't do that,' Polly agreed. 'What do I get if I come? You've got to make it something really good, because you wouldn't want to be grounded again would you?' she said slyly, her big eyes staring innocently at Daisy's multi-coloured eyelashes.

But Daisy had looked at the clock and knew her options had expired. She wanted to leave, and leave now. Her patience evaporated and she grabbed Polly by the hair. 'You're coming with us Polly, and you're going to be really good and do just what I tell you, and you're never going to mention this to anyone, not ever or . . . or . . .'

'Or what?' Polly held her breath.

Daisy grinned, frighteningly. 'Or, you know that mouldy cat that you and Harriet half-dug up last night?'

'Ye . . . es . . . ?' Polly mumbled.

Emma, one step ahead, smiled equally maliciously.

Daisy was still grinning. 'Well I saw a film once, and there was a very silly man in it who told tales when he shouldn't have and one morning when he woke up there was a horse's head in bed with him, all horrible and bleeding. In your case you could end up sharing your bed with that putrid pussycat. Imagine that.'

'Yeah, that's right.' Emma slid closer to Polly and whispered in her ear. Polly could smell her musky perfume. 'You wouldn't like that, would you Polly? I know I wouldn't.'

Chapter Fifteen

If he'd known that Serena was coming, Alan would have thought of some excuse, a previous engagement that was impossible to miss. He could understand that for some men, the sort more used to playing 'away fixtures', the thought of sharing a dinner table with both a wife and a focus of lust was overwhelmingly thrilling, a real kick to the old and flagging virility, but for him it was heartstoppingly hazardous. Suppose he got drunk and said something really stupid, like calling the wrong one 'Pudding'? Adultery, even the planning stages of it, obviously didn't come naturally to him. He was a shambling amateur at it. Who were those men who ran sleek-stockinged mistresses and dared to book smart hotel rooms by the hour for conscience-free afternoon sex? Both women were looking equally desirable, Jenny with her lion-coloured hair, already starting to look sexily dishevelled in her low-cut black velvet dress, and Serena in silky pink, the jacket not quite covering something lacy and black underneath that looked enticingly like underwear. Jenny's body was known, familiar. Serena had the advantage here of being the more tempting through being untried.

Guilt gripped Alan's intestines and made him peevish, blocking off his appetite. He'd been really looking forward to going out with Jenny, liberated from all guilt-inducing fantasies for once in a way that reminded him of taking well-earned time off work. He liked his wife; much better than that, he loved her. What he felt for Serena was completely separate, and the two women had no business facing each other and exercising their social graces across a restaurant table. If he'd known, he could have conjured up a wedding anniversary, or a godchild's birthday treat, or a suddenly dead Irish aunt with a compulsory three-day wake in Kilburn, and simply taken Jenny out to Riva in Barnes as he'd planned. He wished he was there now, watching the men admiring Jenny and looking forward to *linguine* with crayfish in a deliciously creamy tomato sauce. It would all have been so conveniently close to home, too, not two counties away out there in God-forsaken pony club territory, with something that may or may not be Vivaldi giggling shrilly from sub-standard speakers. Bernard really should have left discussing the office finances till Monday, it surely couldn't be that much of a crisis, Alan thought as he sat sulkily crumbling his bread roll (freshly baked on the premises, the menu promised) and wondering if he dared to risk the garrulousness that came with even the smallest amount of alcohol.

He thought he recognized Frankie as the woman waiting on the pavement the night he had driven Serena home. She'd definitely been that sort of squarish shape, though he hadn't seen enough of her to notice the pretty, feathery haircut, or the huge green eyes. Serena introduced her at the table as simply, 'My friend Frankie; we share the flat.' He had been under the impression that Serena had bought her flat herself, so Frankie must be a lodger brought in to help with the mortgage. Typically sweet of Serena not to mention that, thought Alan. He flinched nervously in his seat as, next to him, she swished one silky leg across the other under the table, terrified that he would unconsciously (who was he kidding?) find his thigh drawn towards hers under cover of the tablecloth and that Jenny, all-seeing and all-knowing, would see and know all.

Sandwiched between Bernard and Frankie, Jenny

wondered, rather cattily, why the lovely Serena was manless on a Saturday night. Perhaps she had an absent husband; a fiancé in the Navy would rather suit her, she thought, somebody who looked good in a uniform, doing something important defending the Gulf on the *Ark Royal*. She looked like the well put-together Surrey sort who would have no trouble with Officers' formal dinners, or telling a Captain from a Commodore at thirty paces. She had a plummy little ex-deb voice, just falling short of being gushing as she asked Jenny about her family.

'And has Polly recovered from her exams?' she enquired politely, making Jenny feel immediate and unreasoning resentment that Alan must have discussed his family with her. Instead of sensibly imagining them over coffee in the office or whiling away the journey to a client's audit, she instantly pictured the two of them indulging in cosy chats among crisp linen pillows on Serena's bed, making languorous after-sex conversation, with Alan recounting amusing little tales of disordered family life. Jenny tried not to seethe, tried to control her wandering imagination. It was only one evening, it could and would be got through.

Bernard, Serena and Alan had the advantage of knowing what they had met to discuss. 'We'll just get the boring stuff out of the way quickly and then we can get on with enjoying ourselves,' Bernard announced jovially, as if pleasure in the dinner could be put on hold and resurrected at will. 'Just got to sort out whether we've actually got work premises to return to on Monday or not.' He laughed as if, deep down, it was quite unthinkable that the firm could really be in dire trouble, as if this never really happened to people like him.

Jenny, for one, felt dismissed from the discussion across the table, and after ordering food from a waiter who quite rightly curled a scornful and amused lip at the shameful Restaurant Watch slip, knew she was relegated to making conversation with Frankie and Monica. Her brain cut out momentarily while she pondered whether she should have ordered the sea bass instead of lamb, and returned seconds later to find Monica comfortably launched into listing her weekly timetable.

'And on Tuesdays and Thursdays it's Meals on Wheels, then Fridays I do the hospital run.' She did a girlish giggle and confided, 'They call it the After Eighties clinic, a bit like the mints, because that's the minimum age for our old dears. The charge-nurse calls them the Still With Us brigade, because that's what everyone says to them; "Still with us are you dear?", you know, everyone from the ambulancemen to the consultant. Naughty really, I know,' she laughed cosily, her necklace with dangling fruit-drop beads cheerfully bouncing at her throat.

'Rather patronizing, don't you think?' Frankie's icy voice chipped in as she leaned forward earnestly. 'Just because people are old, surely that's no reason to treat them as if they've no more intelligence than domestic pets?' Jenny turned to Monica, who looked slightly puzzled, as if she wasn't sure she'd heard properly. Frankie had a coldly serious look on her face, her pale pink mouth tight with righteousness. Jenny felt sorry for Monica, who, naïve and well-meaning soul that she was, had no streak of artful wit with which to defend herself.

'Are you in social services by any chance?' Jenny asked Frankie with an innocent note of interested enquiry.

'Physiotherapy. I work with stroke survivors. We don't call them victims any more, of course,' Frankie answered. 'It's a matter of positive attitudes.'

'It must be enormously rewarding, helping the poor

old things regain their faculties.' Monica had recovered and smiled eagerly, making a misplaced bid for Frankie's good opinion. Frankie glowered at her. Not over-rewarding for the patients, Jenny thought, having their broken-nerved limbs coaxed back to useful life by a therapist who thought it was a political crime to call someone 'love', however carefully respectful they were being while they were not doing it.

From across the table small hints of disastrous financial insolvency were making their way to Jenny's ears. Just the odd word, like 'bailiffs', and 'receivers' and 'liquidity factor'. The situation at the office sounded even worse than Alan had been telling her: more clients than ever not paying up. The overheard snatches told her that, unless the firm came up with the annual office rent, plus inevitable extortionate increase by Monday lunchtime, eviction would surely follow. No wonder Bernard couldn't wait another forty-eight hours to discuss it with Alan. What kind of accountancy practice goes broke? Jenny wondered. She listened to them discussing the hiring of motorbike couriers to dash round picking up as much money as indebted clients could pay to prop up the bank balance, and felt very much like she was having the final, over-lavish banquet aboard the *Titanic*. The waiter hovered, dawdled with the wine and listened, with a superior smirk on his face, which broadened as he caught on to the prospect of this collection of punters not being capable of paying their bill. Alan and Bernard and Serena pored over a pocket calculator so tiny that they could hardly read the figures, and Jenny heard Alan complain that it was useless, it was solar powered and running down. You'd think, she mused to herself, that a bunch of chartered accountants could either run to a proper state-of-the-art computer notebook, or be able to do the old-fashioned adding-up thing with a bit of paper and a pencil.

'We're late,' Daisy said, sprinting down the road and dragging Polly after her. It wasn't easy running in the boots, and her little toe on her left foot was already rubbing. By the end of the evening it would be raw.

'We're not. Parties are always dead boring at the beginning; nobody's there and nobody's drunk!' Emma shouted breathlessly, trying to keep up with her and having to stop and gather up her layers of ancient jumble-sale skirts. They were at the far end of Sophie's street, and could hear the music. Boys were loitering in the road, swigging from cans of beer which would later be kicked into hedges, and working themselves up to being offensively noisy. One of them called out to Daisy, jeering, 'What's that? Your kid?'

'Kid sister,' Emma called back.

'Shut up, Em!' Daisy hissed at her furiously. 'I don't want the world to know. I'm going to dump her as soon as I get inside.' She pulled crossly at Polly's hot little paw to hurry her up. She'd wanted to get there early, before some other girl, one of the slaggy, done-it-all sixth-formers probably, moved in to get off with Oliver. He'd think by now that she wasn't coming.

Sophie had obliging and accommodating parents who had agreed that it would be nice for her to have a birthday party. Like all similar parents in the neighbourhood, they considered it scandalous that there was nowhere for teenagers to go at night that didn't involve either breaking the law (pubs, clubs) or breaking the environment (the riverside, the Common). At least with parties they knew they were safely at someone's house, not risking a knifing hanging around in town, and if the party was at their own house they didn't even have to argue over who stayed sober enough to drive out into the 1 a.m. cold, police-patrolled Saturday night air to collect their child. So, refusing to go out and leave

Sophie alone to cope with gatecrashers and trouble, they trailed upstairs to camp unseen in the unused and underheated au-pair suite in the attic, with an ancient television and an Indian takeaway, turned up the volume and assured each other that everything would be fine. The guests were all nice children, from good schools, who had been taught a healthy respect for alcohol. They didn't fear drugs. Sophie had told them that only thick young kids sniffed glue, and had rather snootily laughed off the idea of Ecstasy 'only people who go to raves and wear orange lycra take Es,' she'd sniffed scornfully. If Sophie did run into any problems they would be safely there to deal with it, and if not, well they'd promised their anxious daughter that they wouldn't interfere, wouldn't terminally humiliate her by so much as showing their faces. The noises drifting up the stairs were what the optimistic parents hoped to hear; well-cared-for teenagers having a good time, laughing, a bit of squealing, lots of music (Jimi Hendrix – they smiled knowingly to each other, does anything change?), but no glass breaking, no screams, no roaring of boys indulging in excess-testosterone aggression. They settled themselves comfortably in the ancient pinewood and corduroy Habitat chairs, long abandoned from the first sitting-room they'd ever furnished together, and looked forward to watching, uninterrupted, a gloomy French film on BBC2.

Oliver and Ben were in the kitchen leaning against the fridge when Daisy walked in to get herself a drink. She completely ignored them both and simply helped herself to a bottle of K cider from the supply on the draining board along with, as an afterthought, a can of Coke for Polly, then left the room again.

'There you are,' Oliver bragged to Ben, 'told you she likes me. Lucky I came prepared,' he said, leering and tapping the top pocket of his denim jacket. Ben took a swig from his beer bottle and thought he preferred not to know about Oliver's contraceptive supply if it was going to be used on his sister, though it might come in useful if he got astoundingly, beyond-belief lucky with Emma. When, he wondered, would he be like Oliver and feel able to amble into any old petrol station and casually pick up a packet of Mates as if it was quite the natural thing to buy along with a Crunchie bar? When, please God, he thought, taking another large swig, would he need to?

Polly sat cross-legged underneath the desk in Sophie's bedroom and quickly finished her Coke. She knew she'd made an absolutely unbreakable promise to keep well out of the way and not be a nuisance, but surely she wasn't expected to sit there all night? She sat very still, thumbing casually through Sophie's diary and listened carefully as two boys sat on the bed and smoked a sweet-smelling joint, discussing how much Ben had been charging for it and whether they could get it cheaper from one of the dealers down on the estate. After they'd left the room she uncurled herself and wandered to the top of the stairs. Down below her through clouds of cigarette smoke, she could see that the house was now pretty well full. No-one would notice if she went down and found somewhere more interesting to be. She crept down and snaked her way through the mass of people. From a chair safely hidden behind a large frondy plant in the sitting-room, Polly could see Daisy being closely talked to by a boy with very dark hair and the kind of eyes that don't leave your face when they're talking. Daisy was smiling up at him, gazing intently back and looking, Polly thought, quite horribly soppy. He was probably telling her enormous lies about how wonderful she was. If he was, Daisy would believe every single word, so they'd probably be snogging soon and that would be something to report to Harriet. Polly was thirsty again but didn't want Daisy to catch her, so she looked around and found a bottle on the window ledge just behind her. It didn't seem to be anyone's, nobody pounced on her crossly when she picked it up and sniffed at it. It wasn't Coke, but it would do.

Ben was successfully squashed up against Emma in a corner of the dining-room. It wasn't dark enough for doing anything adventurous to her body, and there were too many people all squawking noisily around them and banging into them. The air was swirling and heady with cannabis fumes. The obvious thing would be to entice her up to one of the bedrooms. He felt his hands getting clammy at the thought, but he'd had a few courage-gathering drinks and could only ask, it was now or never. 'Shall we go somewhere quieter?' he whispered into her hair, despising himself for his corniness. He held his breath and waited for her to laugh in his face and tell him to drop dead.

'OK,' she whispered back unexpectedly.

Perhaps she hadn't realized what he meant. He took her hand and led her to the stairs, where an embarrassing number of sniggering people watched them go up together. Just at the bit where the stairs curved, Ben happened to glance back and into the sitting-room. What was Polly drinking from that bottle he wondered? She was Daisy's responsibility though, he decided, absolutely not his, not at a moment like this. It crossed his mind then that back in the kitchen just forty-five minutes ago, he should have thought to borrow a condom from Oliver. There really was just the most wonderful outside chance he might need one.

'So, are we so completely broke that we'll have to go without dessert?' Monica enquired cheerfully as Bernard snapped shut the calculator and started pouring more wine.

'Frankly, yes,' he said, though his face had an amused

233

and unconvincing look, as if he didn't really expect to be believed. Monica seemed to take that to mean 'Frankly, no' and continued to butter her bread roll thickly, but Alan was looking quite pale, and Jenny felt mildly aggrieved that the situation at work was obviously so much worse than he had been admitting, as if she was just a fluffy little wife who needed to be protected from such knowledge. Alan could be out of work and searching for a job this time next week, and he'd still be telling her not to worry about it. A serious career of her own should have been taken up a long time ago, not just dabbling in a spot of teaching from home as a kind of frill with which to add decorative extras to their family life. She prayed briefly that the sending out of her CVs would be fruitful. Just as the waiter put before her a plate of lobster ravioli, her stomach contracted at the thought of even more years of Polly's school fees. She didn't need a calculator to tell her that she and Alan were going to need (at current prices, and the fees went up annually) at least £33,600 to educate their third child, and that wasn't available from Social Security, so she added another quick prayer for Polly's exam results to yield a scholarship.

'. . . Well I suppose we'll have to draw straws for who has to give up their company car, ha ha ha!' Bernard was saying. Jenny watched Alan grin fawningly and felt annoyed. Was Bernard so close to retirement that he actually no longer cared? He must have some treble-protected multi-bonus pension scheme he was dying to get his hands on, she thought, but what about the rest of them? 'Bought Monica a little runabout, such a good wheeze, we use it all the time,' he said.

'Classic car,' Monica murmured through a mouthful of salmon ravioli.

'Oh yes? I've got one, an MG Midget; restored it myself!' Frankie told her proudly. Jenny could just imagine Frankie, all square in mechanic's overalls, hauling herself under a car with a big bag of spanners.

'Got her a Morris Traveller. Nothing fancy, moss in the joins and a spot of woodworm, but the insurance is a dream.' Bernard leaned across eagerly.

'Do it up and it's worth a fortune. I should know,' Frankie said.

'Ah, but that's the thing!' Bernard announced triumphantly. 'You qualify for Classic Car insurance, and if you do less than five thousand miles . . .'

'But whoever does?' Jenny asked.

Bernard looked round furtively and took a quick sip of wine before confiding, 'If you do less than five thousand, the insurance is absolutely down to peanuts. You simply *disconnect the clock*! Now isn't that a good old piece of accountancy advice for you? Free too!'

'It sucks,' said Frankie, in honest disgust. Jenny thought about the dingy used car lot at the back of the estate where the residents traded beaten-up Fiestas for beaten-up Escorts. Notices on each windscreen denied responsibility for the mileage on the cars' clocks, and Ministry of Transport officials checked it over on a regular basis, along with the police. The place seemed to be under constantly changing management. Eventually nice, trustworthy Monica would sell her priceless Morris. The ad would say something along the lines of 'careful lady owner, exceptionally low mileage' and her word would not be doubted.

There was a bit of a silence after that. Jenny watched Serena applying pâté to a tiny square of toast, her long, pink-polished, fingernails holding it delicately as if the harsh little crumbs might chip at her nail varnish. Jenny imagined those hands caressing her husband, wondered if even in the deepest thrashings of passion she handled Alan with such daintiness, fearful of damaging her manicure.

'And what do you do?' came a polite, social question from Frankie to Jenny.

'I teach flute – when I can get the pupils,' Jenny told her. 'At the moment I'm getting the impression that music lessons are among the little extras that get cut back when times are hard,' she sighed. 'It's the same in schools, sadly, the state ones can't afford the outside staff, and parents struggling to pay school fees can't afford lessons as well, so only the children of the super-rich are learning to play anything.'

'Must be getting like back in the historic days when music was purely an accomplishment for affluent young women,' Monica chipped in.

Frankie retorted sharply, 'Unless you were a man and were allowed to turn yourself into a genius composer. I always wondered why girls who showed prodigious talents like Mozart's were never encouraged too, then we might have some female composers of real substance as well. There must have been some surely.'

'Too busy putting in the necessary hours of embroidery and poetry-reciting I expect, preparing to catch a husband,' Jenny replied and then laughed. 'Plus, if any parent, governess or tutor could get a boy to sit still for more than ten minutes and get engrossed in one activity, they were probably only too happy to encourage them to stay there and get on with it. I know I would be!'

From across the table Serena leaned across and speared a slice of lemon from Frankie's plate. She sat sucking at it without wincing, listening to them laughing. 'That's what it was all about though, wasn't it?' she said suddenly, 'Learning to entertain a husband. It isn't much different now, really, there are still women out there – can you believe it? – who live off their husbands! Can you imagine not earning one's own living? Otherwise it's just prostitution!'

Jenny looked at her for signs of irony, but there was nothing but the expectation of approval on Serena's smiling, porcelain face. Monica was shuffling her napkin around and frowning. 'There are other important things beside earning a living in the financial sense. A husband's income can be shared with his wife for more than just sex,' Jenny said.

Monica beamed agreement, saying, 'Well yes, absolutely. There's children for one thing, and charity work once they're grown up. I'd have thought you feminists would value child-rearing as a valid occupation.'

Jenny thought for a minute and said, 'Also, it could be considered socially responsible to stay out of the job market if you don't really need two incomes. The most important thing there, surely, is that it's not just women who should be allowed that choice. Although not many families these days can exist on one income.'

Alan was watching her, she could feel his gaze and his attention on her. Frankie reached across her with a forkful of monkfish and Serena's cherry mouth opened to bite it.

'Mmmm. Adore it,' she murmured silkily. Frankie smiled lovingly at her friend and Jenny felt she'd been violently clouted by a sudden recognition. Frankie and Serena shared a lot more than just an apartment. Oh poor Alan, she thought, he clearly had absolutely no idea.

Polly was getting to like cider, even though it tasted a bit sour at first. It left a lovely sharp appley flavour in her mouth and made her feel happy, like when she was allowed champagne on family birthdays. Daisy and Oliver were somewhere in the blurry distance, interestingly entwined on a sofa. She'd tried creeping up and listening to what they said, to see if they were discussing sex, but Daisy had told her to sod off and go and find somewhere to sleep. Polly actually was quite tired now, but back on her chair when she closed her eyes the room seemed to lurch over her head, as if she was forever swooping backwards to the top of the big wheel at the fair. The music was too loud, and there was a constant buzzing of voices, pierced sometimes by the kind of shriek that wrenched her all the way back from the edge of sleep. She decided that perhaps she should go and find a quiet bed to lie on just for a little while, and crept up the stairs past a mass of gabbling girls who were talking about the best age for losing virginity. Polly knew she must be unbelievably tired; she didn't feel any real urge to hang around and listen to them like she normally would, but just continued up, holding carefully onto the banisters as the fairground feeling whirled along with her even when she was walking around.

'Ben!' she called into Sophie's bedroom, 'are you in there? I'm tired! Is it nearly time to go home?' No-one answered, so she tip-toed across the dark room to the bed, climbing onto it and looking forward to nestling into a pile of coats that people had left there.

'Polly! Will you get off!' Polly thudded heavily on to the floor and looked up at Ben and Emma, their blurry faces close together, peering down at her from the bed. They should have said they were there, hiding under the coats, why didn't they?

'Oh God, she's completely pissed! Where's Daisy?' Ben demanded grabbing Polly's wrists.

'Dunno. With some bloke downstairs,' Polly slurred back at him.

Emma switched on a bedside light and Polly's curiosity flickered briefly alive again as she noticed her fumbling about under her shirt and refastening her black lacy bra. That would be something else to tell Harriet, was her last waking thought.

'Should we get Sophie's parents, do you think?' Downstairs, Ben watched a furious Daisy unwrap herself from Oliver on the sofa. Oliver grinned lazily up at him and winked.

'Don't be stupid, Sophie would kill us. And then they might tell our parents too,' Daisy growled at him. 'We'll just have to take her home and put her to bed.'

'I don't think she can walk,' Emma pointed out, looking to where Polly sat propped against the stairs, her head lolling like an old rag-doll's on her chest.

'Then Ben will have to carry her,' Daisy snapped. She bit her lip and tried to think quickly about how much money she had with her. A taxi would be the best thing, especially as her poor toe hurt more than ever, though a driver might refuse to take Polly in that state. Suppose she was sick all over the cab? And maybe it was illegal for Polly to be that drunk, he might tell someone and there might be police trouble again. And it was nearly midnight, so they'd get charged more.

'We'll all go. Shouldn't be too difficult if Ben and I support her.' Oliver took charge, in the hope that he would earn enough gratitude from Daisy to take him right on to fourth base next time they got together, or even on to a home run. There wasn't a lot of progress to be made anyway, lying on a very public sofa with people falling, dancing and yelling all around them, though the signs had been extremely promising.

Daisy, Oliver, Emma and Ben tried to look casual and unobtrusive as they walked Polly down the road towards home, terrified that marauding police with nothing better to do at midnight would stop and ask what they were up to. Ben and Oliver took an arm each, and Polly's unco-ordinated feet hardly needed to touch the pavement. Her tousled head flopped up and down and she moaned quietly and constantly. By the time they got to the end of the Close, Daisy was limping painfully, her little toe now rubbed down to what felt like the bone. She was sure it was bleeding all over the inside of her lovely boot, and that her foot was sliding around in a puddle.

'You should have asked Sophie for a plaster,' Emma told her, holding her arm and helping her to walk.

'I know, I know. Hang on a sec, I'll take them off. I can't stand it any more, and I'll do better without them,' she said, plonking herself down onto the kerb. So when Carol and Paul Mathieson drove the Peugeot carefully and soberly round the corner by Sue's house they immediately came across the sight of Daisy sprawled on the pavement inspecting her foot, Polly slumped against the fence leaning on Ben, and Oliver and Emma sharing the lighting of a cigarette.

'Are you all right? Is there anything we can do?' Carol asked politely, looking at Daisy's exposed foot.

Polly stiffened suddenly and sat up. 'I feel really sick,' she wailed. Ben looked at Daisy, and they both looked at Carol, all telepathically agreeing that they couldn't even think of taking Polly home in that state, whatever the consequences.

Chapter Sixteen

Paul was astounded. If he wasn't absolutely certain that she'd only had one small sherry in the interval, he'd have thought Carol was quite paralytic. Taking all these people into the house at this time of night! Whatever was she thinking of?

Carol was being briskly practical, even in her silk frock. The child was clearly very drunk, and the teenagers didn't seem to have a clue what to do with her. They just skulked against the wall and draped themselves uselessly over the banisters. And they were so big. 'It might be better if she is actually sick,' Carol told Daisy. 'That way, she might not feel so dreadful tomorrow, and at least some of the alcohol will be safely out of her. It's really quite dangerous for her to be in this state.' Daisy and Ben stared, ashamed, at the hall rug. Carol bustled Polly into the downstairs cloakroom and propped her up against the sink. 'Paul, go and get a large glass of warm water will you?'

No 'please', he noted sorrowfully, automatically going to the kitchen to do as he was told. She'd been in such a good mood too, after *Charley's Aunt*, chatting away in the car and hinting that it would be nice to be home, in the warm. To their warm bed was where he'd planned to take her next, till they'd come across this rabble in the road.

'Are you going to give her salt water?' Emma asked Carol, trying to take an intelligent interest.

'Definitely not! That could kill her, the salt gets through to the kidneys before you know it and she

241

could die of dehydration. Don't ever make that mistake,' Carol told her. Emma moved closer to Daisy for comfort, and they went and sat on the stairs together, Daisy rubbing her bleeding toe and hoping it wouldn't drip on the beige carpet. She put her hands over her ears as Polly started vomiting noisily.

'Won't your parents be home by now?' Paul asked Ben. 'Wouldn't it be best if your own mother took care of her?'

Where had they taken her, he wanted to ask, they all smelt of a sordid party, the wafts of stale cigarette smoke and alcohol that were coming from them all. Surely they could have taken better care of Polly than this? Daisy was definitely off Marcus and Sebastian's babysitting list.

'Don't be silly, Paul,' came Carol's voice. 'They don't want Alan and Jenny to know about this. There's no need for them to. After all, I don't think this is likely to happen again, is it?' She put her head round the cloakroom door, pink fluffy towel in hand and gave Daisy a surprisingly conspiratorial grin.

Ben was shocked. Carol had always seemed so prissy, so rule-bound. He wasn't sure he liked her like this. He'd been waiting for her to start the telling-off. He liked to rely on her unchanging staidness, the certain knowledge that there was a 100 per cent guaranteed no chance at all of seducing her (or better still, of her seducing him). That way the impossible fantasies stayed exciting.

She needs the boys home more often, Paul thought as he watched Carol fondly and tenderly stroking Polly's damp hair away from her unfocused eyes and flushed face. Something to take care of that isn't just me and those bloody cats. He sighed and went up the stairs, wondering if it was worthwhile switching on the electric blanket; Carol only liked sex in a pre-warmed bed, otherwise she shivered and found it impossible to loosen up, and complained that her feet stuck out of the duvet edges and got cold. He passed the bedroom door and went on up to his attic. He might not be allowed actually to tell Alan and Jenny about their dreadful children, but it couldn't possibly go unreported in the files. It was an Incident, it had Happened. He took down the yellow folder (number 14, Collins) and sat down at his tidy desk, sorrowfully conceding that this was the only kind of entry he was likely to be making that night.

Outside the restaurant, Jenny handed Alan the car keys and he gave them straight back.

'Look,' she said quietly, unlocking the car and giving final goodbye smiles to Bernard and Monica who were loading themselves into their ancient Morris Traveller, 'I don't want to have a silly argument in the car park, with everyone standing around saying goodbye, but I really think I'm too much over the limit to do the driving.' Alan slid into the passenger seat, saying, 'We should have sorted it out earlier. I thought we had and that it was your turn. I'm over the limit too, and if I lose my licence, well . . .'

'Are you saying that it's less important if I get banned for a year than if it's you?' Jenny argued, thinking of all the school runs that could no longer be done, the Sainsbury's bags that would have to be lugged home on the bus with all the tartan-trolley old age pensioners, the impossible last-minute pleadings from Daisy and Ben, '*Please* Mum, I said I'd meet Emma at 5 and it's gone that already.' Who else was there to do all that? And did any of them really matter? Other people got by.

'No, it's not that, I'm terribly tired, though,' Alan said feebly, leaning his head against the cool, misted side window. 'And anyway, you're a better driver than me.'

'Flattery,' she growled. 'OK, I'll drive, but I'm not happy and it'll take ages. You'll have to talk to me, keep me awake.'

Jenny swung the car out into the unlit road and tried to see beyond the headlights just where the road went. Alan, already half-asleep, grunted, and she reconciled herself to a long journey in which she had to drive and talk to herself.

'Funny, isn't it,' she said to Alan's inert body. 'People like us do this all the time, think they're just about OK, and take the risk anyway. Kids from the estate nick cars and drive around in them and the police treat them as if they're handling a murder-weapon. Which they are. But then so are we. We get fines and a ban for a while and they get Care and detention centres. It only really hits us in the insurance premiums in the long run, but they are probably made permanently unemployable.'

'Mmm,' Alan murmured, not really listening. He was still thinking about Serena being whisked away from the restaurant in Frankie's immaculately renovated MG. If he'd taken Serena out in something sporty like that, instead of the sensible BMW, perhaps she'd have admired him as a bit more dynamic, more thrusting. All the years he'd despised the sort of men who bought cars as sexual power symbols, assuming they were making up for inadequacy, but perhaps, now that he was middle-aged and lacking any other visible sexual totems, he could concede that they had a point.

Jenny drove carefully, though not so slowly as to draw unwelcome attention to the car. At every turn she expected to be chased by a flashing blue light. Alan snored gently beside her, dreaming, she imagined, of pretty, slender bailiffs with sleek, dark hair tied up in silk scarves. She glanced at him, wondering how a man who could so ably support his family (so far) could prove to be this dense about a woman. Love may be blind, as they say, but infatuation must also be incredibly short-sighted. Poor Alan, she thought, would it eventually be any consolation when he found Serena did not fancy him to know that she didn't fancy anyone else who happened to be male either? At least that way he wouldn't take the rejection personally, which was a shame, Jenny thought, rallying a spot of malice. Being snubbed was the very least a potentially cheating husband deserved.

Slumped unprettily beside her, Alan twitched occasionally, like a sleeping cat, and she marvelled at the way he could simply cut out, like a torch, once he had made sure someone else was doing the worrying for him. As she passed the estate and pulled in to the Close just after 1.30, Jenny saw a light in her attic go out. Ben, she assumed, home from the party he'd been going to and reading on into the night. She hoped he'd had a good time.

'Daisy, I'll collect you from school and we'll go straight to the police station from there,' Jenny said over breakfast on Monday. 'And Polly, are you sure you feel all right now?'

Jenny put her hand on the child's forehead, but there was no sign of a fever. There hadn't been yesterday either, which had been surprising, for Polly had spent the whole day lying on her bed with the curtains closed, cuddling her old panda and saying that she felt too sick to eat.

Alan had said he smelled cigarettes on her hair and thought that Daisy, bored with babysitting on Saturday night, had let Polly have a go at smoking. 'Good thing it's made her feel so ill,' he'd decided. 'She won't want to try it again.' Jenny wasn't so sure he was right in either assumption, and annoyed poor suffering Polly by making her move her head up and down every hour or so, checking in case what she had actually got was the dreaded meningitis. Daisy had spent the day skilfully avoiding both parents, doing unusual amounts of homework in the sanctuary of her room, and going out to Emma's for lunch. But on Monday morning, Polly was looking pale but better, and the mysterious illness wasn't going to stop her going back to school.

'I don't mind if you have a day off,' Jenny told her. 'You might be sickening for something.'

'Just sickening, more likely,' Ben said.

'Perhaps there's something going round. Daisy, are you all right? It's so warm in here you can't possibly need that scarf.'

Polly ignored Ben's comment but was adamant that she had to go back – there was a maths test that she couldn't miss. Daisy, unloading the dishwasher, her neck swaddled in one of Jenny's favourite cashmere scarves, snorted in disbelief. 'You want to go back for a *test*? Are you mad?'

Polly gave Daisy a very intense look and said slowly, 'Not *just* for the test. I need to see Harriet.' Daisy went pink and pulled the scarf a bit tighter.

'Do I have to go and see the police in my school uniform Mum?' she asked. 'Can't I come home and change first?'

'No, sorry, they said 4 o'clock, and it's the only way not to be late. And besides,' she added with a look that left Daisy easily guessing what was coming, 'it's a good idea to look like a person who is normally quite responsible, as if this was just a one-off behaviour lapse. If you dress in your usual stuff, complete with boots, they'll think you're a born troublemaker and that this is just the first of many times they'll be seeing you.'

'OK, OK,' Daisy said, sighing mournfully. 'I'll make sure they think I'm Miss Goody-Goody of the year. Just so long as you all get off my case.'

Jenny went to hug her, and Daisy, rather stiffly, submitted to being touched. 'It's only that they don't have a lot of imagination. And people tend to be snobs: they'll recognize that uniform and expect you to be law-abiding,' Jenny told her. 'If you go along looking like a rebel and a problem, they won't see beyond that. They don't have the time and they don't know you like we do. Present them with a nice-girl image and they'll leave you alone. It's easy.' Daisy nodded and went to get her school bag. Perhaps it wouldn't be such a bad day, perhaps she'd see Oliver during the lunch break. Then she could show him the marks he'd made on her neck and ask him to be a little bit more careful next time.

Polly couldn't say much in the car. Jenny was listening to *Today* and concentrating on the traffic, but Polly knew better than to start telling Harriet about Saturday night. Mothers always knew when there was something interesting to tune in to, and not just in terms of radios. Harriet easily got the message that there was some information worth waiting for from the way Polly was pulling faces and whispering cryptic hints to her. At school, the moment they were out of the car Harriet pounced.

'What have you done, why are you making important faces at me?'

'Wait till we're inside,' Polly said, hoping to collect a wider audience on the way in. She grabbed Harriet and pulled her into the school building, where they weren't really allowed to be till the first bell had gone. She hesitated at the door, looking round slowly and furtively, and thus making sure that six or seven of her more alert classmates had seen her and become interested enough to follow, then arranged herself above them on the staircase in the central hallway, where she could both tell all, and keep an eye open for the approach of teachers.

Fiona Pemberton, up on the staffroom landing, wasn't surprised to look down and see Polly Collins holding court on the staircase. The child had no trouble collecting an audience and had been a real star in the Christmas pantomime – all that dancing probably, she thought, though if the child was to continue into the senior department she would have to stop taking time off school for ballet exams. There was already quite enough showing-off in that family; Daisy's blue hair had already been noticed, and the executive staffroom decision made to ignore it. Polly's exam results had been unexceptional, a vivid imagination had been shown in her English essay (title: *Rabbit Robs The Riverbank*), but her maths had been dismal. The letters offering places had already gone out, but Polly was on the Borderline and Siblings List, and decisions as to the last-minute offers were to be made that day. They tried to include little sisters, however dense, where possible. Fiona lingered by her office door, in practised headmistressy silence, pretending she was only casually overhearing what Polly said.

'So by about midnight I was really drunk!' Polly was saying. 'Totally pissed! It was really good. And when I was in the bedroom I breathed in loads of dope, so I was *well* out of it . . .' Fiona gasped, clutching the sheaf of exam papers to her thudding bosom. She peered over the banister rail, just to double check she was hearing the right person. It seemed hardly credible.

'Did you see any sex?' Harriet was demanding eagerly. Fiona held her breath and waited in dread for the reply.

'Not exactly. Though Daisy's friend Emma was under the coats with Ben, and her bra was undone in the dark,' came a slightly disappointed voice which soon cheered up again as she then proclaimed loudly, 'But there was *loads* of the oral sort!' Fiona fled swiftly back into her office, collapsed with shock into her Parker-Knoll recliner and therefore missed Polly going on to say with enormous authority, ''Cos really you know, mostly they just *talk* about it.' The audience was enthralled, just as Polly had intended them to be. Her headmistress, however, who had thought that in her fifteen years of running the school she could no longer be surprised by what she saw and heard, was now quaking by the telephone, barking an abrupt message to her secretary, demanding an immediate call to the Collins parents, requesting them to make an appointment as soon as possible to come into school and see her about Polly's future.

Just enough money had been raised to bail out the firm for the next quarter. The rent on the building was now astronomical, as if the recession had never happened. 'Cuts will have to be made' was the catchphrase echoing round the building, and staff looked at each other shiftily, calculating who would be the first to be asked to leave as an economy measure. One of the measures, reflected Alan, should perhaps be a move away from the prestigious W1 address to a cheaper post code. Surely the clients would appreciate their accountants making the kind of money-saving measures that they were always being ordered to make? He put this to Serena during a break between client meetings.

'What do you think?' he asked, as he dealt with the coffee machine in his office. 'Do you think they'd leave us in droves just because of a move, say, from Mayfair to Mortlake?'

To his dismay, Serena's face crumpled into misery. 'It won't make any difference to me where you all go,' she sniffed tearfully, fumbling in her pocket for a tissue. 'I was the last in, so I'll be first out. And I haven't even finished my training.' The sniffing crescendoed into sobs and Alan, as he would for any woman, he justified later, went automatically to comfort her. He wrapped his arms round her trembling body and held her close to him, patting her gently, and softly muttering the appropriate soothing words. He could feel bones as Serena's sobbing ribcage rose and fell under his hands. A small sly devil in his head made him quickly check the doorway for anyone looking, before stroking her more urgently. She smelled of hyacinths, and he inhaled the heady perfume blissfully, nuzzling close to her neck. Romantically inclined, he would ideally have chosen a better venue than his dusty office, with its tired cream walls badly in need of fresh paint, and neglected, yellowing Yucca plant, for Serena to fall weeping into his arms. Blake's hotel would have been good: dark and expensively sensuous, or perhaps a patch of ancient English woodland on an icy-bright, golden autumnal day. Meanwhile, Serena was still crying, so he crushed her closer to him, feeling all the length of her long slim body pressed against him. He no longer cared who saw them and he sighed ecstatically as his hand travelled down her back and slid up again, under her loose silk shirt till he encountered warm bare flesh.

'What the hell are you doing?' she barked at him, somehow, suddenly, half-way across the room. 'You were *touching* me! *Groping* me! How *dare* you!'

Alan stood awkwardly, backed up nervously against the wall between two framed gold discs, not knowing what to do with his hands. 'Er, sorry . . .' he mumbled limply, 'I thought . . . it's just that I thought . . .' He didn't know what he thought, not really. He'd thought she fancied him, but now it seemed so unlikely, so ridiculous that he couldn't even begin to tell her that.

'You *thought*? No you didn't, you just *assumed*. You *assumed* that because I'd gone out to a couple of pubs with you that I was willing to leap into bed. I'm not. I don't leap into bed with men at all, actually.'

'Sorry,' Alan mumbled inadequately, trying to work out what she'd meant.

Serena glared at him, recovering and considering and then said slowly, 'Sexual harassment, that's what it is. When I have to leave here, *if* I do, it's going to be with an awful lot of compensation for this!' She was almost spitting the words at him. Alan was recovering his balance, and something told him that she'd more than slightly over-reacted, hadn't she? Or was she right? Was sexual harassment a criminal or civil offence? Why had he never bothered reading about such cases in the papers, as if they could never involve him? Serena slammed the door hard as she stalked out of the room and as he shivered in the resulting draught, he wondered who she'd gone to tell first, her uncle Bernard, or the entire office full of younger staff where her desk was. Either way, Alan was in major trouble. He sat at his desk and hid his mortified face in his hands. He could still smell Serena's perfume, and wished he could shoo it out of the room and out of his life. Jenny would find out now, and hate him. And nothing had happened. Nothing ever happened. There was going to be all this trouble, for absolutely lousy rotten bugger-all. He wished he'd never gone into accountancy after all. If things like this could happen, what was the point of ever having relinquished his daydreams and gone like a good, careful boy for what he'd counted on as the safe option? He reached into the rubbish bin for his discarded copy of *Accountancy Age* and disconsolately started looking for a new job.

*   *   *

Up at the Tennis Club, Sue and Jenny finished their free sample Step Aeorobics (low impact) class and went to treat themselves to a gossipy fifteen minutes in the jacuzzi before conscientiously tackling a ten-length swim. The club was crowded with women concentrating hard on the serious business of making the best of themselves, dutifully toning their bodies in order to keep their husbands and lovers interested and to continue fitting into a size 12. The gym was humming with expensive machinery, and the thwacking sound could be heard of tennis enthusiasts over on the indoor courts, practising their fiery backhands against a ball-machine, or, in a couple of lucky cases, the well-muscled club professionals. Less athletically inclined women were queuing to discover disappointingly that the 'French' option in the beauty salon was merely a way of applying nail polish.

'Well, I'll not be doing that again,' Jenny said from the changing cubicle. 'If I want to get fit jumping about on steps I can always Hoover the stair carpet more often.' She wondered how imbecilic the class must have looked to a passing casual observer, a bunch of too-rich women hopping up and down on toy-like, primary coloured plastic blocks in time to music. No wonder some of those young mothers with over-loaded prams she saw disappearing into the high-rises on the estate looked so scrawny: one week of the lift being out of action would shift more kilos than several hundred pounds' worth of these silly exercises. Exhausted nevertheless, she peeled off her leotard and squeezed into her swimsuit, wondering if any of this could at least guarantee that she wouldn't have to give in and buy a larger size next spring.

The pool was steaming gently, and was hectic with the flailing limbs of small children as yet too young for either the Froebel or Montessori nursery schools, all wearing orange arm bands and having swimming lessons with their eager mothers.

'Come on now Tamsin darling,' called one of them in weary exasperation, 'we'll do it together. Ready? Now – one, two, three and UNDER!' Jenny watched, remembering doing exactly the same with each of her three, as Tamsin's mother held her nose and bravely ducked under the water, coming up with a face full of tangled blonde hair, running mascara and a disappointed frown. Tamsin, still dry-headed, all of three years old and sucking her thumb, bobbed up and down at the edge of the pool, smirked triumphantly at her mother and shouted, 'Your face is all black paint!'

'Poor thing,' Sue said as they padded past towards the jacuzzi, 'glad all that's behind me,' she said and then added mysteriously, 'and yet, who knows? Maybe it isn't.'

'What do you mean by that?' Jenny challenged her as they lowered their over-stretched bodies into the churning cauldron. She had a sideways glance at the only other jacuzzi occupant, a sunbed-tanned young mother obliviously reading *Hello!* magazine while her eye-make-up trickled down her cheeks from splashed droplets of water. 'Are you pregnant?'

'Not yet!' Sue said with a broad grin. 'It's going to be first things first. I've been dying to tell you. I'm getting married!'

'*Married?*' Jenny squawked. 'God, whatever for? And whoever to? The new one?'

'Of course the new one!' Sue said, languidly stretching out a leg from under the water to see if it needed waxing again. 'And don't go telling me I've only known him five minutes. I know all that. At my age, our age I should say, we should be able to tell gold from goldfish at a glance.'

'Odd saying,' Jenny said, puzzled. 'When is it to be?'

'Saturday after next, we've got a special licence,' Sue told her. 'Like I said, why hang about? The only reason for delay would be if I couldn't find a suitable outfit, but I've got a neat little sexy suit lined up at Whistles, they're altering it for me right now. Collect it Monday, marry in it Saturday. Party at my place in the afternoon. Whole street welcome. Simple as that.'

'Breathtakingly! He must be pretty wonderful. Who is he?' Jenny demanded. 'And where will you live? You won't be moving away, will you?' She felt suddenly anxious, worried that she was about to lose the only friend she could rely on both to behave as badly as she did and never to judge her.

'Ah. Now there's a thing. You know him, in fact you could say I met him through you,' Sue said, with a wary grin and suddenly staring with great and suspiciously guilty interest at the foaming water. 'He parked his car outside my gate, and I just happened to be on my way out, and, well, there it is.'

Jenny could almost hear the cogs in her brain slowly grinding round as she reluctantly made her way to the truth. 'Oh God. I don't believe it. You've nabbed David the Welshman. No feet. But he came to see me the other day!'

'Yeah, well he likes you!' Sue said blithely. 'I told him it was all right, after all I didn't know at first if it was going to last.' She looked worried. 'You don't mind, do you? I mean with you it *was* only for the money, wasn't it?'

The copy of *Hello!* fluttered and moved interestedly, and an astounded streaky face peered round the edge. Jenny giggled, and said deliberately loudly, 'No, it's not a problem. It was purely business. I hope you'll be very happy etc. etc. I'm just surprised, that's all. Well, amazed really. I didn't think people bothered to get married any more.'

'Oh well, deep down, he's very old-fashioned, you know. Like me,' Sue told her, laughing at her own absurdity.

The two women climbed out of the turbulent jacuzzi and started the lazy up-and-down swimming that passed for exercise in the warm pool. The mothers and toddlers had left, relieved to have successfully filled the dragging few hours between their au pairs going to English classes and lunch. Once she was reassured that Sue wasn't intending to move house, but instead move David in with her (so handy for the rehab. unit up at Roehampton), Jenny started to wonder if it was going to be a problem, having, only yards away up the road, a man on whom she had actually performed fellatio in exchange for folding money. They would meet constantly, there would be suppers and barbecues and Christmas parties and sundry opportunities for all the indiscretions that could be blurted out wherever too much drink was available. With any luck, though, David would have similar lurking fears about Jenny, and they could co-exist in a state of truce, each holding hostage to their wicked little piece of knowledge, and hope they never came to bitter territorial wrangles over road-widening, tree-lopping, or Close residents' planning applications.

'Look at that.' Sue swam alongside Jenny at the shallow end, and pointed to the jacuzzi. The *Hello!* woman was still there, but the magazine was damply abandoned in a puddle beside her. She lay stretched out on her front in the steaming bubbles, her head resting on her folded arms on the poolside, eyes closed and her mouth opened slightly. Like a dreaming child, oblivious to all around her, she was making small sighing noises, her face busy expressing little bolts of pleasure.

'See that? You do understand about David don't you Jen? I don't want to end up like that, reduced to having lonely sexual experiences in a public jacuzzi.'

Jenny giggled. 'Oh I don't know,' she teased, 'doesn't look all that bad to me. Perhaps after this swim . . .'

Chapter Seventeen

When Jenny collected Daisy from school, it was hard to tell which of them was the more nervous. Daisy skulked quickly into the car in case anyone saw her being ignominiously picked up by her mother, and slumped in the passenger seat, peeling and chewing the skin round her thumbnail. Jenny, with the uncomfortable feeling that Big Policeman already had his eye on her, drove cautiously, stopping for extra long moments at road junctions, and using her indicators far too early, as if she was on a driving test. Daisy still had the scarf wrapped snugly round her neck, chilled, Jenny assumed, by the idea of having to go and say her piece to the police. The blue hair was neatly tucked away under it, at least, so that was something. Jenny herself, with her long-standing dread of being given the once-over by a judgmental inspector who fancied himself as a domineering TV cop, could still smell chlorine from the pool. By the time she and Sue had breast-stroked their ten lazy lengths, she hadn't had time to rinse it off her hair, and it gave off reassuring wafts, reminiscent of purifying disinfectant.

Waiting in the reception area for the impossibly young desk sergeant to go and find the inspector, Jenny had another look at Daisy to make sure she was presentable. It was hot, and the orange plastic chairs were against a bubbling and gurgling ancient radiator, the huge and curvy sort that reminded Jenny of infant schools. The walls were painted bright, cheery yellow, as if to counteract the feelings of apprehension and fright that must pervade the place and its visitors.

'It's baking in here,' Jenny complained, waving her hand in front of her face to make a breeze. 'Daisy you'd better take that scarf off or you'll faint.'

'I'm OK, really. Don't fuss,' Daisy said, kicking at the floor and rocking backwards and forwards nervously. Jenny got up and wandered round, reading all the posters on the walls: a big bright cartoon one reminding children about locking their bikes and getting them post-coded, a slightly malevolent one about the benefits of Neighbourhood Watch and another inviting anyone over 5′4″ (and presumably without a criminal record) to do their bit and join the Specials. She resolved to suggest it to Paul Mathieson, then perhaps it would take his mind off trying to root out imaginary criminal goings-on in the Close.

The noise of Daisy scuffing her feet rhythmically on the floor stopped suddenly as she got up and started pacing the room.

'Won't be long now,' Jenny reassured her. 'I can't think what's keeping them, it's way after four. Try not to worry.'

'Not worried,' Daisy snapped. 'Just can't stand the noise that radiator makes. It reminds me of Ben's tummy in the mornings.'

Jenny could hear booted feet returning heavily along the corridor. 'Looks like they're ready for you,' she said. Daisy looked hot, and the thought crossed her mind that the poor girl really might actually keel over. They'd just have to put up with the blue hair. Whatever did it matter, really? 'Here let me take this,' she said helpfully, reaching for the scarf before Daisy could stop her.

'No!' Daisy squealed, hands clutching, but it was too late, and Daisy stood in front of the sergeant and inspector brazenly revealing not only the blue-tipped hair but

258

also a scarlet string of huge and hectic love-bites round her otherwise pale, slim neck.

'Oh God,' breathed Jenny as Daisy shot her a look of pure venom. 'You'll probably get Life.'

What Daisy got was a good telling off for cheating British Rail, nothing else. She was to stay out of trouble for ever more, or at least till she was eighteen, when her record would be destroyed and her crime deleted from the computers. ('Oh sure,' Daisy had mumbled when this was explained to her.) The inspector wasn't there to inspect her sex life, and besides there wasn't much he hadn't seen before. A row of hickies on a nine-year-old neck would have been something to worry about, but Daisy was nearly fifteen, and whatever else were teenage years for if not the chance to go around showing off their over-active hormones? Nevertheless, as Daisy slumped out of the police station with her anxious mother, the inspector felt glad relief that he and his wife had only produced sons.

'How could you?' Jenny said to Daisy in the car. 'Whatever do you think you look like? And who is he and when was it?' The two avoided looking at each other, Jenny concentrating hard on driving home as fast as was safely possible, glad that her eyes could not be drawn to the livid vivid marks of passion on her daughter. Daisy was more worried about Jenny finding out about Sophie's party than anything else, and had to invent quickly.

'I'm going out with someone. Have been for ages,' she quickly spat out her lie. 'Sometimes we see each other in school lunch breaks.' She stared out of the window, disgustedly watching a lone man picking his nose in the next car. 'He's at school with Ben, one of his friends,' she added slyly, making a bid to get round Jenny on grounds of snobbery. The boys at Ben's school were what the Close would collectively consider 'suitable'.

'Goodness, I don't mind who you go out with, or what you do, as long as you're careful,' Jenny told her more gently. 'You know that. But those marks! They're so, well, so . . .'

'Common?' Daisy bravely and loudly challenged. 'You don't mind what I do so long as nobody knows?'

This was something uncomfortably like the unpalatable truth, and Jenny pushed it out of her mind as she squeezed the car through the weary rush hour traffic and across a snarled-up road junction with faulty traffic lights.

'Disfiguring, that's the word,' Jenny finally came up with. 'And so blatant. Haven't the staff at school noticed? Whatever will they think of you?'

'Don't care. And no, no-one's noticed. That's what the scarf's for.'

Well that was something, Jenny thought, at least Daisy knew when to cover things up. They were home now and Jenny rushed in to the house to see if Alan had left any news about the office on the answerphone. There was just the brief message form Fiona Pemberton's secretary, requesting Jenny and/or Alan to make an appointment about Polly. The secretary had an infuriatingly apologetic voice, almost as if she was afraid she would offend even by so much as breathing down Jenny's phone. 'It's *vis à vis* Polly,' she'd whispered, adding ludicrously, as if Jenny would need reminding, 'Your daughter. In form four.'

'I'll call them in the morning.' Jenny pressed the off button and then called to Daisy, 'Defrost some of the chicken and do a salad will you please, Daisy, while I get Polly from Ceci's? Thanks!' she added, on the hopeful assumption that Daisy would have heard her.

At Ceci's there was a festive, celebratory air, as if it was someone's birthday. The front door stood wide open and as Jenny walked up the garden path, pushing her way through the overstocked borders of leggy lavender, she could see figures running about, criss-crossing the hallway in a flurry. Ceci, who was normally to be found being languid on a sofa while children were chaotic in another room, bounced excitedly to the doorway to meet Jenny. 'Did you get your letter?' she asked, her face split by a triumphant beam, her big round eyes sparkling with triumphant delight.

'What letter?' Jenny enquired, carefully bypassing the voluptuous tangle of clematis that was just about to flower around the doorway.

'School! The results! Harriet has passed – I can't believe it!' Jenny smiled, genuinely pleased for Harriet, but well aware that what Ceci would have really found hard to believe would have been her daughter's failure. Jenny hadn't had a letter from school that day. Did that mean Polly had failed her exam? They hadn't even considered what would happen if she did, and it was too late to apply anywhere else, even the local comprehensive. 'Oh yours will probably arrive tomorrow,' Ceci said kindly. 'Just a postal delay I expect.'

'I did get a phone call – Mrs P wants to see me. Strict orders, via the answerphone,' Jenny confided.

Ceci looked slightly miffed. 'Goodness, probably got a scholarship then, that's what it will be. We were hoping for one for Harriet, but we'll have to try for the assisted place scheme instead.' As they walked to the vast, walnut-and-wenge kitchen through the sumptuously decorated hallway, Jenny couldn't hide her amazement. Ceci's house had at least six bedrooms, plus nanny flat, there was a lavish swimming pool built into a conservatory extension, and Ceci's annual tan was given a kick-start every February in St Lucia.

'Assisted place?' Jenny asked incredulously before she could stop to think about being polite. 'How on earth could you swing that?'

Ceci smirked guiltily. 'Holiday cottage. You know the one in Wales? Told them that Howard has left me and lives there full time. I'm just a lone mother, you see,' she said with mock tragedy on her face, 'making ends meet on a teeny bit of maintenance . . .'

'But that's . . .' Jenny began.

'Not quite terribly 100 per cent honest? Oh darling, everyone's doing it! And I do put an awful lot of effort into charity work.' She tapped a petulant foot and said sulkily, 'Otherwise I'll have to get a job . . .'

Yes, you'll have to get a job, Jenny thought, like the rest of us. Though not quite like me, she amended hurriedly to herself. She couldn't quite see Ceci deglossing her lipstick round some paying customer's penis.

Alan was home early. As Jenny swung the Golf into the driveway she could see his BMW was parked neatly in front of the garage. (No quick getaways, no getaways any more at all, perhaps?) Alan was concentrating in the kitchen, doing something complicated with red peppers and fennel.

'Stinky fennel! Yuck!' Polly skipped around the room holding her nose dramatically. 'Can't I have spaghetti hoops?'

'I wonder if Raymond Blanc has this trouble,' Alan sighed dispiritedly.

Jenny was saddened by his disconsolate face. Polly could usually make him laugh, however dreadful the day had been. 'What happened at work? Did you all solve the cash flow thing?' she asked, fetching them both a rather early Budweiser from the fridge.

'Solved that. Not for the first time. Bernard's bloody useless. Couldn't run a bath, let alone a business,' Alan said, peeling his peppers and avoiding her eyes. 'But there's something else,' he glanced at Polly, then rather shiftily at Jenny and Jenny felt her heart thud and her insides tighten. This was going to be it. The moment she sent Polly off to watch *Neighbours*, he would be telling her something she absolutely wouldn't want to hear. Surely she'd been right about Serena, hadn't she? The love of Serena's life was Frankie, wasn't it? Not Alan? She felt herself crossing her hot, sticky fingers, childlike with nerves.

'Polly, you're about to miss *Neighbours*,' she said with just enough courage. Then it was just a matter of waiting and listening.

Alan made his humble confession in the conservatory facing Jenny across the cane table and a bowl of tulips, which were the colours of rhubarb and custard. Jenny picked her flute up from its stand and used her skirt to polish the mouthpiece, preferring not to watch Alan's face. He told her flatly what had happened in the office, using the same downbeat, depressed tones to describe both the financial crisis and his clumsy pass at Serena. '. . . So it looks like there will have to be cuts, and after the ridiculous, stupid thing I did it also looks like Serena won't be the one who has to leave. I think it's the only decent thing to do, really, don't you? Sort of honourable resignation?' This sort of formal pomposity didn't at all suit Alan, slouching in his tattiest old rainbow sweater at the table, picking guiltily at the falling tulip petals.

'Bit late to think about honourable and decent isn't it?' Jenny said waspishly. 'Whatever did you think was honourable and decent about cheating on me?'

Alan sighed and stared into his glass like a miserable old drunk. 'But I didn't. That's the point.'

'No it isn't. You tried to, and it hurts. *That's* the point. The fact that you failed dismally has nothing to do with it. If you'd succeeded, when, if ever, would you have told me? And what would have happened to us, to the family? What do you think will happen now?' Jenny snapped.

Alan stared at the table, like a caught-out schoolboy, shredding a fallen petal and choosing his words. 'It was just fantasy, something separate,' he said. 'I don't honestly know what I'd have done if she'd responded. Not very likely, though, was it? Be honest.' He looked up and stared at the blurry outline of himself reflected in the darkening windows and grinned ruefully, a sad hopeless grin, full of a new awareness of his own fading attraction.

'Not so very unlikely,' Jenny said softly, feeling his need for consolation and, from long and loving habit, sympathizing. 'You're not that gruesome. You are a fool though, Alan, did you honestly have no idea that she was a lesbian? Didn't you twig at that restaurant? Did she say nothing at all about her home life?'

'No, well not really.' Alan fidgeted with his glass, looking baffled. 'She'd mentioned the flat-mate. People have them. How was I to know?'

'Sexual harassment.' Jenny tried the words aloud. They sounded important. What would a tribunal think? According to Alan he had made one fumbled and ill-timed pass in his office, taking a sympathetic hug too far. There could be so much more to it than that, but, like any wife, she could either decide to know only what Alan chose to tell her, or torture herself with an imagined torrid version of her own. Jenny wondered what Serena's story would be. She'd find out for sure if Serena really did take things further. The cosy, homey aroma of Alan's cooking suddenly seemed nauseatingly cloying.

'I'm just going out,' she said, getting up so quickly that the tulips shed their remaining petals. 'Just round to Laura's. She's got the cheque for when we rented the kitchen for that breakfast cereal ad.' Already she was half-way out of the back door, gulping desperately

264

needed fresh air while Alan mopped at the pollen. 'Won't be long . . .'

Eventually, given time, Alan's minor transgression would all be forgiven, Jenny knew, because it was all too understandable, clichéd even. And if she wanted their life together to continue, the burden of getting over this would fall on her. Why were men so predictable? she wondered, crossly snapping off twigs of sprouting fuchsia and wisteria as she walked up the road. Whenever she read a magazine feature on the classic things that husbands did at certain stages of their lives, she tended to dismiss it angrily as stereotyped rubbish. After all, no-one was allowed to generalize like that any more about women, were they? And now here was Alan, having the kind of unimaginatively standard mid-life crisis that he could have copied from a manual. Perhaps it really was all there, the final chapter, an appendix in the back of his DIY book.

'Going somewhere nice?' Jenny was startled from her reflections by Paul scurrying to catch up, walking beside her.

'Just to Laura and Harvey's,' she said, not feeling the need to report to Paul exactly what her reasons for the visit were, but also feeling that he expected her to. She felt conscious of Paul next to her, his head bent round at a strange angle, like a zoo monkey peering round a tree stump, willing her to look at him. She allowed him a neighbourly smile, and wearily noted his odd expression, on the edge of wanting to tell her something, as if he knew something that she didn't know, and was dying for her to ask him to tell her. I'm not in the mood for asking, she thought.

'Carol was saying she hasn't seen you lately,' he said at last.

'No, well, busy life, you know,' Jenny answered,

glad to have reached Laura's gate. Paul stood by the gate, reaching over to unlatch it for her, determinedly gentlemanly, but groping awkwardly at the hinge side. She flicked at the catch and quickly opened the gate, Paul still beside her hovering awkwardly, as if not sure whether to unleash his secret or not. He reminded Jenny of Ben when he was little, quite unable to stop himself revealing what he had bought her for her birthday. Suddenly a loud, roaring groan came from inside Laura's house.

'Oh God, whatever's that?' Jenny said, peering, alarmed, at the lighted window. Suddenly a naked leg could be seen, kicking high and fast and disappearing just as quickly.

'Trouble!' Paul said decisively, sprinting up the path.

'No wait!' Jenny called, laughing. 'Suppose they're . . .'

At the front door, which Paul had unhesitatingly rung, the two of them heard more oohing and aahing. There was, Jenny had to admit, no doubt that this was pain, not pleasure. Unless they were one and the same to Harvey, who knew?

'The man said no-one's to come in.' The door had opened and a small girl in a Liberty smock stood blocking their way, solemnly repeating what she had been told to say.

'Is Mummy home, Emily?' Jenny asked the child.

'What do you mean "the man said"? Which man?' Paul demanded of the little girl, who promptly burst into frightened tears. 'Right that's it. I'm going in. Could be murder in there,' Paul declared, as if he was ready to storm the gates of hell.

'No Paul, wait,' Jenny said, grabbing his arm, but it was too late and with the groans and roars reaching a crescendo, and the sound of glass breaking, Paul flung open the door of the Benstones' sitting-room.

Laura emerged from the kitchen with Charlotte, a

smaller version of Emily, looking calm and serene, just as Jenny and Paul were taking in the scene on the polished wood floor. Harvey was lying on the floor on his front wearing only a pair of Fred Flintstone boxer shorts. His gingery-furred legs (which for a moment reminded Jenny of Biggles) were gathered up behind him and across them, forcing his weight onto Harvey's shoulders, was a delectably muscled young man in bulging purple cycling shorts but nothing else, scowling up at them crossly. It looked to Jenny like torture, and it also looked like the kind of torture people pay to enjoy, though surely not with the entire family also at home?

'Er . . . sorry to intrude,' Paul said, for once quite deflated.

'Emily!' yelled a blushing Harvey, his eyes rather glazed from effort. 'What did Jeremy tell you about coming in here?'

'T'ai chi massage,' Laura explained simply from behind Jenny. 'Terribly good for his back. All that sitting around typing does him no good at all. Have you come for your cheque?'

Back at home Jenny folded the cheque into her building society book and did a few additions. There was enough, she calculated, to keep the family for maybe a month if Alan was really suddenly unemployed, and together with savings and a couple of life insurance policies, there could be enough for Polly and Ben's school fees for the rest of the year, and perhaps even further. This was the moment for regretting that she'd been so insistent that Ben stayed on at his school to take A-levels, when he'd so much wanted to leave and go to the sixth form college. When it was Daisy's turn they'd let her. How casually she and Alan had committed themselves to finding the necessary eleven thousand extra pounds that the two years would cost! And what would Ben get at the end of it? Three good A-levels, exactly the same as he would have got free at the tertiary college. She looked out of the bedroom window, down the Close to where Mrs Fingell could be seen stuffing another of her newspaper-wrapped parcels into her dustbin. I must tell her about the bottle bank, Jenny thought. I don't mind taking them there in the car for her. Mrs Fingell looked up and waved to her before disappearing back into the house. Her sitting-room light was on, and the curtains open. Perhaps, Jenny reflected, retired tarts still liked to spend time sitting at lighted windows, remembering the bad but busy old days. She had a sudden rather sad mental picture of Mrs Fingell sitting under a red light with her skirt hitched up over her support-stockings, squinting at a knitting pattern as she turned the heel on a lemon bootee for her latest grandchild. She must visit her soon, Jenny thought, sensing loneliness along the road.

Fiona Pemberton had had years of practice at expelling pupils. She had collected quite a wide range of methods, all skilfully based on letting parents know, as if bestowing some kind of secret privilege, that they could do far better for their child than educate them at her school.

Alan and Jenny, dressed with the same sort of smartness they would have adopted if they'd been summoned to attend court, waited in front of Fiona's desk while she chose her words carefully, very much the headmistress and not at all the neighbour. Her office, inconveniently placed at the top of the school so that visitors arrived panting and wilting from climbing the two flights of stairs, was positively sumptuous compared with the tatty squalor of the rest of the building. Fiona had peaches-and-cream-striped wallpaper, a determinedly feminine shade of baby pink carpet that no over-nervous first-year would ever dare be sick on, and a framed array of the best of the sixth form A-level work. On shelves stood appealingly lopsided jugs, brightly painted ceramic plates and several clay cats on loan from the school pottery room. Jenny smiled expectantly, waiting to be told that clever Polly had achieved at least the school drama award, which would give her free extra speech and drama lessons and a guaranteed starring role in every school play for the next seven years. She tried to keep out of her head the vision of Fiona's husband haggling on her doorstep for sexual services.

Alan, gloomy about his future and confident only of disaster, was therefore less shocked than Jenny when Fiona began her well-rehearsed speech, both arms resting on the desk and her ample bust stacked firmly on top of her blotter.

'. . . abilities that would be far better catered for in a more artistic environment . . .' Fiona was saying, her face lengthened into her well-practised 'this hurts me more than it hurts you' expression.

'Polly will be quite a loss to the school, such a, er, lively pupil.' She stopped to sigh, as if this was on a well-learnt script, and continued with a decisive 'But . . .' just as Jenny was opening her mouth to protest. 'But it is our responsibility, our duty, to put the child first, even at the expense of losing one of our more colourful pupils. That is the creed upon which this school, and its consequent success, is based.'

Alan looked out of the window, watching cars whizzing through amber traffic lights, and wishing he was in one of them, heading perhaps for the distant wilds of Scotland, with just Jenny.

Fiona wasn't entirely without scruples, especially when she had to share the Close with these people, and had now moved on to the practical suggestions, leaning forward eagerly to sell her idea to Jenny and Alan. 'Polly will do reasonably well academically wherever she is. But the academic field is not where her main interests lie, as I am sure you know.' She paused to smile, waiting for them to agree that here was a headmistress who really understood her young charges, before delivering her chosen solution. 'Have you thought of a school for the performing arts? I happen to know the principal at . . .' and before Jenny could so much as ask a question she had reached down to scrabble in her desk drawer and handed over a large and glossy brochure featuring students on the cover dressed as the rude mechanicals from A Midsummer Night's Dream.

'Well, no, we hadn't thought of it, not at all,' Jenny told Fiona, surprised to find that she still had a voice to use, so dismayed as she was that they were having this conversation at all, and flicking obediently through the prospectus.

In what seemed like seconds, Jenny and Alan had been expertly dismissed, whirled down the staircase by the secretary and were out on the street wondering what to do with Polly for the next seven years.

'I wonder why Fiona wants Polly out. Do you think it's because of Daisy – worried that criminal behaviour runs in the family?' Jenny asked Alan.

'Possibly, Daisy's a bit wild, maybe. And Polly's reasonably bright but no genius. Perhaps the school is over-subscribed with Oxbridge hopefuls and there's no room for the good all-rounder.'

'Or in Polly's case, the slightly below average all-rounder.'

'Anyway, what do you think?' Jenny asked Alan, watching him glance through the brochure again as he walked back to the car. 'Do you think it's Polly's sort of thing? Hours of singing and dancing and drama and dressing up? Longer hours than regular school, too?' She waited for him to prevaricate, to pass the responsibility over to her, as it fell within the domain of home-and-family. Before, when the children had been at the school-changing stage, he had left everything to Jenny, telling her he was sure she would be better at making the right choices than he was, and so never having to endure the hectic scrums of open days. But then, with a decisiveness that surprised her, Alan looked up and announced with a broad smile, 'I think it's exactly Polly's sort of thing. She'll absolutely love it.'

Chapter Eighteen

What was it about weddings? As Sue and David exchanged their optimistic vows in the clinically pale green register office, Jenny dabbed at her eyes with a tissue and felt her eyeshadow dissolving. Daisy hissed a cynical 'Oh God, Mum,' secretly eager to impress Sue's younger son home from boarding school, and not wanting her embarrassing parents drawing the wrong kind of attention to her. Sue looked radiant, as a bride should, in cream silk moiré, pleased with herself and everything else. Her blue-rinsed mother in a lavender-and-pink flowered Queen Mother hat, beamed all round at everyone, delighted with her daughter, as if this wedding was Sue's first real one, and the other two had been merely insignificant trial runs. Outside in the mellow spring sunshine, the proud old lady roamed regally, waving an elegant kid-gloved hand at all the guests and mishearing all the introductions. 'A lady registrar!' she exclaimed loudly to Fiona Pemberton, perhaps recognizing equally queenly qualities. 'We haven't come across one of those before, have we Susan dear?'

Sue's new husband David, now successfully down to just one stick, had no trouble with the register office steps, and posed happily for photos in the formal garden along with most of the Close residents, Sue's pair of large sons, and a riotous selection of Welsh supporters who had arrived noisily by hired coach. The photographer set up his tripod, directed grudgingly by Paul Mathieson, who felt that, as owner of the precious Nikon and subscriber to *Amateur Photographer*, he should have been invited to do it.

'You've got to be in these as well, Jen. Got to have all the witnesses!' Sue called as Jenny stuffed her damp hanky back into her bag.

'In a bit, shove up close together!' the photographer ordered, and Jenny found herself squashed against David, smiling apologetically at him.

'That's a huge favour you did me,' he whispered to her as the photographer bustled about arranging people. Jenny felt her heart step up its beat rate and she just knew she was in for a dread lifetime of neighbourly embarrassment.

'No, I don't mean that!' he went on, laughing. 'No, I mean if it wasn't for you I wouldn't have met Sue! Best thing that ever happened to me, believe it.' His face, when he looked at Sue, was so unashamedly thrilled that Jenny could feel tears threatening to choke her again.

No-one had looked at her like that for quite some time. Alan had come pretty close the other night after he'd told her about Serena and the likelihood of losing his job, gratified, relieved probably that Jenny hadn't immediately told him to sling his rotten hook. But that sort of look, the David to Sue look, you didn't get that after years of murky marriage; it required some sort of naïve and joyful expectation somewhere.

'Smile everybody!' the photographer roared above the chat, and Jenny hoped that on the photos she wouldn't be the one who looked as dewy as a person with brand new contact lenses.

'Talking to Hugo the other day.' Laura, gliding like a tall-ship in many layers of expensively mangled butter-coloured silk, approached Jenny later at the reception which had spilled over into Sue's garden.

'He says to send love to your Polly and he'll be sending a rough-cut video of her advert any day now. She was awfully good, he says. Everyone adored her.'

'How sweet of him!' Jenny replied taking a glass of champagne from the wobbly tray carried round by Sue's younger son on leave from his famous public school, (and trailed at an admiring distance by Daisy, who liked his rarity value). 'Hugo might be interested, actually. We've decided to send Polly to a school that specializes in the performing arts. She's thrilled with the idea, can hardly wait for audition day.'

Polly could be seen across the garden, showing off her splits and cartwheels in her best dress to Sebastian and Marcus, who were enjoying frequent glimpses of her purple knickers.

Laura's face was arranged in a little questioning pout, her lips puckered amusedly, and then she smiled broadly as if she'd just unfathomed a riddle. 'Oh! I see, for a moment I thought you meant a stage school!' she trilled.

'Stage school? Who on earth is going to a stage school?' Carol Mathieson, forgetting to watch her powder blue suede high heels on the lawn, tripped into their conversation, spilling a fizzing trickle of champagne down the front of her navy blue sailor jacket. She waited expectantly to be told whatever news was going.

'All those lovely long-necked girls from the Royal Ballet school in Richmond Park,' Laura went on dreamily. 'They stand at the bus stop with their hair in neat little buns and their feet out in third position. *So* pretty. Polly *is* a lucky girl.'

Carol looked at them both expectantly and Jenny felt ganged-up on. 'She's not going to White Lodge,' she announced firmly. 'She *is* actually going to a stage school. And before you say anything, it isn't all hair in ringlets and constant auditioning to be the next

Milky Bar Kid.' I'm sounding defensive, she thought, voicing some of the prejudices she'd had herself only days ago. She caught sight of George Pemberton leering his approval at her from behind a tray of canapés. Fiona noticed and tweaked him viciously back to attention, ordering him to help do the rounds with the food. Jenny decided it was time to go and find someone else to talk to. She was also wondering where Mrs Fingell had gone. Sue had definitely invited her to the party, and she'd been there at the ceremony, exuberant in a cherry red hat. 'Sorry, must just dash back home,' she said to Laura and Carol, whose expressions were stuck in astonishment, as if she'd just told them that Polly had had her name down since birth for the nearest Young Offenders' Institute. Jenny retreated. 'Got to go and collect Sue and David's present. Didn't want to take it along to the register office with me. See you later.'

She picked her way carefully through the crush round the doorway, hearing as she went the unmistakable voice of Carol confiding to Laura '. . . teaching the pupils to speak frightfully badly, so they can get parts in *EastEnders* . . .' Just wait till Polly's the juvenile lead in some upmarket BBC2 period drama, she thought, or playing Juliet at 13. One day they'll be showing off that they've known her since she was this high.

Jenny walked carefully down the road in her favourite going out but-only-if-there's-somewhere-to-sit-down shoes. Could it be true, she wondered, as she tottered painfully up to the front door, that one's feet actually grew a bit as one got older? Surely a size 5 at age 23 was going to be still a size 5 at 42? She left the front door open, kicked off the shoes in the hall and, noticing the answerphone flashing at her, flicked the 'on' button. The tape was getting mangled and most of the message was lost, but Jenny heard just enough to catch the gist ('wondered about whether you felt up to taking on an entire boys' school ha! ha!'). 'Not today thanks!' she said to the machine, and switched it off abruptly. Hurrying now, she went into the kitchen to collect the present. Absorbed both in her blissfully released toes and in searching the dresser for the gift-wrap ribbon, she wasn't at first aware that anyone else had come into the house behind her.

'Thought I'd join you, having a little breather from the hordes,' a familiar voice said from the kitchen doorway. Jenny, startled, swore with anger as she trapped her hand in the drawer.

'George! Why are you creeping up on me like that?' she demanded crossly. 'You've got a nerve, following me here!' She actually felt quite alarmed. George was already drunk, swaying slightly, and his breath was gusting heavily. 'Thought while we've got a few minutes alone . . .' he said, looking her up and down slowly. Jenny backed nervously towards the conservatory, hoping to sidestep him as he followed her in and then make a dash for the front door. 'Wouldn't take long . . .' George said, with a rather desperate pleading note in his voice. He reached for the zip on his trousers, still keeping his rheumy old spaniel eyes on Jenny's face, hoping for some sort of expression of surrender.

'Not a chance, George,' she said firmly, then watched incredulous as he brought out from the baggy folds of his ancient special-occasion trousers a fully erect penis, all raring to go as if, *Blue Peter* style, it was one he'd prepared earlier.

'Cooee, only me!' came the hugely welcome (to Jenny) voice of Mrs Fingell from the front door.

'Bugger! The old witch!' George said, dashing, dick in hand, to the seclusion of the conservatory.

'You in here?' called Mrs Fingell as she came bustling along the hallway, opening and closing doors as she went. 'I saw the front door open,' she said as she reached the kitchen. 'Just popped home to see to the dog.' Then seeing Jenny propped feebly up against the Aga and looking pale, added, 'You all right? Seen a ghost?'

'No I'm not really,' Jenny confessed shakily. 'I was just in here getting some ribbon for the present and guess who followed me in?'

Mrs Fingell's face broke into a knowing smirk, but before she could voice her guess, a long, deep groan emanated from the conservatory. Whether it was a groan of agony or ecstasy was hard to tell, but Jenny, quailing at what sounded like the results of over-excitement, prayed she wouldn't have to go in there with a mop.

'Disgusting old man, following me here like that,' she said furiously. 'Stay there and I'll get him out and make him go away.' She strode angrily into the conservatory about to confront George, grateful to have Mrs Fingell there to give her courage, but George wasn't as she expected, shamefacedly adjusting his clothing, but was instead lying half on and half off the sofa, a twisted grin on his face and his eyes gazing sightlessly at Alan's potted herb collection. His penis, now at half-mast, lay pink and obscene against his best-trousered groin.

'Good God,' Mrs Fingell exclaimed sharply from just behind Jenny, 'he's stone dead!'

I mustn't panic, Jenny thought, followed by the fervent prayer that surely this couldn't be happening to her.

'Well, the first thing we'd better do is make him look decent, poor old bugger,' Mrs Fingell said, taking over with authority.

Jenny could feel her whole body start to tremble. 'I'm not touching him, not touching *that*,' she said, wondering if this was what it felt like before you actually fainted. 'Are you sure he's dead?' she whispered, though she didn't really need to; there was absolutely no doubt.

''Course he is. Heart attack I should think, a bit drunk and a lot over-stimulated. All he can expect at his age.' Mrs Fingell sniffed disapprovingly, even though George must have been quite a bit younger than her. She took off her coat and rolled up the sleeves of her best cardigan like an old-fashioned hospital matron about to tackle a challenging enema, and approached George. Jenny closed her eyes and shuddered, avoiding the sight of Mrs Fingell attempting to tuck George's penis neatly back into his trousers. 'Damn, he's got it stuck. No wonder he snuffed it, that zip must have nipped like a ferret,' she said. Jenny half-opened her eyes and met the sight of her neighbour rather brutally waggling the piece of pink flesh and battling with the stuck zip. 'Look at that! Completely trapped. Not much we can do about that, we'll have to leave it. Or cut it off,' she suggested hopefully, looking at Jenny with a grin of gleeful malevolence.

Jenny started to come to her senses. 'We can't do that, and we can't really leave him here. Poor old soul, who'd want to be found looking like that? And God, imagine what everyone will think has been going on!' The warmth flooded back to her face and she sat down heavily on one of the cane chairs. 'And Fiona! She wouldn't be able to think anything but the worst! I refuse to have anyone believe that I've been having an affair with George!' Jenny got up and paced up and down the small room. 'Perhaps we could move him. In the long run it'll be kinder for everyone. It's probably illegal though. Will you help me?' she pleaded urgently with Mrs Fingell.

''Course I will,' Mrs Fingell replied, accepting a hand up from the floor and adjusting her incongruously cheerful scarlet hat. 'I know,' she said, tapping her temple to help the thought out, 'if we can get him

278

across the road and leave him behind his lilac tree, everyone will think he dropped dead having a pee in his own garden. What do you think of that?' Mrs Fingell looked pleased with herself, but Jenny could see flaws.

'But why would he have to pee in his garden. Wouldn't he have a door key?'

Mrs Fingell cackled. 'You know Fiona Pemberton as well as I do dear, George isn't allowed a key, 'cept in emergencies.'

'We'll have to hurry,' Jenny said. 'Alan will be round looking for me, it doesn't take long to giftwrap a set of table linen.' Then she started to realize the impossibility of the project, her voice rising with panic. 'How on earth can we do this? Someone's bound to see us!'

'No they're not. They're all getting pissed at the wedding party and that's safely up at the end of the road. I'll get one of the trolleys from my garden. Hang on here a sec and get that rug up while you're waiting. Be just right to wrap him in.' Mrs Fingell, having issued her orders and taken command, walked back through the hallway, at a far brisker and stronger pace than usual. Jenny felt desperate to follow her, and trailed after her into the hall to find some comfortable shoes. Cowardly, and horrified at being left alone with the fish-eyed corpse, she wanted to go and snuggle up against the Aga for comfort, but instead had to move the cane chairs and table into the far corner of the conservatory to get at the big cream rug. She sidled past George, avoiding his fixed gaze, and then, unable to stand it, she went back to a drawer in the kitchen and covered his face with a freshly ironed tea towel depicting various Cornish harbours.

Luckily, Mrs Fingell's garden nearly always contained at least one abandoned supermarket trolley. Carol Mathieson was always tut-tutting about them. The one she manoeuvred up Jenny's garden path had a full set of working wheels and was only slightly bent around the handle. It would do very well. Back inside the house, she and Jenny pulled George down from the sofa and arranged him across the end of the rug before rolling him up firmly. Jenny bit her lip to stop herself feeling sick, and tied string tightly round the ends of the rug to stop him from sliding out. The parcel looked like a flaccid and badly stuffed uncooked pastry Christmas cracker, the sort of thing that only Delia Smith can make successfully.

'Lucky he isn't very tall. Or wasn't, I should say,' Mrs Fingell puffed as they loaded George onto the trolley. 'Fits nicely.' She stopped for a breather, leaning on the wall and sighing lustily. 'I always liked that rug.'

'It's yours,' Jenny told her immediately, grateful that she wouldn't have to live with it and be reminded of this awful day for ever more. How she'd explain its absence to Alan didn't even begin to rate as a problem. Getting George's cooling corpse unseen across the road did, however, and as the two women guided their heavy, clanking load along the pavement, Jenny wished and wished that supermarkets had understood the need for silent rubber tyres on their trolleys.

'What've you got in there then? Cleopatra?' Jenny froze, terrified, as Paul Mathieson, his vast Nikon suspended importantly round his neck, stalked down the middle of the road towards them from his own house.

'Yes, that's right, just transporting a body or two,' Mrs Fingell told him. Jenny felt herself gasp involuntarily. Mrs Fingell winked. 'And where are you going with that great thing?' she asked Paul, nodding towards the camera.

'Oh just going to take some impromptu photos at the party. Official photographers are all very well for the formal stuff, but you can't beat the ones taken by a competent friend; more natural,' he said, proudly stroking the lens of his camera. Then he raised it to his eye. 'Want me to take one of you two? Good light out here . . .'

'No!' Jenny yelled, putting her hand up in front of her face melodramatically, then recollected herself. 'I mean, don't waste it on us here, save it for the party. We'll be back there in a few minutes, soon as we've delivered the rug. Really good idea about the photos, I'll look forward to seeing them; we all will,' she flattered him, knowing his mind's eye was already looking ahead to an evening of neighbourly photo-viewing, complete with sherry and Carol's best finger-buffet. She prayed he wouldn't offer to lend a hand with the rug, wouldn't take over hauling it into Mrs Fingell's sitting-room and helpfully insist on unrolling George Pemberton's mortal remains all over the floor. Vanity, as Jenny had gambled, easily got the better of Paul and he eagerly strode off along the Close back to the party. 'Whyever did you say that about transporting bodies?' Jenny gasped as they struggled on to the opposite pavement and along towards the Pemberton garden.

Mrs Fingell sniggered, irreverently. 'I've always found,' she said, 'that when things are at their worst, if you just tell people the absolute truth they will never believe you. They don't want to.'

'Well, let's just hope he doesn't look back,' Jenny replied, but he didn't.

The really hard bit, as it turned out, was going back to the party and acting as if nothing had happened. Jenny suddenly wished, as she rejoined the celebrations, stuck a social smile on her face and delivered the wedding present, that she hadn't panicked and had simply left George where he had fallen and phoned for an ambulance. She could see that the adventure had made Mrs Fingell quite jaunty, and dreaded what truths she might try testing on everyone after a glass or three of champagne.

'Of course, you know what they say, don't you love,' Jenny overheard her confiding loudly to Carol Mathieson. 'Red hat, no drawers!' Carol was looking in horror at the old lady's scarlet hat and blushing vividly as Mrs Fingell winked broadly at her.

Fiona Pemberton, securely unaware that she was now a widow, had got Daisy trapped against a fence and was talking to her in strong terms about her mock GCSEs. Jenny didn't have to hear every word to know that some of them consisted of 'important not to slacken off at this stage' and 'thorough revision now means less ground to cover later.' Nor did she have any doubts that the accompanying words in Daisy's mind were any different from 'Sod off you old bat, leave me alone.' Poor Fiona, Jenny allowed herself to think, surely she'll miss having the daft old man to boss around? Or would she celebrate, indulging in uncharacteristic frivolity, perhaps spending the long Easter holidays taking an extravagant cruise in the Caribbean and saucily plaguing the life out of gay young pursers?

No-one had noticed how much Ben had drunk. He'd lost count, accepting and losing track of glasses of champagne as trays came round and were offered. It was a noisy, busy party and the first one at which he hadn't, as neither child nor adult, felt hugely out of place. Usually when he was dragged along to this sort of thing, he found himself wishing he was still Polly's age and able to dash off and play daft games with any other available child. Adults were stiffly polite to each other and talked about education, au pairs, houses, the awfulness of Nassau and the best route to Provence, and any other teenagers usually skulked in corners as shyly as he did. This time, though, he was sparkling, witty even; some of the younger Welsh girls were laughing with, not at, him. He put that down to his success with Emma. If it wasn't for Polly's abrupt interruption, he'd have definitely, easily, he felt, got

282

to what Oliver called third base with Emma. He felt almost as good as if he actually had, and there'd be other times, now they were actually seeing each other.

Bravely, buoyed up by the success of a joke-telling session with some of Sue's new in-laws, Ben stopped in the kitchen to chat to Carol Mathieson. 'You like jokes? Here's one,' he said to her. She smiled, because Ben was a nice boy deep down, she was sure of that. 'Come out here and I'll tell you,' he said, emboldened by her smile and by the inflaming fact that her pearly silk blouse had enough buttons undone to show the edge of a pristine white, untrimmed, sensible bra. Carol followed him to the hallway, prepared to be daring as it was a party, and secretly a bit flattered that a good-looking teenage boy should seek her out.

Ben propped himself up against the stair-rail and leaned towards Carol. 'What's the difference between a clitoris and a pub?' he whispered intimately into her ear. His face could feel the air whistle past him as Carol's shocked head whirled round to face him.

'*What* did you say?' she shrieked at him. 'No, don't repeat it! *Please!*' she ordered as Ben opened his mouth to say it again. He'd shocked her, he realized, which he had to admit was almost as exciting as the white bra.

'It's only that men can always find their way to the pub,' he finished feebly, hoping that at least *now* she'd see the funny side. She didn't. What, he wondered was wrong? The Welsh girls had laughed like drains. He thought drunkenly about the words of the joke, perhaps he'd said it wrong. He knew it would come over better from a woman, but the idea of *him* telling it was to distance himself from the sort of men who hadn't a clue about women's anatomy. Oliver had told him it couldn't fail, but obviously it could, with knobs on. He was too drunk for intellectualizing. Carol was now tapping her suede foot and waiting for an apology. Or was she, he wondered. If she was *really* 100 per cent shocked, surely she'd be in the garden by now, complaining to Jenny about the appalling way she'd brought up her eldest child. Ben moved even closer to her, intending to manipulate her into the cloakroom. He pushed gently at the door thinking Carol could be slid inside the small room before she knew what was happening, but instead the sudden roar of flushing water could be heard and the door was abruptly opened from the other side. Ben cannoned past Carol into a man who, from his size, was probably a reserve Welsh prop forward, before ricocheting drunkenly down to rest on the floor, his head jammed beneath the wash basin and a pink fluffy towel draped over his hair like Laurence of Arabia. Hopeless, he thought, bloody-sodding-useless-stupid-dickhead. He'd give up the pursuit of older women, he resolved, as he unwound painfully from his undignified position on the floor. People were looking and tripping over his great long feet. He would stick to Emma from now on, this was obviously a lesson. However, staggering up awkwardly from the floor, he caught sight of Carol in the cloakroom mirror. She adjusted her hair, put a finger to the corner of her mouth to remove a lipstick smudge and then winked naughtily at her own reflection. When do you ever know the right stuff about women, he thought, trailing unhappily into Sue's sitting-room to find a phone and ring Emma for comfort.

It was time for Sue and David to leave for their honeymoon in Italy. Jenny was feeling the effects of both champagne and shock, and knew that it could only be a short time before someone made the dreadful discovery of George spreadeagled sadly beneath his lilac tree. At least it wasn't raining. However awful George had been, Jenny could never have abandoned him under that tree to become pathetically sodden. Fiona Pemberton was still at the party, getting on extremely well in a corner with David's Uncle Matthew, who was a headmaster in Cardiff. Jenny had heard various snatches of their conversation in which they were comparing National Curriculum problems and the desirability of bringing back the 11-plus. She seemed oblivious to the fact that her husband hadn't returned. Perhaps she wasn't expecting him, or perhaps she didn't care. Either way, perhaps Uncle Matthew would be usefully available later to provide comfort for the new widow. Mrs Fingell was dozing in the dining-room, her feet up and her shoes off and her cherry red hat sitting on the table, complementing perfectly a bowl of scarlet tulips. I wonder what she's dreaming about, Jenny wondered.

In the garden, Polly sneaked up behind the stone bench and whispered delicately in the ear of Sean, Sue's younger son, 'Just now, when you put your baseball cap on, I realized I'd seen you recently in our house. You were the one in the leather,' she told him.

'Why are you whispering?' he asked her.

'Because,' she went on in a mocking sing-song voice, 'I know what you were doing!'

'No you don't,' he told her in a way that confirmed to Polly that she did.

She went on, close enough for him to smell chocolate ice-cream on her breath, 'Measuring out that stuff that they all smoke, and selling it to Ben. He sells it at school, I heard about it; everyone knows. But they don't know where it comes from. Only I do, so far.' She held out her grubby little hand and requested with her most charming smile, 'Only a fiver.' The boy, digging into his pocket for some of his ill-gotten earnings, sighed and knew he was beaten, just for now.

The wedding guests filled the front driveway and overflowed the pavement into the road as Sue and David prepared to leave. Jenny hugged Sue and wished her luck and Sue threw her bouquet to one of David's pretty young cousins while everyone cheered.

'We'll go home now, shall we?' said Alan, putting a cosy arm round Jenny and squeezing her gently. It was getting so near to the moment she was dreading, the inevitable scream when someone, Fiona most likely, discovered the body behind the tree. The Welsh contingent and some of the boozier neighbours went back into the house, turned up the music and seemed set to party on till dawn. But to Jenny, it felt comforting to be walking home along the Close with her entire family around her, even with Polly and Daisy trailing behind and squabbling.

'Did you get that message from the school?' Ben asked her. 'I forgot to tell you old Jeavons was going to call. Sorry.'

'Who is old Jeavons? Please don't tell me you've been expelled as well . . .' she said anxiously, easily convinced now that it was always right to expect the worst.

'No, no, he's head of music. The other bloke they've got has gone and got a record deal so they need a new music teacher fast. They'd got your CV.'

'Well that's brilliant! I'll give him a call first thing on Monday,' Jenny said, just managing to stop herself from saying that thank goodness at least someone in the house would be employed. Alan didn't need that kind of put-down, and in spite of everything, Jenny thought, didn't deserve it. Something was going right, at last, she thought, feeling like smiling for the first time in hours.

Ahead of them, still with his camera bumping heavily against his chest, Paul Mathieson proudly surveyed his territory. He walked, slightly unsteadily, along the middle of the quiet road, occasionally dashing to the gutter to collect stray litter, or peering over a fence to check whether a car door was actually locked or not. Jenny felt her insides tighten painfully and she held her breath as Paul caught sight of a Snickers wrapper blown by the wind just into the Pembertons' lilac-framed gateway. Any second now, this would make Paul's day. Quite soon, less than half-an-hour away, the Close would be full of flashing blue lights, ambulances, police, stripey ribbon cordons, a weeping widow needing sherry and comfort. The balconies on the estate across the main road would be lined with gleeful sightseers, and there'd be pictures in the local (perhaps even the national) papers. Beside Jenny, Alan watched Paul and chuckled deeply.

'Look at the silly old sod, he's like the Queen inspecting the troops. Can't think why he bothers, nothing sinister ever happens in a place like this.'

THE END

A SELECTED LIST OF FINE WRITING AVAILABLE FROM BLACK SWAN

THE PRICES SHOWN BELOW WERE CORRECT AT THE TIME OF GOING TO PRESS. HOWEVER TRANSWORLD PUBLISHERS RESERVE THE RIGHT TO SHOW NEW RETAIL PRICES ON COVERS WHICH MAY DIFFER FROM THOSE PREVIOUSLY ADVERTISED IN THE TEXT OR ELSEWHERE.

☐	14721 4	**TOM, DICK AND DEBBIE HARRY**	*Jessica Adams*	£6.99
☐	99822 2	**A CLASS APART**	*Diana Appleyard*	£6.99
☐	99564 9	**JUST FOR THE SUMMER**	*Judy Astley*	£6.99
☐	99629 7	**SEVEN FOR A SECRET**	*Judy Astley*	£6.99
☐	99630 0	**MUDDY WATERS**	*Judy Astley*	£6.99
☐	99766 8	**EVERY GOOD GIRL**	*Judy Astley*	£6.99
☐	99768 4	**THE RIGHT THING**	*Judy Astley*	£6.99
☐	99842 7	**EXCESS BAGGAGE**	*Judy Astley*	£6.99
☐	14764 8	**NO PLACE FOR A MAN**	*Judy Astley*	£6.99
☐	99619 X	**HUMAN CROQUET**	*Kate Atkinson*	£6.99
☐	99854 0	**LESSONS FOR A SUNDAY FATHER**	*Claire Calman*	£5.99
☐	99836 2	**A HEART OF STONE**	*Renate Dorrestein*	£6.99
☐	99839 7	**FROST AT MIDNIGHT**	*Elizabeth Falconer*	£6.99
☐	99910 5	**TELLING LIDDY**	*Anne Fine*	£6.99
☐	99795 1	**LIAR BIRDS**	*Lucy Fitzgerald*	£5.99
☐	99759 5	**DOG DAYS, GLENN MILLER NIGHTS**	*Laurie Graham*	£6.99
☐	99801 X	**THE SHORT HISTORY OF A PRINCE**	*Jane Hamilton*	£6.99
☐	99800 1	**BLACKBERRY WINE**	*Joanne Harris*	£6.99
☐	99887 7	**THE SECRET DREAMWORLD OF A SHOPAHOLIC**	*Sophie Kinsella*	£5.99
☐	99737 4	**GOLDEN LADS AND GIRLS**	*Angela Lambert*	£6.99
☐	99697 1	**FOUR WAYS TO BE A WOMAN**	*Sue Reidy*	£5.99
☐	99952 0	**LIFE ISN'T ALL HA HA HEE HEE**	*Meera Syal*	£6.99
☐	99819 2	**WHISTLING FOR THE ELEPHANTS**	*Sandi Toksvig*	£6.99
☐	99872 9	**MARRYING THE MISTRESS**	*Joanna Trollope*	£6.99
☐	99720 X	**THE SERPENTINE CAVE**	*Jill Paton Walsh*	£6.99
☐	99723 4	**PART OF THE FURNITURE**	*Mary Wesley*	£6.99
☐	99834 6	**COCKTAILS FOR THREE**	*Madeleine Wickham*	£6.99

All Transworld titles are available by post from:

Bookpost, P.O. Box 29, Douglas, Isle of Man IM99 1BQ

Credit cards accepted. Please telephone 01624 836000, fax 01624 837033, Internet http://www.bookpost.co.uk or e-mail: bookshop@enterprise.net for details.

Free postage and packing in the UK. Overseas customers allow £1 per book (paperbacks) and £3 per book (hardbacks).